13 MURDER MYSTERIES

Look out for other titles in the Point Crime series:

***The Beat:** Asking For It*
David Belbin

Dead Ringer
Dennis Hamley

***Patsy Kelly Investigates:** Accidental Death*
Anne Cassidy

Fade to Black
Stan Nicholls

POINT CRIME

13 MURDER MYSTERIES

edited by J. Moffatt

SCHOLASTIC

Scholastic Children's Books
Commonwealth House, 1–19 New Oxford Street,
London WC1A 1NU, UK
a division of Scholastic Ltd
London ~ New York ~ Toronto ~ Sydney ~ Auckland

First published in the UK by Scholastic Ltd, 1996

ISBN 0 590 13419 1

Typeset by TW Typesetting, Midsomer Norton, Avon
Printed by Cox & Wyman Ltd, Reading, Berks.

10 9 8 7 6 5 4 3 2 1

CONTENTS

ACKNOWLEDGEMENTS

All of the stories are original and appear for the first time in this volume.

The following are the copyright owners of the stories:

Dead On Arrival copyright © Stan Nicholls, 1996
Why You're Here copyright © David Belbin, 1996
Scree copyright © Philip Gross, 1996
The Cult copyright © Malcolm Rose, 1996
Lovers' Leap copyright © Lisa Tuttle, 1996
Die Laughing! copyright © Amber Vane, 1996
Still Life copyright © Laurence Staig, 1996
Spoiled copyright © Jill Bennett, 1996
Dead Lucky copyright © Sue Welford, 1996
A Touch of Death copyright © Ann Evans, 1996
X is for Execution copyright © Alan Durant, 1996
Colonel Mustard in the Library copyright ©
Dennis Hamley, 1996
Dead Like Me copyright © Nigel Robinson, 1996

DEAD ON ARRIVAL

It was almost ten o'clock and they still hadn't got themselves mugged.

Paul checked his watch again, wondering if their attacker would show. And what he'd look like.

He was aware of Lynn glancing at him, her expression quizzical, curious at his obsession with the time. But she didn't speak. Rex Howard, walking on her other side, nearest the road, was also silent. The clack of Lynn's stilettos against the damp pavement was the only sound any of them made.

As usual, Matheson Street was practically deserted. It was the right place at the right hour. The only thing missing was the mugger.

Paul felt light-headed. He couldn't believe he'd agreed to such an insane idea.

A middle-aged couple came out of a doorway opposite. The woman had a rolled umbrella, but the drizzle was too mild for her to bother using it. Engrossed in a whispered conversation, they hurried off.

Paul sneaked another look at his watch.

Rex Howard transferred his briefcase from his right hand to his left. Lynn adjusted the strap of her shoulder bag, giving Paul a fleeting, secret smile in the process. He responded with a weak grin before quickly looking away, convinced she could read what he was thinking from his face.

A man turned the corner ahead. Despite his green

jogging suit he made no pretence at exercising. He strolled in their direction, his hands the busiest part of him as he fumbled with a small bag.

This could be it.

The man sauntered past, concentrating on opening his packet of crisps.

Paul was relieved. In the cold light of a dismal Monday morning the whole thing was starting to look like a practical joke.

He hoped it had been.

Somebody else appeared. He was in his mid-twenties; scraggy thin, unkempt in a soiled leather jacket, frayed jeans and once white sneakers. Lank black hair hung to his shoulders, and as he got nearer it was obvious he hadn't shaved. He walked with his head down. As he approached, he thrust his hand into a pocket and increased his pace.

He had to be the one.

Paul knew there was no backing out. But everything would be all right as long as he kept cool and followed the plan. He caught a glimpse of Howard and Lynn. Neither seemed to suspect anything.

The young man stopped, blocking their path. He began to take something out of the pocket. It snagged in the lining. There was an awkward moment as he struggled to twist it free.

Even though he knew what to expect, Paul needed a second to take in the significance of the object the man produced.

It was a gun.

An ugly chunk of dark blue metal with a barrel that gaped like the Channel Tunnel. A cumbersome thing, seeming too large for his trembling, pallid fist.

At sight of the weapon they froze. Lynn's hand flew to

her mouth. Rex Howard swung the briefcase behind him, shielding it with his body. In his head, Paul rehearsed what would happen next, and prepared to act.

The robber's tongue flicked over dry lips and he said, "You were warned, Howard."

Warned? Paul didn't understand. The man was supposed to demand the briefcase.

Holding the revolver in both hands, he pointed it at Howard's chest. In a bolder tone he added, "Remember, you won't get off so lightly next time."

Next time? The mugger was working to a different script. Paul wasn't sure how to react. Should he make his move or not? His brain raced, weighing the options.

Then Rex Howard strode forward. His greater height and muscular physique were in total contrast to the stranger's puny frame. And when he wore his tough, no nonsense expression, as he did now, he could be really intimidating.

He stretched out his free hand. "Give it to me, son."

Surprised, the mugger retreated a step, hugging the gun to himself like a child with a favourite toy.

"There's an easy way and a hard way of doing this," Howard told him, edging closer. "And I don't much care which you pick."

"Stay where you are," the man replied feebly. Howard's self-confidence had shaken him. He extended the revolver once more, relying on it for the conviction his voice lacked.

"You little idiot," Howard sneered. "Now, are you going to give me that thing or do I have to take it?"

Paul's insides churned. None of this made sense. He had no control over the situation, and that wasn't how they'd planned it. But perhaps there was still time to step in and—

"Get back!" the man yelled.

Lynn clutched Paul's arm, her fingers sinking deep into his flesh. He didn't notice. The scene mesmerized him.

Then the shot came.

It was so loud their ears rang. The young man's hands bucked from the recoil. A whiff of cordite perfumed the air.

Howard gasped as though winded by a punch. He staggered, dropping the briefcase. A red stain soaked through his crisp white shirt.

Lynn screamed.

Howard went down.

The gunman seemed hardly less shocked than they were. The colour drained from his face. Fear mingled with the wildness in his eyes.

It occurred to Paul that he and Lynn might be next in line for a bullet. But the mugger turned and fled.

This wasn't what they'd agreed. Everything had gone horribly wrong.

Lynn kneeled by Howard's still form. Paul gaped at her. A crimson pool spread across the wet paving stones.

"For God's sake, get an *ambulance*!" she begged.

That snapped him out of his trance. He remembered a telephone kiosk two blocks away and started to run.

As he pounded the street his mind returned to the events of thirty-six hours before.

He could barely hear himself think.

It was quite early, but the Zodiac Club was always crowded on a Saturday night, especially when a band as popular as Hoodoo Harmony played there.

Pam, the new barmaid, held Paul's ten pound note up to the light before putting it in the till and counting out the change. She smiled, and poured his glass of soda. He mouthed, "Thanks," and turned back to the band.

Charmain Kimball, Hoodoo's lead singer, belted out an up-tempo number that had the audience on their feet. Her waist-length auburn hair whipped provocatively as she danced across the tiny stage.

But Paul's mind wasn't entirely on the music.

Someone shouted into his ear, "Why so glum, chum?"

"Vince? Hi! *It's been a while."*

Apart from better quality clothes and a neater haircut, Vince Dean hadn't changed much since they last saw each other at school.

"Must be over a year," Vince said. "How you doin'?"

"OK."

They settled on vacant stools. "What you up to these days?" Paul asked.

"Working here, as a matter of fact." Self-importance puffed his chest. "Trainee management."

Paul nodded, hoping he looked sufficiently impressed.

"How 'bout you?" Vince added.

"I'm a sort of trainee myself. An apprentice, really. With Sapphire Printworks."

Vince's grin faltered. "Rex Howard's place?"

"Yeah. Know him?"

"Slightly." He took a thoughtful sip of drink and returned to his original question. "So, what's up? You were looking pretty low just now."

"Was I?"

"Like you had the weight of the world on your shoulders. And if there's one thing I'm good at, it's reading moods." He raised his glass again, but kept his eyes on Paul. "If you want to talk about it, mate, I'm a good listener."

"Well..." Paul hesitated, then decided there was no harm in a chat. "Things aren't going that well at work, to be

honest. The job's all right, but some of the people there are always having a go at me."

"Giving you a hard time, like?"

"Yeah. They keep telling me what a wimp I am, harping on about me being timid and that." He paused. "They've even got a nickname for me. Bashful."

Vince smiled.

"It's my first job and I don't know how to handle this stuff. It isn't exactly doing a lot for my self-confidence. Mind you, I think some of them are just jealous because of Lynn."

"Who's she?"

"She works there too, in accounts. We're sort of ... going out together. At least she *seems to see the real me behind this wimp thing. But I'm worried that even she'll start believing what they say."*

"What about Howard?"

"Can't tell him. He's a man's man, if you know what I mean. He'd think I really was *a wimp for not standing up for myself."*

"I bet," Vince muttered. He placed his empty glass on the counter. "Well, Paul, I might be able to help you. But I've just got to talk to somebody. Stay here, I'll be right back."

"Just a minute, Vince, I don't—"

"Hang on," *he repeated and hurried away.*

Mystified, Paul watched him elbow into the crowd. He was starting to regret having said so much. It wasn't as if they were ever exactly close. In fact he remembered one of their teachers describing Vince as somebody you couldn't entirely see around. That summed him up pretty well. Still, if he had one of his little schemes going, Paul couldn't see how it affected him.

He shrugged and concentrated on the band.

* * *

Paul and Lynn sat in silence on uncomfortable red plastic chairs.

The casualty department was full, and people spoke in hushed tones. From time to time a nurse or porter passed briskly. Somewhere in the distance the hospital's public address system boomed indistinctly.

Paul's mind was a churning soup of guilt and bewilderment.

Lynn touched his hand. "OK?" she whispered.

"Suppose so. Think he'll pull through?"

"I don't know. He looked bad." She sighed and sank back in the chair.

The silence renewed itself.

Paul glanced at her and thought of the ways in which they differed. She was a few years older, and outgoing. He was more introverted, and some said he was immature. But Lynn saw beyond that, as she often told him, and frequently referred to his "potential". That made him feel good.

They both had eyes an identical shade of blue. And the same sandy hair, his collar-length, hers cut short. Her face was what he thought they called elfin; vaguely pixie-like with fine, small features. Petite, that was the word. She looked cute as a button in her black one-piece trouser suit.

Pity the effect was spoilt by the bloodstains.

He had to tell her the truth. But no sooner had he made the decision than a white-coated doctor appeared.

"Are you – " he consulted his clipboard – "Paul Grant and Lynn Clark?"

They nodded.

"And you came in with a Mr Rex Howard, your employer."

"Yes," Lynn replied quietly. "How is he?"

"I'm terribly sorry, Miss Clark, but I'm afraid Mr Howard was DOA."

"DOA?"

"A piece of jargon, forgive me. DOA means dead on arrival. We did all we could, but the bullet passed through several vital organs. I'm sorry."

Oh my God, Paul thought.

Lynn sniffed and clutched his hand again.

"The police have arrived," the doctor continued. "Do you feel up to talking to them?"

"Yes," Paul managed. "Yes, of course."

They were led to an examination room. A plain-clothed woman in her late thirties was waiting for them. She was tall, and severe of dress and facial expression. A well-built uniformed policeman stood beside her.

"I'm Detective Inspector Rose Garfield," she explained, "CID officer in charge of the investigation. This is Sergeant Hamilton."

Paul and Lynn were told to sit. Garfield and the sergeant remained standing.

"I know you're shaken by what's happened," the inspector said, "but we have to move fast in a case like this."

Sergeant Hamilton flipped open a notebook.

"I understand you were coming back from the bank when the incident occurred," Garfield stated. "Did your boss often draw large amounts of cash?"

"It was how he paid the wages," Lynn stated, falteringly. "He was a bit old-fashioned that way. And he always took one or two of us along when he went to the bank. I suppose he thought that was enough security."

"Yet the money was left behind." It wasn't a question; Inspector Garfield was thinking aloud. But she stared hard at them when she spoke again.

"Tell me, had either of you seen the mugger before?"

They shook their heads.

At least Paul was being truthful as far as that was concerned.

Vince returned and said he wanted Paul to meet somebody.

As they made their way to the office, Charmain Kimball began a slower song and the lights dimmed, taking the dazzle off her pure white leather cat-suit.

Cigar smoke clouded the back room. Vince introduced the two men sitting at a card table inside. "This is the Zodiac's owner, Mr Cameron Rolf, and that's Tony Shaw, the manager."

They were dressed in designer smart casuals. Rolf, the older man, had distinguished silver-grey streaks in his hair and wore a scattering of gold jewellery. Shaw's style was quieter but equally expensive. Paul thought they looked like a pair of affluent used-car salesmen. But their greeting was friendly as they invited him to sit.

After a few pleasantries, Rolf got to the point. "Vince explained your problem, Paul."

"I wouldn't say it was a problem, *Mr Rolf, it's just –"*

"No need to be embarrassed, we're all friends here. And I'm not so old that I can't remember what it's like to be a teenager lacking in confidence."

Shaw and Vince laughed dutifully. Paul managed a nervous smile.

"You know," Rolf went on, "I was in a similar state when I was about your age. Unsure of myself, overawed by everybody. Then one day I faced down a couple of bullies. That bit of bravery did me no end of good in other people's eyes." He reached for an ornate cigar box. "I was reminded of it just now when Vince told me you could use some help."

"Well, I'm not sure I actually need *help. And, no offence Mr Rolf, but why do you want to help me?"*

"Because you're a friend of Vince, and because I get a kick out of helping young people. Look at Hoodoo Harmony, for example. I'm their manager."

Paul didn't know that. "What did you have in mind?"

"I've been acquainted with Rex Howard for years; we local businessmen all tend to know each other. And if I read him correctly he's the sort who'd be impressed by one of his employees doing something ... heroic. Right?"

"Yes, I think he would."

"OK. All I need to know is the next time you and he will be in a set place at a set time. Somewhere away from the printworks, but not too public."

"Well, I'll be going to the bank with him this coming Monday morning. But I don't see what that has to do with –"

"I'll be straight with you, kid. Like I said, I know your boss, and there's a little bit of friendly rivalry between us. Rex pulled a stroke on me a while ago; a sort of practical joke, you might say."

"He never struck me as being the prankster type."

"He is, believe me. And I can see a way of getting my own back, with your co-operation. Don't look so worried! What I have in mind can only reflect well on you." He exhaled a whiff of blue cigar smoke. "I expect you'll be going along Matheson Street on Monday, right?"

"Er, yeah. Between nine-thirty and ten."

"Good. This *Monday you're going to get mugged at gunpoint."*

Paul's jaw dropped.

The others burst out laughing.

"Don't worry," Rolf grinned. "The mugger's actually an out of work actor who owes me a favour. And the gun's real enough but it won't be loaded."

"But –"

"All you have to do is disarm the phoney robber, who I guarantee will put on a great performance, and let him escape. Without *the money, naturally. After that, you're a champ to your boss and girlfriend, and your workmates are going to shut up."*

"I –"

"The police are so overworked they'll be happy to write it off as a foiled robbery." Cameron Rolf's plan continued to spill out in an irresistible flow. "The actor's going to the States in search of work next week, so that's no problem. As to old Rex, well, I'll let him stew for a couple of days, then ring him. He'll see the joke in a phoney stick-up. And I won't tell him you knew it wasn't real, so you'll still be a hero." He puffed at his cigar and beamed triumphantly. "What do you say?"

The way Rolf put it, it sounded a real winner.

"Umm ... yes," Paul said. "Why not?"

"Brilliant! Now, there's just one little thing I'd appreciate you doing in return."

Of course, Paul didn't tell the police any of that. It made him an accomplice to murder, even if that wasn't what he'd intended. And he still hadn't the courage to explain things to Lynn.

Garfield had kept them hanging around all day Monday. So Paul couldn't get to the club to find out what had gone wrong.

Sapphire Printworks was a glum place on Tuesday morning. Most of the female staff were sniffling and all the men were ashen-faced. Nobody did any work. As Rex Howard was a widower with no known relatives, the main topic of conversation was who got to take over the company.

Paul and Lynn ended up sitting in one of the offices with several others, including a woman called Yvonne from the art department. She was taking the news particularly badly.

"It's such a terrible shame," she sobbed. "Poor Mr Howard. As if it wasn't sad enough him losing his wife and having to give away their child all those years ago." She blew her nose in a well-used handkerchief. "He was like a father to us girls."

Someone reached out to comfort her.

The comment reminded Paul that Lynn was an orphan, and she'd hinted at a pretty unhappy childhood. He was probably the only person she could talk to about the tragedy. Him, of all people. What a lousy twist of fate.

The door opened. A secretary ushered in Inspector Garfield and Sergeant Hamilton. Paul held his breath.

"We're here to question the staff," the inspector announced curtly. "And I want a further word with Mr Grant and Miss Clark. Mr Grant first, I think. Can we clear the room, please?"

Then she fixed him with a hard stare and said, "Let's go over it again, shall we?"

Paul didn't know if he could hold out much longer.

It seemed a small favour in return for what Cameron Rolf was doing.

Paul simply had to deliver a package across town, to a guy named Ken at Alley Cat recording studios.

The package contained a demo tape for a new band Rolf was thinking of managing. He needed someone trustworthy for the job, bearing in mind how valuable a demo could be, and nobody else was available.

Paul was flattered. And there were worse ways of

spending a Sunday morning.

But he got a real surprise after making the delivery. As he was on his way out, Charmain Kimball and Hoodoo Harmony's guitarist, Myles Edwards, were coming in.

And Charmain spoke to him.

"Hi," she said, smiling. "Didn't I see you at the Zodiac last night?"

Paul was taken aback. "Er, yeah. And the band was great."

"Thanks."

Edwards stayed silent. He looked impatient and rather surly, just like his stage image.

Charmain nodded at the studio door. "In the biz?"

"Me? No." He remembered Rolf's warning not to tell anybody about his errand. "I was just visiting. I'm with a printing company, actually. An outfit called Sapphire."

"In that case you probably know Vince Dean," she replied.

"Yeah." Paul was puzzled. "But nothing to do with work. We went to school together."

Edwards spoke for the first time. "It's a small world then. 'Cause Vince worked at Sapphire last year."

"Before I joined," Paul mumbled.

"That boss of yours, Rex Howard," Edwards said. "Vince hates *him."*

"Why?"

"Fired him, didn't he? Accused him of stealing, in front of everybody. Vince's still bitter about it."

Paul wondered why Vince hadn't mentioned any of this. It planted a seed of suspicion in his mind.

"What's your name?" Charmain asked.

"Oh. Er ... Paul Grant."

"There you go, Paul." She handed him a small printed card. "See yer."

They went into the studio.

The card was a party invitation for her place the following weekend.

And tomorrow he was going to be a hero.

Paul was ecstatic.

He came away from the interview feeling like a wrung-out dishcloth. And uncertain whether Garfield suspected anything. Passing Lynn in the corridor, he told her he had to go somewhere and would ring later.

It was late afternoon when he arrived at the Zodiac Club. The place had just opened and there were no customers. Vince stood by the bar, far from happy at seeing his old school friend.

"What the *hell* went wrong?" Paul demanded.

"With what?"

"Yesterday, of course! What else would I be talking about?"

"Was there something special about yesterday, then?"

"Don't mess around, Vince, you must have heard. Rex Howard's *dead.* What happened?"

"You tell *me*, mate." He was playing dumb, but couldn't hide his nervousness. "Feeling a bit under the weather, are you?"

Paul's anger rose. "I want to see your boss. *Now!*"

"Suit yourself."

Less than a minute later he came back with Rolf. Tony Shaw tagged along. They looked jumpy and bad-tempered.

"You really landed me in it!" Paul flared.

"And *you've* got a nerve coming into my place and talking to me like this!" Rolf snapped.

"Just a minute! On Saturday night you said –"

"Maybe you were in here on Saturday and maybe you

weren't. Either way, we didn't talk. Get it?"

"But –"

"Let me make myself clear, son." His voice was menacing. "Howard getting topped was a shame. But it had nothing to do with us. You try to drag me into this and I'll deny everything. I'll say you *were* in here the other night, going on about how much you hated your boss and what you'd like to do to him. And my staff will testify to that if necessary. Won't you, boys?"

Shaw and Vince nodded.

"So much for us all being friends," Paul said, bitterly.

"Life's tough, kid," Shaw told him. "Now push off."

At that moment Pam Watkins, the barmaid, wandered in.

"Give security a shout would you, Pam?" Shaw asked her.

She summoned the bouncer. He was all muscle, the sort of shaven-headed dimwit who moved his lips when reading a comic.

"John, escort this kid off the premises," Rolf ordered. "And *you*," he pointed at Paul, "keep your mouth shut."

As he was marched out, Pam whispered, "It might be better to mind your own business in future, love."

Then he found himself on the street.

Paul wandered aimlessly after that, trying to figure things. He knew it was only a matter of time before Inspector Garfield suspected his involvement. If she already didn't.

It was dark when he headed for home, and his route took him past the quiet road Sapphire Printworks occupied.

An unmarked van was parked outside.

Two men were ferrying boxes to it from the building.

He recognized them as drivers from the transport department, although he wasn't sure of their names.

There was something furtive about the way they acted. So much so that he stayed hidden in the shadows until they drove off.

It gave him another mystery to chew over.

He saw the pair at work the following morning, but didn't speak to them. It was just before the police arrived again. In force.

Garfield announced that the premises were to be searched. No one could leave without permission.

Paul and Lynn, along with weepy Yvonne, settled in the staff room.

"Life's funny, isn't it?" Yvonne declared. "I mean, what a time for that contract to arrive."

"Contract?" Paul said.

"The company's secured a big order," Lynn explained. "Enough work to keep us busy for at least a year. There's a lot of money involved."

"And Mr Howard isn't here to see it come through," Yvonne moaned, "after everything he put into negotiating it."

"I slaved over that order too, you know!" Lynn snapped. "Nobody ever appreciates what *I* do for this place!"

Yvonne dissolved into tears. "Sorry I spoke, I'm sure," she snivelled. Hanky to face she hurried out.

"Damn," Lynn muttered. "Now I've upset her. But everyone seems to think Mr Howard ran the business single-handed."

Paul put his arm around her. "Don't worry about Yvonne; you can apologize later. And I know how much effort you put into your job."

"Thanks." She smiled, and the warm sparkle he liked

so much came back into her eyes. He kissed her pretty upturned nose.

"We're all on edge after what's happened," Paul said. *And some*, he thought.

"You're right," she agreed. "Why don't we get away for a while tonight and catch that movie?"

It was the last thing he wanted to do. Nevertheless he nodded.

"Good. Meet you outside the cinema at seven."

He almost blurted out the truth there and then. But his nerve failed again. And shortly after, Garfield called Lynn into the office.

He saw Lynn only once more that day, just briefly when the inspector finished with her. She looked uneasy.

The police let everyone go in the afternoon. Lynn had an errand and left in a taxi. Paul decided on a humbler means of transport.

He was queuing at the bus stop when he spotted him.

There was no mistake. He was wearing exactly the same clothes. Even so, Paul would never forget his face.

It was the man who shot Rex Howard.

The killer moved swiftly through the pedestrians on the opposite pavement. Head down, collar up, hands buried in his pockets.

Paul followed him.

He didn't know what he hoped to achieve. It wasn't as though he could tell the police where the man went. Because if they caught him, Paul's involvement was likely to come out.

But he trailed him anyway.

He kept his distance, careful not to be seen, and eventually they came to a park. At this time of day there was no else about. The man jogged to a covered shelter and went in. Paul approached cautiously, zigzagging from tree to tree.

The shelter was built like a miniature house. There were doorless entrances front and back, set into waist-high brick walls with frosted glass above.

Paul hesitated for a moment. Then a gust of wind sent a piece of coloured paper fluttering out of the building. He snatched at it and missed. Another flew past and also eluded him.

Creeping to the entrance, he saw more on the shelter's concrete floor. They were twenty pound notes. Dumbstruck, he stepped inside.

A trail of notes led to something lying by a wooden bench.

The man. Sprawled on his back. A knife in his chest.

Very dead.

Shock hammered Paul's senses. He couldn't believe what he was seeing. Just a few minutes ago this lifeless corpse had been a living, breathing human being.

He looked around fearfully, but there was no sign of anyone. Whoever did this had a number of escape routes and hiding places. There were plenty of trees and bushes, along with several gates, one leading into a nearby housing estate.

What was he going to do now? If he called the police, and they linked the dead man with Howard's murder, where did that leave him? A suspect in two homicides, probably. He stood looking at the corpse and shaking.

Then somebody walked into the shelter. She was dressed in a park warden's uniform and her scream was ear-splitting.

Paul threw himself out of the other door and ran like hell.

But not before she got a good look at him.

* * *

The police would be hunting for someone of his description. He didn't dare go home. Or Lynn's place, or anywhere else he could think of.

Then he remembered the card in his pocket.

He glanced around anxiously and pushed the bell.

Charmain Kimball opened the door, gave an uncertain smile and said, "Hi, Paul. The party's not tonight, you know."

"Right. But, er..."

"Hey, you look pale." She stepped aside. "You'd better come in."

They settled on cushions in her flat's chaotic living room. A rock station played in the background.

"So what's wrong?" she asked.

"I'm taking a chance coming here. But I'm in trouble." He dried up. He'd backed his hunch that she'd be sympathetic. Now it seemed crazy on so brief an acquaintance.

"Relax," Charmain said. "Tell me about it."

Still shaken, he searched for the right words. Then he realized the radio was carrying a news flash.

"...found stabbed to death in Oak Lane park has been named as Bobby Attwood, who was an actor by profession. Police say there was no apparent motive. They've issued the description of a suspect in his late teens. He has blond hair, is clean-shaven, and wore..."

"Attwood," Charmain muttered. "The name seems..." She saw Paul's face. "You look worse than when you came in. What *is* the matter?"

"I'm—"

The doorbell rang.

She sighed and went to answer it, returning a moment

later with Myles Edwards. He was hot and bothered, as though he'd been running. And he didn't look too pleased to find Paul there.

"We were going to do some song-writing," Charmain explained, turning off the radio. "But you've obviously got a problem, so let's hear it."

Paul's uncertainty about Edwards must have shown. "You can trust Myles," she assured him.

What have I got to lose? Paul thought. He took a deep breath and told them everything. They listened attentively, not interrupting even during the more shocking and baffling parts of his tale. Their silence continued after he finished, and it occurred to him that all he'd done was convince them he was a dangerous lunatic.

Then Charmain gave a low whistle. "Wow. That's some story."

"But do you believe it?" Paul asked apprehensively.

"If I were just going on what you've told us ... no, frankly. But on intuition – " she gazed at him intently – "I think I do. I trust my feelings when it comes to people."

"You've got to admit it's all a bit far-fetched," Myles observed. "Mind you," he quickly added, "*nothing* would surprise me about Rolf. If you knew the way he's been managing our band—"

"Let's not go into *that* now," Charmain said, glaring at him. "What's important is Paul's situation. And I think the only thing to do is talk to the police."

"Yeah," Myles agreed. "I'm not exactly a great fan of the cops, but that has to be the best way, Paul."

"They'll never believe me. I can see myself getting nailed for two murders."

Charmain and Myles exchanged glances Paul couldn't read. He wasn't sure he was happy about them being so anxious for him to give himself up.

"You've got a point," she conceded. "So what *are* you going to do?"

"If I could confront Rolf again perhaps we might get it sorted out. But I doubt whether he'd see me. Only ... maybe he would if I turned up with you two."

Myles frowned. "That sounds a bit of a hassle."

Charmain was more positive. "I think we should do it. And tonight's a good time. The Zodiac's not open on Tuesdays. But once we get in, you're on your own, Paul. OK, Myles?"

"I think it's nuts. Go if you must, Charmain. I'm staying here."

"All right." She lingered for just a second, regarding her fellow band member coldly, then added, "Come on, Paul, we'll take my car."

They left Myles wallowing in moodiness.

Seven-thirty and Paul hadn't arrived. Lynn paced the pavement in front of the cinema. He'd been so nervous and preoccupied since Rex Howard's death. The police *must* have noticed it too.

Her mind was still on the conversation she'd had with Garfield earlier. The policewoman implied that what had happened to Howard could have been some kind of inside job. She told Lynn to contact her if she came across any information that might be helpful.

Now the news had broken about the murder in the park.

It was all starting to come together in a way Lynn didn't like.

She looked up as a red Mini sped past. Paul was sitting in the front passenger seat. There was a fleeting impression of a female driver. But they didn't stop.

Something important had to be going on for Paul to miss their date.

She cursed under her breath and hailed a taxi.

"Follow that car!"

"I've waited years to hear that!" the cabby beamed, pulling into the traffic.

Five minutes later the mini parked outside the Zodiac Club. Lynn got the taxi to stop at a safe distance, and watched as Paul and the girl went inside. Then she paid the driver and made for a nearby telephone box.

Her eyes on the club's entrance, she punched the number she'd been given.

When it was answered she said, "I'd like to speak to Detective Inspector Garfield, please."

Paul regretted standing Lynn up. But he hoped she'd understand, given the circumstances. Even if the next time she saw him was in jail.

Charmain hit the club's bell. The door was opened by Pam Watkins, who cast a disapproving look Paul's way.

"He's with me," Charmain announced as she swept in, Paul in her wake.

"Mr Rolf's not going to like it," Pam told them ruefully.

"Not like what?" Rolf said, emerging from the office. Then he saw Paul and his face darkened. "I thought I made it clear—"

"You must know Bobby Attwood's dead," Paul cut in. "We have to sort this, Rolf. You owe me that."

"I don't owe you anything!" He turned to Charmain. "What are you thinking of, bringing this kid here?"

Shaw appeared, drawn by the commotion.

"Have this pest kicked out," Rolf demanded.

"It's the doorman's day off, remember?" Shaw told him.

"You won't get rid of me so easily this time," Paul said, casting a hostile glance at the manager. "Don't expect me to go quietly."

"Then we'll do it mob-handed," Rolf threatened. *"Vince!"* he bellowed. "Where *is* that idiot?"

Paul's old school friend came out of a door at the far side of the room. He walked toward them slowly, his hands behind his back.

"Move yourself, Vince!" Rolf snapped. "And help us throw this character out!"

The buzzer on the door sounded. Pam went to answer it and someone pushed their way in.

"Lynn!" Paul exclaimed.

She ran to him.

Rolf was furious. "What is this, a zoo? I want you all to *leave*!"

"This is about *two* murders now," Paul said. "You can't heavy your way out of it."

"I think I'd better call the police," Pam decided and headed for the bar.

"*No!*" Rolf yelled.

"That's right," Vince told her, "you leave that phone alone!"

"Vince...?" Rolf was startled.

"I ain't taking the rap for no murders!"

Then Vince Dean brought out the shotgun he'd been hiding.

Paul wondered if the nightmare would ever end.

Vince swept the gun slowly from side to side, covering all of them. "Anybody moves, they're dead!"

"What *is* this?" Rolf said. "And how did you get that shooter? I had it locked in –"

Pam grasped his sleeve and pulled him back. "That hardly matters now, does it? Don't antagonize him."

"Yeah," Vince snarled, "don't push me. Didn't know I'd heard, did you?" He jabbed the weapon in Shaw's direction. "You and him, talking about how you were going to frame me for murder!"

"No, you've got it all wrong."

"I haven't, Mr Rolf." Vince's face showed as much hurt as anger. "You'd let me go down for Attwood's killing. You know I've made some mistakes in the past and ended up in court for 'em. I'm the perfect suspect as far as the cops are concerned!"

Paul thought Rolf was about to be shot.

But Vince was moving away. "I'm not hanging about to be arrested. And don't nobody follow!" He sprinted to the door and wrenched it open.

Two policemen were walking across the pavement towards the club.

Seeing the shotgun, they dashed for the shelter of their patrol car. Vince slammed the door.

"You can't slug it out with the Bill!" Rolf told him.

"*Shut up!* I need time to think. Sit down. All of you!"

As they started to obey, the telephone rang.

Vince pointed the gun at Shaw again, who was nearest. "Take care of that," he ordered.

Shaw snatched the receiver. "Yeah?"

"I didn't say answer it!" Vince protested.

"It's the police." Shaw listened for a few seconds, said, "I'll tell him," and hung up. "That was an Inspector Garfield," he explained. "We're surrounded by armed cops. She said you better give yourself up."

"And get done for murder? No way! Sit down with the others."

Paul knew that if he didn't speak now he might never

get another chance. "Maybe we can get this sorted," he said.

Vince stared at him blankly. "What?"

"You and I are in a similar situation, mate. We're both in danger of being accused of something we say we didn't do. But if we could work out who the real murderer is –"

"Leave it alone, can't you?" Rolf sneered.

Paul ignored him. "Surely the truth can only help, Vince?"

"That's all we need," Shaw mocked, "ruddy Sherlock Holmes!"

"Shut it!" Vince barked. "We'll hear what he's got to say."

"Thanks," Paul said. "Er ... I think better on my feet."

Vince nodded.

As Paul rose, a police siren could be heard outside.

"For a start," he began, "it seems logical that whoever was responsible for the murders of Rex Howard and Bobby Attwood is in this room."

There was a buzz of reaction. A wave of the shotgun silenced it.

"What I mean," Paul continued, "is that when Attwood killed Howard, he was being used by somebody else. Then he was silenced." He regarded their attentive faces. "Let's work our way through this. When you persuaded me to make sure my boss was in a certain place at a certain time, Rolf, you were arranging a classic set-up."

"I don't have to listen to this!" Rolf protested.

"Yes, you do," Vince reminded him, levelling the gun.

"All that stuff about helping me, and playing a practical joke on Howard, was hogwash, Rolf," Paul added. "I think you and my ex-boss had something criminal going."

"That's bull!"

"Spit it out, Cameron!" Shaw blurted, watching the gun nervously. "You're wearing Vince's patience thin."

"All right," Rolf sighed. "Me and Howard *were* involved in something a little ... outside the law. Tony and Vince played their part, too. But that's all I'm saying."

Paul backed his instinct. "I've an idea what it was. Howard was a printer. And there were bank notes around Attwood's body. You were into counterfeiting, weren't you?"

After a moment of grudging silence, Rolf quietly admitted, "Yeah."

"And no doubt the two drivers I saw taking boxes out of the printworks the other night were part of the scam, clearing evidence before the police got too nosy. What about that package you had me deliver?"

"The printing plates. Guy at the studio hides them for us."

"So you double-crossed me. Is that what Howard did to *you*? And the reason you had him killed?"

"I didn't tell Attwood to *murder* him! You're right thinking Howard was squeezing us; he refused to print the notes until he got a bigger share. But I didn't want him dead, I swear!"

"But why invent that phoney mugging *unless* you were setting him up to be murdered?"

"To give him a warning. Howard was a very careful man. He made sure he was never in a situation where we could threaten him. I needed to get him in a vulnerable position, and when you came along it seemed a golden opportunity. Attwood was supposed to shoot at Howard to give him a fright. I would have rung him later and said that if he didn't behave, next time it'd be real bullets. It was to let him know I could *get* to him, see?"

"Knowing he couldn't complain to the police. And *I* could hardly go to them and say I'd been involved in a fake mugging that turned out to be an exercise in putting the frighteners on somebody."

"Right. But for some reason Attwood mucked it all up by loading live ammo."

"I don't think so. From the look on his face he was as shocked as we were. I reckon Attwood was as much of a patsy as me."

"Well, I didn't make him one. *Or* have anything to do with his death."

"How come you were going to blame me for Attwood's murder?" Vince asked.

"Because the cops would figure it just the way your friend here has. Once they found out Howard and I were in a scam together, they'd think I bumped him off. I had to give them a sacrificial lamb, kid."

"Why you..." He raised the gun.

"Just a minute," Paul said. "Rolf isn't the only suspect." He squared up to Vince and tried not to be intimidated by the weapon. "I've got to say this, Vince. You worked for Howard, and he humiliated you in front of the staff. Perhaps you switched the ammo in Attwood's gun and now you're trying to wriggle out of it."

"No! Howard fired me, yeah. Said I was dishonest. Had it in for me, the pig! But I had nothing to do with him getting shot. On my life!"

Paul nodded, noting that their captor's hands were shaking. He turned away. "And what about you, Pam? You're an unknown quantity. I wonder if you had anything to gain from Howard's death."

"Not from his death," she replied, "but I certainly had an interest in taking him out of circulation. I didn't want to do this, but I've no choice." She pulled a plastic identity card from her top pocket and flashed it at him.

"You're a *policewoman*?"

"Undercover. We've suspected this club was the centre of a counterfeiting ring for some time."

"*A nark!*" Rolf exploded. "And we trusted you!"

"That was the idea," Pam responded coolly. Then she addressed Vince. "You're holding a police officer hostage, and that makes your offence a lot worse. This has gone on long enough. Give it up."

"Like hell I will," Dean growled. "If the cops know one of their own's in here I reckon they're gonna be less trigger-happy. We stay put until this thing's sorted." His hold on the shotgun tightened. "One way or another!"

"Where's the mystery?" Charmain declared. "Rolf's the man behind all this." She glared at the club owner. "We know you're a crook from the way you've fiddled the band's accounts."

"Oh, and you're so pure, are you? You had good reason to bump off Howard yourself!"

"How come?" Paul said.

"Howard was another backer of Hoodoo Harmony," Rolf explained. "He owned fifty per cent of the band. But he was holding out on paying them the money he owed. You would have found it very convenient to have him dead and me in jail, wouldn't you, Charmain?"

"Don't be ridiculous!" she said.

"It gets you out of a contract you couldn't otherwise break," Rolf continued, "and leaves you free to get a better deal with a bigger agency."

"And the band knew Bobby Attwood," Shaw put in. "I've seen them talking to him after gigs."

"Is that true, Charmain?" Paul asked, remembering her reaction to hearing Attwood mentioned on the radio.

"Well, yeah," she admitted. "But we only knew him *slightly*. He was just a fan. I couldn't even place his name earlier."

"Maybe you're lying, and you knew him well enough to interfere with the gun." As she shook her head, he recalled something else. "And when Myles arrived at your flat this afternoon he looked like he'd been running. Where from? An appointment with Attwood in the park, perhaps?"

"Course not! Myles was just late. He's *always* late turning up for things."

"Still, Myles doing the deed and you providing him with an alibi fits neatly."

"Don't be stupid, Paul! We're musicians, not murderers. And you shouldn't listen to *him*!" She glared at Shaw. "He had his own reasons for getting rid of Howard."

"Go on."

"Shaw's ambitious, and he's got a junior partnership in this club. I came across the papers when I was nosing around the office, looking for proof that the band was owed money. The agreement says Shaw gets control of the Zodiac if Rolf can't undertake his legal responsibilities. And being in prison for murder would certainly put Rolf out of the picture."

"Don't believe any of that!" Shaw protested.

Rolf scowled. "It better not be true, Tony. I've treated you like my own son!"

The comment sparked something in Paul's mind. He held up his hand. "OK, let's all calm down. It seems just about everybody had a motive for getting Howard out of the way and then killing Attwood. But I think I know who's responsible."

They immediately fell silent.

"I'm sure now that this whole business was based on a *triple*-cross."

"I don't understand," Pam said.

"We'll get to that in a moment. But if my theory's right, we have to go back quite a long way to find the beginning of the story." He took a deep breath and gathered his thoughts. "At work the other day a woman called Yvonne reminded me that Howard's wife died giving birth to their only baby. That child was put up for adoption. I think because Howard blamed the kid for his wife's death."

"An innocent baby?"

"Sounds crazy, I know, but it tallies with the kind of man Howard was. Anyway, let's assume the child grew up knowing this, and resenting it, and over the years their thoughts turned to revenge. Eventually, this person discovered who their real father was, sought him out and got close to him. Probably the original intention was purely murder. But Howard had a thriving business. So there was an opportunity for revenge *and* making lots of money."

"Hang on," Pam interrupted. "Once it was known this was Howard's only heir, they'd immediately become a suspect."

"That's why it was so important that Howard should seem to be the innocent victim of a street robbery. And with the mugger dead too, the police couldn't prove anything, no matter how suspicious they might be. All the person behind this had to do was wait a few months, maybe a year, say they'd just realized who their natural father was and claim his inheritance. It'd look like a big coincidence, I grant you, but nothing the Law could argue with."

"But all this depends on the heir knowing about the deal you made with Rolf."

"No, they only had to know *Attwood*, and well enough that he'd tell them about it. Then they just had to switch the blanks for live ammo and let him do the job for them. As I said, Attwood was a patsy."

"Then he was killed."

"Yeah. It's possible he tried to blackmail the person who set him up. His body was surrounded by bank notes when I found him, and I bet they were counterfeit. I expect he went to that park believing he was going to get paid off, and the murderer took a bundle of fake notes to lure him into a false sense of security. They must have scattered in the struggle, and would have been gathered up, except I arrived and the killer had to leg it."

"The picture you paint of the suspect could apply to most people here," Pam observed.

"Not me!" Rolf interjected. "Howard and I were about the same age."

"Yeah, you're out of the frame for this," Paul agreed. "Someone I have in mind got much closer to Howard than you ever did."

He turned and looked into the face of the person he thought he'd known so well.

"Didn't you, Lynn?"

"*What?*" she gasped. "Come on, Paul, don't mess about!"

"You're a good actress, Lynn, but don't try playing the innocent this time."

"You must be insane!"

"Not me," he whispered.

Vince stepped forward, lowering his gun. "Are you sure? She don't look the killing kind to me."

He made a bad mistake in dropping his guard. Before anyone could react, Lynn's hand flashed out and snatched the shotgun from his grasp. She turned it on the group, her face twisted with maniacal rage.

"Yes, I engineered Howard's death, and I'm glad! He had it coming."

Paul was shocked by the sudden change in her character. "But your own *father*..."

"He was never a father to *me*! And the people I was adopted by made my life hell! I swore I'd get even with him. Once I discovered who he was I traced him and spent a couple of years worming my way into his trust as an employee."

"And I was right about you knowing Attwood?"

"He was an old boyfriend. A fool. A loser, like you. But we kept in touch, and he boasted about Rolf paying him to threaten my oh so precious father. It was easy to switch the ammo. As a matter of fact the timing was perfect, because that big printing order was about to come in and I'd already decided the time had come to do away with Daddy."

"Did Bobby try to blackmail you?"

"Yeah, you got that part right, too."

"You're sick," Pam said. "Put down the gun."

"No! I'm getting out of here, and I'm using a couple of you as shields. Including *you*. The cops are less likely to fire at one of their own."

"You haven't got a chance," Paul told her. "They'll cut you to pieces out there!"

She aimed the gun at his head. "You won't be around to see it. I had hopes for you, Paul. I thought you were smart. We could have done a lot with that company together. Now I can see you really are just an interfering little wimp after all. And you've ruined everything! *I* got the police here, thinking they'd arrest you for the murders and take the heat off me. That hasn't worked, but I'm still going to make you pay!"

Vince put himself between them. "No, you're not."

"Out of the way, you dolt!"

Vince moved towards her.

"Lynn, don't do it!" Paul cried.

She squeezed the trigger.

The shotgun gave a hollow click.

It clicked again and again.

Vince reached out and took the weapon from her. "It wasn't loaded," he said. "I'm not *that* stupid."

Paul watched with a heavy heart as Lynn was bundled into a panda car.

A crowd was gathering. Rolf and Shaw, wearing handcuffs and bickering, were being led to a waiting police van. Two officers cuffed Vince.

Pam Watkins indicated Paul. "So, what about our friend here?" she asked.

Inspector Garfield gave him one of her stern looks. "I don't have to tell you what a fool you've been, Grant. I should do you for criminal conspiracy. Not to mention wasting police time." Then she surprised him by doing something he hadn't seen before. She smiled. Faintly. "But as you were instrumental in nailing a killer, and we've smashed a counterfeit ring, I doubt there'll be charges."

"Thanks." Paul glanced at Vince as they marched him to the van. "You know, Vince was always a bit of a div, but he's basically harmless."

"The gun wasn't loaded," Pam said, "and nobody

got hurt, so that should help his defence. Shouldn't it, guv?"

"Expect so," Garfield replied, her attention fixed on Paul. He was watching the panda car as it sped off.

"What's going to happen to her?" he asked, his voice tight with emotion.

"That's up to the courts, but I suspect she'll be found more in need of treatment than punishment." She paused, her look of sympathy deepening. "It must be rough for you, finding out your girlfriend's ... unbalanced."

"Yeah." He spoke quietly. Then he met the policewoman's eyes. "But I'll get over it. In fact, I think this whole thing's going to make me stronger."

"I believe it will," she said softly, and turned away.

A light shower began to fall. Paul tilted back his head and let the cool rain cleanse and soothe his face.

It felt good.

WHY YOU'RE HERE

The West End shopping arcade was on the verge of closing. Grey metal shutters waited to be pulled down. The lights in expensive stores were either dimmed or dead. As the last cleaner left the building in the early evening gloom, five figures converged on the entrance. Each held a white, embossed card.

The five eyed each other with a mixture of suspicion and shared purpose. As they walked down the sparkling gangway to their destination, each one had doubt in their eyes. Rather than wait a few moments, all five crammed into the lift, as if they were worried that it might never return.

Inside the lift, none of the five so much as looked at each other, must less spoke. But they couldn't avoid smelling. The oldest woman, who had come straight from work, bore a faint odour of antiseptic soap. The bigger of the two men had beer on his breath. The other smelt of stale aftershave. The two remaining women wore freshly applied perfume with a subtle scent. One perfume was much more expensive than the other, but few people would be able to tell the difference. These women could.

They all smelt of something else, too, as the lift reached the basement, and the doors opened, releasing them. It was a distinct smell, and they all knew what it was, even those who had not come across it before. They smelt of greed.

Almost opposite the lift was a branch of Ballard Brothers, one of the West End's most exclusive stores. Each of the five heaved a sigh of relief to see the store still fully-lit, a uniformed attendant in a red cap holding the door open. The five swept past the attendant into the store, handing in their cards as they passed. Each was secretly satisfied when the door was locked behind them. It meant that no one else was to arrive. They had the place to themselves.

Inside the store, they looked around them, expecting someone there to greet them. Any moment now, someone would come in. Perhaps there would be a glass of champagne. In the meantime, though, they examined the merchandise on display, for this was an exclusive gift store, full of desirable items.

The five wandered around, examining the goods. Three of them acted as though they belonged in the store, lingering over some objects, dismissing others with barely a glance. The bigger man and the youngest woman seemed less at ease, as if they were shoplifters working out how much they could stuff into their pockets.

Thomas, a stocky young man wearing working clothes, picked up an electronic personal organizer, then put it down again, deciding that the item was not expensive enough. Imogen, a smart but tired-looking woman of indeterminate age, examined a Cartier watch. It was too showy to wear for work, she decided, and would have to be kept for special occasions. Keith, a thin, flashily dressed man, looked at a large globe with a mahogany base, wondering whether it would fit on the desk in his office. Polly, a fresh-faced, blonde girl, was looking at the jewellery counter. Harriet, who was older than her, better dressed and, in a conventional sense at least, more beautiful, joined Polly in looking at the locked cabinet.

"I like your perfume," Polly told her. "Chanel?"

Harriet nodded, then pointed at the bracelets, with their four and five figure price tags.

"Do you think these are included?" she asked Polly.

"The card did say anything in the store," Polly said.

"Are you a regular customer here?" Harriet asked.

"You must be kidding," Polly said. "I bought some cufflinks for my father's birthday in one of their branches once. That must be how they got my details."

Thomas, having decided to go for the combined wide-screen television, satellite decoder and video, tried to chat up Imogen. She was tall and thin, but not stringy, with a narrow nose and long, tied back, brown hair. Not his usual type, but he'd never been picky.

"Found anything you like?" he asked.

Imogen put down the watch and gave the smallest of shrugs. "I'm surprised that there's nobody here to meet us," she told him.

"There was, wasn't there? On the door. I reckon they're giving us a bit of time to look around."

"Yes," Imogen said, politely.

Thomas kept talking, even though, if he'd understood body language, he would have realized that Imogen wasn't interested in him, or, indeed, any man.

"I've never won anything in my life before. You could have knocked me down with a feather when I got the card. Imagine. *Pick anything in the store.* Now that's what I call a hundredth anniversary celebration. I've never shopped here, you know, but I've done deliveries. You reckon Mr Ballard himself will make the presentation? I expect he's in the back now, waiting with lots of media."

At this mention of the media, Imogen gave a small, disdainful shiver. She turned away from Thomas, just in time to see Keith pointing at the lift they'd descended in.

"Did anyone see that?" he asked, anxiously. "The light's gone off. It's shut down."

"Probably an economy measure," Harriet told him.

"Somebody should be here to greet us, though," Polly pointed out. "The card did say to arrive at seven precisely. Or are we expected to choose what we want and take it away when we're ready?"

"I don't think so," Thomas commented, trying the heavy glass door. "This is locked and bolted."

"They'll be in the back," Keith announced, with a salesman's pragmatic optimism. He went to try the double doors which led to the rear of the store.

They wouldn't open.

"Did everyone get the same card?" Harriet asked, her voice conveying both curiosity and mild irritation. *"You have won a special draw. As part of our hundredth anniversary celebration you are invited to choose any gift of any value..."*

"The same," the others all agreed.

"I expect that someone will be along any moment," Polly said.

While they were waiting, Imogen re-examined the merchandise. Keith told Harriet about computers. Thomas tried to chat up Polly, unaware that she only dated men who wore suits to work and belonged to the same church as her. Getting nowhere, he looked for a toilet. He'd had a couple of celebratory pints before coming here and his bladder was bursting. There wasn't one.

When they had been alone in the store for forty-five minutes, Harriet, bored by Keith, began to burrow behind the counter. She pulled out a Ballard Brothers bag.

"I don't want to disturb anyone," she said, "but look at this: *Established 1876*. The hundredth anniversary was decades ago!"

As the five looked at each other, a new smell seeped from their bodies into the stale, no longer air-conditioned atmosphere: the smell of fear.

"We could be here until Tuesday," Thomas announced, telling the others something they'd already worked out for themselves. "It's a bank holiday Monday. The arcade'll be closed."

"Has anyone got a mobile phone?" Keith asked. "I've left mine at home."

No one answered.

"Is that a phone over there?" Polly said, pointing at the counter.

Imogen rushed over to it and picked up the handset. "There's a tone!" She began to dial feverishly. As she did, her face betrayed frustration, then despair. "I think it's internal only," she said, finally, and put the phone down. Then she added, "Hold on."

"What is it?" Harriet asked.

"Look." Imogen held up several envelopes which had hitherto been concealed beneath the phone. "I think they're addressed to us. Is there a Harriet Carpenter here?"

"That's me," Harriet said.

"Keith Bretton. Dr I. Wheeler – that's me. Polly Smythe. Thomas Green."

All the envelopes were handed out. The recipients showed signs of relief. There was a spark of hope in their eyes. Maybe they weren't trapped. Maybe they would get their prizes, after all. They each read the letter.

I expect you're wondering why you're here. I'll explain. You all have something in common, and it isn't that you've won a prize from Ballard Brothers. You are here because each of you has done me wrong.

How have you harmed me? Perhaps you bullied me when I was at school. Or maybe you failed to protect me from a bully. Thanks to you, I started, but didn't finish a university degree. Maybe you turned me down for a job which I badly needed. Maybe you saw me coming down the street and crossed the road, not wanting to speak to me. You thought I didn't see, but I did, and it hurt.

Maybe you were my lover and treated me so badly that I've been unable to form a relationship since. Maybe you were my friend, but dropped me. When I was at my lowest ebb, you didn't return my calls. Worse, I became a standing joke with your friends, until the gag wore thin, and you forgot me altogether. Maybe you let me down in another way. Maybe you did more than one of these things.

You don't remember me, do you? Never mind. This is my revenge. You are to work out who I am. If, together, you can agree on my name, and get it right, I will release you all. If not, you will remain here until Tuesday morning.

Your stay will not be a comfortable one. There is nothing to eat, or drink. There are no sanitary facilities, nowhere to sleep. You will become ill. But sixty hours of discomfort is a small price to pay for the pain you've caused me.

You will think of escape. You will be wasting your time. I shall explain why. The only job I could get was as a security guard. Given this small chance, I worked hard, and proved to be good at my job. Now I am in charge of security at the West End arcade. I even have a set of keys to Ballard Brothers. You cannot reach me. I am sitting securely in an office in a back room, watching you read this on the security video. I have installed microphones, and can hear your every word. The other guards who should have been on this weekend have been given leave. We will not be disturbed.

You don't remember me, do you?
Try to. Your life might depend on it.

Harriet finished reading first. She was standing next to Keith, and turned to him. "Is yours…?"

A glance showed that his letter was identical to the one she'd received. When they had all finished reading, the five looked at each other.

"That last line," Harriet said. "Is it a serious threat?"

"With no food or water for sixty-odd hours," Imogen told them, "death is a serious threat. The heating's not on, either. There's a risk of…"

"No need to get so negative," Keith told them. "It's obviously some kind of practical joke. This bloke's…"

"Who said it's a man?" Imogen asked. "There's nothing in the letter to indicate the author's sex. My guess is that the person behind this is the one who let us in. Did anyone look closely at them?"

No one had.

"The doorman could easily have been a woman," Imogen said. "She could have had long hair hidden in the cap. All I can remember is that they were of medium build."

"You've got a point," Harriet said. "But there are five of us here – three women and two men. Doesn't that suggest that the writer is a man?"

"Surely it suggests the opposite?" Polly commented. "If the writer's a woman, her enemies are more likely to be women."

"I think it's a woman," Thomas said. "A man didn't write this *I haven't been able to form a relationship* rubbish."

"Maybe not the kind of men you meet," Harriet said, tartly.

"Listen to her," Thomas muttered to Keith, trying to enlist his support. "Stuck up cow."

Keith ignored him.

"I suggest," Harriet went on, "that we all have a think – see if we can quickly identify this person – they're obviously unhinged, if that helps."

"I think," Polly interrupted, "that we ought to be very careful what we say about our captor. He or she is probably listening."

"Point taken," Harriet agreed.

For a few minutes, no one spoke. As if by agreement, they walked around the shop, each looking for a way out. Ballard Brothers had seemed so large when they walked in: a cornucopia of consumer goods. But now it became clear that this was one of the smaller branches, and it felt claustrophobic. The letter proved to be right on another point. There was no apparent escape route.

The glass in the windows might have been designed to stop bullets. Imogen slung a bin at it. Not a scratch. Thomas threw a metal chair, the heaviest object in the shop. It had no effect. The double doors at the back of the store could not be prised open. There were no air vents, no manholes or false walls which could be knocked through.

They were well and truly trapped.

"I think," Keith said, as the minutes ticked by, "that we'd better do as the letter says."

Reluctantly, everyone agreed.

"It might not take long," Thomas suggested. "I mean, as soon as we land the right name, the rest of us'll probably recognize it."

The others didn't seem certain of this, but no one demurred.

"Let's talk about what we do," Keith suggested. "I'm in software – run my own small company with a fairly high staff turnover. Could be someone I sacked, or made redundant when we downsized after the crash."

"I'm a lorry driver," Thomas said. "For Mitchell transport. I've never employed nobody. Had a lot of girlfriends, mind."

"I'm a psychiatrist," Imogen told them. "I've had hundreds of patients."

"I'm a bank clerk," Polly mumbled. "I don't have responsibility for granting people loans or that kind of thing. I don't have any power. I think I'm here by mistake."

"How old are you?" Harriet asked Polly.

"Nearly twenty-three. Why do you ask?"

"Because whoever is doing this is unlikely to be taking revenge on anyone much younger than him or herself. It helps to give an idea. I'm twenty-seven. I lecture in Sociology at Exeter University."

Imogen, it turned out, was twenty-eight, the same age as Thomas. Keith was twenty-six.

"We've got a good idea what age our captor is," Harriet said. "Twenty-two to twenty-eight. That's a start. Now we have to think about names."

"This is embarrassing," Imogen complained. "We don't even know what sex this person is. I don't want to share my private life with strangers."

"Do you have a better idea?" Harriet asked. "If we're lucky, it won't take long. And as for embarrassment – none of us are likely to see each other again, so who cares? The more honest we are, the sooner we get out.

"I'll start if you like," Harriet went on. "I've only been lecturing for two years, but I can think of two students who got thrown out and might think they have a legitimate grudge against me. They could believe that I let them down by not speaking up, or giving them enough help, or something. One was called Simon Harper. The other was Jeanette Cohen. Mean anything to anyone?"

No one spoke.

"I dropped a girl called Melanie once," Keith admitted. "Melanie Green. She was very cut up about it. But that was ten years ago."

No one recognized the name Melanie Green.

Keith and Harriet looked at the others, waiting to see who would make the next true confession. No one did. Eventually, Polly spoke.

"Can I make a suggestion?" she asked. "Why don't each of us write down a list of people who we think it might be? Then we can see if the names match up."

"Brilliant," Harriet told her.

"Who's got some paper?" Keith asked.

"We can use these," Imogen said.

The psychiatrist took five Ballard Brothers carrier bags from behind the counter and handed them out. She was annoyed she hadn't come up with this idea herself. Even so, she smiled at Polly as she handed her a bag. The girl impressed her.

When they'd found enough pens, the five prisoners ripped the bags open and began to write. Some found writing easier than talking. Some didn't. Some wrote more quickly than others. After four names, Polly ran out. She could remember no friends she'd dropped. There were no jilted lovers. It had to be someone she'd let down in another way. Who?

Thomas filled in a dozen names, mostly of women. But he had trouble remembering surnames, particularly when he thought back to people he'd bullied at school.

Imogen wrote calmly in large, clear letters. Part of her admired the low cunning of the revenge being exacted on the group. Imogen knew who her enemies were – professional rivals, dropped lovers, snubbed schoolgirls. She had kept a list in her head. But she didn't think of patients as enemies. If it was a patient, then there were so many, she couldn't remember half of their names. Had she let people down? Of course she had. In her job, it was inevitable. You couldn't be there for patients every minute of the day. She cared, honestly she did. But she was run off her feet, stressed to the eyeballs, and so tired all the time...

Keith wrote slowly, trying to remember the names of people who used to work for him. The trouble was, he was terrible with names. But he hadn't sacked that many people. If someone else mentioned the right name, he was sure to recognize it.

Harriet wrote quickly. She had not been lecturing for terribly long. The names of most students were still lodged in her brain. She wrote down every person who she remembered not getting on with – who knew which one might have a grudge against her? She tried to remember the names of all her ex-boyfriends and the first name of a girl she'd been cruel to at school. Everyone else had hated the girl, too, but memory did funny things. She might bear a grudge against Harriet simply because she was usually so nice to people.

After half an hour, they were all finished. Harriet, used to public speaking, began to read the lists out.

"If you spot a name you know, but haven't written down, stop me, and I'll make a note of it."

Harriet felt a certain satisfaction as she read the names. With such excellent methodology, they were bound to find the right person. She only hoped that the captor would keep their word and let them go. She was supposed to be meeting her lover later. He would worry. She had told no one where she was going.

"Richard Hewitt, Tracey Watt, Myra Connell, Peter Dodd..."

The others listened with folded arms, shivering a little, for the store was starting to become cold. Name followed name with few hints of recognition. Harriet made strokes by several which someone thought might be familiar. Now and again, someone asked for a name to be repeated.

"I knew a Patrick Hyde once."

"This one would be forty-five."

"No good. Mine's only thirty."

The fourth list to be read was Keith's. Halfway down, Harriet stopped. "Petra something. That wouldn't be Petra Jones, would it?"

"S'right."

"That name's on my list, too."

"Tall, skinny girl. Bit of a lefty."

"That's the one." Harriet read the rest of Keith's list, then hers. No other names matched.

"That's our solution, then," Thomas said. "Has to be. Let's tell her."

"No," Imogen insisted. "Not until we've worked out that we all know her. The name means nothing to me. Tell us about her, Keith. Why did you put her on your list?"

"She organized a Union at my firm," Keith said. "Tried to get people to strike. When we had to downsize, she was one of the first to go. Took us to an Industrial Tribunal, earlier this year, but we won. I expect she holds a grudge."

"And you?" Imogen asked Harriet.

"I taught her, in my first year at Exeter. She'd barely scraped into the second year and was spending all her time on political activity. I gave her a couple of written warnings for not handing work in, missing a tutorial, that kind of thing. I tried to talk to her, but she wasn't responsive. I don't think she was thrown out. I think she left of her own accord, because she knew she was going to fail her second year exams."

"Describe her again," Thomas said.

Harriet did. Keith added to the description.

"She was from London," both agreed.

No one else could remember her.

"She sounds like a fem," Thomas said. "I don't go out with fems."

"She might be my age," Polly said, "but I've never heard of her. I mean, she might have been in the year below me in school, but..."

"It doesn't sound like one of my patients," Imogen said, "and it's not somebody I know."

"Let's try again," Harriet said. "The other names mentioned were..."

She read out the names which had a stroke by them. People made tentative suggestions. Keith had cheated on his wife with somebody called Cheryl. Asked for a description, he admitted that he was too drunk to remember. Thomas had dumped a Cheryl once. Polly admitted that, as a child, she'd stolen a bag of sweets from a boy called Nick, who she didn't like. She made the others promise not to tell anyone, as she was worried that the bank might sack her if they knew she'd ever stolen, no matter how long ago it was.

Harriet, in her first year as a lecturer, had had a fling with a student called Nick, who just might have been Polly's Nick. However, he had recently got a first class honours degree, and didn't seem to hold a grudge against her.

Thomas, it transpired, had once got a girl called Penny pregnant. He didn't know what had happened to her, but she might be the same Penny who Imogen remembered as a particularly disturbed patient. Keith once hit a boy at school called Phillip. They worked out that this could not be the same Phillip who Polly had refused to dance with at the bank's Christmas do.

At two in the morning, exhausted, they agreed to sleep. Sleep wasn't easy. The lights were on full. The bucket in the corner, which used to contain a Japanese tree, had been emptied for use as a toilet, and its smell filled the room. They were all thirsty. And it was cold. They pushed pride aside and huddled together for warmth. Using Ballard Brothers bags as pillows, each dozed intermittently.

Polly and Keith both heard a distant phone ring twice, but assumed they'd dreamt it. They could not hear the low voice which answered.

"That's right, officer. All closed up. The boss? I'm in charge. Yes, there was some kind of after-hours do at Ballard's. I don't know how many. Still there? You must be kidding. They'd all gone by half seven. No one's allowed to stay after half seven. Check? I've got the screens in front of me. The building's completely empty. Come and see for yourself if you like."

In Ballard Brothers, Thomas was snoring. In a few moments, he would wake Harriet. Keith was starting to get cramp and shuffled uncomfortably. Imogen had her eyes closed, but was wide awake. She had trouble sleeping at the best of times. Only Polly dreamt. She was in a crowded compartment on the Underground. The tube train travelled quickly but never stopped, yet none of the other passengers seemed in the least worried. There were fifty-five hours to go. The five's captor had a sip of hot chocolate, then settled on a camp bed for a nap.

There was nothing to indicate that it was morning. The shop remained brightly lit, but cold, for the fluorescent lights gave off little heat. Polly still hadn't spoken to any of the other prisoners, but now she had to. One of them was trying to feel her up. She woke with a start to find Thomas's hand wandering in his sleep. Polly was the first to get up. Imogen was second. Harriet had been awake for a while. When she heard other people moving about, she tried to stand, stepping on Thomas, which woke him. Keith had another attack of cramp and shot upright, stamping his leg on the floor to soothe it.

Imogen, in a chillingly matter-of-fact voice, explained that everyone ought to save their urine. If they remained trapped here for another forty-eight hours, then, without liquids, they would dehydrate and die. Urine was pure, and safe, she assured them. One by one, the five crept behind the counter and filled the Ballard Brothers' crystal decanters as best they could.

Sunday passed very slowly. New lists were drawn up. None of the names matched. Keith was convinced that they would soon be rescued.

"My wife knew where I was going," he told them. "She'll have called the police. They'll come down here for us. They're bound to."

The others, who lived alone, hoped that Keith was right. How much did Keith's wife love him, they wondered? Enough to kick up a fuss? Enough to persuade the police to open up a locked shopping arcade on a bank holiday weekend?

Imogen was the first to be sick, Thomas the second. All five were beginning to turn a pale yellow. Finally, Polly cracked. She approached one of the security cameras, the one which most obviously had a microphone attached beneath it, and began to shout.

"Let us out, why don't you? We've played your silly game. You've made us ill. You've won. We're not going to come up with a name now, are we? I don't know what I've done, but I'll tell you something else – nothing I've done in my life deserves this kind of punishment. Nothing!"

She began to cry. Gently, Harriet led her away. Although it was only early evening, Imogen suggested that everyone slept. They were all tired and weak from lack of food.

By four in the morning, everyone was wide awake and feeling like death.

"Let's start again," Harriet said, to barely disguised moans. "Either this person is someone who none of us remembers, or they're on one of our lists, but the others don't recognize the name. There could be reasons for that – people do change their names. Women marry. People get religion, need to hide, whatever."

"How do we start?" Thomas moaned. "Haven't we tried everything already?"

"I don't know," Harriet told him. "I've been thinking about it all night. Consciously, or unconsciously, all of us must be hiding something. We are connected. Otherwise we wouldn't be here. I want everyone to dredge their memories again, and begin talking about the worst thing you've ever done to another person, something you haven't mentioned before."

The other four looked shiftily from one to the other. Imogen, in particular, seemed to resent this younger, better-looking woman taking control. Harriet took a deep breath and began to talk.

"Last night, I remembered something from eight years ago which I'm not proud of. There was this bloke, when I was a student. He was always hanging around trying to make conversation with me after lectures. He was nice enough, but I didn't fancy him. Then my boyfriend dumped me. He was also on the course. So I asked this other guy out. He was delighted. He didn't realize that I was only doing it to get back at my ex. And it worked. My ex got so jealous that he made a big play for me, said he'd made a mistake, all that stuff. And I dumped the other bloke just like that. He seemed devastated."

"What was his name?" Imogen asked, in her most clinical voice.

"That's the problem," Harriet said. "I don't remember. I've suppressed it. I'm sorry."

"Would you remember if you heard the name?" Polly asked.

"Maybe. I don't know. Your turn."

Polly shook her head. "I can't think of anything. I'm sorry, I know this sounds holier than thou, but *I'm not a bad person*. I can't think of anyone I've harmed who I haven't mentioned already." She paused. "You want to know the only thing I feel guilty about? Yesterday, I missed church. There hasn't been a Sunday since I was five years old when I haven't been to church."

Polly wasn't speaking to the others, Harriet seemed to realize. She was speaking to whoever was watching the security cameras. Harriet looked at Thomas.

"You?"

Thomas looked perturbed. "There were a few kids I used to push about at school. Nothing serious, you know. Just a laugh."

"She asked for the worst thing you've ever done," Imogen said, cuttingly.

Thomas glanced around. Polly gave him a withering, contemptuous look. He decided that there was no percentage in holding anything back.

"There was this girl once," he muttered, "a hitcher. I thought she was playing games, that she really wanted it. She said she didn't, but I got carried away."

"Name?" Keith demanded.

"Jane, Judy ... I don't remember. She never reported it. She knew it wasn't ... you know ... things just got a little out of hand." Thomas appeared uneasy for a moment, then looked angrily at Keith. "Your turn."

Keith looked at the floor, not saying a word, while the others stared at him.

"I'm pretty successful," he said, finally, in a matter of fact voice. "I meet a lot of people, all the time. All of my friends are business contacts, one way or another. I've lost touch with most of the people from my childhood. Now and then, someone I used to know comes to me for a job, but I get an employee to turn them down, shield me from them. It's not a good way to run business, the old school tie, not any more."

"Come to the point," Harriet said. "The worst thing..."

"There is no worst thing," Keith insisted. "If I had the files, I could check the names, that's all I'm saying."

"There must be something," Thomas said. "Everyone's got skeletons in their cupboard. Am I the only one who'll admit to something bad?"

Keith looked agitated. He spoke, his voice rising hysterically.

"All right," he said. "What would you like me to tell you? I never bullied anyone at school – I used to get bullied by big kids like you. I've never taken a woman by force. I've only been with two women in my life and I married the first one. Whatever it is I'm supposed to have done, I've forgotten, all right? I've forgotten!"

The room went quiet. All five of them breathed the foul, fetid air. Once, this had seemed like a spacious, glitzy store. Now it was a dingy, disgusting dungeon. Eventually, Imogen spoke.

"I have an inability to form close personal relationships. I make pick-ups in clubs and never stay with anyone longer than a weekend. One of my pick-ups could have become fixated with me, I suppose, but I doubt it. I doubt that anyone thinks I'm worth it."

"What about your job?" Keith asked. "You must make enemies at work."

"All the time," Imogen said. "I make mistakes, I'm human. Recently I refused to admit someone and he killed himself the next day. But we're overstretched. Do you know how hard it is to get a place on a psychiatric ward these days? You need to be a potential serial killer, not a suicide. I didn't spot this bloke's problem, but, even if I had, there might not have been a bed. And, after all, suicides save the state money. He was doing the system a favour."

"What was his name?" Polly asked.

"I don't recall."

"Only," Polly went on, "you made me think of some-something bad I did ... or didn't do."

"I thought doing bad things was against your religion," Thomas sneered.

"It is," Polly tried to explain. "But what I did... In the catechism, they call it a *sin of omission.* I was on the Underground a few weeks ago, coming home from work. It was crowded. I was waiting near the tunnel entrance.

The man standing next to me walked to the edge of the platform and stepped in front of the train. It was horrible. I had to give evidence at his inquest."

"But how was that your fault?" Harriet enquired.

"I could have stopped him," Polly insisted. "I could see what he was doing. Other people could too. There was a moment when I could have reached forward, grabbed him, pulled him back from the brink. But I didn't."

"Because you thought he had the right to kill himself?" Imogen asked, carefully.

"No," Polly said. "I don't think anyone has that right."

"Why then?" Keith wanted to know.

Polly looked uncomfortable. "I suppose," she told them, "because I didn't want to get involved."

They were all silent. They had been in the shop for thirty-five hours now, and there were at least another twenty-five to go. Each was acutely conscious of this.

"We're not getting anywhere," Thomas complained. "We're not going to find out who it is. We're all going to suffocate."

"Your suicide," Imogen said to Polly, ignoring Thomas. "What was his name?"

"It doesn't matter, does it?" Polly told her. "After all, it can't be him. He's dead."

"I'm still curious."

"He was called Peter Miller," Polly said. "Was he the man who you refused to admit?"

Imogen closed her eyes. She looked all played out. "Possibly," she said, when she opened her eyes again. "Now I think about it, I'm almost certain he was. Not that it makes any difference."

"That's it then," Keith said. "We've gone through

everybody we know and we've managed to find two people who two of us have met. Not a lot, was it?"

"Actually," Thomas interrupted. "I think there was a Peter Miller at my school. Skinny kid, always had his head in a book. Got picked on all the time. He left in the middle of a year."

"The boy who I only went out with for a week," Harriet said, softly. "I think his name was Peter. Thin, with a wobbly chin. Very straight hair. Green eyes."

"That's him," Thomas said.

Polly and Imogen nodded agreement. Harriet sank her head into her shoulders.

"Look," Keith told them, exasperatedly, "this is pointless. I mean, Polly saw the guy crushed to death. It can't be him, unless..."

A haunted look spread across Keith's face. No one spoke for several minutes. Finally, it was Imogen who asked the question.

"Do you know a Peter Miller, Keith?"

Keith frowned. When he spoke, his voice was childlike.

"I went to a third-rate public school. There was this bloke arrived in the middle of the third year. We used to call him Windy Miller. Very clever but a big daydreamer. People used to take the mickey all the time. But I got on with him all right. He used to help me with my homework. Then he went to university and we lost touch. He had no reason to bear a grudge against me."

"He wasn't one of those people who wrote to you, asking for a job?" Polly asked.

Now Keith looked embarrassed. "I told you, I don't look at those letters, on principle. I get someone else to deal with them. He might have been, but if he didn't have the right specialist credentials..."

"What's the point of all this?" Thomas asked. "This bloke we're talking about – even if it is the same one – he's dead. He can't be doing this to us."

"I think he is," Harriet said, slowly. "I don't know how, but..."

There was a chilling pause.

"Say the word," Imogen said.

"No," Polly insisted. "I don't believe in them. They're against my religion. You're messing with my head. Stop this."

"It's too much of a coincidence," Harriet told the others. "If all five of us did know this bloke, did harm him in a significant way..."

"We all have to agree," Thomas said. "That includes Polly. We all have to make the accusation."

"But I saw him *die*," Polly said. "If it's him, then..."

"Say it," Keith told her. "Say it for all of us."

Polly looked round the squalid, stinking gift store. She had nothing left to lose. Without speaking, the five of them huddled together in the cold, dead morning, with Polly at the front. They all looked up, but it was Polly who spoke to the camera.

"We think," Polly said, "that you are Peter Miller."

There was a noise from the back of the store. A key was turned, then another. The tumblers inside the locks tumbled. The great black double doors opened.

A man in uniform stepped out.

It was not the man they thought they remembered. This man was in his fifties, not his twenties. Yet, seeing him again, they all realized that he was the person who had let them in, the one who they had paid so little attention to thirty-five hours before.

"Who are you?" Polly asked him.

"My name is Peter Miller." The voice was polite,

almost servile. "That was my only son's name, too," the man added.

None of the five spoke.

"You've seen me before," Mr Miller told Polly in a flat voice, "at the inquest. You explained to the coroner how you could have prevented my son's death, but didn't."

"It wasn't like that," Polly protested.

"It never is," the bereaved father told her. He turned to Imogen. "You saw my son for five minutes, and judged that his depression should be treated with a few tablets. You are more to blame than she is."

Imogen's mouth opened, but no words came out.

"As for you," he said, turning to Keith, "you were one of Peter's only friends. But you dropped my son, losing touch with him when you left school. When, in desperation, he humiliated himself by writing to you, asking for a job, you didn't even reply. You helped drive him to the edge of that platform."

Keith said nothing.

"You," the old man said, turning to Harriet, "you probably hurt him most of all. He worshipped you for months, but you barely gave him the time of day. Then you flattered him, seduced him and finished with him, all in the space of a week. You probably didn't even notice when Peter dropped out of university at the end of that term.

"Thanks to you, he spent years drifting, trying to find himself, and failing, always tasting the bitter residue of that rejection. He was still writing about you in his diary during the last week of his life.

"Yes," Peter Miller went on. "My son kept a diary – thirteen years of words, going back to when he was fourteen. In the end, the diaries were almost his only posessions. I read them all after he died. I wanted to find out what had made him the way he was. Peter always blamed himself, you see. Anything which went wrong, he blamed on his own failings.

"But my son was clever, imaginative, talented. I knew there had to be other reasons. And they were there, everywhere, a page a day, the people who helped to ruin his life – not because they hated him, but because they didn't care. There, almost on the first page, you were, Thomas: teasing him, bullying him, endlessly putting him down, shattering his self-confidence."

When Mr Miller paused, Polly spoke. "You blame the five of us for your son's death – but we can't be the only ones."

Peter Miller shook his head. "No. There were many others. You were the ones I was able to track down."

"Is it over?" Imogen asked, quietly. "Can we go?"

"I will keep my word," Peter Miller said. "You can leave. If you choose to go to the police, this is where they'll find me. I expect I've committed a crime, though I don't know what it is. I wanted you to understand what you did to my only son. That's why you're here."

The five were silent. Their captor went to the doors, opened them, then left. A few moment later, the lights on the lift came back on. From his security booth, Peter Miller watched the five bedraggled prisoners as they traipsed out of the shop, then squeezed, forlornly, into the lift.

Inside the cramped compartment, the five didn't look at each other, or speak. Polly was the only one who considered calling the police. But she would need to talk to the others about it, first. Opening her mouth would mean taking in more air. And the air in the lift was rank, unbearable. It had all the fetid odours of five people who had been locked away without a bathroom for two days.

The air smelt of something else, too, a smell which none of the five would ever forget. It smelt of guilt.

The lift came to a halt on the ground floor and its doors slowly opened. The five were relieved to see that the arcade's grey shutters had been lifted. Without a word, they scurried out into the grey morning, the empty city streets.

Each went their separate way.

SCREE

Crash. It's some horrible hour of the morning. In my dream there is a picnic, all the family, all the aunts and uncles I've never seen. We're in the zoo and suddenly the animals go wild, rattling their cages till the bars burst and they pour out, monkeys, buffaloes, the tigers… I open my eyes and there's Mr Barratt storming through the dormitory, like every morning since we've been in the hostel, rattling my bunk frame with his metal-pommelled walking stick.

"Look lively, this isn't a holiday camp." He grins. Outdoor pursuits for inner-city layabouts. Mountain air. Put some backbone in us. A week of this, we won't be problems any more. I stumble to the floor. "Mohan, you great lump of lard."

"Yes, sir," I start to say, but he's striding off already, and there's Gary grinning down from his top bunk. "Lard. Cow fat. Nice one!" As I bury my head in my T-shirt, he whispers, "Don't you worry. That git's going to get it one day."

There's a clattering downstairs. "Breakfast!" Mr Barratt bellows. "Last one down's on washing-up." Gary vaults over my head, Mal is out of the door and the girls will be down there already, unless Tash is staging one of her protests. It'll be scraping the porridge pot again for me.

No one looks up when I come in. "Hey, pass me the sugar, Mo," says Tash without turning round.

"Let her get it herself," says Colette in her prissy headmaster's daughter voice. "Mo's not here to wait on you, you know."

Tash slams her spoon down. "Look here, pizza-face, my ancestors were slaves on some sugar plantation. If I say pass the sugar, someone better jump!" There are damp brown lumps in it; people put their coffee spoons straight in. I'm just passing the bowl to Tash when Mr Barratt strides in.

"Sugar! Water and salt, that's the way. Don't know you're born, you kids." He looks me up and down. "Who's this?" he says. "The waiter? You're not in the restaurant now, you know." I close my eyes. No one in my family runs a restaurant... *Crash.* I'm not sure how but there's the sugar on the floor.

"Oh, God, Mo," someone groans. "You're useless."

Kath the warden comes through the door with a dustpan and brush, and I get down on hands and knees.

"Eat up, you two." She has to mean Jack and Jill, nobody else is "you two". They're twins, you see – identical, because Jack is a girl.

"You can't make us eat this," says one of them. "We have Bran Flakes at home," says the other. They always say "we", never "I".

"Sorry," said Kath, "this is all there is. You need something inside you. You're going on a real climb today." The twins mutter something to each other in that language they've got no one else can understand, then push their bowls aside. "Leave them alone," says Tash. "You can't rule their life." "That," says Mr Barratt quietly, "is where you're wrong." Behind his back Gary belches. Mr Barratt brings his fist down on the table so the porridge shudders. Mal starts to clear plates. "Now *there's* a good lad," says Mr Barratt to him so the rest of us can hear.

I try to respect Mr Barratt. It's very important, respect. I do try, but it is hard.

Cold dripping grey outside the kitchen window. At first I think it's steam from the washing-up but from the porch it looks the same. "It's piddling down," says Gary. "We can't go out in this."

Mr Barratt just laughs. "Ground mist," he says. "It should break around two thousand feet. Then you'll see what's in store for you."

There's the usual lecture about clothing, how we've brought all the wrong things, especially jeans. When they get wet they shrink and you get hypothermia. Exposure. He's always on about exposure, so he can do this *when-I-was-yomping-to-Port-Stanley* routine. Then again, there are penguins in the Falklands, so of course you'd get exposure there. Only Mal's got proper trousers, from the Army Surplus store.

"Mr Barratt..." Kath's in the doorway behind us, with a strange look on her face. He stops, annoyed. Nobody interrupts him. "Mr Barratt," she says again, sort of urgent. "I think you'd better see this."

The others crowd into the kitchen and I have to push to get a look. I'm only just in time. As the draught from the door cools it, the condensation on the window is vanishing and with it the words someone has scrawled – big letters, some capitals, some not.

ONe Of uS GOt to DiE

Nobody speaks. It's like the silence we get in group therapy in the special class at school, when they try to embarrass someone into saying something. It can last a whole hour sometimes. So it's a real relief when Mr Barratt snorts. "Stupid!" You're not meant to call people stupid nowadays, but he says it again. "Stupid kids. All they need is a bit of hardship. That'll sort them out. Boots on, you lot. Bags, cagoules. Get a move on." For once I'm almost glad.

Scree... It's the noise when you scrape your fingernail down a blackboard; you can feel it in your bones. Mr Barratt's been talking about the *scree* and now we know what he means: a steep slope, half a mountain made of bare, sharp, slippy stones. We're going to climb it. Now.

He was right about one thing. Just as the track gets really steep the mist starts changing, going bluer, brighter, then we're out of it, like coming up from underwater. Everyone stops to gasp a bit.

The valley looks as if it's flooded, with the mist churned up so the other hillside looks like cliffs with white waves breaking. The twins are gazing out at it, their identical fair hair falling straight, almost hiding their identical pale faces, and their pale blue eyes trained on the same spot far away. There should be a boat with sails coming across the mist to carry the two of them off to a land where they'd really belong and everybody spoke their language. Somewhere else, not here.

"Watch your feet on the scree." Mr Barratt is thirty paces on up the steep track. With his stick, he prods the scree, so a flat heavy stone starts to slither, taking others with it, with a sound like a dog growling deep in its throat. A warning. Gary giggles, testing his trainer on a loose stone, but Mr Barratt's got deadly hearing. "Just you dare," he calls. "There's no social worker on this mountain. Now, climb!"

For the first stretch he's ahead, stopping now and then to shout. "Put your backs into it. Go, go, go." Mal is second, Colette next, though Tash keeps level with

Colette to bug her. We're straggling. Gary stays last, behind me, but he's doing it on purpose till Mr Barratt comes pounding back down. For a moment they're eyeball to eyeball. Gary's big, but Mr Barratt looks like he's made of rope, all grey and twisted tight and fraying slightly. Gary blinks first. I can't hear what Mr Barratt says but Gary goes red. Most of us when Gary goes that colour, we run for it. He could lash out at any moment. Mr Barratt knows this, he's seen the files on Gary, but he does it on purpose, putting him down in front of the others, pushing him almost to breaking point, daring him: go on, snap! Gary looks at the ground, and ... Mr Barratt smiles. Man-management, he calls it. That's what the Marines taught him, he said in one of his speeches. He says he'll make a man of Mal. Maybe even Gary. What he'll make of the girls, he never says. And not a word about me.

Half an hour into the serious climbing, no one talks much. The ones at the front stop at each twist in the path, their tongues lolling like dogs. It's hot while we climb, but there's a cool wind that feels like water if you purse your mouth and drink it, though you're thirsty again straight away. The front ones wait for the rest to catch up, and move off as I get there. Tash isn't winding Colette up any more – a bad sign – and doesn't respond when Colette gets a crack back in about her smoking. From time to time the twins lean close together and whisper in their private code. They can talk properly when they want to and everyone says they're very intelligent. I just wish I knew what they were saying. Sounds like birdsong to me.

Soon no one thinks of anything except the pain. It isn't my legs so much as somewhere in my chest, a ripping feeling as each breath goes in. Once I slip and a little stoneslip starts and I freeze, in case Mr Barratt has noticed. But nobody looks round. They're trudging on with their heads down, each in their own little puddle of sweat and bad temper. Even Colette's got shadows round the armpits of her Beauty Without Cruelty T-shirt. Glistening trickles run out of the gaps between Tash's tight nappy plaits but as I look she rounds on me suddenly. "Watch it. Else it might be you, right?" *What might...?* I'm about to say when I remember the kitchen window. Right, Tash. Just then Mr Barratt comes jogging, yes, *jogging*, past us. "Co–o–me on. I thought you were *good* at climbing," and he makes a little movement with his arm. For a moment everything goes wobbly, like a heat haze. I look round at Tash, but she hasn't noticed, or else she's ignoring him. *Monkeys,* that's the word he didn't say.

The scree is narrowing as we climb, with sheer rock closing in on either side. As the shadow of the rockface touches us, I notice there's a crack in the corner above us. "O–o–oh no," says Gary. "Not up that. We ain't got gear or nothing. It's not safe."

"That's right." Tash is getting her breath back. "You got no right to make us. Health and Safety..."

"Nonsense. We're nearly there," says Mr Barratt.

Mal's being a good boy. "We can't turn back now."

"I can put up with it," says Tash.

"Mr Barratt's a qualified leader." This is Colette. "If he says it's safe, it's safe." She looks at Tash and Gary, haughty. "Are you afraid?" Mal and Colette on one side, Tash and Gary on the other. They all look at me.

"Of course not," comes a sweet voice from behind me. It's Jill, or is it Jack? "No," says the other one. "We're not afraid."

"There you are!" Colette gives Gary and Tash her

best withering look. Mr Barratt smiles to himself. Man-management has won again.

The crack's quite safe, though we'll have to leave our bags down here. *Nobody* could fall, Mr Barratt says. The worst that could happen – here he looks at me – is to get stuck. The others snigger.

Mal goes first. A minute later, his face appears from a ledge we hadn't seen at all from below. "Hey, it's wicked up here," he shouts. Gary is already shouldering up. Then everybody helps the twins.

"Move your backside," Mr Barratt mutters from behind me. "You're not in your corner shop now."

I met this Sikh boy once who showed me his dagger. "Do your parents know?" I said. He laughed: all of them had one, they were warriors. I find myself thinking about him for some reason, as I wriggle up that crack.

"Wow..." gasps Gary, as we spread out on the ledge. Even Tash has gone quiet. No one is squabbling or fidgeting. We just stand and stare. Above our heads, an overhang leans down so that it's almost but not quite a cave. "Listen." In a dark recess, water is splashing into water. For a moment Mr Barratt's face has a look I've seen on people in a temple or a shrine. "Living water. Drink. You'll never taste anything like it."

"But it's unhygienic," Colette says. Mr Barratt shakes his head. "Purest water on earth. Straight from the rock." It's strange, it may be the echo from the cliff, but no, his voice is different, almost gentle. I realize with a shock: he loves this place. The hard man has a soft spot after all. "Gary," he says, "you're thirsty."

"Er, I'm OK. Got some Coke in my bag, sir."

"Mal, what about you?" Mal balances on wet stones. He gasps as the spray hits his face, then shakes his head and grins. Colette and the twins come up, and me too, but the water's so cold and so hard that it stings. I can see Mr Barratt's disappointed in us. "Water of life," he says. "Nothing like it any more." He looks out at the world. "All spoiled. Spoiled by people like you. Your Coca Cola, your video games." I want to say, *No, sir, you're being unfair*, but he's turned his back on us and thrust his head right under, drinking deep. Off his guard. You could almost like him for a moment. But Gary had been waiting for a chance like this all week. There's a grunt, a thud, a splash.

Gary's taken a step back already, looking round with that *what-ref-me?* look that footballers do after a foul. Mr Barratt is full length in the narrow pool. For a moment it's hard not to laugh, until we notice he isn't moving. Then he groans but the water is pouring straight on top of him, beating him down. He coughs and grabs out vaguely. There's a second as we all look at each other, then everyone's fumbling, slipping, losing their hold, then heaving. He comes upright, staggers a few steps, then his legs buckle. He sits propped up, shuddering, dripping.

He doesn't shout. It's scarier than that. Gary's stood there like he's in front of the class any ordinary day, his head down, waiting to be blasted. "'S an accident," he mumbles, but Mr Barratt hardly seems to hear. "Listen," he says in a quick level voice. "This is an emergency. Keep calm." One of the twins gives a whimper. "We must get down. Quickly," he says. "Keep me moving. If I give a different order later, disregard it. If I start sounding sleepy and drunk..." Tash lets slip a little snort of laughter, but he ignores her. "If that happens, I'm going into hypothermia. Someone else must take command." He gives a sudden shudder. As he looks up, round the circle of us, a shadow passes through his eyes, as though a hawk was circling between him and the sun. "Wind chill..." His teeth chatter in spasms. "Gary, you're the strongest. You go first."

A cold wind is blowing up the crack. "Lower him slowly." Gary's voice sounds thin and edgy, not like him at all. Sometimes Mr Barratt mutters an order – "Left han' down..." – that no one quite hears. Suddenly he slumps; Mal and Colette lose hold; "Hey, careful!" Gary shouts. With a bone-jolting jerk, Mr Barratt slithers a few feet and sticks in the crack.

"Ssssokay," he says mildly. "Very snug."

"Christ!" says Tash. "Do something, someone. He's got that hypo thing."

The twins start screaming. "Calm down," says Mal. "Look, shut it," says Gary, but they're in a panic and it's spreading. Then Tash gives one of them a slap across the face, and they both shut up together. Colette goes into head-girl mode, but no one's listening. It could have been minutes, it could have been hours, but suddenly we're struggling for the crack, all knees and elbows and swearwords. The worst bit is squeezing past Mr Barratt, who has started singing to himself. "I did it my–y–y way..."

I glimpse the twins above me and think I should be polite, let them go first, but then the nearer one slips and slithers against me, so I have to help her down and that feels good. The moment I ease her feet down the scree, though, she's edgy, looking for the other one. You don't see them apart. They're like one person. It's easier to imagine one leg walking off without the other than to imagine Jack without Jill. Or vice versa. "Where are you?" she waits, and straight away there's Mal's voice, just out of sight round a bulge in the rock. "I've got her. This way's easier." My twin scoots. A minute or two later they both reappear.

Then it happens. A miracle. My twin skips over. "Thank you, Mo," she says and kisses me right on the lips. We're so close I can see delicate violet veins in the skin of her eyelids and, on one, a cut where Tash's ring caught her.

There is a small *splat*... A drip of something hits the twin's hand where it's resting on my shoulder, and a little splashes on my face. It is wet but not cold. The twin opens her pale blue eyes and looks at it, puzzled. Then she screams. Everyone is staring up the crack. Wedged up there, Mr Barratt's head droops at a funny angle. From it comes a steady splash of blood.

"Battered!" The police inspector bangs the table. He paces up and down the hostel lounge. You can see he's watched films where the detective does that, weighing up the suspects. He's going to be *psychological*, even I can tell.

"Fine man, your Mr Barratt. Ex-Marine. Sergeant, I believe. Devotes his life to helping the likes of you. Then..." He pauses at the window, gazing out, just like they do on TV. "Why anyone should want to do ... this to a man like that..." he says. "Beggars belief."

"Please, sir," Mal says. "Couldn't it have been a falling stone?"

"Falling stone? Come off it, lad. You saw his face." The twins shudder and start gently weeping. "Battered," says the inspector slowly. "Blunt instrument. The man's own walking stick. Repeated blows to head and face. So let's cut out the funny business, shall we? One of you prize specimens, *at least* one of you, knows who."

"Gary," Colette says quickly, "Gary pushed him." "Shut your mouth," Gary snarls. "Stuck-up bitch.

Everyone knows I was at the bottom when ... when it happened. Wasn't I? Well, wasn't I?"

"Thank you," says the inspector. "That'll do. I think we've established that much." He looks round. "What I normally look for, in these cases, is a *grudge*. A grievance. Maybe not just against the individual, but against the things he stands for. In this case, the British way of life, maybe..."

"Screw you!" Tash jumps to her feet. "You all want it to be me, don't you? 'Cos I'm black. 'Cos I'm a girl and 'cos I don't take shit from no one. OK, say it, it was me. Go on, I want to hear it. Then I can get up in court and do this..." Her clenched fist punches at the ceiling. "I'll be a hero then, see? Go on!" She thrusts her arms out, ready for the handcuffs. "Say it, someone say it. Please." There's no sound but rain pattering the window. Suddenly Tash crumples. "Trouble is, it's not true, is it? *Should* have been me who got the racist bastard, on behalf of all the niggaz. Me or Mo."

There's a jolt beneath my ribcage, like being punched from inside. Tash has started again, but it seems like miles away. "What about Mal, then? Teacher's pet? Maybe he got tired of being patronized? And the rest of us hating him." Mal's gone white but he can't get a word in, and anyway Tash's tirade has swept on. "Or Colette. Goody-goody Colette. Headmaster's daughter, is she? Huh! That's just what her mum says and the two of them are as crazy as each other." Colette shrieks; Kath grabs her just as she lunges at Tash, fingernails raking, and suddenly everyone's yelling at each other, with the inspector standing gawping like an umpire who's lost count at Wimbledon. The room's all hot and swaying, there's a ringing in my ears and things look clear, but far away.

"Mo?" says Kath. "What's the matter?"

One day when I was younger these big boys were teasing me, and it was hot like this, too hot, and the playground started swaying, and…

"Quiet, all of you," snaps the inspector. "That boy's trying to say something."

"Please, Inspector… Please, what do they do if someone's done a crime…" It's very quiet now. "…and doesn't know?"

"Don't be stupid," says Colette.

"I'm not stupid. I think it was … I mean the person who … who did it, you know. I think it was me."

There's a long hush. I wait for sirens to start up, constables to dash in… Nothing. "Inspector," Kath says softly. "There is something in his records. Incident of violence in the playground." I put one of them in hospital, people tell me. Me, I don't remember. "That's why he was recommended for this group."

"It wasn't him," says Jill, or Jack. "He was helping me down. I was with him all the time."

"No, you weren't," says Colette. "You were the last one on the ledge when I came down … you or the other one. If it isn't Mo, it's one of you."

"You aren't accusing *the twins*?" says Kath. Gary snorts, "Come off it…" Tash says, "You really are crazy."

"But … but she's right." One of the twins is speaking. Everyone turns. "She did … she did see one of us up there." Suddenly she can't go on. Her face is whiter, and her blue eyes larger, than I've ever seen before. "Can't say it," she blurts. "Can't, can't…" Kath puts an arm around her shoulder, shakily. "You can," she says gently. "If it was you…" The twin shakes her head fiercely, then burrows it into Kath's woolly jumper. "Worse. Worse." Very timidly, she looks up … at the other twin.

A shudder passes through her. "We … I mean, I … I'm sorry, Jill," she says, faintly, and she's sobbing. "I tried … I can't … I tried to cover up for you. I told them I went down with Mal. But I went down with Mo." She looks at me, pleading. Those beautiful eyes. "I was with you, wasn't I? Tell them, Mo."

"Mo! I was with you. Not her. Me!" Jill's eyes are on me now, identically blue, identically beautiful. I can still feel the touch of her lips … or was it Jack's? The only girl who's kissed me, ever.

Then I remember something. "Excuse me. Both of you, please close your eyes."

Jill's eyelashes quiver, her delicate lids have tiny violet veins. I bend closer to Jack. Same lashes, same eyelids … with the little nick of Tash's ring. Jack. "You were with me."

There's a shriek, more hawk or gull than human. Jill is glaring with a wild hopeless look – at Jack, not me. Jack flinches into Kath's arm. "Help me," she wails. "She'll kill me…" Jill's shriek changes into something like a cry of pain, then she ducks past the inspector's outstretched grip and is out of the door. The porch door slams, and there's no sound but the driving rain.

"Poor dear." Kath is stroking the twin's hair. "She won't hurt you. You're a brave girl, Jack."

"Not Jack. No more Jack and Jill. I'm me now. Jacqueline. My proper name."

It's the small hours. A search party is out but there isn't much hope, not with the mist and the rain. They say she headed back towards the scree. If Mr Barratt got exposure so fast in broad daylight, well… They say it's quite a pleasant way to die, exposure, you go numb and cosy. Better than being locked up, I guess. Locked up without Jack, her other half, for ever. Case closed, says the inspector. He sounds pleased with himself. Another victory for psychology.

No one thought they would sleep, but one by one it hit them, even Jack. Kath thought we should stay in the lounge, and she laid blankets over them as they fell asleep. She's curled up on the sofa, snoring too. It's only me awake. There's a break in the rain, and moonlight through the curtains. It feels peaceful. Calm.

No, someone else is stirring. Quietly they slip their blanket off and shuffle to the kitchen. After a moment, I creep out to see.

Jacqueline is staring through the window with the moonlight in her hair. She doesn't hear me, and I don't dare move. She's gazing out into the darkness, where Jill might be lying. Jill the murderer. Her other half. Jack looks so frail, lit up by the moon, so lonely. If I could put my arms around her, hold her tight... I move up step by step behind her, silently. She leans forward and breathes on the glass. Very faintly, an inch from her lips, a shape shows. A ghost O. Jacqueline breathes. f uS GO, reads the window. Then I recognize it, still there in the grease left by a finger, so that just a breath can bring it back:

ONe Of uS GOt to DiE

She wipes out the evidence, very carefully, with her sleeve, then turns. In the moment before she catches sight of me, I see her face. It's bright with more than moonlight. There's a smile of victory.

It's all there, written in her ice blue eyes: the story of her life, her weird half life, a life only half hers ... till now. Yes, one of them had to go. "No more Jack and Jill." One of them couldn't imagine a life without the other.

The problem for her was: the other one could. Of course Jill ran off crying. She wasn't guilty, just confused and afraid. She was betrayed. Imagine: if your left arm accused your right arm of murder? Wouldn't you run away? Poor Mr Barratt. He had to go too, just a means to an end, to get rid of the other twin. Those eyes of Jacqueline's saw herself trapped for the rest of her life, not a person, simply half of Jack-and-Jill.

It's wonderful, really, thinking how she did it. They always did say the twins were clever. Jack was the last on the ledge. She saw Mr Barratt helpless, grabbed a rock and did it. She saw the other twin with me. Yes, she knew that someone would work out it must be one of them, eventually. That's what she wanted. It was just a lucky chance that Mal got her down the quick way. She always planned to plant that kiss, to take Jill's place in the eyes of the only person it mattered to. Me.

But still, that kiss... My miracle, her alibi. I'm tingling all over, and I don't know if it's love or fear, as I look into those Snow Queen eyes. "Don't worry. I won't say a word," I whisper quickly, very quickly. Because this is a girl who would do anything, who *has* done anything, to be free.

THE CULT

Jules decided to make her bid for freedom when Ruth brought her next tray of food. Till then, she tried to shut out Daniel Campana's incessant preaching that was being piped into her cell like muzak. The sound of his words was soothing at first but, when Jules refused to be lulled by it, the easy rhythm of his voice became irritating. The message of his words was a different matter. Behind his vision of harmony in the world, there lurked something sinister that horrified her. She vowed never to surrender to his views.

Jules had got herself into this mess because she'd lost her faith in the world. She would see only misery and cruelty on the news. It used to make her so sick that she couldn't eat. Her parents were wealthy enough to have her symptoms treated at a private clinic. They could do nothing about the cause, though. They were too busy making pots of money for themselves to be concerned about bigger problems. For Jules, their lifestyle did not provide the answers. World-weary, she'd run away to find a more caring way forward, to find something to believe in. She found this branch of the Divine Truth and Justice Sect. It had seemed idyllic. Forty young people together in the old mansion, abandoning the rat race and material things, accepting each other, praying for the common good, eating pure and natural food, leading a modest life. She had almost been seduced by it when one of their sessions with the master had alerted her to a dangerous undercurrent in the sect. Just before her full initiation, Daniel had announced that the growing number of conflicts around the globe foreshadowed the end of the human race. The venerated prophet, in a plain white kimono contrasting with his straggling black hair and beard, had predicted a global catastrophe at the end of 1999. Few humans, he'd said, would see the year 2000. Worse, he'd welcomed the apocalypse. He had presented it as a necessary and beneficial cleansing of the Earth. Jules could not agree. She was repulsed by conflict and would not submit to the inevitability of disaster. She thought that the sect existed to point the world towards a better future by eliminating hostility, not by eliminating human beings.

From that moment, she'd lost her faith in the sect as well. It wasn't right for her because it was not working to counteract the coming evil. Yet, from the moment that she'd tried to leave, she realized that the sect would do everything in its power to stop her. Hugh Goldsmith, the smooth manager of the sect, had taken her forcibly and locked her in the bare cell. Since then, she had been denied sleep, exposed continually to Daniel's words, and brought simple meals by Ruth.

When Ruth reappeared, she was carrying a tray with a salad and glass of water. Jules scowled at her and declared, "You can't keep me here against my will, you know. It's called kidnapping."

Ruth bent down to put the tray on the floor and whispered, "Look..."

Jules had to strike when her opponent was unsteady. She did not wait to hear Ruth recite some words about obedience to the master. She did not wait till Ruth had regained her balance. Jules sprang at her and pushed her as hard as she could. Ruth fell backwards, somersaulted and slammed into the wall. She lay on the floor like a rag doll. Jules hesitated. She hated violence and feared that she might have hurt Ruth, yet she forced herself to leave. She had to take the opportunity to escape. At the doorway, she glanced back regretfully. Ruth was such a mild, inoffensive girl, but she was also beginning to stir. It spurred Jules into making a dash for it.

Like Jules, Natasha had long fair hair. To reduce the resemblance between them, she had it cut so short that it did not even reach her ears. Then she starved herself for four days. When she looked the part, she hung around outside the clinic like another sad victim who could afford expensive treatment for eating disorders. It wasn't long before she was befriended by three members of the cult who homed in on the disaffected girls who attended the clinic. Almost all of the girls shunned the cult's recruitment team but Natasha allowed them to coax her into the park where they introduced themselves as Charlotte, Ruth and Paul. She allowed them to ply her with questions and talk with her about the beauty of untroubled life in the Divine Truth and Justice Sect. Within a week, after dithering and doubting in two further sessions with them, Natasha ended her feigned resistance. She agreed to go back to the mansion with them – just to see what it was like.

As they crossed the park, Paul paid more attention to the wildlife than to the new recruit. At one point, he picked up a nervous, mangy cat and stroked it lovingly. "Poor thing," he muttered. "People who don't look after their animals should be... Anyway, there's room in the animal house for him, isn't there, Ruth?"

"Yes, of course."

Charlotte, who seemed to be the leader of the group of

three, smiled at Natasha and commented, "Two rescues in one day. Good work."

Clearly, they regarded Natasha as another stray – one more troubled girl in search of sanctuary and companions who would care about her. She did her best to play the role. She put on a nervous smile, almost purring over her salvation.

As soon as she entered the grounds of the cult's mansion, Natasha experienced a compelling atmosphere of peacefulness. Immediately, she recognized that Jules would have found it irresistible. Natasha acted as if she too were enchanted, while she wondered how the sect raised enough assets to run such an awesome building, and why every face that she saw belonged to a vulnerable youngster. She thought that she knew the answers to both questions. The Divine Truth and Justice Sect attracted disillusioned kids and probably absorbed their money as a first step towards enlightenment and a more spiritual life. Most older people would be too cynical to accept the tranquillity at face value. At nineteen, Natasha could see both points of view. She tried to keep an open mind, even though she was naturally suspicious. After all, she'd infiltrated the cult to investigate Jules' disappearance. In the last reliable sighting of her younger sister, she had been spotted by the receptionist walking away from the clinic with a couple of members of the cult. The police said that they were already looking into the sect but Natasha had not seen any evidence of a serious investigation. That's why she had decided to undertake one herself.

Soon, Natasha was taken to an older man. He was about forty, she estimated, and he wore a designer suit. He introduced himself as Hugh Goldsmith, the manager of the whole set-up. "Well," he began, "I'm told you're

Natasha and you've come to see how we live. You're welcome. Take a look and talk to anyone. I think you'll like what you see. We're a happy community. It's part of our philosophy to accept and embrace anyone, so we'll make you feel at home straight away. I'm sure you'll want to join us. But don't rush into it." He grinned. "As you'll see, no one rushes around here. We're very relaxed. You check us out and then I'll ask a few questions about you. If we hit it off… But there's no rush. Paul will be your guide."

Natasha was perturbed by Goldsmith. He was far too slick – a smart operator. He exuded efficiency and menace.

He turned to Paul and remarked, "I see you've found another cat in need of our care and attention. Give him to Ruth while you look after our guest. You know Ruth looks after the animal house."

Reluctantly, Paul handed over the tangled ball of fluff. It was evident to Natasha that he resented Ruth's position as keeper of the cult's animals. He seemed to believe that he would be the better choice.

Paul showed her round the big old house. There were so many corridors and rooms that it would be easy to get lost in it. Everywhere they went, the decor was bright – mainly green, yellow and blue – and members of the cult chatted chirpily. They never seemed to grow tired of wearing their benign grins. There was no sign of unsettled or unwilling inhabitants. And no sign of Jules.

At one point, Paul indicated a suite of rooms where they weren't allowed to wander. "That's where Hugh has his office and Daniel lives."

"Daniel?"

"The master. He spends most of his time meditating. You'll see him later. He talks to us each evening. You'll be allowed to watch."

"Does everyone go?"

"Of course," Paul answered. "No one would miss the master. What's more, if you join us, you'll meet him face to face. It's ... a marvellous experience. He's so ... I don't know ... mystical. Virtually holy."

Natasha nodded as if she understood what he was talking about.

"I'll show you the animals," Paul said eagerly.

Outside, there were pens for rabbits and the larger creatures, and coops for the birds. The chickens wandered at will. Inside, the dogs and cats had kennels. Gerbils, hamsters, mice and rats had cages. Fish glided in aerated tanks. Frequently, Paul stopped by an enclosure and murmured a few sympathetic words to a favourite pet.

As they turned into a different section, Natasha caught the sound of Charlotte and Ruth talking heatedly. In an insistent tone, Charlotte was saying, "What happened, then?"

Before she saw Natasha, Ruth replied desperately, "How should I know? She was cornered. I suppose she ran in because there was nowhere else..."

Behind Natasha, Paul coughed to announce their presence. Immediately the two girls put an end to their conversation and resumed the obligatory grin. Presumably, they did not wish to reveal any internal discord. "Hello there," Charlotte called. "Enjoying the tour?"

"Mmm, yes," Natasha answered, wondering what their sharp exchange was about. She did not dare to pry, so instead she peered into a gloomy, glass case on her left and enquired, "What's in here?"

"Insects," Paul replied. "Spiders. That sort of thing."

"Ugh." She turned away.

"We've got a few snakes further along, as well." Paul

chuckled but then, more seriously, declared, "Ruth and Charlotte, they were just talking about a rabbit, you know. It got out of its cage. Then it got scared."

Natasha got the impression that Paul was trying to find excuses for the girls because he was disappointed that something on her tour was less than perfect. She shrugged as if not interested in petty events. Looking over the whole menagerie, she commented, "It's like the ark in here. A few of everything. Apart from rhinos and elephants. Unless they're somewhere else," she quipped. "Why do you keep them?"

"They're all God's creatures. All precious. Daniel says we're like a miniature world within a world. It wouldn't be right if we didn't have animals."

"I suppose not," she replied. Pointing at a closed door near Ruth, Natasha enquired, "What's through there? Lions and tigers?"

This time, Paul did not giggle. "No. It's our animal surgery. Nothing grand. Just a laboratory where we can treat them when they're ill."

Again, his expression suggested that he was disgruntled. Natasha guessed that caring for the sick animals was not one of Paul's responsibilities. Obviously, he loved all of the animals and it vexed him that he was not allowed to be more involved. After a moment, though, he resurrected the permanent grin of someone who was enjoying an endless private joke. It made him look half-witted – or deranged.

"What do you think?" Paul asked. "It's a super place to be, isn't it?"

"Mmm. Serene. But … I must admit, I'd like to see Daniel first."

"That's OK," Paul responded. "You won't be disappointed."

* * *

All forty members of the sect assembled in the large hall. There were no chairs. They sat cross-legged in rows on the wooden floor. They still wore their cloying smiles, and several clutched bibles. With the entire group in one place, Natasha used the opportunity to scan the room for her sister. There was an expectant hush as if God Himself was about to appear. Only Natasha's gaze was not fixed avidly on the stage where Hugh was orchestrating the event. She sighed inwardly when her eyes had surveyed everyone. Jules was not among them.

When Daniel stepped on to the platform, Natasha was taken aback. No, he wasn't a god but he resembled pictures of Jesus Christ, except that he was rather plump. He had long dark hair and an imposing beard. The air was electric. In utter silence, everyone in the hall focused on the master. Daniel prowled across the stage twice before lifting his head and pronouncing his words of wisdom. "Greed and envy!" he exclaimed as if trying to claim the attention of the congregation even though his audience could not be any more attentive. He followed it up with a tirade against people who put profit and possessions before the good of the planet, society and their own souls. Daniel nodded his head vigorously at the end of each sentence as if to stress its importance. The action made his hair fall about his shoulders and his beard bounce on his chest. "God," he proclaimed, "does not reside in the free market. He resides in the hearts of the meek, in nature, in the Earth that's being bled for gain."

All very laudable, Natasha thought, and guaranteed to be popular within this isolated sect.

Now animated, Daniel continued, "We have all seen the havoc wreaked on the Earth by the greed of humans. Out there, they rush around with their money, looking serious, important and powerful. They're not. They rush around with guns and bombs to protect their plundered riches and fruitful lands from the envious poor. Their money oils the machine that keeps rich nations rich and poor nations poor. Their money oils the machines that make weapons. Their money oils conflict. Nature looks on and groans as if at a troublesome child. One day soon, her curiosity with human beings will dwindle. Her patience will be exhausted. The entertainment value of man will reduce to zero. Then nature will retaliate. Even now she is preparing to rid herself of the curse of the human race." Daniel paused, wiping away the perspiration from his forehead. "I have foreseen it. In 1999, humans will witness real power. Nature will swallow up every last one of those puny, sinful people. Puny minds. Sinful lives. All gone. The Earth will enjoy the next millennium without them. Purified. And so we must look to our own purity," Daniel concluded, nodding feverishly. "We must prepare ourselves. Each of us will survive – or perish with the rest – as we deserve." He finished with a plea for even more selflessness, worship and virtue. Then he slipped away, leaving an enormous vacuum.

Natasha was astonished at his impassioned performance. She was also astonished at his message. There was little doubt in her mind that he really believed his crazy prediction. He delivered the news of the end of the human race without regret. He even seemed to relish the prospect. His followers appeared to accept and welcome it too. Instinctively, Natasha felt that if her sister had heard his grim theory, she would have run scared. She would have made a dash for home. But she hadn't come home and there was no sign of her in the cult. She had disappeared. Fearing the worst, Natasha shuddered.

She was not given long to ponder on her sister. She was surrounded by Ruth, Paul, Charlotte and Hugh. "What do you think?" they asked enthusiastically.

To Natasha, Paul appeared to be particularly elated. She guessed that his simple soul would be delighted with the prophecy that animals will inherit the Earth. His sympathies did not lie with humankind.

"It's ... a lot to take in at once," she struggled to reply.

Hugh smiled his slippery smile. "I can understand that," he murmured. "Why don't you stay with us tonight? Be our guest. It'll give you time to think. We can talk after morning prayers and breakfast."

Feigning gratitude, Natasha nodded appreciatively. "Sounds good, but I haven't brought..."

"We can supply all you need," Hugh interjected. "Charlotte can get on to it immediately."

"OK," Natasha agreed. "Thanks."

Alone in a plain room, Natasha wept a little. She felt like a loner in a dangerous environment. The tension of keeping up an act was taking its toll. And she thought that something horrible had happened to her sister. So far, she had not dared to ask anyone about Jules. She could not afford to arouse suspicion by displaying curiosity, and it was too early to decide if she could trust anyone in the sect. With the exception of Goldsmith, she had not yet identified which members of the flock were actually wolves in sheep's clothing. She was wary of Charlotte, though, because she had an unnerving air of authority. She reminded Natasha of a school prefect. Daniel was too distant and complex to fathom. To Natasha, Paul and Ruth seemed much more uncomplicated and sincere. Perhaps she would confide in one of them first.

* * *

Natasha had guessed correctly that Hugh Goldsmith's questions would concern her parents, wealth and whether she was willing to renounce both of them. She surmised that his motivation was more to do with money and power than saving souls. She had stock answers prepared and seemed to pass the manager's test with flying colours. Asked for her verdict on the sect, she declared that she would like to stay and embrace its principles. She gathered from Goldsmith that her membership was a foregone conclusion. She wondered what he would have done if she had refused. She got the impression that she would not have been free simply to walk away.

Hugh told her that she would be called an associate member. After further initiation, including the handing over of her worldly goods, prayers, and a session with Daniel, she would become a full member.

Natasha nodded. Inside, she quaked. What had she got herself into? And, once she had found out what she needed to know, how would she ever get out of it?

Charlotte found her an inelegant outfit that made her look like everyone else. Unadorned and innocent. She was given some light tasks in the garden to get her used to the austere life and a work schedule. In the evening, Paul asked, "Beginning to enjoy it?"

"Mmm. I met some terrific girls growing the crops. Good company. I'm going to like it here." She practised the sect's silly smile.

"Good," Paul replied, beaming. He was feeling proud to have brought the master a promising novice.

Lowering her voice, Natasha whispered, "I had a friend who came here as well."

"Oh?" Paul mumbled cautiously.

"Name of Jules. But I haven't seen her. Do you know where she is?"

"Jules." For a moment, Paul was taken aback. "Er... Yes, there was someone called Jules. A couple of weeks back. You'd have to ask Hugh about her."

"OK, but what happened to her?" Natasha persisted. "I hoped I'd join her."

"Well, unfortunately, we can't please everybody. We didn't suit her. She was here for a few days but then left us."

Natasha nodded. "I see." She did not know him well enough to decide if he was lying. "Never mind," she added. "It's not that important." Despite Paul's reaction she was convinced that Jules had never left the cult.

The next day brought a real shock. They were informed that, in the night, Ruth's heart had simply stopped beating. She had died suddenly and unexpectedly in her sleep. All of the members of the sect were excused work to attend a service in her honour. Even so, there was no mourning and no sadness. Daniel and Hugh presided over a celebration of Ruth's life and her journey to a better place. There were no ambulances and no police, either. Seemingly, the cult preferred to deal with its own tragedies in its own way. Her body was cremated straight away and her ashes were scattered on the garden. Throughout the whole process, everyone maintained their smiles. The broadest smile belonged to Paul, now in charge of the animal house.

Natasha had to retire to her room. She had known Ruth, an apparently healthy individual, and regretted her death, but there was something else. Deep down, she wondered if Jules had met the same fate. A mysterious death followed by a rapid and convenient cremation. Maybe yesterday Natasha had walked among her sister's ashes in the garden. In the privacy of her room, she flopped miserably on to the bed. She was dismayed.

In the morning, regaining her resolve, she decided to step up her investigations. In the garden, she asked a few of the girls about Jules. Each time, she got the same bland response. Jules had arrived, sampled their way of life, and then left. After the third time of hearing, Natasha wanted to scream, "No, she didn't! She's my sister, so I should know!" Of course, she restrained herself.

At two o'clock in the morning, she crept out of her room, determined to explore the mansion without an escort. It was a still night. A bright moon and occasional lamps in the corridors provided enough light to guide her. No longer resonating to the naïve cheerfulness of the inmates, the deserted passageways seemed cold and eerie. Most of the doors were shut but some had been left ajar. Natasha padded along as quietly as she could. She made for the animal house. She was drawn to it because Ruth had worked there, because it was the only place where she had witnessed friction among the sect's members, and because instinct told her that it was worth investigating. She was especially curious about the surgery that Paul had called a laboratory. Somehow, it didn't fit. A community that was proud to be primitive should not boast laboratory facilities.

As she was leaving the main quarters and entering the wing that led to the animal house, she froze suddenly. There was a noise from one of the nearby bedrooms. It was only a cough but, in the dead of night, it sounded like the loud bark of a dog. And it might mean that someone was restless or even awake. Natasha could not imagine what would happen if she was discovered. She might end up like her sister. Disappeared. She stood still like a shop-window dummy for at least half a minute.

Unlike a plastic model, though, she was trembling with nerves. Yet there were no further signs of stirring from the room so she continued stealthily into the next wing. There, the musty smells of the animals drifted towards her. As she tiptoed among the cages, there were scrabbling noises. Probably the rats. A few of the rodents, frightened by her presence, bolted into their nests, thudding into the sides of their cages in panic. The place was lit by the shimmering white glow of the aquariums and the faint red glimmer from the insect and reptile cages where leaves rustled creepily as furtive nocturnal species scuttled and slithered.

Natasha felt furtive herself. She did not know what she expected to see. There were no weird rituals, no blood sacrifices. Nothing but rows and rows of harmless animals. She padded towards the surgery. Just as she was reaching out for the handle, the rhythm of animal sounds changed, alerting her to some disturbance. A few seconds later, she heard the light footsteps of another human being among the creatures of the ark. She stepped behind a cage and found herself inches away from a writhing snake. Staring at its hypnotic eyes and flickering tongue, she gulped instead of crying out. After all, she was separated from it by a pane of glass. She ducked down to avoid looking at it and to conceal herself further as the other sleepless person came closer. She tried to subdue her breathing as the night stalker also walked towards the door of the surgery. As she glided past, her face was illuminated strangely by the light of the insect house. It was Charlotte, on patrol in the early hours. Probably, Natasha thought, she was checking that everything was quiet. Natasha shook like a trapped and terrified animal.

By the door Charlotte hesitated and looked round like

a soldier on duty. Natasha had to hold her breath to stop herself gasping. For an instant, she thought that Charlotte must have caught her scent. But a moment later, the sect's prefect opened the door and went inside. Natasha almost sighed with relief. She realized that the most sensible plan of action was to scurry away as quickly as possible before Charlotte discovered her, but she was determined to take a peek at the surgery. Anyway, she was not sure that she could summon the courage to repeat this escapade on another night. Deciding to stay till the coast was clear, she squatted on the floor without making a sound. It was more nerve-racking than waiting with toothache outside a dentist's surgery.

Charlotte was inside for just a few minutes but it seemed like hours. Pins and needles had gripped Natasha's feet before the door swung open and Charlotte emerged. Without pausing, she passed between the cages and continued her prowl of the premises.

Unsteadily, Natasha got to her feet. She pressed her toes against the floor to shift the cramp. When she could walk again, she limped to the door and squeezed into the surgery. Even in the dark, she could tell that it was an enclosed room. There were no windows to let in moonlight or to let out tell-tale signs of her trespass. She felt the wall beside the door till her fingers found the switch. When she turned on the lamp, her eyes snapped shut. It was too bright after the weak radiance of the aquariums. It took several seconds before she could open her eyes without squinting.

She was appalled by what she saw. The gasp finally escaped from her mouth. There was an operating table like a sacrificial stone and a glass-fronted cupboard that contained lots of bottles of chemicals. It was covered in yellow and black labels warning of biohazards and toxicity. Worst of all, a dog, a rabbit and several rats were strapped into cages so that they could not move. Where electrodes were attached to their bodies, they had been shaved down to wrinkly grey skin. The loss of hair made them look malformed. They were pitiful but at least they were alive. With imploring eyes, they watched Natasha as she shifted quietly and with increasing revulsion from specimen to specimen. She didn't understand the purpose of the room but it was not an ordinary surgery and it turned her stomach. Tearing herself away from the last pathetic and imprisoned animal, she tried a second door in one corner of the laboratory. Gently, she turned the handle but the exit was locked. Her curiosity was still keen but she was forced to give up. She could learn no more tonight. Besides, she had taken as much as she could bear and it was dangerous to linger in that awful place. Charlotte could return at any time and discover her. After a last look round the surgery, she turned out the light and stole back to her bedroom.

Despite being exhausted, physically and mentally, Natasha could not sleep. Whenever she closed her eyes, she saw the experimental animals and the ominous bottles of chemicals. Restless, she began to formulate a theory. Her eyes wide with the horror of her own reasoning, she wondered if someone in the cult was doing his – or her – best to make sure that Daniel's prophecy would come true. Whoever was in charge of the surgery could be engaged in sinister experiments aimed at studying the effects of poisons on animals. Perhaps the idea was to develop one that was deadly to humans but harmless to animals. But, even if she was right, what had it all got to do with Jules' disappearance? It was then that she had the worst thought of all. It made sense that the poison would have to be tested on humans as well. Maybe the ultimate test had been carried out on an obstinate recruit – Jules! Ruth might have been second. That's why her body had been cremated so quickly. It would have destroyed all traces of the poison.

Natasha tossed and turned in her hard bed. She hoped that she was entirely wrong. She hoped that her imagination had been fired unduly by her night-time foray. It was possible that Jules was just lying low, alive and well, but Natasha found that hard to believe. It was possible that Ruth had merely been unwell or, if she worked in the animal laboratory, she might even have had an accident with the chemicals. It didn't have to be murder. Yet Natasha's instinct told her that it was. She was gravely suspicious of Hugh and Charlotte. If they oversaw the surgery and Ruth had objected to their cruelty to the animals, then one of them would have had to remove her. Natasha had seen for herself that Charlotte frequented the laboratory. It could be one of her jobs. Natasha could easily imagine that Hugh was in command and that Charlotte carried out his warped wishes.

Natasha was too full of ideas and foreboding to sleep. Instead, while she waited for the dawn, she planned her tactics for the next day.

The other workers in the garden did not seem to mind that they were working amongst Ruth's remains. They dug and sowed enthusiastically as if they could blend her spirit into the crops to come. Natasha avoided treading where she thought Ruth's ashes might lie. On purpose, she chose to work behind the main building where she had a clear view of the wall of the surgery. From the outside, she tried to judge the position of the inner locked door. Leaning for a minute on her spade, she estimated that the door must lead into a short block of rooms that connected the surgery to the wing containing Goldsmith's office. The windows in the block were small and high. If they'd had bars, they would have reminded her of a prison.

When someone tapped her on the shoulder, she jumped, inhaled sharply and let go of the spade. Slowly, it keeled over, churning some earth as it went. Natasha spun round, then breathed a sigh of relief.

"Sorry," Paul said. "Didn't mean to frighten you." He smiled sweetly at her. "Just wondering how you're getting on."

"Fine," Natasha answered, forcing a grin. "I was daydreaming, that's all."

"That's good. Contemplation."

"How are *you*, anyway? Are you coping with the animals, now Ruth's ... gone?"

"Of course. It's good. I'm sure Ruth would approve."

Again, Natasha inflicted a smile on her tired and anxious face. "Do you have to take charge of the surgery as well?"

"Not really," Paul replied. "I help out, but it's Hugh who does the real work. He was some sort of doctor before he gave it all up to live here. Why?"

Natasha shrugged. "Just interested in what you do."

Still looking like a child who has just been given a precious gift, Paul said, "Talking of work, I must get back. Catch you later, Natasha."

"OK." Watching him retreat, Natasha noticed Charlotte standing by one of the doors to the mansion and spying on her. Feeling uncomfortable to be watched, Natasha bent down, picked up her spade and quickly returned to her work. There was something about

Charlotte that gave her the creeps. Only Hugh could match her cool self-confidence. To avoid returning her stare, Natasha dug vigorously. At least the gardening gave her time to figure out her next move.

After the vegetarian meal and Daniel's ardent appeal for humility in the face of the coming Purification, Natasha retired to steel herself for another midnight raid. It was difficult to stay alert as she waited for sleep to descend on the house. She dozed and drifted, but she was determined. At half past one, she shook herself awake and headed quietly for the suite that housed Hugh's office and Daniel's room. If she could not access the secret corridor from one end, she decided that she'd have to try from the other. The only problem was that she'd have to go where Paul told her that no one was allowed to go. If she got caught, there could be no excuses. She was risking everything.

She hesitated by the forbidden area, but not for long. Her mind was made up. She took a deep breath and, as lightly as she could, padded into the annexe and past the first two doors. She turned a corner and, by the dim lights in the corridor, saw another door. Suddenly, she was sure that she had found the other way into the locked area. Very gently, she turned the handle and felt the door give. She opened it just enough to slip through and then shut it again. It felt like sealing herself into a tomb.

There were three rooms on the left. All three doors were solid and shut tight. The first was locked but, strangely, Natasha thought that she heard a voice inside. Sweating, she moved rapidly on to the next. This time the door opened. Inside it was dark but again there was a voice. The same voice. She held her breath, fearing that someone would leap out and grab her. Yet nothing happened. She recognized the voice as Daniel's. From the tone, she also realized that it was a recording. She breathed again.

The dark room seemed to be empty so, making sure that she'd closed the door, she fumbled for a light switch. Eventually she found it. Praying for good luck, she turned it on. The bare, dangling bulb revealed a simple white room with one high window like a ship's porthole. There was no bed, no furniture. It was more like a solitary confinement cell – but without a place to rest. A cold room. The cruelly vacant walls seemed to hem her in. High in one corner of the room there was the speaker that relayed Daniel's message. Over and over again.

Natasha guessed what she had found. She had heard on television that cults were in the habit of brainwashing reluctant members. This was the place where it happened. She could imagine someone, perhaps an abducted youngster, being locked in, deprived of company and force-fed the master's words for days until submitting to his will. It was a terrifying thought. Shuddering, she left. She did not try the third door. It was the same as the other two. At the end of the short passageway, there was the locked door that led to the laboratory. Natasha's spine tingled. It struck her that those who did not succumb to the brainwashing could be taken straight into the laboratory ... maybe as human experimental animals.

Really, she wanted to turn and run. She wanted to charge out of the house and never return. But she curbed the impulse. She still needed to discover her sister's fate. She retraced her steps.

She crept past Hugh's office and headed for the relative safety of her own wing. Just as she passed the last room, the door opened and Daniel himself, in white kimono, appeared in front of her like a spectre. Natasha stopped, turned bright red and inwardly began to panic. For a second, Daniel looked surprised but then he smiled. In a faraway voice, he remarked, "You're the new associate member. You must be here to see me."

"Er ... yes," Natasha stammered. Clearly the master had no concept of the time. He did not wear a watch on his wrist. He had probably been lost in meditation. He had the detached air of a god. A world war could break out around him and he would probably not be aware of it.

"Come in," he invited. "No need to be nervous, my child." He looked on her kindly and touched her shoulder tenderly.

Natasha tried not to shiver or withdraw. She staggered into his room.

It was large, almost completely white, and nearly empty. There was a chair in the centre of the room and a huge ornate bed to the right. Underfoot there was a luxurious carpet and one wall was composed entirely of mirrors. It made the room seem twice as large. In the furthest wall there was a window and outside there was blackness.

Daniel looked at Natasha and then at the window. "It is late – or very early," he declared. "But it's not important. Time is not important. Whatever the time, it is *now*. That is sufficient." He sat in the chair, facing the mirror, and motioned her to sit on the floor in front of him. "Closer," he instructed.

Natasha shuffled forward on the carpet and sat cross-legged. She waited anxiously in case he was about to condemn her.

"You're called Natasha," he began. "And you know that there's a big bold world out there." He waved his arms to indicate life outside the sect's mansion. "It's a world that many girls of your age would find seductive. Television, radio, newspapers, parents, brothers and sisters, modern gadgets and money. Why do you want to reject all that?"

To answer, she tried to imagine what Jules would have said. "It's all stress and the pursuit of money out there. Very ugly. And the news is full of hate and intolerance."

"Mmm." Daniel peered into her face.

She felt as if her brain were being scanned by a remarkable man.

"To take a place among us you will promise solemnly never to leave, to put all of your wealth into the common purse, and to put Divine Truth and Justice before your family, before your own life and even before your own needs. Are you prepared for that?"

Natasha swallowed. For the sake of her sister, she lied. "Yes."

Daniel did not reply straight away. For several long seconds, he regarded her like a father watches a new-born daughter – with feelings of curiosity, wonderment and love. Eventually, he murmured, "You are new. Perplexed. You must have questions for me."

Natasha looked for the first time directly into his face. He seemed genuinely to care about her. It did not fit with what she had just discovered. "You really believe that the human race will be wiped out, don't you?" she asked.

"Look into my face and tell me yourself."

Natasha took a deep breath and followed his instruction. She could not detect a trace of deceit or malice. It was an honest and open face. "You do," she concluded softly.

"There will be a spreading disease. It will decimate humans – as they deserve to be decimated. The wicked will be cut off from the very Earth. The pure and humble will be the next generation. In the new world there will be an end to crime, violence and sickness. There will be homes, enjoyable work and good food for everyone. There will be peace between people and animals."

Natasha understood now why he welcomed the devastation that he had predicted. He hoped for heaven on Earth and this was what he was offering to his followers. She was becoming convinced that she had been right last night. Someone in the cult seemed to be engaged in making sure that Daniel's prophecy would actually happen. She believed that someone was planning to infect the world, protect the cult members and emerge unscathed – to inherit the Earth. Yet she was certain that Daniel would have no part in it. He only announced the future. He did not try to shape it. He was not aware of the seamier side of the sect. He probably did not even know that his tape-recorded words were played and replayed to obstinate members, saturating them with the aims and ideals of the sect till they agreed that it was right for them after all.

Surprising herself, she heard another question coming from her own lips. "Did you have a talk like this with a young woman called Jules?"

"Jules." Daniel looked puzzled for an instant and then said, "No. The Lord welcomed her into His kingdom just before we could welcome her into ours."

Natasha stared at him, hardly believing her ears. "You mean..."

"She passed into a better world."

Natasha spluttered and burst into tears.

Concerned, Daniel proclaimed, "Come now. We don't cry for the dead. Perhaps they should cry for the living."

Amid her sobs, she said, "How did she die?"

"She was called. Like Ruth, she was ill. Chosen. Such things are beyond my power to see."

"They told me she'd left," Natasha wailed.

"And so she did," Daniel replied. "She left this Earth. No one has lied to you. Because she wasn't a full member, we couldn't mark her passing as we did with Ruth. Hugh arranged a private cremation and I said a few words to aid her journey." He reached down to Natasha and muttered, "Take my hand."

Natasha did as she was told. His hand was small, stumpy, soft and comforting. She almost wanted to check if he had scars on both palms.

The prophet was quiet for a while as he contemplated her hand. "She was your friend," he deduced. "I'm sorry that you no longer have that friendship but don't be sorry for Jules. She has achieved paradise." Then, without warning, he declared, "You don't belong here." He said it without accusation. It was just a matter of fact. He stared into the mirror as if it were a window on a world where all wisdom lay. Then he gazed fondly on Natasha and, using his uncanny second sight, he murmured, "You only came to investigate the death of your ... friend. I sense she was your sister." Seeing her tearful nod, he added, "I will speak to Hugh. You would not be happy here. You must leave us. He will organize it. Now, you must leave me."

Feeling empty and wiping her cheeks, Natasha trudged back to her room. She didn't care who saw her now, but the corridors lacked all life anyway. No one saw her grief.

Daniel was right. She would have to leave. But she did not yet know everything. And she didn't know if Hugh and Charlotte would simply let her go. She feared being thrown into one of those sterile cells and slowly stripped of her own free will. Perhaps Jules had had to endure it as well – until someone used her body for an experiment. Natasha gulped. She hoped that she would not be the next guinea pig.

A sharp knock on the door woke her in the morning. She had not been able to sleep for a long time after the session with the master of the cult. She was still dead to the world at dawn when the sect came to life. "Who is it?" she called, fearing that Hugh or Charlotte had come for her already.

"Me. Paul."

She sighed with relief. "Just a minute." The sect's clothes were so simple that it only took a moment to dress. When she was decent she opened the door and welcomed him into the room.

"Are you OK?" he asked.

"Listen," Natasha said, ignoring his question. "I think I know what's going on round here." She had to trust someone because she needed to spill out her story.

Paul grimaced. "Really?" His dark eyes retained mystery.

"Yes. I know what really happened to Jules. You were told Jules left but she didn't. That was a cover-up."

"Oh?" He did not invite conversation by asking her a question. It was as if he was not interested or he knew already.

"Jules died – just like Ruth." Suddenly less animated and more sober, she added, "They're *both* dead. And I reckon they were both killed in that so-called surgery of yours – or the rooms just round the corner."

"But ... the surgery's there to cure, not to kill," Paul objected.

"Not kill animals, no. But humans ... that's different."

Suddenly Paul laughed. "There's no violence here, Natasha. You're imagining things." Then he held out his hand to her. "Come on. I'll take you to the surgery. I'll show you you're wrong about it."

Natasha hesitated, looking askance at him for a moment. He was not going to allow her to refuse so she let herself be led towards the animal house. At times, Paul almost dragged her in his enthusiasm. Obviously he was keen to dispel the slur against the surgery and his good work with the animals. Or... There could be another reason for his haste. Suddenly, Natasha was struck by an awful idea. Perhaps Paul was behind the deaths. She wondered if her distaste for Hugh and Charlotte had blinded her. She didn't know why Paul might have murdered Jules but he could have killed Ruth. He was jealous of her. Ruth's death had secured his promotion to the animal house. And he would certainly approve of any arrangements that would allow animals to displace humans on the Earth. Now, she was being taken by him to the surgery where she believed that the killings had taken place and the downfall of the human race was being plotted.

"Er ... I've just thought, Paul," she muttered, "I'm not sure this is the best time. I'm supposed to be helping in the garden now. Perhaps we should postpone it?"

"No, I don't think so," he replied. "No time like the present."

He'd always been a bit odd, but everyone in the sect was strange in some way. Now she realized that there might be something much more ominous about Paul than mere eccentricity.

They were between the reptile and insect enclosures. No one else was there. It was no use crying out for help. "Paul! I..."

"Don't blurt out," he ordered. "You'll scare the animals." Then he smiled that innocent smile which made him look completely insane. Still holding her hand tightly, he whispered, "Come on."

"But..." Natasha could not finish her sentence. She lost her voice as they approached the laboratory door.

Suddenly the door opened and Charlotte emerged. "What *are* you doing to our Natasha?" she asked Paul.

"I ... er..." He paused and then admitted, "I was going to show her the surgery. She believes some peculiar things about it."

"Does she, now?" Charlotte rejoined. "But you know only you and Hugh are allowed in there. Anyway, this will have to wait. Hugh needs to see her right now."

Natasha was surprised to be grateful for Charlotte's interception. Feeling like flotsam on a changing tide, Natasha followed Charlotte in a different direction. The quickest way to Hugh's office, she knew, was through the surgery and past the cells but Charlotte took the long route.

In the business-like office, Hugh dismissed Charlotte and then glowered at Natasha. "What's the meaning of visiting Daniel without permission?" he bawled at her. Without waiting for an answer, he added, "And what's this about you nosing around for Jules?"

Natasha had avoided one threat only to face another. "She was my sister."

"And that's why you came here. You told us lies! You misled us in a vile way. We do not have liars here."

"You *do* have liars here," she protested. "*You* told everyone Jules had left. She didn't. She died."

Goldsmith grabbed her roughly and yanked her towards the cells. "She did leave," he insisted. "She left permanently." He opened one of the grim doors and whispered in her ear, "You'll stay in here until you learn how to behave!"

"No!" she yelled.

But she had no choice. He pushed her unceremoniously into the cell and slammed the door.

Natasha could not tell how long she was subjected to Daniel's drone. It was probably not much more than 24 hours, but it seemed like for ever. The continuous preaching hijacked every part of her mind until there was nothing else. Her own thoughts were brushed aside, subsumed to Daniel's ideas. She was ready to agree to anything if only someone would let her out.

When the prison was eventually opened, her spirit had evaporated. Hugh appeared in the door frame and he informed her that he was taking her to the surgery.

"The surgery?" she mumbled, as if she could not quite recall what or where it was.

He nodded, gripped her by the arm and dragged her out of the cell. She could not resist. He pulled her into the laboratory and plonked her limp body into a seat that resembled a dentist's chair – but this one had straps. Before she came to her senses, Hugh had secured her forehead, ankles and arms to the chair. Then, like coming out of a carefree dream and recognizing dreadful reality, she twisted and turned but it did no good. She was strapped down like those experimental animals. She *was* an experimental animal! And Hugh was by the cupboard, wearing gloves and some sort of protective gear. Her eyes would not focus properly but, through a haze, she could see him drawing up a pale yellow liquid into a syringe.

"No!" she screamed.

Hugh smirked at her. "Ah, you're back with me. Good. It's better if you're conscious. You can tell me what you're experiencing as the toxin invades your body."

He was quite mad.

"This is what you did to Jules and Ruth," Natasha stammered, hoping to delay him.

"Yes. You're privileged to feel exactly what your sister felt."

Gradually reclaiming her own brain, she prompted, "Because she wanted to leave, no doubt, but what about Ruth?"

"Discovered what I was really doing here. She objected, silly girl."

"You're trying to poison the world!" Natasha cried.

He held up the syringe so that the vicious needle pointed at the ceiling. To remove any air bubbles, he squeezed the plunger and a little of the poison squirted into the cupboard. "Not all the world," he replied. "Just humans. Daniel has foreseen it. There *will* be Armageddon. It's my purpose to make sure it happens."

"That's … crazy. You'll kill yourself – and everyone else here!" Still she tried to stall for time.

"Wrong. I'm developing an antidote for me – and others who deserve it. I'll preside over the next generation of the human race."

"I bet Daniel doesn't know all this. He wouldn't approve."

"Daniel's far-sighted. He can see the future but he can't see what's under his nose. His visions help me to see what *I* must do, that's all. He doesn't *need* to know I'm the key to the future he predicts. Neither does anyone else."

Satisfied with the syringe and its contents, he took a step towards Natasha. He pulled up the sleeve of her dress and revealed an attractive white arm. Grinning insanely, he remarked, "Beautiful flesh. Pity." With his left hand he pinched together some skin of her arm and, with his right, he brought the needle to it.

Natasha screamed.

Before the sharp needle pierced her skin, there was a shout from behind her. "Stop! Drop the syringe. I'm a police officer. It's all over."

Hugh hesitated and then laughed. "You?" He sneered. "After her, it's all over for *you*!" The needle scratched Natasha's arm.

There was a crash that, in Natasha's confused and terrified mind, sounded like an explosion. But it wasn't. The police officer had flung a heavy cage energetically across the surgery and it crashed into Hugh's head.

Immediately, he dropped to the floor and the cage fell on top of him. At Natasha's immobilized feet, Hugh Goldsmith's head lolled to one side and let out a groan.

In the next moment, Charlotte appeared at Natasha's side, saying urgently, "Are you OK?"

Natasha could not speak. She just grunted.

Charlotte bent down and examined Hugh. The syringe that had rolled away from his hand was empty. When she turned him on to his back, there was a bloodstain on his white coat. He had fallen on the syringe and the poison had discharged into his stomach.

Immediately, Charlotte stood up. "There's an antidote somewhere." She searched among the jars in the cupboard.

"Is he worth saving?" Natasha moaned.

Still sorting the bottles, Charlotte replied, "I'm a police officer, not a judge." Filling another syringe, she muttered, "I want to see him in court to answer for all this." Roughly, she jabbed the needle into his arm and squeezed the liquid into him. "I don't know what I'm doing," she uttered, "so I can't do any more for him. It's just a matter of waiting now."

* * *

Sitting opposite Natasha, Charlotte explained herself. "I got the job as infiltrator because I look young and, when I want to, vulnerable. It was supposed to be an investigation into a few missing kids but I sniffed something much more serious than abduction. I got myself well in with Goldsmith so I could find out everything. I was a bit too late for Jules, though, I'm afraid. I got evidence that she was being held against her will but she died before I could do anything about it. I wheedled something out of Ruth. Jules made a run for it but, cornered by Ruth and Hugh, her only option was the lab. Hugh followed her in and Ruth never saw her again."

"You went along with everyone else's story that she'd left. You didn't try to warn me."

"I didn't know you were carrying out your own investigation. And I couldn't break cover till I had more to go on," Charlotte responded. "Then Ruth must have finally admitted to herself that Hugh was doing more than treating sick animals. They must have had an argument about it and ... Ruth became number two. Goldsmith couldn't tell everyone that she'd walked out like he did with Jules. Jules wasn't committed to the cult but Ruth was. No one would believe that Ruth would up and off without a word. He had to admit that she'd died. But her death gave me my best lead. One night, I took a look at the lab, and then you and Paul almost caught me setting up a hiding place in it. Luckily, you didn't. That's how come I was in there at the end, watching and listening to everything Goldsmith did to you."

"So Paul had nothing to do with it?" Natasha asked.

"No. Like Ruth, he looked after the animals. Took in the sick ones for Goldsmith to work on. Eventually, he'd have cottoned on to Goldsmith's real purpose and then he'd have met the same fate, no doubt."

Natasha shook her head sadly. "What about Daniel and the sect?"

"There's no law against it as long as abduction isn't involved. That was just Hugh Goldsmith's little game. Daniel didn't even know about those cells. I couldn't pin anything on him. Sure, he knew that Jules died but he accepted Goldsmith's word that she was ill. He wasn't really part of the conspiracy to keep quiet about it, either – just that no one asked him till you did. And there's no law against predicting things." Charlotte shrugged. "Perhaps he's right. Perhaps there'll be a plague, but at least the Divine Truth and Justice Sect won't start it now."

"What'll happen to Goldsmith, do you think?"

"I've just been to see him. He's recovering, sort of. Not a pretty sight. He's going to be paralysed, apparently. I think his punishment's already begun but, when he's fit enough to appear in court, he'll be tried for murder and attempted murder." Charlotte sighed wistfully and then added, "All of which reminds me that I'm supposed to be working. There won't be much hope of a prosecution unless I get your testimony. I'm going to start now. OK? This," she said, pointing to a switch in the interview room, "will turn on a tape. Are you ready?"

"If he's paralysed, is there any point?" Natasha murmured.

"Just think what would have happened if he'd perfected his poison," Charlotte replied in her police officer's authoritative voice. "I think the point is the truth. Especially if it deters any other cranks in cults. Don't you?"

LOVERS' LEAP

I had a bad feeling about the expedition from the start. Me and the wilderness were not exactly made for each other, and normally I would have steered well clear of an exercise in character-building meant to introduce a group of poor wee city mice to the glories of our natural heritage. But Chloe begged me to come along, and Chloe is my best friend – we've been pals since we were two. I had this idea that she might need me along to take care of her, and, as it turned out, I was right.

It's funny how when your friend breaks up with a bloke you're not only allowed you're *expected* to say he was a useless excuse for a human being and you can't figure how she stuck him for so long – but until the break-up is final you're not to hint that you have the least suspicion he might not be Mr Perfect.

Chloe loved Dave. Dave was the bloke in charge of our expedition. He was gorgeous, yes, and intelligent, witty, strong, and charming … too charming by half. Maybe because it doesn't come easily to me, I don't trust people who flirt with everybody. And I really didn't like the fact that Dave already had a girlfriend.

"He doesn't love her any more," my friend assured me. "But he doesn't want to hurt her pride, so he's going to let her be the one to officially end it."

"What if she doesn't end it?"

Chloe sighed at my ignorance. "Of course she will, probably in a couple of weeks, as soon as exams are over.

She doesn't love him – if she loved him, she wouldn't have gone away to university, would she?"

I was sure plenty of people went away to university leaving loved ones behind, but I didn't say that. I wasn't trying to make her feel guilty for stealing another girl's boyfriend – I just wanted her to see that she could do better than Dave.

"But if she doesn't love him, why do the two of you have to sneak around and pretend you're not involved?"

"We're not sneaking around because of Jenna! Dave told me he could get sacked if it came out that he was involved with anyone on the expedition. It's stupid, but there you go. It's not *his* fault. And anyway, we only have to play it cool until the weekend's over. That's why I need you to come – you'll help me to be good."

"I've a better idea. We'll both stay home, and you won't even be tempted."

"Not on your life. I wouldn't trust that Laura Ferguson..." She shut her mouth quickly.

I stared at her. She had sounded so cool, so calm about Dave's actual girlfriend, why this snarl of jealousy about someone else?

"Dave's only human," she said defensively. "And she's *that* determined ... I know she'll throw herself at him if I'm not around."

"Honestly, Chloe, if you can't trust him..."

"It's not about trust! Only things are still so new between us, and Laura is such a predatory cat ... it would be stupid to take that kind of risk, to leave him alone just now."

I hated hearing her talk like that. If Dave could be tempted away from someone like Chloe by someone whose bra-size was bigger than her IQ, she should let him go. The problem with stealing someone from another lover is that once you know how easily it can be done you must always be worrying that someone will do it to you. But Chloe was not stupid. She must have decided that Dave's love was worth suffering a certain amount of jealous fear, and who was I to tell her otherwise? I didn't even have a boyfriend. So I kept my mouth shut.

Twelve of us went up the mountain on a warm, still day in June. The sky was overcast and there was something almost menacing in the quiet air.

Besides Chloe and me and Dave there was the aforementioned Laura Ferguson and three other girls whom I knew only from the planning meeting of two weeks earlier: Katie Abernethy was the sturdy, capable brunette in red spectacles; Megan Murray was the willowy blonde; Fiona Johnstone was an athletic-looking girl with curly red hair. The five boys had made even less impression on me than the girls, and it took me a little while to sort them out: Jim and Roy were both brown-haired, brown-eyed, unobtrusive and ordinary looking – at first I could only tell them apart by remembering that Roy was Katie's brother. The tall, painfully shy one who blushed and flinched if anything female so much as looked too closely at him was called Graham. Ian was the very tall redhead with a good stock of jokes, stories and rousing songs – he was also Katie's boyfriend. I don't think Malcolm – short, dark-haired, with a round, generally impassive face – was anything quite as formal as Megan's boyfriend, but he was always watching her, and his feelings, beneath that stolid exterior, were pretty powerful, as we would learn.

All of them, even Laura with her penchant for playing helpless, were far fitter than I was, and as we set off the trail up the rising slope of the mountain, I quickly fell behind. Chloe would say I was exaggerating to call it mountain climbing. According to her, we were hill-walking. There was a path, only occasionally wide enough for two to walk abreast, and it was seldom necessary to use both hands to scramble up a particularly steep bit. There was absolutely no rock-climbing, although sometimes the path hugged bare walls which would have made a rock-climber's heart leap but which made mine drop into my stomach. This was the easy route, said Dave, the one requiring no skill. The path *he* preferred rose far more steeply on the far side.

At first, as I toiled along, Chloe dropped back to wait for me, but I knew how frustrating she must find it and I urged her on.

Dave came back just then, the good shepherd in search of his lost lambs. Chloe and he exchanged a few phrases so stilted and banal that they could have been a secret code. Their eyes met, and I could practically see the sparks between them ignite in the sultry air. For a moment I felt a pang of envy. Even frustrated desire seemed better than my solitary freedom. Maybe, I thought, love really was worth whatever you had to do to get it.

Then Chloe mumbled something about needing to stretch her legs and shot off. I suspected it was only by running away that she could keep from throwing herself at him, but for the moment I was stuck with Dave. He must have found me incredibly hard work. All that effortless charm and flattery rolling off his tongue, and me turning into a stone toad behind him. Having glimpsed him, briefly, through Chloe's eyes as the ultimately desirable object, I was too self-conscious to relax. What if I started liking him? What if I started liking him *too much*? Or what if Chloe, seeing me laugh at one of his jokes or melt a little under one of his compliments, *thought* I did? I couldn't risk it. Chloe, I knew, was not rational on the subject. Laura Ferguson! The idea of that bimbo posing a threat... But Chloe thought she might. Chloe was in love, and love was blind. Finally Dave gave up and left me to my own devices.

"Take as long as you like," he said. "As long as you stick to the trail you won't get in trouble."

Eventually – miserably swearing that I would never, ever, climb another mountain in my life – I made it to the little house which was our base camp, and began to look for Chloe.

She wasn't with the boys who were building a campfire, or inside helping Fiona and Megan inflate air mattresses. Dave was leaning against the wall outside, deep in conversation with Laura Ferguson. I went over to them. "Where's Chloe?"

He shrugged. "Around somewhere. Malcolm said he was going off to pick blackberries – could be she went with him."

The hairs on the back of my neck were prickling. I didn't know why, but I felt sure something was wrong. "Did you see her go? Did you see her at all since you got here? Did anyone?"

"Chloe's a big girl," said Laura. "She can take care of herself." She spoke to me, but smiled, wrinkling her tiny nose, up at Dave.

And then I heard her; we all did. "Help! Help!"

Seconds later, she came charging into view, coming from the far side of the mountain.

Dave strode over and caught hold of her. "What's wrong? Are you all right?"

Chloe stared at him, wild-eyed, her face contorted with fear or anger. "You shouldn't have asked her to come. How could you? I never meant to hurt her – if she's dead, it's *your* fault."

"Chloe! Calm down. What are you talking about?"

"Jenna," she spat. "Your girlfriend."

He let go of her. "What's she got to do with anything?"

By now, everyone had gathered round, but they seemed unaware of an audience, locked in a private, personal battle.

"She was here when I reached the bothy," said Chloe. "Waiting for you."

"You've never met Jenna. What makes you think –"

"She told me! She said her name was Jenna. I asked was she on her own, and she said not for long. She said she was waiting for her boyfriend who was taking a bunch of kids on a hike. Now, what does that sound like to you?"

"Pure fantasy," said Dave coldly. "I didn't invite anyone to meet me here."

"Maybe she didn't wait for an invitation. Maybe she wanted to check up on you."

"That's simply not possible."

"Oh, no? You think you know her so well, you think you can predict exactly what she'd do? Maybe she's not as uninterested in you as you like to pretend. Maybe she got jealous and decided to pay you a visit."

"By hiking up a mountain? Jenna couldn't walk across a car park by herself. My girlfriend's in a wheelchair. I don't know what you're trying to prove, Chloe, but I'd thought better of you."

He turned his back on her stunned silence. Laura cast Chloe a shocked, pitying glance, then went after him.

"What actually happened? Why were you calling for help?"

It was one of the boys who spoke; I didn't look around to see, but I thought it was Roy. For a moment, watching Chloe's stunned expression, I thought she wouldn't be able to answer. Then, the panic creeping back into her voice, she said, "That girl – Jenna, or whoever she is – I think she's hurt. I ... saw her slip and fall and then ... I think she must have knocked herself out when she fell. She wasn't moving."

"Can you take us to her?"

She nodded.

"I'll bring the first aid kit," said Katie.

"I'm coming, too," I said. Although I'd felt ready to drop with exhaustion a few minutes earlier, curiosity spurred me to make the effort. I was desperate to talk to Chloe. Her story didn't make sense; something was missing.

But she shrugged off my questions during the short walk down the other path, calling a halt after less than five minutes. "It was here," she said. We were in a more forested area than any we'd seen yet. Bramble bushes, gorse, and even some small trees blocked the view, unlike the more open slopes on the other side. "It was somewhere around here that we – that she slipped. Look, there, you can see where the bracken is crushed, that's where she landed."

We gazed down at the spot where someone, or something, might have lain. "Where is she?"

"Maybe she didn't really hit her head – maybe she was just pretending to be unconscious when I called."

"Why would she do that?"

"I – I don't know. But she must be all right – she's gone." There was unmistakable relief in her voice.

"Are you sure this is the right spot?" asked Katie.

"Yes!"

"If she hit her head she could be concussed. People can do that, pass out and then get up and wander around for a bit before passing out again. It's very dangerous. We'll have to try to find her."

"Let's call her name," said Roy. "What was it again?"

Chloe flinched. "Jenna."

Roy called loudly and the name bounced and echoed around us, time and again. But there was no reply. Midges and flies, drawn by our body heat, began to feast. I fidgeted, eager to get away, and the others felt the same.

"She's probably halfway down the mountain by now," said Chloe.

"Or back with the rest of her party. Maybe they found her before we could," said Roy.

"She was by herself," said Chloe. "She didn't have a party. She'd come up on her own, looking for Dave."

"Then we have to find her," said Katie. "If she's here all on her own, with a possible head injury, we have to keep looking until we find her. What's a few midge bites compared to saving somebody's life?"

"I'd better go back and get Dave, don't you think?" said Roy. "He'll know what to do."

"I think he already knows," said Katie. "I think we all know. Right, Chloe?"

"Know what?" asked Roy, sounding baffled.

"Yeah, what are you talking about, Katie?" I asked.

Katie kept looking rather mockingly at my friend. "Chloe? Want to change your story?"

Chloe flushed a deep, dark red.

"Or," said Katie, "maybe we should just forget the whole thing? Pretend this never happened?"

"Are you calling me a liar?"

"I've been very careful not to."

"Why should I lie? Why should I make up a story like that?"

"Well, love can make people do all sorts of things."

"What do you mean?" She'd gone red again.

"Oh, come off it," said Katie. "It's obvious. I think your friend Olivia and I are the only ones on this hike who aren't in love with the leader."

"Please," said Roy.

"The only females," Katie amended.

"Look," said Chloe. Her flush had faded and she sounded controlled and dangerous. "Dave and I have a *relationship*, this isn't some silly one-sided crush, it's a mutual understanding, and we've talked about Jenna. I know all about her –"

"But not that she's in a wheelchair."

"If he wasn't lying."

"Your trust in him is touching."

"Let's go back," I said uneasily, but Katie and Chloe paid no attention.

"If he didn't lie to all of us, then he lied to me before. He never mentioned she was in a wheelchair."

"Not mentioning something is not always the same thing as lying. Maybe it never seemed relevant before. Or maybe he wanted to keep you on a string, and thought you'd feel too guilty about stealing a crippled girl's boyfriend. Look, I don't care what you and Dave get up to, or what lies you tell each other, but please could you not waste everybody else's time and energy? Come on, let's get back to the others."

Chloe stood as if rooted to the spot even after they'd gone. I tugged at her gently. "Come on. The midges are eating me alive."

Finally she looked at me. "You believe me, don't you?"

"Sure." Even if she had some reason for lying to Dave, I didn't think she'd involve the rest of us in it, and I found her active, pursuing Jenna more believable than Dave's suddenly wheelchair-bound girlfriend. But there were things about Chloe's story that made me uneasy. It didn't make sense; something was missing. "But I don't understand – why did you go with her?"

"What do you mean?"

"Why leave the bothy with her? Why didn't you just wait there? Why walk down this path – away from the rest of the group? And how did she fall? What happened?"

She was just opening her mouth when we heard the sound of someone coming up the path behind us.

"Jenna," whispered Chloe, and clutched at my arm.

But it was Malcolm who came into view, toiling up the path. He stopped short, looking briefly as startled to see us as we were to see him before the usual blank, bland expression settled like a mask over his face.

"Where've you been?" I asked.

"Oh, just having a look at the other route. I stopped before it got too steep."

"Did you meet anyone?" Chloe asked. "Or see or hear anyone else on the way?"

He shook his head. "Not a soul. Just me and the wilderness. It's great, isn't it? There's no one else on the mountain but us."

I don't know if Chloe and Dave were avoiding each other because of the Jenna incident, or if they were just keeping things cool as originally agreed, but the end result was the same. Sensing a gap, Laura Ferguson moved to fill it. She was constantly at Dave's side that evening, ready to hand him whatever he reached for, laughter for his next quip always bubbling on her lips. I can see that he might have found it difficult to discourage such a determined admirer, but he didn't have to kiss her, did he?

It happened after lights-out, when we were all inside the bothy at last, snuggled down in our sleeping bags – all except for Dave, who was making absolutely sure that the fire was out, and Laura, who'd elected herself to help him. It must have been nearly midnight, although it wasn't fully dark. It probably seemed dark enough outside, but with the bothy door open, for air, the darkness outside seemed like light to those of us within. Dave and Laura were framed by the door like actors on a narrow screen. I saw their lips meet, saw how he pulled her to him and ran a hand caressingly down her spine.

I looked to my left, hoping Chloe was already asleep, but the whites of her eyes gleamed softly in the dimness, and I knew she had seen what I'd seen.

The next morning, Laura was gone.

It took a little while before we noticed. Her sleeping bag was empty when I woke up, but so was Chloe's, and at least one other, although later when I struggled to recall it, I couldn't have sworn as to which one it was. People were coming and going as they had been all through the early hours, answering calls of nature or getting drinks of water.

But when everything else had been packed away and Laura's gear conspicuously still littered the ground, we began to compare notes and realized that no one had seen or spoken to her all morning.

Dave became grimly efficient, dividing us into four search parties and giving instructions.

"If she's injured, do not try to move her. Blow your whistles and send one person back to base to report."

A chill had fallen not only across our hearts, but also outside. The sultry summer weather of yesterday was already like a dream. The temperature must have dropped by ten degrees, and heavy clouds were massing overhead.

Laura was found just before the weather turned totally nasty. Her body was lying on the rocks at the bottom of a steep crevasse, unreachable. But it was obvious from the way her arms and legs were twisted, and from the blood which darkened and matted her fair hair, that she was beyond any help a rescue party could bring.

All the groups had returned to the bothy to huddle in an anxious silence, still absorbing the shocking news, when the clouds opened and hailstones fell.

After the hail came driving sheets of rain, and we knew we were stuck for the time being, as it would be too dangerous to attempt to descend in such weather.

"I could make it down on my own, and contact rescue services," said Dave, at which Megan burst into tears and threw herself on him.

"Oh, don't leave me, please don't leave me," she cried.

Beside me, I felt Chloe go rigid. I also noticed Malcolm's normally placid face settle into a murderous scowl as Dave, oblivious to the emotions he was setting off in others, held Megan gently, stroked her hair, and bent to murmur some comforting words in her ear. Eventually, she sat up, but she didn't let go of him, and he made no effort to free himself from her entangling grasp.

"Of course I won't leave you if you don't want me to," he said. "I only wanted you to know that it is possible. If I needed to go for help, I could, quite easily. But there's no real urgency, is there? After all, this rain can't last for ever. A few more hours or even a few more days won't make any difference to poor Laura."

For something to do, and to cheer us up, Dave broke out the food and began preparations for lunch. He was only doing his job, but it struck me as callous. Even worse was the way his hands, ever so casually and ever so often, kept encountering bits of Megan who had become, since Laura's death, his constant companion. I hated to see it, but I couldn't blame her: we were all upset and in need of comfort, and if she preferred the charismatic Dave to the silent Malcolm, who was I to object? But I did resent the ease with which Dave switched his attentions – after all, he'd been kissing Laura only hours before! And although I kept trying to push the thought out of my head, I felt uneasily that by showing so much interest in Dave, Megan was putting herself in danger.

Some time after we'd eaten, Chloe was making her way towards the door when Dave stopped her. "Where are you going?"

"Where do you think?"

"I don't think it's a good idea for you – for any of you – to step out of here on your own. Not after what happened to Laura."

"Because the person who killed her might try to kill the rest of us, too?"

Katie dropped a tin plate which clattered noisily on the hard floor.

"I'm not assuming that anyone killed Laura. It could have been an accident."

"A fall like that in broad daylight doesn't just happen! You know as well as I do Laura was killed – and you know why."

He went to her quickly and spoke softly, but not so

quietly that I couldn't hear. "Stop it, Chloe. Things are bad enough already. At least wait until we're safely down before you say something you might regret."

I saw her trying to resist him, but at his nearness, the stiffness went out of her body. He touched her lightly on the shoulder, and she nodded and then moved away. "I won't be long."

"I'll come with you," called Megan, before I could open my mouth. Malcolm said nothing, but he also rose and followed the two girls into the slackening rain.

They were gone rather a long time. Then they burst in, Malcolm carrying Megan in his arms and stumbling slightly under her weight, with Chloe just behind them. Megan's skin looked white as paper.

"What happened?"

Dave rushed forward to relieve Malcolm although he seemed reluctant to let his burden go, while Megan strained forward, turning her head to gaze up at Dave. Her lips parted and she seemed about to speak, and then she slumped, a dead weight.

Chloe and Malcolm both cried out.

"She's fainted," said Dave. "Somebody get the water bottle, please, and a flannel."

Gently he lowered her on to an air-mattress. Her eyelids fluttered and she tried to sit up a few seconds later, but he restrained her. "Take it easy." Then he looked at the two who had been with her. "What happened?"

"Chloe bashed Megan on the head with a rock," said Malcolm. His face was ugly, contorted with anger. We all drew in our breath with horror, except Megan, who only moaned and shut her eyes, and Chloe, who said flatly, "That's a lie."

"Did you see this?" Dave asked Malcolm.

"No, but it's obvious. She's so crazy with jealousy she

can't stand seeing you pay attention to anyone else."

"Just the facts, please, Sherlock. I thought you went out after them to keep an eye on the girls – so why didn't you see what happened?"

His round face pinkened. "Um, well, she was, you know – I left the girls together, and I went for a quick pee. I thought they'd be safe!"

Dave looked at Chloe. "What did you see?"

Chloe bit her lip. "We heard someone rustling in the bushes – Megan heard it too – and then I heard someone call my name, and – really, I was only gone for a few seconds! And then I heard Megan groan, and rushed back and found her on the ground, with a rock beside her, with blood on it."

"You were supposed to be watching out for each other. If you'd only done that this would never have happened," Dave said sharply.

Chloe flinched. "I guess you'd rather it was me who got clobbered instead of your precious Megan!"

"Don't be stupid. I didn't want either of you hurt. I'm responsible for each and every one of you, and you seem to be going out of your way to make my job impossible!"

"How dare you!"

Dave ignored her, bending down to Megan. "Did you see anyone? Hear anything? Do you remember what happened?"

"Chloe heard someone. She said she'd just have a quick look around. I thought it would be all right – anyway, it's bad enough trying to pee outdoors without somebody staring at you. I'd just finished and I heard footsteps – I thought it was Chloe coming back, and then, before I could turn around there was this horrible thud at the back of my head." She winced and shut her eyes.

"You didn't hear anybody calling Chloe's name, did you? No, of course you didn't," said Malcolm. "Neither did I. Nobody heard anything because there wasn't anything to hear. Megan heard Chloe's footsteps just before Chloe hit her. She's just lucky she didn't go the same way as poor Laura."

When he stopped there was a horrible silence. I couldn't believe that Dave wasn't standing up for her, so I rushed in. "That's ridiculous! Chloe wouldn't kill anyone! She didn't!"

"Forget it," said Katie, almost kindly, to me. "I know she's your friend, but face facts. Maybe she'll get off on a plea of temporary insanity. You might as well confess, Chloe – you were about to this morning, weren't you, before Dave stopped you? You're the murderer. Who else could it be? You and Laura left the bothy sometime early this morning – both your sleeping bags were empty – and only you came back. Then you go out with Megan and Megan comes back with her head bashed in. Who else could have done it?"

"You're forgetting Malcolm," I said.

"No I'm not. Why would Malcolm want to hurt the girl he loves?"

"Maybe he was mad at her. He didn't kill her. And he wasn't in love with Laura. He's just as likely a suspect as Chloe – more!"

"Oh, stop, Olivia," shouted Chloe. "Malcolm didn't kill Laura, and neither did I. It was Jenna – Jenna's the killer! – and she would have killed me, too, if I hadn't fought back – I'm sure of it! I never meant to hurt her – honestly I didn't – only she wouldn't let me be, she just followed me down the path and kept taunting me, saying those horrible things, which I know couldn't be true, how she and Dave used to laugh about me – I knew they were lies, but she kept on and on until I lost control. I didn't mean to hurt her, I just wanted her to stop – I just pushed at her, I wasn't thinking, I didn't realize how close she was to the edge until she fell … I…" Chloe faltered. She looked dazed, swaying on her feet, as if she, rather than Megan, had been clubbed. "I didn't mean to kill her … but … but I didn't kill her, did I? I didn't even hurt her, not badly, because she wasn't there when we went back!"

"No, she wasn't," said Katie. "Not Jenna. But Jenna never was on the mountain, except inside your head. If she had been, you'd have pushed her over the edge. You wanted to kill her, didn't you? And when you saw Laura making up to Dave it was just like watching him with Jenna, whom you'd never met. Something in you snapped. When you saw her going out in the middle of the night, you went after her. Maybe you were just going to talk to her, but she said something horrible to you, and you gave her a push and … you didn't mean to kill her, but you did. But getting rid of Laura didn't get rid of your problem. You were still insanely jealous, and Dave's a natural flirt, and when you got a chance to strike out at Megan, you took it. That's the truth."

"No," said Chloe. Her voice was a frail whisper, carrying no conviction. Tears ran down her face and she shook her head helplessly.

There was a terrible silence in the little hut. No one spoke. Megan turned her face to the wall and wept, and everyone else shuffled around quietly, eyes down. I tried to comfort Chloe, but she wouldn't be touched. When she shook me off the third time I went over and sat by the door by myself and stared out at the falling rain.

It seemed that everyone except me believed Katie's interpretation of Chloe's words, but I simply could not.

Chloe was not a murderer. If she'd done it accidentally, surely she would have come running back to rouse everyone to try to save Laura, as she had done after Jenna's fall?

Of course, Katie and the others refused to believe in Jenna's presence. According to them, Chloe had been lying. But now that she'd confessed to pushing Jenna, her earlier story made sense. They'd quarrelled over Dave, and they'd fought. But the shock of believing she might have hurt Jenna had sent Chloe running for help. I couldn't believe that my friend would then plot to kill Laura – and attack Megan, too. It didn't make sense. But why would anyone want to kill Megan?

I turned and looked back into the hut, and my eyes fell on Malcolm, sitting beside Megan, gently holding her hand. Could he have done it? No matter what Katie said, the evidence against Malcolm was just as strong – or as weak – as that against Chloe. Jealousy could have driven him, too. Maybe he never intended to kill Megan, but only to make her helpless, so he could look after her? There was no reason for him to want to kill Laura, but who said murderers were rational beings? What if he was crazy, some sort of split personality, hiding a serial killer underneath that quiet exterior? What if he'd just killed Laura because she was available, because he saw her outside, and he could? A shudder ran through me as I remembered meeting Malcolm on the path when we were looking for Jenna. What if Jenna, stunned and helpless after her encounter with Chloe, had been his first victim?

Whoever it was, I thought, whether it was Jenna hiding on the mountainside waiting for her chance to kill off every one of her potential rivals, or Malcolm, or some unknown killer, we were all in danger, and the longer we were on the mountain, the more likely it was that someone else would die.

Dave must have come to a similar conclusion on his own, for the rain had only just stopped when he announced it was time to move out.

"The path will be slippery, but if we all take care, we'll be fine. I think we'll be better off moving now instead of waiting another night. If this rain sets in again it could go on for days, and after another downpour like the one we've just had, getting down could be decidedly tricky – parts of the path could even be washed away. Two by two, now, like Noah's Ark. I don't want any of you walking alone. I'll keep moving up and down the path to see how you're getting on."

We were a very different group than we'd been only a day before: no longer joking and carefree, but quiet, frightened, suspicious and, of course, missing one of our party. Twelve had come up, but only eleven would walk down.

Although it wasn't raining, the air was wet with the suggestion of more to come, so we were all wearing our waterproofs. Except for Dave, who was a shining beacon in fluorescent orange, the boys were in dark colours – identical dark blue jackets on Malcolm, Ian, Jim and Roy, dark green on Graham. Katie had a dark blue jacket like her brother and Ian, but the rest of the girls wore brighter colours. It occurred to me that we looked like spring flowers, or Easter eggs. Megan was in pink, Fiona in yellow, while Chloe and I wore matching lavender macs which we'd bought in the sales.

I hung back as we began the descent, and Chloe stayed beside me. This put us at the end of the queue, which suited me fine. I wanted to share my thoughts with her and find out what she thought, but she made it clear she didn't want to talk. "Let's just concentrate on getting safely down the mountain."

It was true that a certain amount of concentration was necessary. The rain had transformed the "easy" path and made it treacherous. I'd thought walking up was hard, but walking down was terrifying. My hands were always ready to save me if my feet should slip, but often when I thrust them out to the sides they flailed uselessly, unable to find anything to hold.

And I felt horribly exposed in my position as the very last of our group. I'd insisted on it, making Chloe go ahead of me, thinking that I might be able to protect her if Jenna was the killer, but now the back of my neck prickled and my shoulders were tense with the expectation of a blow from behind. I could only hope that the killer was far away by now.

We walked for about an hour, saying little, and then Dave came around a bend to ask if we were all right.

"Of course," said Chloe. "You don't need to keep checking up on us."

"It's my job to bring you all safely home again."

"Well, *I* don't need your help. I'm just fine on my own, thank you." She shot him a look of pure dislike and then squeezed past him on the narrow trail.

"How about you, Olivia? Would you rather I left you to your own devices?"

"No, I'd like your help."

He met my smile and came closer. "Do you know, until now I would have sworn you didn't like me."

"I've been worried about Chloe."

"Ah. You didn't want to seem to be moving in on your friend's boyfriend?" He was close enough to touch me, and he did.

I pulled away from him, but slowly, aware of how high we were, how steep this path. Caution was necessary. "No, Dave. I'm immune to your charm. I didn't want to see Chloe get hurt."

"I'm very fond of Chloe. But..."

"But that's the problem, isn't it? Girls you're fond of get hurt. Sometimes they even get killed."

"What's that supposed to mean?"

"Why did you say that Jenna was in a wheelchair? Has she done something like this before? Or threatened to? What have you covered up? Don't you realize that could make you an accessory to murder?"

He grabbed hold of me and the breath stopped in my throat. His face was very close to mine, close enough for a kiss, but the look in his eyes was of fury, not any gentler passion.

"There was no murder! Jenna never killed anybody! She gets a little upset, sometimes, because she loves me – that's no crime! All right, I lied about the wheelchair, because I thought Chloe was lying, but –"

"But when Laura died you must have known –"

"Jenna wouldn't kill anyone," he said desperately. "I wouldn't cover for her if – It was an accident, it had to be. I'm sure of it. Don't say things like that."

"It doesn't matter what I say. Laura's dead, there'll be an investigation. The rest of this group have practically convicted Chloe already."

He let go of me. "Don't worry about Chloe. You saw for yourself she's gone off me ... and there's absolutely no evidence against her. Or against anyone else. Laura had an accident – they do sometimes happen."

"Around you especially," I suggested, but he wasn't to be goaded any further, and turned and walked away from me without looking back.

I stood for a while, feeling a little shaky. I had just started to walk on when a sudden pain low in my back almost knocked the breath out of me. I stumbled and half fell, catching myself just in time.

A rock rolled away down the path. I looked up the mountain.

The higher slopes were still wrapped in swirling wisps of fog, or low cloud, but lower down, brilliant against the grey rock and dark green vegetation, I saw a flash of lavender, the same colour as the coat I wore.

My stomach lurched and my thoughts swirled madly, sickly. "Chloe?" I managed to croak. Then, more loudly, I called her name again. "Chloe!"

Slowly a figure rose from the concealing rocks and heather, a girl in a lavender mac. She had her hood up and I couldn't see her face, but the sick pounding of my heart told me that it must be Chloe. The others were right and I'd been wrong. There was no one else on the mountain.

She threw another rock, and this one struck my arm. I'd had no idea Chloe had such good aim. I cried out in pain and terror.

"Chloe, don't! It's me, Olivia, I'm your friend! You know I'd never hurt you!"

She must have witnessed the embrace – but she'd been too far away to see the hatred on his face, or hear the words we exchanged. All she'd seen was intimacy, and in the madness of her love for him, she could not allow it.

She bent down to find another projectile. I shrank against the wall. I would have run from a stranger, but she was my friend – I had to try to reason with her, even though she was trying to kill me.

"You can't kill everyone he looks at or talks to! Think

about it! If you're going to kill anyone, it ought to be him!"

She straightened up and began to pull her arm back to throw. Knowing how good her aim was, I couldn't wait for it this time. Slipping and sliding on the path, I scrambled away, hunched down almost on all fours. I heard the rock strike the mountain wall just above my head, and I whimpered as I continued to half crawl, half fall down the path.

The path was growing steeper, narrower and more dangerous along here. If a rock hit me hard enough, it would knock me over the edge. But the twists and turns into the side of the mountain also meant that it took me out of view – she'd have to come after me, possibly even descend to the path itself, and by that time maybe I'd have caught up with Dave or someone else.

"Help," I cried, my voice shaking, and as I rounded the next bend I came face to face with Chloe.

I screamed.

She gazed at me, bewildered. Her hood was back, her familiar face full of concern.

"I heard you call me – what's wrong?"

I gaped at her. She frowned over my shoulder. "Who's behind you?"

"Who screamed?" Dave came up behind Chloe, who flattened herself against the wall, pulling me in close with her to enable him to pass. "What's going on?" he demanded.

Then he saw her.

A woman in a lavender waterproof jacket and trousers was hurrying down the path. She had a rock in each hand, and there was an icily blank lack of expression on her pale, pretty face. She was a complete stranger to me, but not to Dave.

"Jenna," he breathed.

As soon as she saw him she was transformed. It was as if she melted. Her taut fingers relaxed, releasing the rocks which tumbled, disregarded, to the ground. A soft smile curved her lips and lit her eyes.

"Darling," she cried, and began to run.

Dave stepped forward, his arms opening to catch her. I think it was meant to be a lovers' reunion, a happy ending to this miserable day. And so it might have been if they'd been in a meadow somewhere, standing level, and not on a slippery, narrow ledge jutting out from the side of a mountain. Had Jenna forgotten where she was, or were her last actions utterly deliberate? She came running at top speed and then threw herself at Dave. The full weight of her body knocked him off balance. He staggered. He might have recovered, but she didn't give him the chance. She didn't let go or draw back. She went on, pushing against him, throwing herself at him until he went over the edge. I think she was kissing him as they fell, locked in their final embrace, to their deaths.

DIE LAUGHING!

"I'm a new man, right? I cook, I sew, I care. I wouldn't mind except my girlfriend's an old woman."

There was a ripple of laughter in the audience. The performer, dressed in a black suit with silver pinstripes, waited for a minute, then plunged on.

"No, really, I don't mean it. She's great, my girlfriend. But ever since I started sharing – like, I mean, sharing the chores, not my feelings, I don't share those yet –" At this, there was more nervous laughter from the floor.

"Ever since I moved into the kitchen she sort of – moved out. She says I'm better there, now that I know my place. And maybe she's right. I mean, cooking never was her thing, now I come to think about it. If you asked her for a prawn cocktail she'd give you a glass of Malibu with a couple of shrimps floating on the top. If you said you fancied a chilli she'd put the stew in the fridge. Last time she told me she was cooking up a big surprise it turned out she was ordering pizza. The surprise came later."

As Jerry Rowden strutted through his stand-up act, the rest of the group stood in the wings of the tiny theatre, listening with rapt attention. Phoebe gazed at each face in turn, fascinated at how he managed to capture their attention.

For a start there was her very best friend Amanda – blonde, pretty, full of confidence. At least, she had been until she started going out with Jerry. Phoebe thought he was doing her no good at all. She was so edgy these days, always worrying about pleasing him. It was hard to see how someone so talented could ever have a moment's doubt, Phoebe thought affectionately.

She and Amanda did a double act, singing funny old music hall songs. Sometimes they added songs they'd written themselves. They'd opened the revue tonight and gone down very well, but Amanda had needed some convincing about that because Jerry hadn't bothered to say anything afterwards. For some reason his opinion seemed to matter to her more than anything.

Then there was Diane – beautiful, strange Diane Egerton – who'd gone out with Jerry for a while last term. For her magic act, Diane was dressed in a black conjuror's suit with shiny top hat. She'd painted her face dead white like a clown's with scarlet lips. It looked a bit strange but the audience had loved it, especially when she selected a volunteer from the front row and hypnotized him. She deliberately chose a big, beefy guy so that she could demonstrate her power over him, her ability to make him sit up and beg like a dog, or whimper and crawl like a baby. When he finally woke from his trance to find he was sucking his thumb, the crowd went wild.

But now, she stared at Jerry with such wide-eyed concentration that Phoebe wondered whether she was still in love with him. Funny taste, Phoebe thought idly. But then, a lot of girls seemed to fall for Jerry for some reason.

And yet the boy Diane was hanging around with these days was far, far nicer. Robert Jacques was the cleverest boy in their year at college. He was very funny, too. He used to do a double-act with Jerry, Phoebe remembered vaguely. But today, staring fixedly at the stage, he wasn't laughing. In fact, he looked pale and withdrawn, as if in another world.

Phoebe wondered whether he was feeling embarrassed about Stella. After all, it was no secret to any of them that Stella had been heartbroken when he'd split up with her earlier that summer and started going out with Diane.

There she was, standing well away from Diane, still clutching the doll she'd used in her act. Stella Ronson, the ventriloquist. But crazy Stella, the computer freak, was no ordinary ventriloquist. Instead of throwing her voice in the traditional way, Stella used state of the art technology to make her dummy talk.

Inside the dapper little male figure she'd fixed a voice-activated microchip, which responded to various triggers so that it sounded as though she was having a conversation with it. The dummy, known as Arnold, was meant to be a sexist bloke constantly putting women down.

"What do you think of the women's movement?" Stella asked him.

"I like it from the waist down," replied the dummy.

"Why are men always late for dinner?" demanded Stella.

"Because they have to show a woman where she stands."

"And where does a woman stand?"

"Behind a man, of course," chortled Arnold.

Phoebe thought Stella's act was brilliant – easily the most inventive item in their repertoire. But she never got top billing. It was always Jerry who came on last. And, although his stand-up routine was incredibly corny, Phoebe had to admit he was a great showman. They would probably never have got a show together if it hadn't been for Jerry. He wanted to be a comic so badly.

Yet his real talent was in organizing people. And getting them to do exactly what he wanted.

Phoebe turned back to the stage to watch the final minutes of his act. She was amazed that the audience was actually laughing. She hated jokes that put down women. But she had to admit he ended the routine with a flourish.

"She doesn't understand what I've done for her," he went on. "I've decorated the flat, chosen the furniture. I mean, she used to think green walls and teddy bear duvet covers were the height of chic. I told her she had no taste when she started going out with me. She said she quite agreed. She said she never realized what happiness was until she moved in with me. And then it was too late! Ladies and gentlemen, goodnight!"

And he strode off the stage to a burst of applause, whistles and cheers. The minute he reached the wings Amanda flung herself into his arms.

"Darling, you were fantastic!" she raved. "They adored you!"

"Did they?" asked Jerry, worriedly. "I wasn't all that sure for the first part. Do you think that food section went OK?"

Big-head, thought Phoebe. But she just said: "Come on – time for the whole group curtain call." She and Amanda, Jerry, Diane and Stella all trooped back on to the stage, held hands as though they were all best friends, smiled and took a bow.

"Ladies and gentlemen, let's hear it for this talented group of young performers – winners of the college and campus revue competition: The Flying Aces!" The organizer of the Festival took the centre stage to introduce the next act, then came scurrying after Phoebe as she dived backstage.

"Phoebe, hi, do you have a minute?" he asked, panting as he caught up with her. She turned to look at him, her heart thumping. She'd fancied him all week, ever since they'd arrived at the theatre. He was very hunky, she thought approvingly – not exactly handsome, but with warm, crinkly eyes and a shock of dark, unruly hair. He was probably a couple of years older than her gang, just enough to be mature without being the least bit boring. Although they'd talked together quite a lot and he'd seemed interested in her, he hadn't actually asked her out. Until now.

"Listen – I'd really like it if we could have a drink together," he said earnestly. "Would you be free after the show?"

"Sure, we're all going to the bar anyway," Phoebe smiled, trying to hide her delight.

"I meant just you," he answered. "But I guess that'll have to do."

Excitedly, Phoebe rushed off to join the others in the theatre bar, right in the basement. She found Amanda, who'd already bought her a beer, and grabbed her by the arm. "Guess what?" she told her. "Michael Halliday's asked me out! You know, the good-looking festival organizer? The one with the hair?"

Amanda didn't respond. She was staring over Phoebe's shoulder with narrowed eyes. Phoebe tried again. "Well, he didn't exactly ask me out," she carried on. "But he does want to buy me a drink and… Hello? Amanda? Are you hearing me? You're not listening to me, are you?"

Amanda turned to her mournfully. "Sorry? Oh, gosh, sorry, Phoebs. It's just Jerry – look at him."

Jerry was deep in conversation with a striking-looking American girl dressed like a soldier, who'd done a very challenging stand-up routine earlier on.

"He's getting off with her, isn't he?" said Amanda tearfully.

"He's a rat," said Phoebe shortly. "And no, he's probably not getting off with her. He's too busy fancying himself. He just likes to go round conquering every available woman, haven't you noticed? But if it's any comfort I expect he loves you really, even though you're probably better off without him."

"Oh, I couldn't do without him!" protested Amanda, horrified.

Phoebe shook her head pityingly. "In that case you'll have to put up with his horrible habits," she told her friend sternly. "Now come on, let's join Stella."

Stella was quietly sipping a lemonade, all alone. As Phoebe and Amanda sat down to join her a seedy-looking man with thinning hair and a moustache arrived at the table. "Hello, people, I'm Dennis Mordant, agent and friend to funny folks." Amanda smiled politely. Phoebe stared at him. She thought she'd heard his name before.

"Mind if I join you for a moment?" he asked, sitting down between Phoebe and Stella without waiting for a reply. "I just wanted to congratulate you on a very fine little revue, very fine." The two girls perked up a little at that. No one else was taking much notice. "I do think you were most creative and original. Your act, my dear, was a masterstroke." This was addressed at Stella, who gave him her usual dreamy smile.

"Yes, you could go far. I think you should definitely develop it." He handed her a card. "Call me if you want any advice. I'll be interested. Oh, and by the way, your friend, the young lad."

"Jerry Rowden," said Amanda eagerly.

"Yes, I caught him last year, you know. He was with another fellow at the time. Now that young man really had something."

Stella sat up straight and looked at him. "You mean Robert? Robert Jacques?"

The agent shrugged. "I don't remember his name. I just remember his timing. Wonderful for such a young boy. I remember saying to the other one, this Jerry, I said you've got yourself a great gag-writer as a partner. You tell him to get in touch with me. I never heard from him, though. Oh well, win some, lose some."

He drained his glass, got up and bowed. "See you, ladies. And good luck. And Stella – I'm waiting to hear."

Stella seemed to stare into the distance as she watched him leave the bar, her eyes oddly blank. But Phoebe had no time to ponder Stella's problems. She was too busy putting on her most dazzling smile and waving at Michael as he threaded his way through the crowded bar.

Soon they were joined by Robert and Diane, who'd spent ages taking off the white make-up and now still looked pale and anxious. Stella, who didn't normally speak to Diane at all, was forced to sit next to her as she whispered something urgently to Robert. Phoebe thought she must be telling him what the agent had said.

"Right, well, the least I can do is buy this round," said Michael, clearly unaware of the tensions around him. "You lot were great! The toast of the night. I just hope you can repeat your brilliance tomorrow."

By the time he'd returned with the drinks, Jerry had joined the group, swaggering a little. "Sorry about that," he said. "Just doing a little business over there. It seems that Marlene Dykes might be able to introduce me to someone in New York..."

Amanda tossed her head away from him as if she was

angry, but Phoebe could see that she was trying hard to control her tears. "Cheers, Flying Aces," toasted Michael. "Here's to you all." Then he turned to Phoebe and added quietly: "Especially to you, Phoebe – let's drink to getting to know each other."

They clinked glasses and sipped their drinks. Then Robert, looking pale and angry, cleared his throat. "Jerry, why didn't you tell me that Dennis Mordant wanted me to get in touch?"

Jerry looked nonplussed for a few seconds, then regained his cocky assurance. "Oh – oh, right, that guy. Well, to be honest, I didn't think it was very important. He was a real loser. Tried to tell me how we should do our act and it was all rubbish. Sorry and all that, but I really don't think it's any big deal. He was just a sad case, trying to come on as a hotshot. Believe me, you were well out of it."

Michael looked amazed. "Did you say Dennis Mordant?" he demanded. "Dennis Mordant? He's just about the most astute agent you can find on the comedy circuit. He's the best at spotting new talent, you just wouldn't believe how many kids he's discovered and started on their careers." He named a few voguish comics. Robert looked tense and angry, Jerry white and defiant. Phoebe glanced around at the others. Amanda was staring anxiously at Jerry, worried for him. Diane was holding Robert's hand protectively. And Stella – Stella was staring into the distance with those blank eyes, almost as though she were somewhere else, in someone else's skin.

"Your friends are a bit, um…"

"Strange?" suggested Phoebe.

"I was going to say that," replied Michael. "But I

didn't want to offend you or anything."

They were wandering down the road away from the theatre, hand in hand. It was much, much later that evening and Michael was walking her home.

"I thought I'd never get you to myself," he confessed. "You really are a close-knit gang, aren't you?"

"I suppose we are, really," Phoebe shrugged. "We've known each other for ages because we went to school together and now we're all at Sixth Form College – Jerry joined last year, after he'd moved away from here to live with his brother. He and Robert are a year ahead of us. It's really since we got this show together that we've got close. And we're far away from home so we're all staying in the same place."

"Yes, I suppose Wales must seem a bit different from the industrial North," said Michael.

"Well, Cleeford isn't all that industrial," Phoebe said. "Unless you count the Sixth Form College. That's a sort of factory – an A-level factory."

"I keep forgetting you're only sixth formers," teased Michael. "I'd better not tell anyone I'm dating a schoolgirl. After all, I'll be in my final year come October." He put his arm round her to show he was only joking.

"But I must say it's pretty impressive, a group from a Sixth Form College beating all the others in the competition. You really are an exceptional lot, I mean it. How do you manage it?"

"Oh, I suppose it's Jerry, really," Phoebe admitted. "He's just great at getting people together and creating a show. And of course he was really keen to win this contest. He's really the only one of us who wants to go professional."

"How about Robert?" asked Michael. "He looked like he might be serious."

"I don't know about Robert," answered Phoebe. "He's got a great career ahead of him – he's expected to get all A's this summer and go to Oxford. But maybe you're right – maybe he is yearning for stardom..."

"How come he's here, if he isn't performing?" asked Michael.

"Well, I suppose he wanted to come with Diane," said Phoebe. "But it's a bit awkward, because he and Jerry used to have this great duo."

"Why did they split up, then?" asked Michael.

"I don't know, really," Phoebe answered. "At the time I thought it was because Robert wanted to concentrate on his exams. But after tonight – I just wonder if it was as simple as that."

They arrived at the front door of a rather imposing double-fronted house. "Do you want to come in?" she asked.

"How did you land such a fancy place?" demanded Michael, impressed.

"Oh, didn't I mention that?" said Phoebe vaguely. "It's Jerry's house. His mum and dad are away and they said we could all stay here, which is very convenient because it's big enough for us all to squeeze in. Jerry stays with his brother in Cleeford during term time because he wanted to get away from home and be independent. He says his parents are cool about it. I should think they were probably quite relieved."

Everyone else was slumped in the living room. Jerry sat on the floor at Amanda's feet, his head in her lap. Diane and Robert were arm in arm on the sofa. Stella was busily tapping away on a lap-top computer. Michael immediately began chatting to Robert but although he appeared engrossed in the conversation, Phoebe could tell he was hoping the others might disappear soon.

"I was wondering about tomorrow," she broke in at last. "Anyone fancy going to the beach?"

Jerry shook his head. "Count me out," he said. "I'll be up in my studio all day and I don't want any distractions. I've got some tapes to go through. I want to listen to tonight's show to see if I can find any improvements. And, er, I thought I might dub a few of my performances for Marlene."

"Well, why don't you all come over to my place for dinner?" offered Michael.

"I'm not sure," said Amanda. "We don't usually bother with an evening meal because we're so busy getting ready for the show."

"Especially me," agreed Diane. "It takes ages to put on my get-up – I don't know why I ever bother to take it off!"

"I didn't have anything very grand in mind," said Michael. "And you could always get ready first. The show doesn't begin until nine tomorrow, so if you arrive around seven-thirty we should have plenty of time."

Everyone said they'd like to come.

"Well, bedtime for me," announced Jerry. "I need my beauty sleep."

"I'll come too," said Amanda hastily.

"Oh, just a moment, Jerry – could I have a word?" Tall, elegant Diane uncurled her long legs from the sofa and glided across the room. "It's about – well, it's to do with my act. I really wanted to get your advice and if you're going to be tied up tomorrow..."

Jerry raised an eyebrow enquiringly and looked her up and down. "Now?" he asked quizzically.

Diane nodded. "It won't take a moment, I promise." And she followed him out of the room, leaving Amanda open-mouthed and hurt.

"I'll join you in a minute," she called after Jerry, rather weakly.

A few minutes later Stella closed up her computer and bid them goodnight, followed by an unhappy Amanda.

"At last!" Michael breathed. "I was beginning to think that would never happen." And then as he took her in his arms and kissed her, the stars began to flicker all around her, and Phoebe found herself melting into his warm, sweet embrace.

Phoebe was in the kitchen the following evening, busily chopping tomatoes for the salad, when Michael crept up behind her and put his arms round her. "You're looking great – from the back," he murmured, his lips brushing her hair. "Mmm – can the front view ever live up to this? Come on, turn round – I want to look at you."

Phoebe was wearing a shimmering silver-grey cat-suit that clung to her thin, muscular frame. Her long, dark hair was laced with silver sequins and she wore high-heeled black boots with silver stars on the ankles. Michael gasped as she slowly turned round to face him.

"You really are something, Phoebe," he murmured, pulling her towards him. As they kissed, the doorbell began to ring insistently. Michael sighed. "It's always the way, isn't it? I just can't seem to get you away from your mates."

"Well, you did invite them for dinner," Phoebe pointed out.

"But it's only six-thirty," protested Michael. "I thought we'd have lots more time. Oh, well – I suppose it just proves I can never get enough of you."

He opened the door and a flustered, tearful Amanda burst in, dressed identically to Phoebe, but in gold instead of silver.

"Amanda! What is it?" demanded Phoebe at once.

"It's Jerry!" Amanda gasped. "The rat."

Phoebe opened her mouth, then closed it again as Amanda went on: "No, don't tell me you know he's a rat. It just makes me worse. But you're right, he is. I went up to his studio – you know, the studio where he was supposed to be alone all day, undisturbed, working? And guess who was there?" Phoebe and Michael shook their heads expectantly.

"That awful Marlene Dykes, the American dream, I don't think. Sitting there, right next to him. Right up close."

"Well, he did say he was going to give her a tape," soothed Phoebe.

"Huh!" retorted Amanda. "I don't care what he said he was going to give her. I know what I saw, and it was not a tape-giving ceremony. They were practically touching. At least, they probably were touching and they just sprang apart when they heard me coming."

"So what did he do?" asked Phoebe wearily. She was used to Amanda's despair over Jerry.

"Oh, I didn't give him a chance to do anything," said Amanda. "I just stormed out and left them to it. I think he probably called after me but I was too angry to take any notice. I've had it with him, Phoebs, I really have."

"Course you have," said Phoebe, as she always did. "But then again, you might just forgive him as usual. After all, you know Jerry. He falls for flattery, doesn't he? He likes to believe he can conquer all women. It doesn't mean he ever actually does anything about it."

But Amanda was determined. "This time it really is the last straw," she said, picking at the tomatoes that Phoebe had just chopped. "Fancy behaving like that – on the last night of the show! I feel like I could kill him, I really do!"

Soon Diane arrived, looking strange and glamorous as she always did in her conjuror's outfit and full stage make-up. "Is Robert here yet?" she demanded at once.

"No, weren't you going to come together?" asked Phoebe.

Diane shook her head. "No, he said he had to meet someone in town. And I always need a good two hours to get ready when I'm putting this lot on. It's really time for a new look, I think."

At about a quarter to eight, Robert arrived. Diane greeted him with a long, abandoned kiss of such passion and intensity that Phoebe felt embarrassed, as though she was somehow peering into their souls. She was aware of someone else watching them, too. Stella was gazing at the couple with a look of almost palpable pain and desolation.

Then, although Jerry still hadn't arrived, they sat down at the table, Robert next to Diane, Michael and Phoebe at either end. Amanda sat next to Stella, who propped her dummy, Arnold, next to the empty chair on her other side.

"God, you are pathetic with that ridiculous doll," Diane spat cruelly. "Don't you think it's time you got yourself a real life boyfriend?"

"Well, I'm not sure if I can afford the insurance," Stella snapped back. "In case he gets stolen like my last man!"

Everyone held their breath, horrified. Robert looked anguished. Surprisingly, it was Amanda who came to the rescue.

"We'd really better get a move on or we'll be late for the show," she announced briskly. "Michael, can I just give Jerry a quick ring?" She looked defiantly at Phoebe. "We'd better make sure he's on his way."

Michael handed her the mobile and she tapped out the numbers. She waited for a minute or so, then began speaking slowly and carefully. She was obviously talking into the answer-machine. "Jerry? Hi, it's Amanda. Just to say I hope you're on your way now because it's eight o'clock, and you're late for dinner."

As she put down the phone an astonishing thing happened. Diane, who until then had been glaring daggers at Stella, her eyes flashing with spite, suddenly began to laugh uncontrollably.

"What's the joke?" demanded Phoebe, intrigued.

"Oh, nothing really," guffawed Diane. "I just thought of one of Jerry's stupid jokes from that routine he does about cooking. It seemed – appropriate somehow. You know, when he says how his girlfriend always complains about him being late for meals when she's cooking. And he says – what's the point of answering?" Diane paused for more peals of laughter. "What's the point of answering, when he was only going to bring it up later!"

It was ten past nine and the evening show was in full swing. The Flying Aces were due on in just quarter of an hour. But Jerry had still not appeared and Amanda was distraught. "Where can he be?" she kept saying over and over again. "Something's happened to him, I know it has."

"Relax, honey – he was just fine when I saw him," drawled Marlene Dykes, who was in the wings about to go on. She ostentatiously removed her lurid piece of Hollywood chewing gum, wrapped it in a piece of green tissue and flicked it into a bin. "But hey – what a fine love affair that guy is having. With himself. I'm surprised the mirror hasn't worn out the amount of time he spends looking at it. If you ask me, he's just so big for his boots he's gonna trip right over them one of these days."

"Well, no one did ask you!" Amanda flared. But Marlene didn't hear her because she was striding out on to the stage in her soldier's garb, and the audience was already laughing at her first crack.

"Cheek!" Amanda muttered to Phoebe. But Phoebe secretly agreed with Marlene. She put an arm round her friend.

"Look at it this way," she comforted her. "If that's how she feels about him she's obviously not having any kind of scene with him, is she?"

"Oh, don't be so sure," Amanda muttered darkly. "She may only just have realized how self-centred he can be. Anyhow, that's not the point. Right now, we need Jerry for the show and he's not here."

"I've got the perfect solution," announced Stella unexpectedly. She was standing just behind them, clutching Arnold as usual. "If Jerry doesn't show, let's have Robert instead."

"There's an idea," Phoebe agreed. "Robert would be great. But where is he? Has anyone seen him since he left Michael's?" Robert had gone out before the others, claiming he needed some fresh air. Phoebe had thought he wanted to avoid any more scenes between Diane and Stella. But now, she realized, he'd been gone for nearly an hour.

"Here he is," said a silky voice on her left. It was Diane, of course, looking immaculate. Robert appeared just behind her, his face even whiter than usual, his eyes haunted by some obscure terror.

"You will go on, won't you?" pleaded Stella.

Robert hesitated. "Of course he will," declared Diane. And so it was decided. There was no time after that for any more discussion. Marlene was finishing her act. She bowed to warm applause, whistles and catcalls. Then Michael was introducing The Flying Aces, and Phoebe and Amanda were on stage, singing their hearts out.

Then Diane performed her smooth, amazing conjuring act, followed by Stella with her beloved Arnold.

Phoebe watched, enthralled as usual by Stella's strange conversation with the computerized doll. Then it was time for Robert. He stood in the wings, his face ashen. Michael announced his name.

And then he just burst out: "I'm sorry. No. I can't do it. Not now." And fled.

Everyone raced after him. "It's OK, darling, it's OK," Diane was soothing him. "It doesn't matter. Just do what feels right, that's all!"

"Oh, you would say that, wouldn't you!" Stella said acidly. "I don't think it's all right, actually. Robert's just blown his great chance. Didn't you see Dennis Mordant in the front row? Didn't you realize what you've thrown away?"

"I – I don't care. It doesn't matter now…" Robert said faintly.

Amanda, too, was ashen-faced. "I think we should get back," she announced, her voice trembling. "I want Jerry. I just can't stand not knowing where he is – who he's with now…"

Michael came to find them, his face full of concern. "Don't worry, mate," he said to Robert. "Can't be helped. Listen." He turned to Phoebe. "Why don't you borrow my van and drive everyone back? I'll join you at your place after the show."

Phoebe flashed him a grateful smile. It was so like him to be considerate rather than angry. He could see they were all a bit strung out.

It only took about ten minutes to drive everyone back to the house. They arrived just before ten-fifteen. As soon as they got through the door Amanda rushed upstairs to her and Jerry's bedroom. Then Phoebe heard that door slamming, and more thumps as she made her way up to the top of the house to Jerry's studio. And then the house shook with one, then another blood-curdling scream.

Everyone started at the noise and then seemed frozen where they stood. Phoebe recovered first, and began racing up the stairs. She flung through the open door and gasped at what she saw. Right along one wall was a bank of state-of-the-art hi-fi equipment including two CD players, cassette players, a reel to reel tape recorder, surround-sound speakers, and rows upon rows of cassettes and CDs.

Jerry's huge, matt black desk sat at right angles to the wall. It was empty except for a telephone and answer-machine, two glasses, one still full of wine, and a tape box. A matching chair rested at an odd angle against the desk. And a hideous figure sat in it.

Phoebe had taken in the scene in just a second or two. Then her eyes rested on the figure slumped strangely in the chair.

Phoebe forced herself to come forward to examine Jerry's body more closely. She nearly retched when she saw what had happened to him. A thick coil of recording tape had been wound round and round his neck, and was somehow attached to the tape recorder on the wall. Jerry himself was tied to the chair with more tape. He'd been strangled. That much was clear.

By now the others had made it to the room and were staring, horrified, at the ghastly scene. Amanda was shaking uncontrollably and sobbing. Phoebe took a deep breath and somehow managed to regain a little cool.

"OK, this is what we do," she said in a voice so shaky it was barely recognizable. "Stella, take Amanda downstairs and give her some tea. Robert, you ring the police. Now. We'd better not touch anything here, but I'll stay until the cops arrive. Someone should..." Her voice broke here. "Someone should stay with him."

Diane raced after Robert, while Stella led Amanda away. As soon as she was alone Phoebe looked round the room carefully, trying to memorize every detail. There were some bright Hollywood chewing gum wrappers in the waste-paper bin – probably left over from Marlene's visit. Phoebe went close up to the body and touched it gently. It was still warm. Jerry must have died very recently. Absently, she noted a peculiar white smear on his denim shirt. Strange, she thought, Jerry is normally so immaculate. *Was* so immaculate, she corrected herself.

Although he was tied tightly to the chair one arm had come loose and was splayed on the desk. His watch had smashed, showing exactly eight o'clock. That, she supposed, must be the time of death. She shuddered.

She had never liked Jerry that much. But he was a friend, a fellow-trouper, part of the gang. And he certainly didn't deserve this foul, ghastly death. Who could possibly have done such a terrible thing to him?

It had to be someone quite strong, she decided. Jerry was powerfully built and kept himself in good shape. So whoever tied him to that chair must have been pretty big. Probably a man, she thought. Although you never knew... What puzzled and sickened her even more, though, was the viciousness of the attack. Whoever had done this knew Jerry well and hated him. Phoebe shivered again.

Her eyes strayed to the telephone and the answer-machine. The green light was flashing insistently so almost without thinking she wound back the machine and listened. There were two messages. Both gave her a shock. The first voice was immediately recognizable. "Jerry?" said Amanda's voice. "Hi, it's Amanda. Just to say I hope you're on your way now because it's eight o'clock, and you're late for dinner."

Late for dinner? thought Phoebe, puzzled. Why does that sound so familiar? But then she was distracted by the second voice. It belonged to Robert. "Jerry? Are you there? Just in case you haven't left yet for the theatre, I'm coming round to see you. There's something I've got to ask you."

An icy finger of fear crept down Phoebe's back. So Robert had been here tonight – when the others were making their way to the theatre. He had more than a grudge against Jerry and he was easily strong enough to overpower him. But not to kill him – surely not that...

Phoebe realized she shouldn't have touched the machine. It could easily form some vital clue to the killer. She'd have to confess what she'd done to the police and they'd be furious. But she didn't really care that much. She was thinking too hard. Somehow, those two messages convinced Phoebe that she held the pieces to this mystery puzzle. All she needed to do was put them together.

As she rewound the machine, still wondering what Robert could have meant, she noticed something small and shiny that had been hidden underneath it. It was a tiny green screwdriver, the kind you used to fiddle round the back of TVs when they went wrong. TVs and computers.

But she had no more time to think. The police had arrived and were on their way upstairs. Immediately a sort of gruesome efficiency took over. A scene-of-crime area was marked out, someone was flashing a camera, someone else issuing technical orders. Phoebe watched for a few minutes, fascinated, until someone spotted her.

"Phoebe Underwood?" said the kindly-looking man. She nodded. "I'm Detective Chief Inspector Graham Ellison. Well done for holding the fort here. You go downstairs now and get some hot tea, and I'll join you down there in a minute. I'm going to have to take statements from you and your friends, OK?"

Phoebe nodded and allowed herself to be ushered out. The next hour passed in slow motion like a nightmare. The Detective Inspector had seen each of them in turn, including Michael who had somehow, magically, arrived in the middle of the chaos. When the detective had finished he came and sat down heavily on an armchair in the large living room where they were all assembled.

"I know you've all had a terrible shock," he said gently. "But you must understand that this is a full-scale murder inquiry and I will require your full co-operation. I want you all to stay here overnight. I'm leaving Constable Watts here to guard the crime scene until tomorrow, when I shall return."

"Do you mean we're all suspects?" demanded Phoebe. He sighed and looked down at his vast fingers.

"Let's just say – you're helping the police with their enquiries," he replied.

Phoebe eyed her friends one after the other with a new watchfulness. There was Robert, drumming his hands nervously on the edge of the chair as he tried to play chess with Michael. Stella, looking tense but serene, was fiddling with her beloved lap-top. Diane lay languidly on the sofa, flicking through a magazine. Amanda was curled up next to her, white-faced and hollow-eyed. No one seemed quite able to leave the room.

"Poor old Jerry," Diane commented, breaking the tense silence. "It's hard to believe he's dead, isn't it?"

"Well, why would you care?" demanded Amanda bitterly. "Oh, don't tell us, you were still hoping that one day he'd get back with you. Some hopes."

"No, not really," Diane replied mildly. "I'm just sorry he's dead, that's all I said. I mean, he wasn't so bad, was he?"

"Oh, really?" intercepted Robert. "That's not what you said when you chucked him. I remember the first time we went out you said what a relief it was after such a jumped-up, conceited, self-regarding, insensitive creep!"

"Please, Robert," answered Diane. "Don't let's speak ill of the dead."

Phoebe suddenly felt a tingle down her spine as she took in what Robert had said. "Do you mean – *you* chucked *him*?" she repeated.

Diane looked suddenly hunted. "Well, yes – but he didn't want that spread about so I agreed not to talk about it. I know, how about some more tea?"

A series of images flashed into Phoebe's mind. Of Diane coquettishly asking Jerry for help the previous evening. Of Diane and Robert – and their intense, passionate kiss. And of Diane, maniacally laughing after Amanda's telephone call.

An idea was beginning to thread delicately through her mind, so delicately she didn't want to disturb it. She just wanted it to make sense. But there was one important fact she needed to establish before she could pursue that line of thought.

"Tell you what I can't understand," she said carefully. "There's something here that doesn't add up. According to Detective Chief Inspector Ellison, the time of death was between eight and ten-fifteen – when we found him." She explained that she'd overheard him saying that it had to be that recent because the body was still warm. But she didn't mention the smashed watch. After all, it didn't prove anything conclusively. On the other hand it might be a vital clue to the time of death – and if so, it was a vital clue she intended to keep to herself.

"Yes, it was," sobbed Amanda. "I should know. I found him first."

"Don't keep on about it!" snapped Diane. "You know the one who finds the body is usually assumed to be the murderer."

Phoebe glanced at her, surprised at her cruelty. Then, for some reason, she remembered the white smear on Jerry's shirt. Of course! Diane and her white make-up! Her mind began to race furiously, but still none of the details made any sense.

"What a stupid thing to say!" said Amanda, more angry than hurt. "It was far more likely to be that horrible Marlene. We know she visited Jerry today. I saw her."

"What time was that, Amanda?" Phoebe asked gently.

"About – about five-thirty, I think," said Amanda, trying to remember. "But she could have done it, you know. I mean, maybe I was the last to see him alive..."

"Stupid as well as guilty!" teased Diane, cruelly. "First of all, she visited him in the afternoon, and he was killed at night. Secondly, if she was about to steal him away from you, it rather obscures the motive, don't you think?"

"Let's get back to the time of death," pleaded Phoebe. "It's very odd, because we were all together then, weren't we?" she appealed to them. "From dinner at Michael's, when we were all there before eight o'clock, then the theatre and then back home. We were all together. Except…"

Her gaze rested on Robert. "Come on now, Robert. I expect you've told the police this already. At least, you're a fool if you haven't. They're bound to find out that you were here tonight. Probably the same way I did. So shoot!"

Robert looked startled, like a hunted rabbit. Then he shrugged. "OK, OK. I'll tell you. It was awful keeping it to myself. It's true. I did come here when I left Michael's. I'd phoned Jerry first to let him know. But when I arrived he was…" Robert's voice broke and he buried his head in his hands. "He was already dead. I panicked. I thought it would look as if I killed him. So I rushed over to the theatre and just hoped no one would ever know. I forgot I'd left a message on the machine."

"But what were you going to ask him?" Phoebe asked, staring at him hard.

"Oh, I'd been to see that agent Dennis Mordant," Robert said. "He – he said he might have a place for me in a revue he's doing in Edinburgh, if he could see me on stage tonight. I wanted to persuade Jerry to do the double-act one more time. But it was too late. So of course, when I got my chance, it looked perfect. But I just remembered Jerry – the way he looked, all trussed up… And I couldn't do it."

"So Jerry managed to ruin another chance for you," commented Stella, unable to keep the bitterness out of her voice. She was still peering hard into her computer. "Anyone got a screwdriver?" she asked. "I think I'm going to have to get right inside this little lot. Can't think what I did with mine."

It was as though a bolt of lightning had shot right through Phoebe. So Stella had lost her screwdriver! The one she used for fiddling with the tiny nuts on computers? Phoebe remembered the little green-handled screwdriver by Jerry's phone. Then she remembered Amanda's message on the answerphone. And suddenly she knew. She knew who had killed Jerry. And why. And, almost – how.

"OK, so Robert has no alibi," said Phoebe carefully. "But let's say we believe him. Let's rule him out. What were the rest of us doing at eight o'clock?"

And as everyone started talking at once about the dinner party, about Amanda's phone call and Jerry's non-appearance, she remembered that bitter, spiteful exchange between Diane and Stella. Who could forget it? So maybe that was it, Phoebe realized. Maybe no one was supposed to forget where Diane and Stella were at eight o'clock – nor that they were bitter enemies.

"Stella," she said suddenly. "I don't think we're getting anywhere after all. Why don't we cheer up Constable Plod out there? I think he'd enjoy seeing your act, don't you?"

Stella shrugged her agreement, and Phoebe slipped out of the room to tap the policeman on the arm. "Er, Constable – come into the living room, would you? Stella's agreed to do her brilliant ventriloquism act for you."

Intrigued, the policeman took his seat next to Michael, and watched intently as Stella went through her paces with Arnold. Eventually she reached the dinner routine.

"Why are men always late for dinner?" Stella asked.

Arnold, prompted by the words, replied as usual. And that was when Phoebe knew, absolutely, that she was right.

"Stop the show," she said quietly. "You've done all you need to do. Constable Watts – you're looking not at one murderer but at two. And possibly, technically, three. Because although Jerry did die at eight o'clock, just as we thought he did, his killers weren't anywhere near him at the time. It was murder by remote control."

She looked first at Diane, who was maintaining a magnificent composure, and then at Stella, hunched once again over her computer. "Those are your murderers," she announced. There was silence. Dead silence.

"You had us all fooled, didn't you?" Phoebe went on. "Doing your big enemies act, when all the time you were conspiring together. You killed out of love, didn't you? Love of Robert made you overcome your hatred for each other. Because you needed each other for the almost perfect crime."

The silence hung in the air now like poison gas. Then a loud, witch-like cackle of laughter sliced into the quiet of the room. It was Diane. "Well, he deserved what he got, after all he'd done to Robert," she said, in a strange, crazed voice. "Besides, if he wasn't so damn vain we could never have pulled it off. You're right, Phoebe. Last night we arranged that I would come to his room this afternoon. It was easy. He'd never got over being chucked by me so it suited him to think I regretted it. When I got there, I looked deep into his gorgeous eyes..."

"And hypnotized him," Phoebe suggested quietly.

Diane laughed harshly. "Well, at least he went happy," she agreed. "Sucker!"

"Presumably you had your white make-up on by then," added Phoebe. "Which got smeared over his shirt. Was that when you tied him up?"

Diane nodded, giggling disturbingly. "Oh, yes – who else but a magician could manage knots like that. But I didn't kill him, you know. I just tied him up and put the tape round his neck. Oh, and then put the other end round the tape recorder spool like Stelly Welly showed me."

"Of course, you didn't want him dead, did you? Not yet. That had to happen when we were all sure of where you were. You and Stella."

"It was my best ventriloquist act ever," said a strange, tiny voice. Stella, still staring at Arnold, seemed to be addressing him. "If I could activate a dummy to respond to certain words, I was sure I could do exactly the same with a computerized hi-fi like Jerry's. That equipment was wasted on him. It made me so angry to think of him going over and over his stupid third-rate tapes when he'd messed everything up for Robert..."

"I knew that answer-machine held the biggest clue," said Phoebe. "Late for dinner."

A strange, unhuman voice responded at once: "Because they have to show a woman where she stands."

It was Arnold, lying on the arm of Stella's chair. Arnold, the dummy.

"You see, he's programmed to those words," Phoebe said. "You simply fixed the tape recorder with a microchip which would respond in the same way. No wonder Diane laughed when Amanda used those words. She saved you a job, didn't she, girls?"

It was Amanda's turn to look horrified. "You mean – it was me who set off the tape recorder? When I rang Jerry?"

Diane cackled again gleefully. "Right first time. We were just going to make the call ourselves. But we were quite happy to have another accomplice."

"Such a coincidence," chimed in Stella. "The words started the tape recorder but there was no tape on the left spool. It was round Jerry's neck instead. So the right spool just whizzed round faster and faster and faster, pulling on poor little Jerry's neck until he died."

"So I killed him," said Amanda flatly. Then she fainted dead away.

Then everything happened at once. The Constable arrested Stella and Diane and led them away after summoning his chief. Robert, looking sickened, insisted on going with them while Phoebe helped Amanda to bed.

It was nearly dawn when Phoebe and Michael were alone again, side by side on the settee. She was almost trembling with exhaustion and shock, yet she was elated, too.

"I thought you were wonderful before all this, Phoebe," murmured Michael. "Now I know you're mega wonderful. I want you to be my girlfriend properly and efficiently. On one condition."

Phoebe looked at him quizzically. "You mean, no more murders?"

"Oh, no, I can take all that," Michael answered seriously. "I just want you to keep out of my kitchen. Your salad is terrible. And please – no more shrimps in the Malibu!"

Laughing helplessly, they fell into each other's arms and kissed – a long, passionate kiss that seemed to put a seal on the horrors of the night, and welcomed in the new day.

STILL LIFE

"It's just like one of those old fairground fun houses, isn't it? Notice it's curved? That's why locals call it the banana building."

Susan Stubbs' eyes sparkled. His mother had worn her wide-mouthed frog face ever since leaving the house that morning. The commentary wasn't that new of course, Jonathon had heard her talking about the place all year.

He shook his head, folded his arms, and stood in the road for a better view. He had to smile at her enthusiasm. It was a warm day, and a gentle London breeze carried the sound of children playing in the park nearby. He brushed his dark fringe back and viewed the place with a touch of suspicion.

"It looks deserted. I mean, the windows are filthy, cracked and ... well it's a bit of a dump, isn't it?"

"That's character, for heaven's sake – character, there's *real* people in there." For a moment she threatened to become serious, frighteningly earnest, then she almost danced back into his face. His mother made sweeping gestures with her hands, something which all artists seemed to do. Jonathon couldn't resist another grin. She stood quietly for a moment, appearing reflective as she tied her blonde hair into a bunch.

"It used to be a warehouse," she continued. "A Victorian warehouse, then a removals store or something. There's subsidence, that's why it leans forward, but until it falls down completely it's home to a community of forty artists – including me. There it is then, the Bretton Park Studios. I can feel the good vibrations just standing here."

His mother was happy, that was clear. But what mattered most was that no longer would she have to spend the winters sat at the bottom of the garden, shivering in a badly modified shed.

Across the road a community centre had just opened its doors, she had spoken of it in the car. Well supported by locals, the two-storey building had been converted from a former police station. There was the Brazilian café at the rear. Suddenly, a car pulled up opposite.

An attractive young girl with long, dark hair waved at them as she got out of the passenger side, then she said something to the driver and skipped across the road.

"Hi," said the girl. "Today's the day, eh?"

"Yes," Susan beamed. "This is my son, Jonathon."

The girl smiled and held out her hand. For a moment she hesitated – Jonathon thought she was staring at him.

"Hello, I'm Astrud. Come and visit us, my father and uncle run the café there. I know your mother's dying to move in to the studios. I'd better go, but call in, make it soon." She tripped back across the street.

"She's nice," said Jonathon.

A cloud of dust billowed into the street, as a pair of glass doors opened at the side of the studios building. This was followed by a vigorously pushed broom. An ashen-faced figure, gaunt with long, silver hair looked round one of the doors, checked that no pedestrians were passing, and then continued to sweep.

Jonathon's mother pointed at the gathering dust cloud. "Down there, look, where that man's just stepped out. That's the gallery."

She drummed her fingers on the roof of their old Volvo. Humming quietly, she locked the driver's door, and skipped round to the rear. The hatchback door yawned open, creaking like a seaman's chest as slivers of flaky rust fell from one of the hinges.

"My studio's on the ground floor, so we won't have to climb stairs. There's three floors, steep stairs, all at an angle. Just as well – my kiln weighs a ton and a half, it's coming next week."

Jonathon shook his head. She hadn't appeared this happy since Dad had finally run off with one of his students. In the back of the Volvo were a number of buckets, mops, with other cleaning essentials in boxes. He began to move a box. A pair of wraparound sunglasses poked out from behind a bundle of dusters.

"What on earth are these?" he asked. "You'll look like a biker."

She sniffed and pushed them further into the dusters. Something glinted beside them, catching the light for a moment.

"What's that? Is that a lampshade in there?"

"Just junk, you know me," she laughed.

The silver-haired man stopped sweeping and looked in their direction. He leaned his broom against the wall and ambled down towards them.

"I think that's Gerry. I've only met him a couple of times. He was on the interview panel. He makes masks and props for films too, but he's also the part-time manager of the studios."

Gerry Finnegan nodded at her, and glanced briefly in Jonathon's direction. He wore a faded denim jacket from which extended spindly legs, in tight frayed black jeans. Knobbly knees peeked through holes. His huge Doc Marten boots completed the effect, making him appear a little like a character in a cartoon. He forced a smile and, after dusting his palms on his jacket, extended a hand in greeting. For a moment he seemed uncertain what to say.

"It's Susan, isn't it – the potter?" he enquired.

His mother seemed alarmed by the question. "Yes. Of course ... Susan Stubbs. Ceramicist, not just pots. Hello there. This is my son, Jonathon. We're dead keen. I thought I'd show him my new work place, and he's handy with a hammer and nail so I thought we might drop some things off. We're coming to the show this evening, of course."

Gerry smiled, but Jonathon noticed that it was without much enthusiasm, his thoughts seemed elsewhere. He coughed nervously and gestured towards a paint-blistered side door to their left.

"You can go in this way, I think it will be easier for you, unloading and so on."

"Thank you," said Susan.

He smiled again, but the edges of his mouth turned down soon afterward.

"Forgive me, I'm one foot on another planet just now, we've been landed with a major problem to do with our exhibition."

Suddenly, a shriek rang out from further down the road. The twin doors of the gallery swung wide and a plump woman with a shock of frizzy hair whirled out on to the pavement like a loose Catherine wheel. She held a sheet of yellow paper in one of her hands, which she waved furiously in the air.

"Gerry! Gerry! Have you seen this? Have you?"

Gerry Finnegan groaned and put his face into his hands, slowly he moved his head from side to side and allowed one eye to peep through his fingers.

"That's Daphne, she's been away for the past few

weeks. She got back this morning. I guess she's just seen the letter. God help us all, she'll freak."

His shoulders dropped.

"Gerry!" called the woman again. "Have you seen this damn letter, it was in my pigeon-hole!"

Within seconds the woman was upon them. Her hair seemed to crackle and twist with electricity, her face a red-veined balloon, containing orbs for eyes, wild and huge.

"Susan Stubbs, ceramicist," volunteered Susan, extending her hand. Jonathon felt that this was an unwise move – whoever she was, this woman was in no mood for polite introductions. His mother's hand froze in mid-air. The wild woman stared at her for a second and then turned on Gerry.

"I know, I know, Daphne," sighed Gerry. "Of course I've read the letter, it was me that had to put those letters into our pigeon-holes, wasn't it?"

The woman appeared to consider this for a moment. Then she stared at the sheet of paper once again and with a semi-animal noise tore it into two. She held the pieces in front of her for a second, and allowed the halves to flutter down between them.

"Can't we stop this, call the Arts Board – make a complaint?"

She dissolved into a stammer of expletives, turned on her heels and disappeared back down the street and into the gallery. From somewhere above came the creak of an opening window. A man's moon face peered down, spectacles perched on the end of his nose.

Gerry looked up and made a huge gesture of hopelessness with his hands. "Hi, Norman. Daphne's just got back – she hadn't heard about Georgina Swayles."

"Georgina? The woman's not fit to pass judgement on

a half-cocked pavement sketch, let alone a mixed media show!"

Gerry made a helpless gesture again.

The moon-faced man grunted. Fixing a wooden stick beneath the sill of the window, he disappeared inside.

"Excuse me," said Gerry, "I've got to sort out this exhibition. Welcome to Bretton Park Studios. I'll unlock the side door for you. Do call down later, I'll be in the gallery with the others."

"I'd love to help," said Jonathon.

Gerry nodded and hurried back to the gallery.

Jonathon picked up the two halves of paper and held them together. He quickly read the contents, and after a moment looked up.

"This is a letter from the local Arts Board." He perused the letter again. "It says here that due to illness Dame Elizabeth Forsythe is unable to judge the West London Galleries Open competition, and a Ms Georgina Swayles, former art critic of *The Manhattan Times* is to take her place. Swayles?"

He thought for a moment.

"I've a feeling I know the name..."

Then Jonathon noticed. His mother had gone silent. The wide-mouthed grin was still frozen on her face, but she had a far-away look in her eyes which Jonathon was not used to. Something was troubling her.

"Mum, what is it, do you know this woman, this Georgina Swayles?"

She said nothing, not at first. The warm breeze of the morning unexpectedly died, and despite the sun, she shivered. The good feeling seemed to have left her.

She coughed and looked around, feeling embarrassed, then snapped back with a smile.

"No, I don't believe so."

* * *

"So, you're here to help your mother?" asked Astrud. She brought him another coffee but this time she sat down.

"Yeah – I'm hoping to go to art college, I suppose it's in the blood; my dad teaches painting at a college – he doesn't live with us. My mum makes pots. I've just finished my exams so I'm killing time – looking round for a summer job."

"It's a good place over there," she said. "Most of the artists are very friendly, they eat in here and I help out. It is, what do you call it, a real 'artists collective'. They stick together, make things happen together. At the moment they are upset about this competition and this critic."

"Georgina Swayles?" Jonathon said.

"Yes, they talk quietly in here, I think she has done bad things in the past. I have seen your mother before. She's a potter, yes?"

"Yes," he said, "she's wanted a studio at Bretton Park for a while."

"The artists, they have worked hard to make the place what it is. Your mama was lucky to get an interview so quick. Sometimes people wait for a long time, a very long time. The committee is strict. Her work must be good to get in so soon, that is unusual."

Suddenly a cry of "Two teas" rang out from behind the counter.

"I must go," she said. "I have to serve, but come over later. Maybe we can have another coffee, but together?"

Jonathon grinned. He felt his face reddening, so with a gulp of half of the mug he nodded in her direction and left.

The gallery was a hive of activity. All around him groups of scruffily dressed figures were positioning plinths, arranging platforms, hanging canvases and generally rushing around.

Some of the exhibits appeared very strange to him. There were papier mâché sculptures which looked like cyberspacemen. Some of the canvases had been daubed with thick layers of paint, and objects had been attached to them. Jonathon had inspected one earlier and was convinced that they were parts from a car engine. On one wall were a series of photographs of people in cardboard boxes, their faces painted silver and gold.

A short woman, with paint-spattered jeans, asked him to hand her a claw hammer. She stepped back to view the painting again.

"Thanks," she said. "You're Susan's son, aren't you? Hang on. Just got to fix this nail. Oh, by the way, your mum's had to go off to get some stuff for us, said not to worry and she'll see you later."

A nearby voice chipped in.

"Jan, if you've finished with that so-helpful young man, he can come here and help me." A dark-haired, middle-aged woman with glasses and huge earrings, waved at him with plump leathery fingers. "Here my love, help me place this bronze on its plinth, it's heavy."

The woman was Mediterranean in appearance, and strong-faced. Jonathon thought she might be Greek. She introduced herself as Nikki. A space had been cleared near the entrance for her to unpack her exhibit, a pine-coloured crate which sat on a porter's trolley. She had already removed the lid, and was now busy pulling out tufts of grey-flecked straw, like stuffing from a sofa.

At the rear of the gallery an archway opened out into another room, and through that a further space could be glimpsed. A tall white-haired man, wearing a business suit, was setting up a camera on a wall bracket.

"What's going on in there?" he asked.

"That's Grant Scott," said Nikki. "Looks like a banker, but he's a brilliant installation and video artist."

"Installation?" said Jonathon.

"It's hard to explain, an installation is a statement and sometimes it can be very powerful. It can be controversial too. It's when a room is filled with objects that are all part of the artist's statement – they are his or her work. A room full of tyres, or painted mattresses, for example. Grant does incredible things with video screens and cameras. His computer videos visitors to the exhibition and then reworks their images into something else. He's reckoned to be another Andy Warhol."

"This is a neat gallery," said Jonathon, as he offered to ease one of the sides off Nikki's crate.

"Yes," said Nikki, "it is. Very neat."

Grant Scott had now appeared at the archway. He called across the gallery to Gerry Finnegan.

"Gerry, telephone upstairs, you just won't believe whose secretary wants to speak to you! Want to guess? Ms Georgina Swayles!"

Gerry Finnegan's face turned to thunder.

"Poor guy," said Jan.

"This Swayles person, she sounds quite a woman. What's she like?"

"Oh, a real poser, a pretentious cow," said Jan.

"Swayles?" smirked Nikki. "A walking fashion disaster, she used to wear all that junk jewellery. Remember those silly rings, huge things on every one of her fingers, all cut glass – looked as though she had chandeliers for knuckles. They must have really hurt her fingers, but it was her kind of trade mark, wasn't it?"

"She had matching earrings too," said Jan. "Hideous things. And red lipstick like a clown. Pah!"

They all laughed, but Nikki's expression had slowly become hard-edged. She was deep in thought.

"She's a bad memory," said Nikki, then added, "You see, my good friend Jonathon, she doesn't like us."

About them the exhibition had been making progress. Paintings hung beneath focused pools of light; ceramics had been placed on plinths and fabrics hung like exotic tapestries against the bone white walls.

A long and heavy oval-shaped trough was being placed beside a bronze. Jonathon thought it looked like a flower bed. Dozens of flowers in the shape of hands "sprouted" from the ceramic earth. Beautiful wine-coloured petals of glass opened to reveal outstretched fingers. Other hands were made of brass, some ceramic, and a few were carved from wood. It was stunningly beautiful.

"Do you like it?" asked Jan.

"It's ... well, it's stunning."

She nodded quietly.

Grant joined them, he looked stone-faced.

"Gerry's beside himself," he said. "He's had a call from Swayles' secretary. She wants to stop by, unofficially, before we open. My guess is that she wants to sniff out who will be exhibiting, so that she can prepare some nasty vitriolic speech. That or some other reason. She's insisted that the place is cleared and she is allowed to look around on her own."

"Can she request that?" asked Jan.

"Yep. The Arts Board says that as she's flown in at short notice, we should accommodate her. They say it's only fair. Of course, they probably don't realize what we have to deal with here. Gerry's furious."

Jonathon tucked the back of his shirt into his trousers and looked at his watch. His mother had not returned.

Jan caught his look of concern.

"You're wondering about your mum?"

"Yeah," he said. "Surely she should be back by now."

"That's OK," Nikki interrupted. "She said she'd see you tonight."

Jonathon frowned. *Typical*, he thought.

Then he reconsidered, no, that wasn't typical at all.

Gerry appeared through the arch and raised his arms for attention.

"Folks! Quiet please! I've an announcement concerning Georgina Swayles!"

A huge groan filled the room.

Jonathon offered to help out further, but Gerry Finnegan was adamant. There should be as few people around as possible when Georgina Swayles was to arrive.

Jonathon felt at a loss, almost abandoned. He put his head round the door of the café, but decided he could not face another coffee. Astrud dumped her cups and saucers on the counter.

"Hi there. Nothing to do?" she asked.

"Just some time to kill."

"I've got to finish up here. But why not take a look round the neighbourhood? The park's good, at the back of the studios. Go take a walk, but call in later, yes? I want to come to the show. You can be my escort, OK?"

This time he did not feel so embarrassed. Instead, he left, stepping on air. She walked with him out into the street and watched as he made his way towards the park. Just as he turned the corner he looked back. A woman in a red dress, wearing a black head scarf had stopped beside the gallery. Astrud remained outside the community centre and gave him a wave. He looked back at the gallery entrance. The woman said something to

Astrud and then stepped inside the gallery.

"Georgina Swayles has arrived, I believe," said Jonathon quietly.

The park was friendly, and the whisper of the early summer breeze was like a hypnotic voice. He decided to put his feet up on a park bench which looked over the back of the studios. He felt strangely tired although the coffee should have kept him awake. It was not long before he slipped into a late afternoon doze.

He awoke with a start, feeling uncomfortable rather than refreshed. Evening was drawing in. He glanced at his watch and could not believe he had been asleep for so long. With a stretch of his arms he braced himself and trudged out of the park towards Bretton Park Road.

Outside of the park, something stopped him in his tracks. Tied to a lamppost was a makeshift poster backed by hardboard, held with string. It advertised the show, but across the copy in black felt-tip pen was written CANCELLED.

"*What's happened to Georgina then?*" he whispered to himself. Just as he passed the late night stores, one of the artists from the studios stepped out of the shop – Norman, a Canadian weaver. Jonathon glanced across the street. The gallery doors were open and a small group of artists were putting up strips of banner announcing "Cancelled" on the walls of the building. Nikki and Astrud stood in the entrance.

"What's going on?"

"Oh, hello," said Norman. "Gerry and his gang must have got round real fast, they're putting up cancellation notices everywhere. You haven't heard? Georgina Swayles pulled out." Norman grinned mischievously. "I've heard she was her usual awful self about everything. She was in there for ten minutes, then said that the exhibits were as crass as she remembered and what was the point. Poor Gerry had to hear all of this stuff from her – then she declared she had better things to do, produced a mobile phone and announced she had changed her mind about being a judge and would be returning to the States forthwith!"

"It's true," said Astrud. "There was a row. It even spilled out on to the street. I came out, she was yelling at him – just over there in front of passers-by. Then she marched off."

Jonathon began to laugh. He wasn't sure why.

Nikki joined them.

"We're popping up the road for a quick celebratory drink, join us if you'd like," she said. "Jonathon, would you mind just hanging on in the gallery for fifteen minutes or so? Gerry or Grant will be down to lock up."

Jonathon nodded. "It'll give me a chance to take an undisturbed look at everything."

"See you," said Nikki.

Other artists poured out of the gallery and disappeared up the road.

Astrud shrugged her shoulders.

"Meet up later?"

"Sure," he said.

"You go and do your duty in the gallery. Call over after."

She returned to the café.

Jonathon was on his own. Evening shadows were starting to fall across the pavements. He crossed the road and stepped inside the gallery, pulling the doors shut behind him.

The place was oddly silent. Only the start-up hum of an extractor fan sounded somewhere in the building. He was startled to hear a voice. It came from the adjoining room. Within, a flurry of colour was suddenly cast on to the walls.

"Is that you Gerry? Grant?" he cried.

He heard only an electronic drone in return.

Jonathon stepped through the arch. It was Grant's installation. He had fixed it to operate periodically. Jonathon watched his own image flash on to a TV monitor as he entered the space. Then, seconds later it vanished and reappeared on a huge bank of computer screens. An electronic voice warbled, "Welcome. We can reshape your spirit. We can redesign you. Look at the computer monitor and choose your option now."

Jonathon looked closer at one of the computer screens. A menu displayed a list of options: *Re-Morph*, *Review*, *Outline*, *Previous Images* and *Quit*. The voice filled the room again, "Select your option now, use the mouse or keyboard."

He looked about for the computer mouse, which sat beside the monitor. At first he felt uncertain what to pick, wondering what they meant, then he laughed to himself and decided to select *"Outline"*. He moved the mouse forward, but his fingers were not used to the device and suddenly it slipped from his control. *"Previous Images"* was selected instead.

"Drat," he mumbled. "What does that do?"

A message flashed up on the screen:

"All previous files have been deleted. A Backup copy of the last file is still available, do you wish to view this?"

Jonathon frowned. Someone had tried to wipe the disk. His natural curiosity burned through.

He typed Y for Yes.

For a moment a series of file names flashed across the screen. Then without warning, a woman's face appeared.

It wasn't anybody he recognized, but the expression was unsmiling. A crackle filled the air and the huge monitor bank came to life. Jonathon stared, and stepped back. The woman's image became large and threatening. She was standing in the gallery, looking up at the camera. Jonathon watched hard. He was unsure what happened next, but something like a scarf or a rope dropped across her face and fell around her neck. Shadows moved behind her.

The computer voice rang out again.

"Close up in progress, prior to Morph."

He wasn't sure what to think, was this part of the show? Then his hand reached out as though to steady himself against an invisible wall.

The woman's face filled the screen bank. It had become a frozen cry. Her mouth was wide, and deep red lips filled the lower half of the monitors. Then he noticed something which threw him completely. She was wearing distinctly large glass or gemstone earrings. Her hands reached up to her throat in a desperate attempt to pull the scarf, or whatever had noosed her, away.

He saw her hands.

He saw her hands and he remembered.

"She used to wear those silly rings, huge things on every one of her fingers, all cut glass – looked as though she had chandeliers for knuckles. Matching earrings."

"Oh, my God!" he whispered. "It's that woman."

Her eyes bulged and closed, and then the head and shoulders shook in a terrible spasm.

The computer screen changed colour for a few seconds and then ran the sequence again. This time the red lips filled the screen and mouthed like a drowning fish. Computer-generated graphics dropped into the picture and it fragmented into a bizarre jigsaw of shapes.

Jonathon cried out. Staggering to the side, he accidentally twirled into the electric cable and pulled it from the wall. There was an instant flurry of activity somewhere inside the computer, then it shut down. A darkening echo filled the silence.

Jonathon froze, uncertain what to do next. A single idea occupied his thoughts. Was this a recording of something that had happened here, or had Grant created it? He glanced back at the mouse again and moved nearer; something made him examine it closer. There was a mark, a stain on the switch. Trying desperately to find a reason, his first thought was that it was his own blood and that he had cut himself. He examined his fingers, but there was nothing. There was a mark on the mouse mat too – three wiped red streaks.

Red wine? he wondered. Artists did like a drink. Then moving back he began to look about him, and squinted at the table leg. He hadn't noticed it before, but why should he? There was something there. Jonathon crossed the room to the light switches and turned the dimmer switch to full. The floor and walls of the gallery became brighter. There was a definite sequence of dark spots which led to a door at the back. He knelt and looked closer, a patch appeared to have been newly washed over.

"My imagination's running overtime," he said.

"Lost something?"

He almost stumbled backwards, and looked back over his shoulder. Grant Scott stood near the front doors. The lights from the main gallery spot picked him out like a character, centre stage. Jonathon swallowed air.

"Er, marks."

"You've lost what? What marks, where?"

"Marks, I've just found some – oh, it's nothing."

Grant marched across the floor and entered the gallery. He seemed anxious, and his brow had furrowed into a look of deep concern. He searched the floor around Jonathon.

"No really, it's nothing."

Grant ignored him and continued to search. He stopped at the table and picked up the mouse. Removing a handkerchief from his breast pocket he spat on the mouse and wiped the stain clear.

"Blood," he announced casually.

Jonathon hauled himself up.

Without comment Grant reached out and showed him the back of his hand. There was a red weal like a scratch or graze.

"I had an accident recently, a week or so ago. Nothing dramatic, Jonathon, I'm afraid the blood's mine."

Gerry's voice came from somewhere at the rear. The back door opened. He stood there with Susan Stubbs.

"Mum!" said Jonathon. "Where have you been?"

His mother said nothing; she looked uncomfortable for some reason. After a second she entered the gallery and glanced at the computer.

"Have you had this on?" she asked.

"I tripped over the lead," he said.

Grant coughed. "There'd be nothing to see anyway. I accidentally wiped the thing."

Jonathon looked down at the floor.

"Is there anything wrong?" Gerry asked. He didn't even look at Jonathon.

"Bloodstains," Jonathon said.

His mother looked pale; Gerry stood motionless.

Grant laughed and held out his hand again.

"Mine – remember I had that scrape helping Nikki with her damn crate!"

"Me too," said Gerry. He reached out and showed a similar wound on the back of his own hand. "Easily done when shifting plinths."

Astrud stood quietly in the doorway. "Jonathon – I've been waiting for you. I thought we were going to do something? Hi, Grant," she said, noticing him behind Jonathon. "How is your computer video installation – have you fixed your downloading bug?"

Grant smiled and replaced his handkerchief in his top pocket.

Jonathon's jaw began to lower. Grant Scott was loosening up, becoming friendlier.

"Yeah. Thanks Astrud, your suggestion worked. Some good programming."

"I thought it might be a problem with the TIFF resolution. It's a common scan refresh problem." Astrud's eyes sparkled as she turned to Jonathon. "I don't work in the café all the time, you know."

Astrud had sat him down in a corner of the pavement bar. There were a couple of artists from the studios inside, but it was still a warm evening, and comfortable enough for them to remain outside, where it was quieter.

Jonathon was trying to concentrate, his mind was racing, trying to reconcile what he knew with what he thought he saw. That *had* been Georgina Swayles on the computer monitor. There *was* blood in the studio, but she had been seen arriving at the studios earlier, and more significantly, leaving. Why were they acting so strangely?

The sound of clinking ice snapped him back. Astrud placed two large fruit cocktails on the table and wiped a space in front of Jonathon.

"Hope you like it, George makes fruit juice taste

exceptionally good. Now. What's going on with you, you've been antsy ever since I called over? Perhaps you're always like this."

He leaned back with a sigh. Then he took a long cool drink, through the coloured plastic straw. His gaze held hers for a minute while he collected his thoughts.

"The woman who called at the gallery," he said. "You know, just after I went off? She had a red dress, black shawl and so on. You did see her leave, didn't you?"

"Yeah, she spoke to me, she asked if it was open or something. Why? What's wrong?"

"Was she Georgina Swayles?"

"So I believe. I mean I've never met her before, but I was told that was her."

"By?"

"By Gerry."

"Was she wearing any odd jewellery, earrings, for example?"

"Yes. She had a red dress, black shawl, as you mention it, these dreadful huge earrings and dark glasses. Anyhow, the pair of them tumbled out on to the pavement and had that terrible row in front of everyone."

"So it was definitely Georgina Swayles."

He thought for a moment.

"You told me she had done 'bad' things. I mean, do you know about her, all this fuss?"

"Some things. They talk to me, the artists."

"About what?" he asked.

Astrud looked about her, then leant back in her chair and signalled to somebody inside the bar.

"Listen," she said. "Listen to what the others have to say."

After a moment Nikki appeared. Her eyes were glassy and far-away.

"Tell Jonathon about Georgina Swayles," said Astrud. "He wants to know why there was all this fuss."

"Georgina Swayles?" Nikki replied. "You mean, slimy, waspish Swayles. What would you like to know? She was an art critic for a crappy but prestigious magazine, *Urban Focus*. She had a lot of contacts, a lot of influence. But she was nastier than a cockroach with a grudge. She dumped on Gerry Finnegan's career, one of many."

"How did she dump on his career?" Jonathon put down his drink.

"OK, let me explain. Gerry was – is – a great mask maker. I mean, seriously great. Some years back he was going to be given a huge contract for a Hollywood movie, it was some Mexican Inca thing, an adventure movie with a big budget. He was to make all the masks – other things too. Then, somebody put a spoke in the works, a hell of a spoke, some kind of vicious rumours about his reliability – about him having a drink problem, all bull. He lost the contract – it could really have turned things around for him."

"It was Georgina Swayles?"

"It most certainly was. We had a wonderful artist here once," Nikki continued. She sloped into one of the chairs and lowered her voice. Jonathon leant forward. "She was brilliant. Her name was Debbie – from the East End. She worked in textiles, only a year out of college. Her work was weaving for the angels, patterns for the gods. Her brother has her studio now."

"Why, what happened to her?" asked Jonathon.

Astrud and Nikki exchanged an uncomfortable moment.

"She was young, insecure. Swayles reviewed an Open

exhibition she was involved with, said that her work was worse than off-cuts from a Petticoat Lane sweatshop. I think those were her exact words. All senseless spite. Then Debbie couldn't take any more."

The breeze dropped, and somehow London seemed silent. The street lamp buzzed nearby and moths were flying into the amber glow.

"They pulled her out of the Thames," someone said.

Jonathon looked up – Jan had joined them.

"Swayles became scared after a while," said Jan, in a quieter voice. "Began to receive mysterious threats and suddenly she got offered this top-notch job in New York."

"Where she's been ever since," said Nikki. "Then a few weeks ago we hear that she's returning to the UK – and, surprise surprise, she's scheduled to judge the West London Open Show. OUR show. Unbelievable."

"And now she's walked out, eh?" said Astrud. "Probably couldn't face you all – celebrate, she's gone!"

Nikki's mouth slowly turned upwards into a huge crescent smile of satisfaction.

"Yes. She's gone."

Jonathon sipped at his drink. Astrud had begun to shift in her seat.

He put his drink down and glanced over at Nikki and Jan.

"Whose sister was she?"

Nikki blinked deeply.

"Pardon? Whose sister...?"

"The girl in the Thames," repeated Jonathon. "You said her brother had her studio now."

"Oh, didn't I say? Grant was her brother. They were very close."

* * *

It was late and Jonathon's head still jangled with uncertainty. He stood with Astrud on the corner, across from the studios. Others at the café-bar had noticed his shifting in his seat, his uncomfortable glances, and Astrud had suggested a walk.

"You really think there's something wrong, don't you?" she said softly.

"Yes," he replied spinning round. "I don't know. Damn it, I'm confused."

She took his hand.

"Where do you live, is it nearby, how do you get home from here?"

"Not far, only Cricklewood. I told my mother I'd make my own way back. Wouldn't mind a long walk, anyhow she's gone off celebrating with Gerry." He paused, his eyes looked down. "*With Gerry. Celebrating.* It doesn't add up."

He looked her full in the face.

"You said you'd seen my mother before?"

"Yes," said Astrud. "Lots of times, especially in the last few weeks. She calls by at the studios. What is it with all these questions?"

Jonathon's head thudded. She'd spoken of the place over the year, but she had never mentioned making so many visits there. Her interview had only been a week or so ago – or so she had said. He thought back to the morning. What was it she had said to him when he first saw Gerry? *"I think that's Gerry."* Surely she'd know his name – and hadn't he behaved as if they had only recently met?

"This is crazy!" he said. "It doesn't make sense."

"Look, can I help?"

"Is there a way in to the gallery? I need to show you something, I want to get into Grant's computer program. Do you know a way in? Look – please trust me, this is important."

Astrud sighed and reached into her bag, she pulled out a bunch of keys.

"I'm a computer programmer at College, I help in my father's café and … guess what?" She jangled the bunch. "Dah dah! I clean Bretton Park Studios in the wee small hours."

He gasped.

"I'm wonderful. BUT…" She squeezed his hand. "Hear me. Nothing illegal, OK – just a look around, but I don't know what we're looking for."

"It might be nothing," he said. But deep inside, a notion which wouldn't go away was beginning to gnaw at him.

A few photographers were working late on the top floor, but otherwise the rest of the building was silent.

"I'm usually an early morning cleaner, not a night owl," whispered Astrud. "But they all know me and so we shouldn't look too suspicious."

They closed the door behind them and Astrud put on the lights.

"Hey," he said.

"Act normal," she hissed. "Just like we're merrily cleaning up, OK?"

They crossed to the computer.

"You really helped Grant program some of this?"

"Just a touch. But I can switch it on, get into the program. Go and pull down the blinds on the front doors whilst I boot it up."

She was incredibly dextrous. Fingers flew across the keyboard and within minutes the monitors were shining with images of the gallery.

"I selected *Previous Images* before. We need to do that again," he said. "What does that mean exactly?"

"That repeats the last collection of pictures the cameras captured over a few sessions. It gets written over eventually. You see the thing plays with the pictures, cut and pastes images – jumbles them up into art!"

"It told me all files had been deleted, then asked me if I wanted to see the Backup file."

"Then somebody's attempts to wipe everything were only partially successful. Let's take a look."

Within moments the same set of scenes he had watched earlier flashed across the screen. Astrud went quiet, Jonathon watched as she observed with wide-eyed innocence.

"That is the woman you saw?" he asked.

"Yes," she said. "Yes, I think so, the earrings, lipstick and – well sort of."

"What do you mean?"

"I'm not sure, perhaps it is. This is horrible – is it from a film?"

"I don't think so," he said. "I think it's a recording of something that happened here."

"Let's take a closer look," she sniffed.

She leant forward and selected zoom with the mouse. Then she panned down to the hands on the screen. The back of the attacker's hand was clearly visible. She pressed a key on the keyboard. In dreadful slow motion the woman's fingers clawed into the back of her attacker's hand. A red weal opened up, which disappeared beneath a wash colour which crept down from the corner of the screen.

A single thought raced through Jonathon's head.

She's scratched him. But is it a him? Grant had a scratched hand. But ... his was an OLD wound – not today's. And what about Gerry's...

Jonathon took a deep breath.

"Look!" Astrud cried.

They watched as another hand came into the screen from the left. Then another seemed to creep upwards from below, plump feminine fingers, then another – a hand in a denim sleeve appeared to tighten the scarf.

"Just how many hands has this person's attacker?" Jonathon hissed.

"It may be just one," said Astrud. "The program copies and pastes images – reworks them. It's impossible to tell. The computer may be making all this. Look, now!"

There were hands and arms thrashing everywhere. The computer graphics had taken over and was making the entire scene a kaleidoscope of colour.

Jonathon sighed, his evidence was being manipulated by Grant's program, the pictures gelled into a galaxy of strange images.

Suddenly, he had an idea. "Is there any way by which we can get a date on when this was recorded?" he asked.

"Possibly. If the computer's clock is running correctly."

She moved the mouse and selected "INFO". A dialogue box dropped down from the menu.

They stared at one another.

"Two weeks ago," she said.

"Two week ago," he repeated.

"Do you want to look in the office upstairs?"

Jonathon scanned the office, nerves razor-edged. The place was surprisingly tidy; he was expecting something dishevelled. Several files had been pulled and lay at the corner of Gerry's desk. One particularly fat file had strips of paper amongst the leaves marking spots.

"Go on," Astrud said. "Take a look at it."

The file opened at a date some ten years ago. He flipped the front over. A grubby label read: *Studio Applications.* Turning back to the earlier place, he quickly read the notes on the sheet of note paper, then turned the page. It was a plainly-typed application form for studio space. The form was headed with the name *Georgina Swayles,* and beneath this was written *Artist – water colours and oils.* At the bottom, in a square stamped "For Official Use" was a tick beside the word "REJECTED".

"Ah," said Jonathon. "Things fall into place. Our Georgina Swayles was once interviewed for a studio space – didn't get it."

"Let me see." Astrud pulled the file towards her. She flicked through the pages. "There's letters here, notes of phone calls. She tried bribery, everything by the look of it. She's described as an appalling artist." Astrud looked up. "I suppose she just wanted to 'have a studio, dahhling' – something to put on her letterhead."

But Jonathon had found something else. He nervously fixed his hair behind his ears, whilst fingering a large file, which looked ancient, dusty and spotted with coffee-cup rings.

"These are notes on Nikki," he mumbled. "There's a record of a complaint to the International Critics Forum. There's more – cuttings and letters. It seems that Nikki had a major exhibition five years ago, *Vogue* magazine did a piece on her, something about Sir Ernest Van Peeble planning to do the feature, but Van Peeble mysteriously pulls out and – yeah, Georgina Swayles got to do the article instead. Gossip columns linked the pair for a while afterwards."

"Don't tell me," said Astrud. "She trashed Nikki's show?"

"Worse than that, she trashed it and emptied it into the river by all accounts. Nikki hasn't exhibited since, it says here. I think they were considering making an official complaint about Georgina being the judge this year."

He looked up. "I think someone decided on another solution."

He gave a snort and replaced the file.

Suddenly, he slapped his hand on to the table.

"I've had a terrible thought. I *have* heard Georgina's name before."

Within minutes he had picked up the phone and heard his father's voice.

"Dad, look I can't explain, I know it's late. I'm sorry. Yes, I'm fine. Look. Does mother know a Georgina Swayles?"

He waited silently. "No. No look. No, I'm not wanting to…"

He listened to his father for several minutes. Astrud watched as he slowly turned white and his eyes grew wide. Finally, he replaced the phone.

"What, what is it?" Astrud lifted her hands to her face.

"Astrud. Try and remember carefully. The sunglasses Georgina Swayles was wearing, what did they look like. Exactly."

"They were just sunglasses. I don't know. Those big ones, you know what are they called – goggles style, like a motorcyclist's."

"Wraparound."

His mouth dried, he remembered the pair he had seen in his mother's box. Then he remembered the lampshade too. He thought it had been a tacky chandelier, but it wasn't. He had glimpsed a large cut glass earring.

"That was my father. He had an affair with a woman named Margaret James many years ago. My parents' marriage was rocky. She was an artist. It was brief, but he claims my mother never forgave them and that was the start of the break up of their marriage. I remember an argument. My God, he even asked how my mother was."

"Who was Margaret James?"

"Someone we're beginning to know. She thought that the name Margaret James was too plain, wanted something that sounded flashy. Thinking it would help her career she became Georgina Swayles." He sighed. "Then she became an art critic."

The office door burst open. Out on the landing stood Gerry, Nikki, Jan and Grant.

"Working late, Astrud?" Grant asked.

Jonathon gritted his teeth and held Astrud's arm.

"I have something to say."

"Sure. You know," said Astrud, kissing Jonathon gently on the lips. "Come on, you guys. Use some common sense. We thought we'd have some privacy. We've just met, we like each other. OK, you've caught us."

The four artists exchanged looks. There was an iron silence.

"Come on," said Astrud, turning to Jonathon. "We'll go elsewhere."

They watched the couple slowly descend the stairs. When they reached the bottom, Grant called after them.

"Jonathon."

They looked back.

"Jonathon, Bretton Park Studios is a community. We work together, we create together, we make decisions together. She would have made our lives misery. She was going to take on a major job as a critic for a national paper. It's good that Georgina Swayles has gone back to the States."

"And of course there's people who saw her go, aren't there?" said Jonathon, more sharply than he intended. Astrud gripped his arm tighter and pulled him towards the door.

"By the way, Jonathon, it's good to have your mother on board," said Gerry.

"And yourself," added Grant Scott. "It's good to have you too. Welcome."

For a moment Jonathon stared at Astrud. He was no longer certain who he could trust.

Georgina Swayles was reported as having returned to New York, but then vanished. She never took up her London job, and was never seen again.

It was not until a year later that she reappeared.

Jonathon had received a sudden call from Astrud whom he had not seen for a long time. There was an exhibition at Studio 77 in Islington. An exhibit from the Bretton Park Studios had been singled out for a special award; she urged him to go and see it, it was fast becoming acclaimed as a masterpiece. She had said something else too:

"We *were* set up, you know. You were right. Remember you said your mother went off somewhere for a week afterwards? Could she just have put on some rings, jewellery and a few other things to have made a short trip back to the USA as Georgina Swayles? That would have perfected the alibi. Georgina didn't go anywhere, Jonathon, enjoy the exhibit." Then she had laughed. "Got to give it to them, it was *very* clever."

It was raining and Jonathon felt churned inside as he walked from the Angel tube station. The gallery was set in a side street, off Devonia Road. He pushed the door open and stepped inside. His shadow stretched along the polished wooden floor, meeting just short of where it stood.

His tongue felt huge and awkward.

Jonathon reached and touched one of the glass hands. It was so solid, clean and clear, somehow strangely comforting. He let his fingers travel across to the brass, and felt the coolness of the metal. Then there was the softness of the textile hand and the carved reassurance of the wooden arm. It was still beautiful, exactly as he remembered.

But now he saw with different eyes. He felt another hand, which somehow appeared supported, encased in some kind of resin. It felt strange, and he wondered what the material was – it reminded him of some kind of embalming resin he had seen used on Egyptian mummies in the Museum. He moved closer. For a second he thought it was a flaw in the craftsmanship, then a closer inspection revealed that it was design. There were indeed tight indents below the knuckles, *as if it had been a hand used to wearing rings.* Another hand with similar marks, protruded beside it.

The realization made him stumble. He fell back with a gasp. As he struggled to catch his breath he noticed that there was a title and an author to the piece. It gave him his answer, of course. He remembered what they had said: *"We work together, we create together, we make decisions together."* The brass plate confirmed this: *"Still Life." By the Artists of Bretton Park Studios.*

SPOILED

"Travellers, in Barker's field!"

"That's something new, old Barker must have died!"

"They probably didn't ask him."

Danny grunted in reply; they probably didn't, he thought. He was guiding his car carefully over the potholed track and couldn't turn his head to look where his sister, Samantha, was pointing. They were passing a field where a collection of battered vans, old lorries and shabby caravans were parked higgledy-piggledy on the sun-burnt grass.

The Mini was jammed to capacity and over with five teenagers plus all their gear and provisions for a fortnight.

Samantha, in the passenger seat next to her brother, had bags of groceries packed around her feet and on her lap. Jenny, their foster sister, sat behind with Tanya, Sam's closest friend. And there, too, with assorted bags rising around him, pinning him in place, was Mike. He was the skinniest of the five, squashed between the girls, squeezing his knees tight together and his elbows into his sides as he clasped his precious lap-top computer to his chest.

"Whew, it's hot!" Jenny spoke for everyone. "Turn it down, Dan."

The endless beat on the radio was getting to her, even though the windows of the little silver car were wide open. It made its painful way between tall Devonshire hedges fringed thickly with pink campion, Queen Anne's lace and meadowsweet.

At the rattle of a cattle grid the track opened out into a cobbled farmyard. Many of the cobbles were missing now and others were fighting a losing battle with dandelions and tough summer grass. Gratefully, the Mini came to a halt within the shadow of the farmhouse.

"Welcome to the Back of Beyond," said Danny, switching off the disco-beat in mid chord.

The car doors burst open.

"I thought it was called Mollers Farm." Tanya stretched herself and shook out her length of flaming red hair. She looked about for the name plate. There wasn't one.

"It is." Samantha was dragging the bags up to the front door. "Should be called Harris Farm for all the years we've been coming here."

"Lovely, lovely Mollers." Jenny spoke dreamily, wandering away and gazing through the surrounding trees to the sloping fields beyond. "Hello, there's a caravan in the field. Did anyone know it was going to be there?"

No one replied. The heavy front door was open and the bags were disappearing into the hallway beyond. Jenny joined them. Tanya was delighted to see the Harris' old holiday house at last. She exclaimed at the view through every window.

Danny hauled the larger bags up the narrow wooden stairs to the bedrooms. Mike followed.

"Where can this go?" he asked, hugging his lap-top to him.

Jenny looked after him doubtfully. It was her idea that Mike should come with them. He wasn't really a special friend, but his rather earnest personality struck her as being less shallow than some of the others in her class. He thought the world of her. Also, she was sorry for him. His mum and dad had split up, and this summer his home had been sold. Years ago Jenny had known what it was like to have her world collapse around her.

Danny and Samantha were easy-going people and had not minded when she asked him along. Besides they were used to Jenny befriending the needy. Between themselves they agreed that she just couldn't help it, it was one of the things she did. But that lap-top was another thing, he seemed obsessed with it. You never knew what people were really like until they stayed with you.

Jenny sighed and turned back to the kitchen where Samantha was pouring out warm lemonade into tall glasses.

They sat around the littered kitchen table sipping the lemonade and allowing the coolness of the stone around them to lift the mid afternoon heat from their bodies.

Danny, the eldest, waiting for his exam results, was feeling good. His tall, rather poetic good looks were all on his side and he knew it. The car was his eighteenth birthday present from his parents. He loved it. Without it they wouldn't be there now. He was going to travel the world in it. The Travellers in the field interested him. He would investigate them. It would be something different from the old routine which, frankly, could be boring.

Somewhere during the last year he had begun to forget the intense pleasure to be gained from long days climbing the high tors on the moor with his sisters, or wading up to his knees in fast-flowing Devon streams looking for crayfish.

He yawned loudly.

Samantha was sixteen and skinny and fair like her brother, but had not grown tall to match him. What she missed in height she made up for in energy. She was thinking what fun it was to be away from adult company at last. She would take Tanya for walks up through the woods and show her the best places to have picnics on the moor that she loved, now that Danny was so... Well, anyway, it was going to be great to have a companion of her own now that he had become ... so aloof.

Jenny put her elbows on the table and rested her chin on her hands. Masses of dark hair tumbled forward over her eyes. She loved it here. She loved every stone. This summer was going to be the best. A great feeling of warmth towards them all filled her. Her lot, her family, her Danny. He had always been her Danny. From the moment when she was nine and he was ten and Mr and Mrs Harris had plucked her out of the childrens' home and brought her to live with them she had loved him. Later, when they adopted her and she had a real family at last, she gave all the Harrises her pent-up love.

But the Moller Summers, as she thought of them, were always the high spot. Long bright days to hide with Danny in the waist-high bracken for Sam to find and chase them out, screaming with laughter. When they grew older they fished in the deep pools, watching water beetles and the lazy trout, never really bothered when they went home without a catch. Happy to read or lounge, listening to tapes, happy to be together.

This last year she had seen Danny blossom into young manhood. Her pride in him was immense. She blotted out from her mind any thought that he might be changing, growing away from them – from her. Here, with the magic of Mollers, everything would be absolutely perfect again. Nothing would ever change.

Later, she would wash the dust off his new car. She would make it gleam for him…

Tanya wasn't pretty. She had a turned-up nose, a wide mouth that overruled her little chin, and freckles. Only her flaming hair marked her out from the crowd. She and Samantha had been friends since they had entered the middle school at the same time. She was a merry girl, good for a laugh, and they made a formidable pair when they got going. Her parents had always insisted on taking her on holiday with them, but this year, she had finally persuaded them to let her go with the Harrises to Devon.

It was better than she had dreamed. The house was so romantic and old and Danny, quite beyond her reach at school, was going to be there every day. She thought his slightly arrogant air quite devastating. The next two weeks were going to be bliss.

Of them all, Mike's thoughts were the most sombre. Now that he was here, he felt unsure. A little spike of panic jabbed him in the chest. He didn't fit in, he knew it. It was wonderful of Jenny to ask him, and she was a wonderful girl, but that made it worse. She would find him out, know he was dull and boring, not a computer whizz or a hacker de luxe. He should have gone to the rented house with his mum. He knew he had let her down.

Samantha reached out and switched on the old radio cassette player. "Give us your Stone Roses tape, Jenny, while we clear a space. The butter's melting – you've got your elbow in it, Mike."

As Jenny rummaged in her holdall, the radio announcer's voice droned on. It was the six o'clock news.

"During an attempted mass breakout from Dartmoor prison…"

Danny laughed. "Our neighbours never give up..."

"Shush!" Sam's voice had enough urgency in it to make them all pause.

"...it was discovered that one prisoner was missing. He is John Cassidy, five feet ten, brown hair and moustache, and very dangerous. Members of the public are advised not to approach him, but inform the police at once if they see him.

"At the Summit Meeting in Moscow..."

The tape slammed into place and music took over.

"How far away is Dartmoor prison?" Tanya asked.

"Not that far as the crow flies, but one mile of moorland is about ten anywhere else." Danny meant to be reassuring.

"They'll have the helicopters out, anyway," said Sam.

Great, thought Mike. A dangerous con on the run. That's all I need.

"Listen!" Jenny held up her finger.

"Give over, Jen." Samantha was almost sharp. "No time for one of your mystic moments." Jenny had a leaning towards the mystical; her down-to-earth family didn't take it seriously.

The steady drone of an engine became audible to them all. Helicopters! They raced for the back door and gazed up into the clear sky. Two helicopters were doing a wide circle a little to the north where the sparse hills of moorland were etched black against the bright skyline.

"He won't get far, they're better than bloodhounds." Danny tugged Tanya's hair in a big brotherly way. "Stick around, Red, you're safe with us!"

Tanya smiled up at him.

"Well," he said, surveying the others, "I'm off out. See you later." He turned, getting his car keys out of his jeans.

"Now?" Samantha felt dismayed. "We haven't made any plans for tomorrow – or anything," she ended rather lamely.

She didn't want the group to split up so soon. She had pictured them all sitting round the table, eating their pizzas and making plans all together, the way they always did. The Danny of last year wouldn't spoil it like this.

"Can anybody come?" Tanya took a step forward.

"Feel free." Danny shrugged; he was not enthusiastic.

"Coming, Sam?" Samantha knew Tanya was urging her, wanting her to go too.

"Oh, OK, then, if you want, but we've only just arrived..."

She looked a little helplessly at Jenny.

That wasn't what Jenny had planned either. If Danny took the car away she couldn't wash it and surprise him. She looked over at him and he caught her eye and winked. She grinned at him – it was a shared moment. She relaxed, things were OK, nothing had changed, she could wash it later.

"You go," she said, "I'll do the chores here. We'll eat when you get back. Don't be too long." She looked at the two younger girls in a motherly way. She was only a year older than them, but fell easily into the role of surrogate parent.

Tanya scrambled in beside Danny. "Where to?" she asked.

Jenny and Mike stood at the door watching as the dust raised by the leaving car settled. Then Jenny walked round the house to the garden, leaving Mike to his own devices.

She had planted some hardy herbs last summer, rosemary, thyme and purple sage, and wanted to see if they had weathered the dry spell. They had and she began to gather some. Apart from being with Danny, being in a garden was the next best pleasure on the list.

"You want something? We're not a zoo, you know, we don't charge admission."

A woman, her hair in an untidy pile on her head, looked at the three teenagers leaning on the gate into the field. A hand-dyed T-shirt fell to her hips over a pair of very faded jeans. She was barefooted.

Samantha blushed to the roots of her hair and Tanya looked away in embarrassment.

But Danny, his hand on the piece of wire that held the gate shut, said "D'you mind if we come in?"

A child, only dressed in a pair of shorts, came to stand beside his mother.

"Feel free," the woman said, echoing Danny's words of a moment ago.

He pushed the gate open and walked through it with the suspicion of a swagger. After a moment of hesitation the girls followed.

Abruptly the woman turned on her heel; she and the little boy walked away towards a group of Travellers who stopped what they were doing to stare at the intruders – for that is what they were beginning to feel that they were.

Self-consciously, Danny strolled around the parked homesteads. Van windows were curtained and washing was hanging out. Cooking smells wafted over them and people stood, leaned, or sat around eating and talking. Several dogs of unknown breeds wandered about, and music filtered through the talk. Music made with instruments not usually found in an orchestra. Tanya liked it, it made her think of space and wind.

No one spoke to them and most of them stared.

Danny began to think they ought to leave. Their reception had not been quite what he had imagined. He had vaguely thought of offers of hospitality, or drinks, or conversation, something, not this veiled hostility. He turned back to the gate.

Someone detached himself from a small group and walked in their direction. He was chewing on a piece of toast as he called out, "Hey, it's Dan, isn't it?"

At the sound of his name, Danny paused. He looked at the approaching figure. He frowned, trying to place him.

"Peter?"

"Yeah, that's right, man. Pete, Pete Holloway, you remember. How're you doing?" He put his elbow on the gate and surveyed Danny as coolly as if they had just said goodbye last week. It had, in fact, been nearly two years since Pete had left school abruptly, before taking his GCSEs.

"What happened to you?" Danny asked, amazed to see him there. "We heard you were..."

"You don't want to believe all you hear, man," Pete said, with a grin. "My mind was getting sick with all that school stuff. I had to blow. It was them or me... That's my van." He waved a hand vaguely. "It's freedom, man, freedom..." He left the sentence hanging in the air.

"Ah," said Danny, he hoped wisely. Sam and Tanya looked at each other.

Jenny put a jar of leaves and seed pods on the kitchen table. The ancient beams of the kitchen ceiling were touched by the evening light. It played over the warm wood of the furniture and the cool grey of the flagstones. Mike was sitting on the window-seat trying to get enough of the waning light to read his computer magazine.

Suddenly, a loud knock on the kitchen door startled them both.

"I'll go." Mike got to his feet.

The stocky figure of a woman stood in the open doorway. Her hair, a very dark brown, was cut in a short manly bob. It was difficult to guess her age. She smiled at Mike and held out a jug.

"Can you spare a little milk?"

Jenny joined him at the door. This was very unexpected. No one ever called at Mollers, the farm-house was too remote.

The woman said amiably, "We forgot to buy more milk today, and the milkman don't deliver – we're the caravanners. Me and my sister, I'm Marg."

"Oh, hello." Jenny tried to be polite, but she was not glad to see a strange, uninvited face at Mollers. "We didn't know you would be here," she added rather lamely.

"Me neither. And we wouldn't be, except we got lost and the motor gave up just by the gate. We pushed us in, it was hot work. It looks as if we're stuck here until we can get going again. Not my idea of fun, I can tell you."

Jenny bridled. Anyone who wanted to be somewhere else than here was a philistine and not worth talking to.

"Got a phone?" Marg asked, peering round them. "In case we need to phone the garage and that," she added.

"Yes," said Mike. Jenny poked him in the ribs and he winced.

"We have a houseful here," she said shortly. "Milk's short. But give me your jug and I'll see what we can spare." She took it and turned back to the kitchen.

Mike was left looking at the stranger. "Er ... did you see the helicopters just now?" He tried to make small talk.

The woman, Marg, looked at him.

"Yeah, noisy brutes."

"Looking for the convict," Mike followed up.

"What's that, then?" Marg's eyes narrowed. "Someone on the run?"

"Didn't you hear on the radio, there's a dangerous man on the loose."

"Ain't got a radio, more's the pity. It's broke. Pauline dropped it in the washing-up – she would!" Marg snorted.

Jenny came back with the jug half full. "You're not very well organized, are you?" She began sharply, but softened it with a smile.

Marg gave her a sideways look. "We can't all be lady of the manor, can we? Thanks, anyway," she added as she turned away.

Mike raised his eyebrows at Jenny.

"I didn't like her," she said defensively. "She looked shifty."

"Just out of her element, more at home in the city I think."

Jenny shrugged.

The campers in the farm field did not call again. No one saw much of them, but Pete became a constant visitor.

"The other one's a blonde," he reported of the campers. Pete made it his business to know what went on. "They've got a rough old cara. Nothing there worth nicking – joke," he said, as Samantha stared at him. "I just crept up by the hedge and peeked in the back window. Those old girls knock back the booze all right. Bottles everywhere!"

"Talk about bottle," Danny said, admiringly, "they could've seen you."

"Nah," Pete was confident. "The radio was going full blast."

"Oh?" said Jenny. She and Mike exchanged looks.

"Hope it wasn't blowing bubbles too," he said and they both laughed.

Four days later the heat had stopped being pleasant and became heavy and oppressive. It hung over Mollers Farm and its inmates like a huge blanket. Everyone was sitting in the kitchen after breakfast, listless and inert.

Pete walked in through the back door. He had given up knocking. Jenny was annoyed by the way he took Danny, Mollers and everything for granted.

"Greetings all," he said, waving a limp hand and flopping down into the only vacant chair. He reached for a mug on the dresser and poured himself some coffee.

Mike couldn't stand him. He hated his matted dreadlocks and rip-torn jeans. He hated the sleeveless, grubby T-shirt and his filthy trainers without laces. He got up and went upstairs.

Over the rim of her coffee mug, Jenny watched him go. She felt totally unable to cope with the situation for once, another reason for disliking Pete. She hated to be out of control of things, and that was just what Pete made her feel. She clenched her teeth. Mike would lose himself in his computer for the best part of the day. He'd be OK. Her grey eyes turned to look at Pete. She dug a mental pit and buried him in it.

His talk of earth spirits and being at one with nature seemed very bogus to her. Unlike Danny and Samantha who could take or leave "nature", Jenny was drawn towards it in a positive way. Intuitively, she understood a great deal about it. She loved making herb teas and using essential oils to burn in her room and make her bath-water sweet. She was in tune with Eastern ways of thought and took classes in yoga and meditation.

Her family teased her about it, but recognized that in that way, as well as in her dark hair, she was different from them and they respected it.

"How's the karma, then?" she asked Pete.

Danny looked at her sharply. He had heard the sarcasm in her voice. He was rather attracted to Pete. Sure, he'd dropped out from school, sure he'd done the drug thing, but here he was, living free, not caring to be part of the great commercial world and happy with it. To Danny, from a well-to-do, respectable, professional home, it had an air of romance about it.

"Great, man, just great." Pete was oblivious to Jenny's scorn. Does he always have to sound like Dylan on *The Magic Roundabout*, she thought viciously.

Samantha pushed a damp strand of hair back from her face. "Let's go to the moor, I need some air. You haven't seen it yet, Tanya, you'll love it."

Tanya looked at Danny. She would go if he would. She was absolutely hooked.

Danny looked at Pete, who raised his shoulders and let them drop.

"I'd love to see it, Dan." Tanya addressed him directly. Her large blue eyes rested on him compellingly as she willed him to look at her. He did.

"You're like some little stray kitten, when you look at me like that, Red."

She smirked at the given nickname and tossed her hair over her shoulder.

Samantha smouldered. What did I ever see in her, she thought suddenly, surprising herself with the violence of her feelings. She's supposed to be *my* friend. She rose and moved over to behind Pete's chair, flashing a look at Tanya.

"Take me to the field, Pete, show me your world, who knows, I might like it." I can play that game too, she thought.

Jenny noted Pete's total lack of interest. Pete only wants what Danny has, she thought. That rules Sam out. She had seen the greedy way his eyes took in Dan's Mini, the house, Danny's designer shirts and his swish camera. But he doesn't know about Danny and me, she thought. That's our secret. We'll always have that. Pete's just a passing phase and that Tanya's like a baby groupie. She smiled a little to herself, secure in her place in Danny's life, remembering the secret codes they used when they were younger. They had been – were, she corrected the tense – inseparable.

Getting no response from Pete, Samantha said, defiantly, "Well, I'll go off on my own, then. I know my way on to the moor."

"We'll go with you," Jenny spoke with decision and stood up. "Come on, Dan, we need a lift in the car, it's far too hot to walk today." She knew that if she took the lead all would follow. She got up and began to load a bag with provisions for a picnic.

"Count me out." Pete didn't rise. "I'll stay and mind the homestead."

Danny felt torn. He wanted to stay with Pete, but he knew the others needed the car. Tanya came up behind him – she only reached to his shoulder. "You are really great, y'know?"

Suddenly Danny felt OK. "Hurry up, sloths, the great outdoors awaits!" He tossed his car keys into the air and caught them.

At the door, Jenny turned to look back at Pete. She

didn't like leaving him alone in the farmhouse.

Pete knew what she was thinking. "Have fun," he mocked her.

No one remembered Mike.

It began to thunder after lunch. Large rolling claps ricocheted off the bare outcrops of rock and travelled down into the moorland valleys. The light seemed to shiver.

Jenny felt deeply oppressed. Thunder always did that to her and this was going to be a bad storm. She always got a headache.

Sam was dabbling her feet in a brook a few yards away from the parking bay, feeling disconsolate and angry. She threw pebbles at the rocks, hating Tanya, who was out of sight with Danny.

Jenny climbed on to a small rocky pile to see if she could see them. They were standing down the slope a little way. Tanya had picked a bunch of heather and was trying to push it into Danny's buttonhole. She was standing on tiptoe to do it and losing her balance. They were both laughing.

"It's going to rain," Jenny shouted to them. "We've got to go!"

As she spoke the rain began to fall in huge, slow drops as large as ten-penny pieces. Then the pace quickened till it was drumming a tattoo on the roof of the Mini. Samantha scrambled in and the other two followed, giggling. They began the drive home through what was soon a deluge. Great streaks of lightning split the sky and the noise of the thunder made the car rock as it battled through the sheets of water.

Mike was alone in the kitchen when they arrived, dripping. He looked nervous.

"When did Pete go?" Jenny asked casually, while the wet ones sorted themselves out. She put on the kettle, eyeing Mike and wondering what was eating him.

"Jen…" It was obvious he had something he had to say.

"Jen, I came downstairs for something and I saw Pete…" He paused.

"Pete what?" Samantha asked, taking down the mugs.

"He was poking around here, putting things into a bag –"

"Things?" This was Danny who had just come in.

"I don't know – things, bits of food, some things that rattled, I didn't get a look at them."

"Did he see you?"

"Oh, yeah. I just walked in on him and he laughed. I opened my mouth to say something to him and … he picked up one of the knives from the wooden knife-block and…"

"He threatened you?" Jenny's eyes narrowed dangerously.

"Not exactly. He played with it a bit, looking at me all the time – he didn't say a word."

"Creepy," breathed Tanya.

"You're making it up." Danny's voice was harsh. "That bit about the knife. I said he could take some fruit and a bit of bread down to his field any time."

Jenny looked at him.

"He took more than that, and I didn't make it up." Mike's voice rose. "When he had gone I noticed that your pile of tapes had gone, and your camera."

Danny's mouth tightened. "My camera's in the car. Pete's not like that!" he stormed at Mike. "He doesn't care about cameras and that, he's beyond those things! Not like you, creeping round the house by yourself, I wouldn't put it past you to stow things you wanted out of sight till later!"

A deafening clap of thunder shook the trees outside and punctuated the silence that followed Danny's outburst.

"Dan!" Jenny exclaimed, pressing her aching forehead. "That's not fair, take it back."

Mike drew himself up. "You don't have to stand up for me, Jenny," he said quietly. He turned with some dignity, to go upstairs. That was it. He was going to pack, and Danny could darn well drive him to a station, rain or no rain.

They all looked at Danny, who blustered a little. "Look, Pete's a friend of mine, Mike had no right..."

"Go after him, the poor guy's in a bad enough state without this. We'll follow and give you moral support, go on."

Jenny gave him a little shove and they followed him up to the floor above.

Tanya began to follow, but then she turned back. This was Harris business and for once she felt outside it. The kitchen was dark and gloomy, shrouded by the rain – it was difficult to think it was the same happy place they had all left earlier that day. She switched on the overhead light. The shadows jumped. Someone was standing there. She gasped.

Pete detached himself from the wall. "Hi, Red," he said.

"Pete." She felt frozen. He was the last person she expected to see.

"Quite a storm." Pete sounded conversational. Tanya noticed, with relief, that the kitchen knife was back with the others.

"You're wet," she said. Pete's T-shirt was sticking to

his shoulders and his face glistened. He took a step towards her.

"Danny's Little Girl Red." He took another step and she backed away. Only Danny called her Red, but she couldn't help liking the way Pete had linked her with him, even though she wasn't sure what he was really getting at.

"You're a little goer, Danny's Red. Danny likes them little, and so do I." Another step took him close to her, she was trapped against the dresser. She began to panic. This was more than friendly.

"Get away from me." Her voice rose to a squeak.

Pete laughed and put his hands behind her neck.

"You smell!" she shouted at him, helplessly.

As his hands tightened behind her head and his face lowered to hers, she screamed and he dropped her and stepped back.

"Pete! What the devil are you doing!"

Danny, with Jenny and Sam behind him, stood in the doorway.

Pete opened his eyes wide and tried to look innocent, but Tanya ran to Danny and clasping him round his waist, began to cry. He put his arms around her, feeling a surge of protective tenderness sweep through him.

"Get out!" he snarled at Pete. "Go to your filthy friends in their filthy vans – you have no idea how to behave in a proper house. Get out!"

Pete opened his hands in a gesture that tried to say, "What's with you, man?" But then, seeing their joint hostility, his face darkened and he turned and left.

A blinding flash of lightning made them all blink. The ensuing thunder rattled the dishes on the dresser and the light went out.

"Don't tell me," Jenny groaned. "There goes the

electricity. Bet the phone's gone too, the lines always go together."

"I'll get the lantern," Sam sighed. This was common practice when the electricity went off.

Jenny went to where the telephone stood on a little table by the back door, and picked up the receiver.

"Stone dead." She bent to check the plug and stood up, her face was white.

"Danny, the line's been cut, look." She waved the unattached receiver at him.

Tanya, with a little cry, buried her face in Danny's shirt front.

Danny didn't know what to do first, go to see the cut line or comfort the girl who was clinging to him.

Jenny let out her held breath in a gush. She didn't know which alarmed her most, the cut line or Tanya clasping Danny's waist.

"Lemon tea," she said briskly. "I'll pick some lemon balm. We need it." She had to get outside to think and cool her head.

She went out into the dripping garden. The rain had stopped, only the disgruntled rumble of thunder could still be heard away in the valleys.

Jenny picked a damp handful from the untidy clump of lemon balm growing near the house. As she straightened up to drink in the fresh after-rain smells she froze. Hanging head down with its leaves and late flowers trailing in the puddles lay the old climbing rose that had clung to the house for all the years she had known it. Storm damage, she thought and went towards it, but it had been slashed viciously, the great stem lying in two pieces. Jenny moaned as if she, too, was hurting.

Shaken, she looked around the garden. Most of the plants that crowded round the walls and windows of

Mollers Farm had been uprooted and left to lie about the path in bedraggled heaps. It looked as if a tornado had passed through.

Danny came up beside her.

"This is your friend Pete's work," she spat at him. "Your nature-loving chum!" She had never spoken to him like that before.

"You don't know that," Danny said desperately.

"Oh, yes I do." Jenny was blazing. "It won't be the only thing he'll do, count upon it. He's always been rotten. We might still catch him at it." She took his hand and they both ran around the house to the yard.

"There!" She almost sounded triumphant as she pointed to the Mini. A long, deep scratch splintered the silver paintwork from bonnet to boot – on both sides.

"He really hated you, you know," Jenny said quietly, as Danny stood there hurt and dumb. "He wanted everything you had from day one." She thought of her wrecked plants. "I don't think he liked me much, either."

Tanya came out and put her arm round Danny. Sam, too, stood bewildered and silent.

Jenny, with a grunt of rage, turned on her heel and went inside, revenge in her heart.

Mike was going. It was early the following morning and he was packed and ready. He had made it up with Danny, and that evening they had all sat playing cards around the kitchen table in candlelight, seeming, on the surface, to be a happy party again. But Mike was odd man out; he knew he should leave.

The storm and the strong emotions of the day before had tired them all and they were late getting up. Mike was getting anxious, he couldn't miss his train. He wanted to hurry things along by getting his bag and his beloved lap-top into the Mini.

Mike regarded the deep scratches in its sides and shook his head. He hated to see wanton damage like that. The Mini looked a bit odd anyway, he thought. What was it? The rain had washed it clean of dust – what was different? He gasped. All the Mini's tyres were flat, ripped to pieces. But there was something else that was odd... He put his hand on the passenger door handle, it gave easily, something was pushing against it from the inside...

He suddenly realized what the other odd thing was. All the car windows were steamed up inside, he couldn't see through them. There was no time to think. With a gentle sighing sound, a body slid from the passenger seat and sprawled half in, half out of the car door. A hand hit the cobbles and lay still. Mike, too shocked to move, took in the swathe of flaming hair.

"Tanya?" he breathed.

Danny rushed out of the front door. "Come on Mike, we're late..." Then he too stopped and stared in disbelief.

"God!" he said at last. He bent towards her.

"Don't touch her!" Mike stopped him.

"But she may be alive – help me, Mike."

"She's not alive, look." He pointed to a narrow wound between Tanya's shoulder blades. Her shirt around the gash was stained with blood...

"Get the others," Danny half shouted. "And phone the police, I'm putting her back in the car. She can't stay like this, I won't let her."

He grasped Tanya's inert body by her shoulders and, as he did so, her face swung backwards, brushing his bare arm, and he nearly dropped her. She was stone cold. Pulling himself together, he managed to lean her back in the seat. There was no head restraint, so her head lolled forward on to her chest. He shut the Mini door and felt very sick.

Samantha, Jenny and Mike stood together in the farmhouse doorway.

Mike said, "We can't use the phone."

"Ask the campers. Their car may be mended now, we could get a lift into town." Danny's sickness was receding and his mind beginning to work again.

Jenny ran to look in the field.

"They've gone," she said flatly.

"What are we going to do? What are we going to tell her mum and dad?" Samantha began to sob. "She was my best ever friend." All recent troubles disappeared before the dreadful enormity of what had happened. "Oh, who could have done this to her?"

Jenny put her arms around her. Her face was chalky white.

"Someone must walk into town." She was looking at Danny. "Now, this minute. Whoever's done this must be running like mad. There's no time to waste," she said urgently.

"Right." Danny grasped at action. He couldn't keep Tanya's face out of his mind, and her blue eyes that had looked at him so adoringly.

"Stay with the girls, Mike," he said, and he sprinted for the door.

Mike looked uncertain. He too wanted to run. He wanted to get as far away from the whole situation as he possibly could. He was cursing himself for not leaving the night before. It was all a nightmare and he wanted to wake up. He hesitated.

"Go on, Mike," Jenny said. "You can leave us, Danny

might need your help. He really didn't look too good and it's quite a long way. The faster you go the faster you will come back. Sam and I will be OK."

Gratefully Mike sprinted out of the yard.

At the kitchen table the two girls sat in silence. Samantha couldn't stop the tears that trickled down her cheeks. She dabbed at them with pieces of kitchen paper.

Jenny made them some strong coffee.

Sam said, "I can't bear to think of her out there, it's getting so hot."

"The police won't be long." Jenny spoke gently.

"It was going to be such a wonderful holiday with Tan…" She broke off. "Now it's a … horror movie."

"Yes," said Jenny quietly. "Yes, you're right. Mollers will never be the same for any of us."

"It's all spoiled," whispered Sam.

They lapsed into their own thoughts.

Pete came into the kitchen and said, "Boo!" They started, staring at him bleakly.

Even when they told him what had happened, when they made it clear that he wasn't wanted there, he didn't go.

"You're a bad lot, Pete what's-your-name Holloway," Jenny flung at him, her anger barely under control. "Stay here till the police arrive, then. They'll have lots to ask you. Who wrecked our garden? Who scratched Danny's car? Where were you when our phone line was cut, answer that. And what about the tyres, did you steal back to do that later with that kitchen knife you were playing with when Mike caught you – did you use it again – on Tanya?"

Samantha put her hands over her ears.

Pete remained calm. "You know who cut your phone

line, Jenny. They weren't just two old ducks in that caravan. I found a blonde wig in the hedge. You don't suppose an escaped con would like the idea of a phone working quite so close to where he was holed up, do you? Or perhaps," he added, an unpleasant smile twitching his lips, "they thought someone was snooping, they wouldn't like that either."

Sam gasped, and he went on, his eyes gleaming. "And why would I want to hurt that little flirt, I could have had her any time! Get your ideas sorted out better than that, nature woman!"

Pete laughed very unpleasantly and pulled the bottom cupboard of the dresser open. He took out a bottle of whisky. He knew where to find it.

"Danny liked her, and anything that Danny liked or owned, you wanted for yourself," Jenny shouted at him, stung. "But you couldn't have her or any of it – so you wrecked it all!"

"Oh, give it a rest." Pete poured some whisky into a tumbler and took a gulp. He grinned.

Jenny spun on her heel and made for the staircase.

Samantha looked after her wildly.

"Jen..." she began, about to ask her not to leave her. She didn't want to be alone with Pete. He disgusted and frightened her.

If Tanya discovered or even suspected it was the escaped convict in the caravan, she thought with mounting fear, he might well have killed her and scuppered the Mini. That way, with the phone cut, he could get far away safely. Panic began to stir way down in her stomach.

Pete had finished the whisky in his glass and was pouring the last drop out of the bottle. He was still grinning as if at some inward joke. The spirit was beginning to have some effect.

"Such a smug, satisfied bunch of no-hopers, aren't you?" he muttered. "With your narrow little minds and comfy little homes. Now you have something that really needs some bottle, and everything falls apart... All ... fall down!" He giggled.

Samantha watched him and said nothing. He was standing near the dresser with the knife-block close by. It was a sturdy chunk of wood with slits for four sharp knives to rest in, their black handles sticking out. He ran his finger over them one by one, looking at her as he did so.

Oh, God, he killed her – her thoughts spun in a circle. He's capable of anything. Perhaps Tanya caught him about to steal Dan's Mini and he stuck a knife in her back – one of those – he could easily get it ... I think he's mad.

She gasped as Pete threw the empty bottle away from him in disgust, crashing it on to the flag floor. Splinters of glass flew everywhere.

"I know where you can get some more whisky, Pete." She spoke hurriedly, grasping at a straw.

"OK, where?" His voice slurred the words.

"In the cellar. Dad keeps it there – to keep cool," she added lamely, trying to sound as if she wanted him to have it.

"I'll show you, shall I?" Without waiting for Pete to answer, she moved gingerly through the splintered glass to the door leading down to the farmhouse cellar.

"I'll get it ... get away!" Pete grabbed her arm and pulled her away from the door. He lifted the latch and peered into the dark space in front of him. Samantha put her arm round the door and switched on the cellar light.

"Down the stairs, turn right," she told him, her heart in her mouth.

Pete began a slow descent. He stumbled once or twice. Sam made herself wait until he was at the bottom of the steps before she switched off the cellar light and slammed the door shut.

"Thank God Dad put a bolt on it," she breathed, as she thrust it across and ran towards the stairs and Jenny.

Jenny was sitting in the middle of her bedroom floor, cross-legged and deep in meditation. Her hands were on her knees and her eyes were closed. Sam burst in.

"I've shut him in the cellar, Jen. Till the police come, he's drunk, mad I think. I've been so scared!"

Jenny's large, grey eyes opened slowly and stared at her. Sam thought she hadn't understood.

"Please come," she begged. "Listen, he's banging on the door, suppose he breaks it down? Oh, Jen, please come!"

"You've shut Pete in the cellar?" Jenny came out of her trance. "Good for you." She began to stand up.

Sam noticed she had been sitting in front of a lighted candle, and in front of it, on the floor, lay a photograph. It was one Sam knew well, one with Tanya and herself, arm in arm, in the garden at home. She saw, with shock, that Tanya's face had been carefully painted out.

Sam's mind reeled. What had she seen? What did the mutilated photo mean? Her wide eyes stared uncomprehendingly into Jenny's.

Jenny smiled at her, and seeing her familiar smile, Sam steadied. She waited for Jenny to say something.

"Oh, dear Sam," the words came out like a sigh, "I'm such a fool. I was so jealous of her, you see."

"Jealous of Tanya?" Samantha was thunderstruck that Jenny should be jealous of anyone.

"This was Danny's last summer here, with us, with me. I wanted it to be perfect. I wanted it to be how it always was, Danny and me – and you, too. But then Tanya went after him, and he liked her and..."

"And so you ... killed ... her?" Sam said it slowly, in disbelief, trying to understand, but thought, I must wake up, I must.

"No!" Jenny cried. "No, what are you saying, Sam?"

"But..." Samantha pointed to the blacked-out face.

"No! I just wanted her away, anyhow, out of our lives. Not dead."

"She is dead." Sam spoke flatly. "Stabbed in the back."

"I know, I know, but I only wished it. I concentrated my mind and willed it – I didn't *do* it. Not to kill her, but to send her away. I didn't even know if ... if it would happen!"

"How can I believe you?" Sam cried in despair. Her safe world was crumbling around her as they spoke. "How could some *bad wishing* do that to Tanya!"

Jenny put her hands over her face. "I don't know, either, Sam. All I know is that I could never have damaged Danny's car like that, never, never, never. Or stab Tanya and put her in it to die."

"What do you mean, to die? How do you know she wasn't dead first?"

"Because ... of the misted windows. She had to have been breathing for a little while..."

Sam's cry of horror stopped her.

"It's too, too horrible!" She sank down on the floor and wept bitterly.

"Come on now, Sam," Jenny said, pulling her to her feet. "The police are bound to find out who really did it. Let's leave it to them. Listen – Pete's breaking down that door, we'd better do something to stop him."

Sam leaned against her weakly and Jenny stroked her hair.

"Come on," she said again. "Two of us are more than a match for him, especially drunk. The others will be back soon anyway. I'll make some—"

"Lemon tea," said Samantha, smiling shakily and they moved to the door together.

Silence had fallen in the cellar.

"He's gone to find the drink at last," Samantha said. "Shall we let him stay?"

Jenny grinned wryly. "Dad wouldn't thank us if all his whisky disappears."

"Suppose not." Sam squared her shoulders and reached for the bolt. "On your head be it," she said over her shoulder to Jenny, "if he comes out fighting." She opened the door.

The next instant she felt an almighty shove in the small of her back and she was tumbling, arms and legs anyhow, down the cellar steps. Her head cracked against the stone floor and she saw stars. The door at the top of the steps shut with a bang and she was in the dark.

But not alone. Pete's legs had got tangled up in hers and they were spread-eagled on the cellar floor together.

"Come on in, ev'body welcome..." Pete muttered drunkenly.

"Oh, my God," breathed Samantha when the stars receded. "Come on Pete, we've got to get out."

But her ankle hurt, she couldn't stand. She shouted.

When she stopped shouting fear, sharp and terrible, gripped her. Someone was tearing paper up just outside the cellar door. From where she crouched she could see some of it being pushed through under the door. That could only mean one thing.

Above the sound of the tearing paper she was aware of a voice whispering, and the whisper was worse than anything. It didn't sound human, it didn't sound like Jenny, but that's who it was.

"Spoiled," she was saying, "sp–oi–led..." over and over again.

"Mollers spoiled, garden spoiled, Mini spoiled..."

"Jenny," shouted Sam. "*Nothing's* spoiled, it can all be mended. Let me out!"

But the whisper went on with its awful incantation.

"Spoiled, all spoiled. Family gone, Sam gone, all gone." And then with a dreadful sort of chuckle, "Tanya gone!" Then conversationally, quite normally, "So easy, so quick, one, two and through and through!"

Sam shuddered. She tried again.

"Jenny we haven't all gone – we love you!" she shouted.

"No, spoiled." The whisper became a howl. "Love sp–oi–led... Danny spoiled. Jenny and Danny all gone!" It was a child crying in desolation. "Danny, Danny, Danny..."

Then came the inevitable sound of matches being struck. One, two, three, before any light took and the fire against the cellar door began to flicker.

"Pete!" Sam shook him, but he lolled over, fast asleep.

She could hear Jenny chuckling as she fed the fire with anything she could. Cookery books, paper off the shelves, then bigger things like tea towels.

"All gone, all gone, no more Sam, no more family, no more Danny," and sobs broke through the laughter.

Smoke drifted into the cellar and the door began to burn.

Sam screamed. She went on screaming. She was still screaming in terror when strong hands beat out the flames and lifted her to safety.

When she felt fresh air around her she opened her eyes and saw that she was in the yard. Mollers Farm was still standing where it always had, and a familiar face swam into vision.

"Oh, Danny. Thank God."

"Mike and I got a lift in Dave's van to the town – wouldn't have made it back in time otherwise."

"Dave?"

"One of the Travellers," Danny said wryly. "They're not all like Pete."

"Jenny!" Sam remembered. "Oh, Dan – Jenny … and Pete's still in there…"

Danny smiled wryly. "Pete's sleeping it off under the hedge. The police will want to have a word with him, his van is full of stuff – not his."

"But Jenny, she … she…?" Sam began to sob weakly into Danny's chest.

Danny's eyes filled with tears. He still couldn't take it all in – didn't understand. Later … later…

"Sh… later, Sam. Jenny's in good hands. The ambulance is coming and the doctor's here now. You need to rest. Mum and Dad are on their way."

Samantha closed her eyes again. She ached all over and her ankle was throbbing badly. Jenny had been right. Everything *was* spoiled. She never wanted to see Mollers Farm again.

She didn't hear the doctor murmur to her kindly before the needle pricked her arm, but she felt Danny's hand stroke her hair. Then she slept.

DEAD LUCKY

"How far is the hotel now?" Simon leaned over the coach driver's shoulder. He peered out at the whirling blizzard of snowflakes caught in the headlights like a plague of white moths.

The driver shook his head grimly. "I had reckoned we'd be there by now." He leaned forward, straining his eyes to try to see through the storm. "But to be honest I haven't got a clue where we are. I just hope we can stay on the road, that's all. If we plough into a drift, we've had it."

Simon sat back down in his seat. He ran his hand round his jaw, then through his untidy mop of brown hair. He felt a pang of apprehension. He didn't fancy freezing to death on some lonely highland road that was for sure.

The girl next to him spoke for the first time since the skiing party had set out.

"What did he say?" she asked.

Simon told her.

"Oh." She gazed out of the side window, then back at Simon. She had very dark hair, almost black. It was cut close to her head. She had strikingly dark blue eyes. She wore a black jacket with military style buttons and a short skirt that looked more suitable for a day at the office than a trip to a highland ski resort. Her eyes widened as she looked at him, almost as if she thought she might have seen him somewhere before.

"I only booked this trip at the last minute," she said, pulling a wry face. "I'm beginning to wish I'd stayed at home."

"You probably took my friend's place," Simon said. "He's got flu and had to cancel."

"That's hard luck ... for him anyway. Good luck for me though." She half smiled shyly at Simon.

"Yep. It's an ill wind, I suppose. Mind you, it doesn't look as if any of us are going to get there if this weather doesn't let up."

The girl sighed and sunk back down in her seat. She hunched her shoulders into her collar and gazed miserably out of the window.

Simon had thought it pretty exciting at first, the snow storm starting almost as soon as they got up on to the highland road. The sky had gradually got darker and darker. You could see the storm coming across the moorland like an approaching cloud of doom. Now, it didn't seem exciting at all. He had saved for months for this trip but everything seemed to be going wrong. First Mark getting sick, now the prospect of not even reaching Highdale, let alone spending a week there skiing. The whole thing was turning out to be a nightmare.

One of the other passengers, Ben, came up the aisle towards him. He had been talking to Ben and his friends in the bus station earlier. There were six of them, all at college together. They had seen Simon was on his own and had invited him to join them.

One of Ben's friends, David, had been reading a story out from that day's newspaper.

"Hey, look," he'd said. "That serial killer's been at it again."

Simon had looked over David's shoulder at the story. The headline seemed to jump out at him: *The Cat Strikes*

Again. The notorious killer, dubbed "The Cat" by reporters because of the way he left scratches on his victim's body, had indeed been at it again.

"A young man in his twenties," David read out loud. "Found with a slashed throat. As usual, the killer left no clues."

Ben had felt a shudder of apprehension. He had read a lot about that serial killer. He had claimed victims all over the country. Worst of all, this most recent murder had taken place not far from where Simon lived. He felt doubly glad to be going away for a while. If the killer was operating in that area he, for one, would be happy to be miles away.

Ben held on to the back of Simon's seat for support as the coach lurched round another treacherous bend.

"This is a bit of a pain, Simon." Ben bent to peer out of the window. He was wearing a yellow baseball cap that looked a bit out of place with his purple and black padded ski-jacket. When Simon had chatted to him earlier he'd revealed a grin like a cheeky school kid, but now he looked serious. He pushed the cap to the back of his head. He and his friends had been pretty noisy when they first set out. Laughing, cracking jokes. Simon wished he'd been sitting with them instead of the silent girl beside him. The gang had gradually grown quieter and quieter as the bad weather set in.

"You're not kidding," Simon said in reply to Ben's comment. He was just going to say something about being stranded when suddenly there was a cry from Rachel, Ben's girlfriend.

"Hey ... look ... lights!"

They all craned their necks. Sure enough, you could just make out a dim orange glow through the gloom.

"Looks like we made it, folks," the driver called out,

sounding relieved.

There were a few whoops of delight and a smattering of applause from the rear.

"Great." Ben slapped Simon on the shoulder. He turned and headed back to his seat. "See you later."

The coach turned slowly into the hotel drive. Simon could just make out two rearing brick pillars with a stone stag's head on top of each one.

"Let's hope they can put us up," the driver said to Simon. "Because we're not going anywhere else for a long time, that's for sure."

The hotel was like something out of a Christmas card. It was built of stone blocks and looked like a miniature Scottish castle. Its towers and turrets were dark-shadowed and mysterious amidst the swirl of snowflakes. The lighted windows seemed like eyes looking through the storm. Drifts of powdery snow had been blown up against the front steps. The branches of the neighbouring conifer trees were already bending with its weight.

A man came down the steps. He was shrouded in a long overcoat and boots. A woolly bobble hat was pulled down almost over his eyes.

The driver cut the engine and got out.

"What's the road like?" the man asked.

The driver shook his head. "Terrible," he said. "We've been dead lucky to get here. It looks like we're stuck for a while. Hope you've got room for us."

"Plenty. We've only got one other guest. Everyone else has phoned to cancel." The man introduced himself. "I'm Bill McMann, the manager. You'd better get those people off and inside before they freeze to death."

Simon, Ben and his friends Lee and David stayed behind to help unload the bags.

"So much for our holiday," Lee grumbled. He was a tall, thin boy, with pale eyes and freckles. His sandy hair was already white with snow. He kept blowing on his hands and rubbing them together for warmth.

"Well, at least we got this far." David moved aside a pair of skis to haul out a huge zip-up bag. "I didn't fancy spending the night stuck in a snowdrift," he panted. "We're miles from anywhere." He pushed back his long hair and bent to haul out another suitcase. "Reminds me of that werewolf film that came out last year. You know, where those guys got lost in a snowstorm and were never seen again. All they found was a pool of blood." He grinned.

"Come off it," Simon laughed, and took the bag from him. He carried it up the steps into the foyer, stamping the snow off his trainers as he got inside.

The girl who had been next to him on the coach was standing by a ragged-looking potted plant. She seemed a bit lost. It was no fun being on your own when something like this happened.

Simon felt sorry for her. "Go and talk to Rachel." He indicated Rachel standing with her back to a huge log fire that burned in the hearth. With her were her friends Liz and Sharon. "We'll have all the bags in in a minute," he added.

"I'm OK." She fiddled with one of the buttons on her jacket. She looked frozen. Her light suit and high-heeled shoes were hardly the kind of clothes to wear in this kind of weather. "I'm waiting to be allocated a room."

Simon shrugged. "OK. By the way, I don't know your name."

"Jane," she said.

"I'm Simon."

She looked at him. "Yes, I know."

Simon smiled. Jane was pretty in a boyish kind of way. He was curious about her. She seemed a lonely kind of person. Maybe they could get to know one another while they were here? In fact, he had a feeling they might all get to know one another very well if the storm didn't let up. The prospect of ever getting to Highdale was receding into the wild, white yonder. Simon was always curious about people. He fancied being a crime writer one day and reckoned that the first step was getting your characters right. And the only way to do that was to study people, talk to them, find out what made them tick.

At last, all the bags were unloaded. People were milling about in the foyer chatting. The manager was calling out instructions for the waitress to bring a tray of hot toddies. The receptionist was busy fixing everyone up with a room.

"We'll meet later," Ben said to Simon as he took his and Rachel's bags upstairs. "We'll have a laugh. It's not exactly the Ritz but if we're going to be stuck here we may as well enjoy it." He looked round, grinning. "The place looks as if it needs livening up a bit."

Ben was right. Apart from the huge log fire, the hotel foyer was dingy and unwelcoming. Dark panelled walls were lined with gloomy oil paintings of highland scenes; cattle drinking from murky-looking ponds; one of a dead stag being dragged behind a horseman with a gun slung across his saddle. When Simon gazed up at the chandelier at the top of the stairs, cobwebs hung from the dusty crystals like grey skeins of silk.

Simon was waiting to be allocated a room when one of the other coach passengers, a tall man with a dark beard wearing a leather jacket and jeans, came up to the desk. Simon had noticed him before. He had been at the back seat of the coach, not speaking to any of his fellow passengers. He had sat hunched up in the collar of his coat just staring at everyone.

As the man came up to the desk his mobile phone rang. He gave an exclamation of annoyance then went over to a distant corner of the reception area to answer it. He was frowning and seemed to be arguing with the person on the other end. Simon wondered why he bothered to have a mobile phone if he didn't want people to ring him.

Still looking annoyed, the man marched back up to the desk and rang the bell loudly.

"Won't keep you a moment, sir." The receptionist already looked harassed. She had been trying to allocate everyone rooms for the past half hour.

The man stood tapping his fingers impatiently on the desk. Then with another exclamation of impatience he strode off up the stairs without waiting to be given his key.

Jane picked up her small suitcase and headed up the stairs.

Simon lugged his rucksack up behind her. His room turned out to be next to hers. Room 13. Simon wasn't superstitious but somehow it seemed appropriate.

The corridor was long and narrow, dimly lit. It had staircases at either end as well as in the middle. Each of the end staircases was overlooked by a narrow window. Simon reckoned they must lead up to the towers. He wondered what was up there. He was fascinated by old houses, castles, that kind of thing. Maybe he'd get the chance to explore later. A figure appeared out of one of the rooms. It must be the only other guest, Simon thought. He started in their direction, then seemed to change his mind and hurried off down the end staircase. Then he saw the man with the beard. He had dumped his case at the top of the stairs and was walking up and down the passageway as if he was counting the rooms. He had turned suddenly and glanced at Simon. Then, seeing he was being watched, he hurried to the end of the corridor and peered out of the side window. Simon stared at him for a minute or two longer. What on earth was the guy up to?

Jane's voice broke through his thoughts. "See you later, then."

"Oh ... er, yes, sure." Simon forgot about the man with the beard and turned to speak to her.

"Sit with us at dinner if you like," he said as Jane put her key in the lock. "No point in being on your own."

"OK, thanks," she said without turning. "See you later."

Simon's room was just as dingy as the rest of the place. He dumped his rucksack on the bed and went to draw the curtains. Outside, it was still snowing heavily. He could just make out the shape of an outbuilding, the edge of its steeply pitched roof softened with snow. There were trees all round, branches weighed down, reaching towards the building as if they were trying to drag it down with them. He could almost imagine he heard the distant howl of a wolf. He shivered. Simon loved open spaces, fresh air, mountains. That's why he had come on this holiday. To feel the wind in his face as he skied down the slopes. Before, snow had always been beautiful, the sight of it had given him a feeling of freedom. Now it was imprisoning him. He felt shut in, ill at ease. He shivered again. This place was giving him the creeps. The sooner he got back downstairs the better. A good meal ... a laugh with Ben and his pals ... he'd feel much better after that.

But Simon couldn't shake off his feeling of unease. It

was still with him, even after they had eaten, an hour and a half later. The rest of the party seemed subdued as well.

The meal had been forgettable to say the least. Some kind of casseroled meat with potatoes and little else. The manager did apologize, saying the expected supplies hadn't turned up due to the state of the roads.

A few of the older members of the coach party were propping up the bar sampling the manager's mature highland whisky. The man with the beard had gone off to his room directly after the meal.

Simon and the others sat round the fire.

"Well." Lee stretched his legs out and lay back in his chair. "What shall we do?'

"Play cards?" Rachel suggested. "I saw a pack on the table in the foyer."

"Boring," Sharon said. She was a short girl with blonde hair, long curling eyelashes and a small, rosebud mouth. She reminded Simon of a Sindy doll, although that could have been because she was dressed in bright pink leggings and a white fluffy top.

"What then?" Liz, a plump girl with glasses, tucked her long hair behind her ear and leaned forward, clasping her hands round her knees.

"Scrabble?" Jane said timidly and was shamed into silence by groans from everybody. Simon grinned at her. She had changed from the smart suit into a pair of jeans and a blue sweatshirt. It brought out the colour in her eyes. Again, Simon thought how attractive she was. Maybe getting stuck in this place wasn't going to be so bad after all. He pulled his chair closer to hers.

There was a pause. Obviously, no one could think of anything to do. Simon reckoned the atmosphere had got to them, too. He watched the waitress come to draw the heavy maroon velvet curtains across the windows. They seemed to make the room smaller … more confined. He leaned forward and threw a log on the fire. Sparks flared as the log caught and flamed. The fire threw dancing shadows across the faces of his newly-found friends.

In spite of the blaze, Simon gave a sudden shiver.

"If David was here, he'd have some ideas," Liz said. "He's always the life and soul of the party."

"Where *is* David?" Simon asked. He'd noticed David hadn't appeared for dinner but hadn't got round to asking why.

"Don't know," Ben said. "I knocked for him earlier but couldn't get any answer."

Simon got up. "I'm going up to get a sweater, shall I see if he's OK?"

"Good idea," Ben said. "He's in number 30."

"Right."

Simon went off up the stairs. He got his sweater, then went along to David's room. On the way, he noticed that someone had left the door of room number 26 open.

"That's a pretty stupid thing to do," Simon said to himself. He went to close it. You read a lot about hotel thefts in the papers, leaving your door open was asking for trouble.

Simon's fingers were on the handle when he noticed something strange. Inside the room he could just see the bedside lamp lying, overturned, on the floor. Curious, he pushed the door open a bit further. It hit something soft. He pushed harder. The obstacle gave way a little, just enough to allow Simon to poke his head round the door and see into the room.

The sight that met his eyes made him gasp.

The body of a young man was lying on the floor.

Simon squeezed through the gap. He stared down,

frozen to the spot. The top of his head went icy cold. It was the worst thing Simon had ever seen in his life.

There was a wide, gaping wound in the young man's back as if someone had plunged a knife in, then twisted it viciously to get it out. A pool of blood, a dark, shining stain, pear-shaped, spread across the mushroom-coloured carpet.

Simon felt sick. You saw violence all the time ... on TV, on videos, at the cinema, on the news. But this was something entirely different. Different and shocking. Real. And the smell, Simon would never forget the smell. Warm and metallic.

The smell of blood.

The victim was lying, face down, on the floor between the bed and the TV. Although his features were hidden, Simon thought he was probably about eighteen or nineteen. He had a mop of brown hair that flopped over his ears and curled into the nape of his neck. He was slim, well muscled, wearing only a pair of jeans. His hands were outstretched, palms upwards as if he had been offering up some kind of gift, or maybe begging for mercy.

Simon turned away for a moment and took several deep breaths. The poor bloke ... being killed just along the corridor and no one knowing about it. Didn't he cry out or scream or something? Or had the murderer taken him by surprise, thrusting a knife in without mercy when his back was turned?

Simon squeezed back out through the door and ran downstairs.

Bill McMann was at the bar.

Simon rushed over and grabbed his arm.

"Quick!" he gasped, his voice louder, more panicky, than he'd intended. "Upstairs, someone's been murdered."

Everyone in the lounge looked at one another in horror.

"You're kidding," Ben said, laughing nervously.

Simon shook his head. "I wish to God I was."

Jane was sitting bolt upright in her chair, a look of fear on her face.

Mr McMann looked at Simon in disbelief. Then he must have seen from Simon's expression that he was telling the truth.

"Show me!" he said tersely.

At the bottom of the stairs, he turned and shouted above the chorus of voices that had risen at Simon's words. "Everyone stay here!"

Simon ran on ahead.

"In here," he gasped when they reached the victim's room.

The manager went in and knelt beside the dead body. He lifted one wrist to feel for a pulse. Simon couldn't think why he was doing that. It was obvious the guy wasn't breathing. Mind you, maybe he should have done the same thing. Simon had just assumed that the bloke was dead. After all, with that great wound in his back, the blood spreading out over the carpet, he could hardly be anything else.

"He's not still alive, surely?" Simon said shakily.

Mr McMann shook his head. "Dead as a doornail. Poor chap." He looked up at Simon. "Who the hell could have done this?" He gazed at the victim for a minute longer. Then, dazed and shaking, he reached for the hotel phone and quickly dialled 999.

"Stabbed, yes..." he said, when he'd been put through to the police. "I'm not sure of his name, I'll have to check the register. I do know he's been here a couple of days. The room doesn't look as if it's been turned over but there's been a bit of a struggle."

By now, several people had ignored his instructions and had come up the stairs. The man with the beard had come out of his room to see what the commotion was about. Simon turned to see him staring at him with a curious look in his eye. Simon's stomach turned over. Surely the guy didn't think *he* had done it?

Ben and Rachel were behind him. They were both craning their necks to see inside the room.

The manager put the phone down.

"Right." He came to the door, shooing everyone out. "There's nothing we can do until the police get here. I'm going to lock this door and I'd ask you to all keep away. I've been told not to touch anything. They're going to get here as soon as they can but by the state of the roads..."

"Shouldn't you cover him up or something?" Rachel said shakily. "It seems ... horrible, just leaving the poor guy like that."

"No, we'd best leave him," McMann said, gently.

The man with the beard was still staring into the room. "And you, sir. If you don't mind." Bill McMann took the man's arm and steered him away. It struck Simon that the man looked more curious than shocked. Everyone else looked pale and shaken.

The man looked annoyed when the manager hustled him away. He strode off down the corridor, went into his room and slammed the door behind him.

McMann was trying to sound reassuring. "I want you all to keep calm," he added. "It's not likely the murderer would have hung around, so you've got nothing to worry about."

"Yeah, but where would he go in this weather?" Ben muttered, as everyone filed back downstairs.

"Exactly," said Simon. "Just what I was thinking."

Downstairs everyone was talking at once.

Mr McMann quickly explained what had happened. Again he begged everyone to keep calm.

"There's nothing anyone can do," he said. Then he invited everyone to have a drink on the house. The man with the beard had come back down and had seated himself at the bar. He had changed from the jacket and jeans into a pair of light trousers and a sweater.

"Double scotch," he said, suddenly amiable. He grinned at the man behind the bar. "On the rocks." He began talking to one of the other guests. Simon didn't blame him for suddenly deciding he wanted some company. Who in their right minds would want to be alone in their room with a killer on the loose?

In the lounge, Simon and his friends sat around the fire. They had been wanting something to happen to liven the place up. Well, now it had.

David had joined them now. He appeared dozy-eyed and confessed he had fallen asleep.

"What's going on?" he asked, groggily.

When the others explained, David's face had lit up. "Wow!" he said. "What did I tell you about that werewolf movie..."

Liz threw a cushion at him. "It's not funny, David. It's horrible." Her lower lip trembled.

"Sorry." David looked full of remorse. "But you've got to admit this place is dead creepy."

No one argued with that.

"You know," Lee said suddenly. He had been quiet up until now, sitting back in his chair looking thoughtful. Now, he leaned forward, his elbows on his knees. "It's really weird. We were reading about that serial killer, remember? Now someone's been murdered here." He shuddered.

"Wait a minute," Simon said. "That killer's victims, they were all young blokes, weren't they?"

Everyone stared at him.

"What are you getting at?" Rachel fiddled nervously with a button on her jacket.

"Well ... maybe..." Simon broke off. He didn't want to scare anyone more than they were already.

"I know what he's getting at," Ben said. "I've been following those murders, too. All those blokes were killed in hotels. Right, Simon?"

"Right," Simon said. He could have kicked himself for not making the connection before. He guessed he must still be in a state of shock.

"Someone's got a grudge against them, that's for sure," Liz said in a small, shaky voice.

Sharon shivered and moved closer to Lee. "I don't like it," she muttered. "There's nothing to stop him doing it again."

Ben gave a nervous laugh. "Come off it, Sharon."

"No, Sharon's right," David said. "The bloke couldn't go anywhere ... it's still snowing like mad. He'd be better to stay in the hotel and act normally." He looked from one to the other, then over towards the bar. "It could be one of them. Or it could be him..." His eyes went over to the guy with the beard, sitting on his own now not far from where they were gathered round the coffee table. He was close enough to hear what they were saying.

David's eyes went back to Sharon, then to Liz,
then Lee...
Simon...
Jane...
Ben...
Rachel...

David opened his eyes wide so they were staring…

"…or it could be one of *us.*"

Everyone laughed nervously.

"David," Liz said loudly. "Just shut up!"

"That serial killer," Sharon said suddenly. "Why do they call him The Cat?"

"Because he goes out at night," Ben joked.

"You shut up as well, Ben!" Rachel reprimanded. "It's *not* funny."

"Because he always scratches his victim's face," David explained. "*After* he's killed them, they reckon." He turned to Simon. "You got a good look…"

Simon shook his head. "No, I didn't. The poor guy was face down on the carpet."

"Well," David said. "I think we should find out."

"What difference would it make?" Jan said. She fiddled nervously with her fingernail.

"None I suppose," David admitted. "But I'd like to know, wouldn't you, Simon?"

"Er … yeah." Simon felt a morbid kind of curiosity. He *would* like to know if the victim had been killed by The Cat. Maybe he could even use it in one of his stories one day.

"Right." Lee leaned forward. "I saw old McMann put the key under the reception desk. What do you say we get it and go look?"

"Ssh," Simon said. "Not so loud, huh?" The last thing they wanted was for anyone to know what Lee was suggesting. He glanced over to where the man with the beard had been sitting but luckily he had gone.

Liz was shaking her head. "Not me," she said in a low voice. "And I reckon you must be crazy."

"We are." David got up. "But I'm *dying* to find out," he hissed. "Coming, Simon?"

Simon got to his feet. "Anyone else?"

The four girls shook their head. "Serves you right if you get caught," Sharon said sulkily.

"He might be waiting for you," Liz said. "The Cat … he might be lurking about."

"There's safety in numbers," David said, breezily. "Come on, you guys."

Liz shrugged. "You're nuts," she said. "All of you."

"I'll keep a watch out for McMann," Simon said, as David went to get the key. He could see the manager sitting in the lounge with a group of guests. They were too busy chatting to notice what was going on anywhere else.

"Right," David suddenly hissed in Simon's ear. "Got it."

Simon was first as they crept stealthily up the stairs. As he reached the top he saw a dark figure at the end of the passage.

"Wait," Simon hissed. "There's someone there."

They all held their breath. They would have a lot of explaining to do if they were caught creeping around carrying the key to number 26.

The figure at the end of the corridor seemed to be examining the window catch for some reason or other. It was so dark along there, Simon couldn't be sure but he thought it was the man with the beard. What on earth was he doing? As Simon watched, he opened the window. He leaned out. Flakes of snow blew in, whirling and dancing in the dim glow of the corridor lamp.

Simon saw him pull the window to. Then he hurried off down the staircase.

"OK," he hissed. "Coast's clear."

At the door to Room 26 they hesitated. Then David put the key into the lock and turned it slowly. He pushed open the door, then stood back.

"You go first," he said to Simon.

"Coward," Simon whispered.

The room was cool. The cloying smell of death still lingered. Heart thumping, Simon clicked on the light.

"You stay there," he said to the other three. "I'll look. The fewer people that touch him the better."

He went apprehensively over to the body and knelt beside it. The blood had soaked into the carpet by now and had dried to a deep, rusty red.

It took all Simon's courage to gently lift the head and turn it sideways. Simon drew in his breath. There, down the victim's left cheek, were two long, deep scratches.

There was no doubt about it, he had been killed by The Cat.

Simon was just about to tell the others when suddenly the light flickered. It flickered again, then went out. The room was plunged into inky darkness. The only light came from the window. A shaft of that curious brightness you get when the world is covered in snow. It shone through, casting a weird shadow across the body on the floor and lighting up the bloodstain like a pool of deep red moonshine.

Simon swore under his breath. He heard Lee call from the doorway.

"That's all we need, a damn power cut. Simon ... did you manage to see?"

Simon got to his feet and felt his way back to the door. "Yep," he said. He pushed the others out in front of him. David fiddled around to lock the door.

"Well?" Ben said impatiently.

"No doubt about it," Simon said. "It was The Cat all right."

"Hell," Ben said. "And he only murders young men ... and he could still be here ... and now there's no lights." He gave a groan. "I wish I'd never come on this damned holiday."

"And so say all of us," David muttered. "Come on, let's get back to the girls."

Downstairs, pandemonium had broken loose. Mr McMann was going around with a flickering cigarette lighter telling everyone to calm down. The receptionist, armed with a small torch, had hurried off to find candles. Soon the place was glowing with candlelight.

"It's the power lines," Mr McMann was explaining. "It's happened before in bad weather. Sorry, everyone ... all we can do is wait."

"Well?" Jane looked anxiously at Simon as the boys arrived back downstairs. "What did you find?"

Simon explained. "Really deep scratches down his face," he said. He gave a shudder. "Horrible. Poor guy."

Liz gave a little cry. "What are we going to do?"

David shrugged. He had been subdued since the discovery. He looked scared. Serious. His jokey mood seemed to have given way to one of fear. Ben was quiet, too. He sat clutching Rachel's hand. Lee sat with his head in his hands.

Suddenly Simon couldn't bear the atmosphere any longer. He left the others sitting in silence. The light from the guttering candles threw crazily dancing shadows into every corner of the room. Outside, a bitter wind screamed through the eaves and rattled the front door. The curtains billowed and a puff of smoke came out into the room in the downdraft from the chimney.

Simon went to look out of the window. Outside the snow had let up. Everything was covered in a thick blanket. The drive had disappeared totally. The cars parked by the steps, the shrubs that lined the drive, all were misshapen lumps of white. It was as if they were on an island, a remote island in the middle of a bottomless sea. He felt scared, more scared than he had ever done in his life. Supposing they were stuck here for days and days? Supposing The Cat struck again? There was no doubt about it, the victim hadn't been dead long before he was discovered. Simon remembered distinctly how the blood had been fresh. It hadn't even had time to soak into the carpet. And David had been right. The murderer could never have got away in this weather. He *had* to still be around somewhere.

Simon turned and studied the guests for a minute. They were chatting, laughing. There almost seemed to be a party atmosphere about the place. Even the guy with the beard was having an animated conversation with a woman in a blue dress. It almost seemed as if they had forgotten what had happened. Except for *his* party. It seemed to have affected them more. Maybe because The Cat's victims had all been about their age. He reckoned the murder must have taken place just before dinner. David had been up in his room but hadn't heard a thing. Or had he? Had he *really* fallen asleep? He seemed a nice enough guy but then you could never really tell...

Simon shuddered, suddenly cold, suddenly wishing he was *anywhere* but here.

"Hey, Simon," Ben called. "We've decided to stay up all night. Lee reckons there's safety in numbers and we can kip down here, there's plenty of room."

But Jane yawned and got up out of her chair. "Well, I'm not," she said. "I'm exhausted, I'll never sleep properly in a chair."

"It's OK for you," Lee said with a wry grin. "The Cat never gets girls."

David seemed to have got some of his old humour

back. "There's always a first time," he joked.

Simon gazed at him. Maybe he wasn't joking at all? Maybe he was deadly serious?

"I don't think that's a very good idea, Jane," Simon said. "Supposing..."

But Jane wouldn't change her mind. "I'll make sure I lock the door," she said. She took her key from the left-hand back pocket of her jeans and waved it at him. "And I'll bolt it from the inside, don't worry."

"Well, if you're sure?" Simon still thought she was being foolish but it was really up to her.

"Do you want one of us to come up with you?" David said.

Jane shook her head. "I'll be fine, honestly."

After Jane had gone they all sat in silence for a while. The porter appeared with a basket of fresh logs and threw a couple on the fire. They hissed for a while then caught, the orange flames leaping up the wide chimney like a holocaust.

Then Liz piped up. "What are we going to do? We can't sit here all night in silence. It just makes things worse."

Ben had sprawled back in his chair. He yawned. "I'm going to sleep," he said.

"I wish I'd brought my book down," Liz said in a disgruntled voice. "I don't suppose anyone would come up with me to fetch it, would they?"

The boys looked at one another. "I will if you like," Simon said. He still didn't like the idea of Jane being on her own. It would be a chance to check that things were OK.

David got up out of his chair. "I'll come too ... safety in numbers, remember."

Ben sighed and stood up. "OK, guys. Count me in."

"Do you want me to come?" Lee asked.

The others laughed. "I reckon three will be enough," Liz said with a smile.

She led the way up the stairs. Simon and David carried candles. Their guttering flames threw giant shadows on the walls of the stairway.

Liz's room was right at the other end of the corridor.

Simon was just about to follow the others along when he heard a strange banging sound. Holding his candle high he was just able to see that the window at the opposite end of the passage was swinging to and fro. He had wondered why the passage seemed so cold.

"Hang on," he said. "I'll just go and shut the window."

It seemed silly afterwards, but he didn't check the others had heard him. He headed off along in the opposite direction. Suddenly the candle spluttered and went out. Simon was plunged into darkness.

Simon swore under his breath. He might have known the wretched thing would never have stayed alight in the draught from the open window.

He turned but the whole length of the passage was black as the ace of spades. The others must have gone into Liz's room to get her book. Simon gave a shiver. It was hard to describe how complete darkness was when there were no street lamps, no moon to light his way ... nothing.

He hurried on, groping his way towards the window. He may as well shut it now he'd got that far.

Suddenly Simon froze. Someone was following him along the corridor. He stopped, holding his breath. He cursed himself again. He must be crazy. Alone in the darkness with a serial killer on the loose. He must need his head testing.

Suddenly Simon felt a hand on his arm. He gave a little yell and jumped backwards, colliding with the wall. As he turned to flee there was a quick, sharp burst of flame as someone struck a match. A pale face was suddenly illuminated … black hair, deep blue eyes…

Simon gave a huge sigh of relief. He gave a kind of hysterical laugh. "Jane … for God's sake … you scared me!"

Jane held a candle in her other hand. She held the match against it. It caught and flared. Simon saw her grin in its brightness.

"Sorry, Simon. I didn't mean to."

"Did the others tell you I was along here?" He turned and closed the window. "We came up to get Liz's book."

"Yes," Jane gave a small laugh. "I'd wondered who the voices belonged to."

"Have they gone back down?"

"They must have done." Jane gazed at him, her deep, dark eyes wide in the light from the candle.

"Great," Simon said. "Leaving me all on my own. It's a good job it was you and not … well … you know."

"You were right, Simon." Jane gazed at him. "I shouldn't have come up on my own. I've tried to get some sleep but it's hopeless."

Simon noticed for the first time that she was wearing her dressing gown. She shivered suddenly as if someone had walked over her grave. She pulled the edges of the gown closer together.

Simon put his arm round her as they went back towards her room. "I reckon that guy with the beard left the window open," he said.

"He must be crazy. It's freezing."

"I know. I saw him fiddling with it earlier on. I reckon he's a bit weird altogether."

"Why?" Jane stood in front of her door. There was no sign of the others. Jane was right, they must have gone back down.

Simon shrugged. "I don't know ... there's just something odd about him."

Jane was smiling shyly up at him. "You don't think he could be the killer, do you?"

"He could be. Anyone could be."

"Even me?" Jane said.

Simon put his hand on her shoulder. "No," he said softly, gazing into her eyes. "Not you."

She stared at him for a moment, then said something that surprised him. "Why don't you come in a minute?" She gazed at him from under her dark lashes. "I'm not sure I want to be alone after all."

"OK," he said.

Inside, she hurriedly removed a laundry bag from the doorway to the bathroom and pushed aside a couple of newspapers that lay on the bed. Simon stood in front of the closed door, not knowing quite what to say.

"Won't be a minute," Jane said. She disappeared into the bathroom. Simon heard the sound of a tap running. He glanced down at the newspapers. Strangely, they were several days old. The front page of one of them carried a story about the serial killer. It was the same paper Ben and the others had been reading at the bus station.

Jane came out of the bathroom. She stood in front of him and lifted her hand to stroke his cheek. Her eyes washed over him. He felt really surprised. He had no idea she thought about him in *that* way. He'd thought they were all just pals ... friends you meet on holiday, then maybe never see again.

"Here..." She softly stroked the left side of his cheek. "The scratches on that poor guy's face..."

Simon swallowed. "Yes."

He frowned. There was something strange about what she'd said. Alarm bells began ringing in Simon's head. Something was bugging him ... what on earth was it?

Then it dawned on him. How had Jane known what side the scratches had been on? He hadn't told anyone the *exact* details. *Deep scratches down his face* ... that's what he had said. He distinctly remembered because Liz's hand had flown to her cheek ... her right cheek, but he hadn't thought to say anything.

Simon's heart began to thud. He suddenly felt he must be going crazy. Jane was still looking at him and smiling. "You know," she said softly. "You remind me of someone."

Simon swallowed again. "Yeah?" he said. All the time his mind was racing. He had realized something else. It was almost certain that someone left-handed would have made those scratches. Jane was left-handed. He remembered she had carried her suitcase in her left hand. He could picture her now, teetering up the stairs in those high heels and tight skirt, holding her small case in her left hand. Her *small* case ... a case never designed to hold skiing clothes ... and that smart suit ... hardly the stuff you'd wear for a long coach trip. Was it because she had booked at the last moment? Had she been in a hurry to get away for a while? To disappear up into the highlands? If so ... why?

Simon took several steps backwards. He blinked and came to. His imagination was running away with him. Those minutes alone in the darkness of the corridor. It must have shaken him up more than he realized. And he'd been reading too many of those murder mysteries he was so fond of. Loads of people were left-handed, probably twenty per cent of the population. And not everyone took skiing gear on holiday, lots of people hired it. It was ridiculous… Jane couldn't possibly be…

She was still smiling at him.

"W–Well," he stammered. "I'd better get back downstairs. The others will think I've…"

He broke off. Jane was still staring at him with those eyes … eyes that seemed suddenly to glow with fire.

Wordlessly, she was reaching into the back pocket of her jeans… She was drawing something out … something long … sharp … gleaming…

"I'm sorry, Simon," she whispered. "But you remind me of him, too … the boy who ditched me a year ago." Her voice took on a far-away sound. "We were on holiday … a hotel…"

Simon spun into action, dodging sideways, as she lunged towards him. She gave a cry and turned swiftly, lurching forward again. Simon felt a sharp pain in his arm. He clutched at it and his fingers came away, red.

He had his back to the door. Desperate to escape, he fumbled for the handle. He'd got to get out, warn the others. The door flew open and he stumbled backwards into the corridor. Jane flung herself towards him.

Then the sound of people saying goodnight to one another came echoing from below. Then the sound of footsteps on the stairs.

Jane went pale, her lips were raised in a snarl. Her eyes flew about in panic. She turned suddenly and fled down the corridor. Simon dived after her.

She was heading for the end stairs. Simon bolted after her, amazed at how fast she could run. His brain was in turmoil. Jane … the killer … no … yes … he could hardly believe it.

At the bottom of the stairs, the side door had been

thrust open. It was snowing heavily again. A blast of bitter air hit Simon's face as he dived through. He lunged forward, following the line of footprints that led to the garages.

The snow was so deep, Simon could hardly run. He floundered on, holding his arm up over his eyes to protect them from the needles of wind-blown snow. His other arm was bleeding badly. He was starting to feel dizzy. His heart pounded in his ears like a crazy drumbeat of death. He was soaked and frozen to the skin. He could hear shouts, his name being called but all he could think of was Jane … Jane…

A flight of steps behind the garage led up to a storeroom above. She had gone up there. He could see her footprints, a place where she had slipped, then carried on. He hesitated at the bottom. There was no way out. She must be crazy if she thought she could get away. But then she *was* crazy. He had seen the madness in her eyes as she lunged for him with the knife. He should wait there until someone else came.

But something drove Simon on. Up the snow-covered iron treads, in through the open door. He hesitated, panting on the threshold. Where was she? She'd got to be hiding somewhere. He couldn't see a thing. Then, gradually his eyes got used to the gloom. He could make out stacks of cardboard boxes, potato sacks, a few crates of tinned food. He had just taken another step inside when he heard a noise. A soft sound behind him. A swish … the harsh sound of someone out of breath. A picture flashed into his mind … the guy in Room 26, lying, face down … the wound in his back. He remembered wondering if the killer had taken him by surprise, plunging the knife in without mercy before he could turn or even cry out…

He whirled, raising his arm to punch away the hand that was poised to kill him. He hooked his other arm round her neck, squeezing as hard as he could. She kicked and screamed obscenities at him. He began to feel more dizzy than ever. Her screams began to fade and he felt his grip begin to give way … she wrenched from his grasp … she was getting away…

Simon heard a shout… "Stop, police!"

He was vaguely aware of another figure leaping forward then a great black curtain came down over his eyes and he remembered nothing more.

"You feeling better, Simon?" The man with the beard came into the lounge.

Simon looked up. "Yes, thanks." He frowned. Why did the guy have a notebook in his hand? And how come he knew his name?

The flesh wound in Simon's arm had been bandaged and he was sitting by the fire with a blanket tucked round him. A glass of brandy stood on the table by his side. He had shrugged off everyone's congratulations, saying none of it had really been intentional. He had just happened to be in the right place at the right time, that was all.

"The wrong place, you mean," Ben had commented with a wry grin.

The man held out his hand. "Holmes is the name," he said. He grinned. "Not Sherlock before you make any comment. Detective Sergeant Bill Holmes. Ashbourne CID."

Simon was puzzled. What was the guy on about? Ashbourne … that's where he came from. And CID? What on earth was going on?

Sergeant Holmes grinned again. He sat down beside

Simon and flicked over a page of his notebook.

"It's you who should really be named Holmes," he said. "If it hadn't been for you we'd never have caught her."

"But I don't understand," Simon said.

"We'd got reason to believe that the killer of the young man in Ashbourne had headed for the coach station," he said. "So I was assigned to the one you all were on. Undercover, of course."

"Oh..." Simon couldn't think of anything else to say.

"I've found all the evidence we need in her room," Bill Holmes went on. "A laundry bag with her bloodstained suit, the arm torn where she had struggled with that poor bloke upstairs. We found the knife in the store-room. The one you knocked from her hand. We're hoping she hadn't wiped it too well. If there's traces of blood on that as well..." He spread his hands. "Bob's your uncle."

Simon took a deep breath. "I thought –" he began.

"That I might be the killer?" Sergeant Holmes threw back his head and laughed. "I saw you looking at me a bit strangely once or twice."

"What were you doing at that window?" Simon asked.

"Seeing if it had been forced," the sergeant explained. "And checking how high it was off the ground and if there were any footprints in the snow below."

"And what about—" Simon began.

But Rachel intervened. "Simon, you still look a bit pale, why don't you have a chat to the sergeant a bit later?"

Bill Holmes stood up. "Right. Anyway, just to say thanks, Simon."

"It's me who should be thanking you." Simon remembered the figure lunging at Jane just as she was getting away.

“What for?” Sergeant Holmes asked.

“For turning up in the nick of time...”

“Isn’t that what we’re supposed to do?” He grinned broadly. “After all that’s what happens in all the best crime novels.”

“Umm,” Simon said thoughtfully. “So it does. I’ll have to remember that.”

A TOUCH OF DEATH

"Oh God! What am I doing here?" Carla Lawson whispered to herself as she stared down at the corpse laid out in the front room.

He looked as if he was made from rubber – unreal. Like one of those grotesque Hallowe'en masks.

Someone had touched up the grey-white skin with rouge. Coloured in the blue lips with lipstick. Concealed the black and blue bruises with powder.

He was dressed in white, his bony old hands crossed over his chest, looking hideous against the beauty of the blue silk lining of the coffin.

The shock of coming face to face with the dead man robbed Carla of her own colour. She felt weak, nauseous. She hadn't expected to find the body actually lying in state. She'd assumed this was to be a normal funeral, not something from the dark ages!

A cold hand touched her arm suddenly and her whole body jerked with fright.

Her boyfriend smiled at her and her knees almost buckled with relief. "Damian! You scared me to death!"

His arms wrapped around her and held her close. "What are you doing in here?"

"I was looking for you. You seemed to vanish the minute we got here."

"I was putting your overnight bag in your room."

"Damian, why didn't you warn me that your grandfather's body would be lying in state?"

"Carla, I did warn you that this wasn't going to be a picnic. I said you'd be better off staying home. But you just pestered and pestered till I gave in."

"I thought you might want me," she said, linking her arm through his. "Funerals are awful things, thought I could cheer you up if you got too depressed – only I didn't quite expect this! Seeing him all laid out in his front room – it's a bit ghoulish, isn't it?"

"It's not ghoulish. It's just one of those traditions that have stuck in this family. Nothing I can do about it. I can't help it if I've got a weird family!"

"And I want to find out how weird," Carla insisted inquisitively, relaxing against him. "Damian, do you realize we've been going out together for four months and your family are *still* a mystery to me." She smiled mischievously. "I thought this would be an ideal opportunity for me to get to know them."

He moved away from her and leant on the open coffin. "You don't need to know them, not yet. It's me you're going out with, isn't it?"

"Of course, but I'm curious. I can't wait to meet them!"

"Then believe me, you'll be just as eager to see the back of them!"

"I don't believe they're as bad as you make out."

He smiled then and pressed a kiss into her hair. "They're worse ... but I'm glad you're here really – and as for my family, just try not to let them get to you."

"I'm sure we'll get on great."

"Let's hope so," he sighed and stared broodily into the coffin.

Carla studied his handsome profile. Theirs was definitely a case of opposites attracting. Damian, tall and blond, with deep blue eyes and long thick eyelashes that a girl would kill for. While she was petite and dark, traces of Italian blood still in her veins from distant ancestors.

They'd hit it off perfectly from the moment they'd met. Perfect except that he flatly refused to let her meet any of his family, going to extraordinary lengths to make sure she didn't.

She was intrigued to know why. And the sudden death of his grandfather seemed an ideal opportunity to find out.

"Are your relatives due today?" she asked. "Or are they just coming for the funeral tomorrow?"

"There'll be a few nieces and aunties for you to meet tomorrow, but my mother's already here – she came to stay right after Grandad popped his clogs. And there's Hannah, of course." He looked into Carla's eyes, adding solemnly, "That's *his* wife – widow, rather. Grandad remarried years ago, our real gran is dead."

Carla bit her lip, unsure of how to react. She decided to murmur a respectful "Oh!" and lowered her head as if in prayer.

A strange kind of sound exploded from Damian, startling her.

He was laughing.

Something had struck him as so hilarious that there were tears in his eyes.

"What's so funny?" Carla asked, feeling that she ought to be joining in the joke. Only, for the life of her, she couldn't see anything even vaguely amusing.

"You!" he said, kissing the tip of her nose.

"Me … why?"

"Because you're acting so funereal. Look at you, you're even dressed in black."

For the first time since they'd met, Carla felt irritated by him. "I often wear black," she retorted hotly. "Black suits me. I suppose I could have worn yellow and put flowers in my hair..."

"You could have," Damian agreed. "No one gives a hoot that the miserable old so-and-so's dead anyway."

"Damian!"

"It's true. He was a bad-tempered, cantankerous old man. No wonder Hannah talks to herself, she couldn't get two civilized words out of him. It honestly wouldn't surprise me if it was her who..." He stopped in mid-flow.

"Who what?"

"Nothing. Forget it. Anyway, I was telling you who's here now. My mother and Hannah. Oh yes, and Liz is bound to be here."

"Who's Liz?"

"She's a relative of sorts, a twice-removed distant cousin or something – more of a family friend, really. She's been around ever since I can remember. And if my mother has anything to do with it, she'll be around for evermore, as the future wife of my brother Jason – or me!"

Carla shot him a startled glance. "What's that supposed to mean?"

"Liz is the only girl good enough for my brother or me – according to my mother." A muscle twitched in his jaw. "Yet another good reason for you not having contact with my folks."

Carla's heart plummeted. At the back of her mind, she'd always wondered if that was the reason Damian hadn't introduced her to his family – because she wasn't good enough. Now she had heard it from his own lips.

"And talking about my big brother," Damian went on, oblivious to the hurt he had unknowingly inflicted upon her, "Jason is supposed to be putting in an appearance later on." His eyes glinted suddenly with a look that could have frozen the coffee in your cup. "That should be fun!"

Carla stared at him. She thought she knew him. In their four months together, she thought she had come to know him well. But by the look in his eye, she didn't know the half of him. And it scared her.

He sighed then, and looked down into the coffin, letting his hand trail over the old man's hands and face. "It's funny, but I like the old boy better now that he's dead than when he was alive."

Watching him, Carla felt an icy chill run through her body. She never realized he had such a cold streak. Cold, callous almost.

"Come on, this is giving you the creeps, isn't it?" he murmured, brushing a stray black curl from her eyes.

His finger on her forehead was cold. Icy cold from where it had touched the corpse.

A touch of death, she thought stupidly, and shuddered.

"How did he die?" Carla asked, as they closed the door on the airless room and walked out into the huge hallway. Doors led off in all directions and in the centre of the hall was a magnificent sweeping staircase like something from a classic old thirties movie. "Old age, was it?"

"Old age – him? He might have been eighty-five but everyone thought he was indestructible."

"So how?"

Damian's blue eyes glinted wickedly, and his voice hushed to an eerie whisper. "Murder, my dear Watson ... murder!"

Carla's mouth dropped open.

He laughed. "Only joking. He had an accident." He

continued looking into her horror-stricken face. "I was joking … you know, a joke, those things that people laugh at?"

But Carla continued staring at him. She'd never noticed what a sick sense of humour her boyfriend had until now.

"Hey, lighten up."

She tried, but it all seemed so disrespectful. There was an old man dead in there, and all Damian could do was joke about it!

Her troubled thoughts were interrupted then, as a woman came down the stairs. She was in her early fifties but dressed much younger in a short red dress, and her golden hair was wild and flowing. The idea crossed Carla's mind that flowers in her own hair might not have seemed so out of place after all!

"Ma, hi!" greeted Damian, offering his cheek.

His mother smothered him with hugs and kisses, leaving dark pink cupid impressions all over his face. Then to Carla's amusement, she produced a tissue, spat on it, and wiped the lipstick from his cheeks.

Damian stood and took it, while Carla did her best not to laugh.

When Mrs Goldby had finished fussing, just stopping short of checking behind his ears, her gaze switched to Carla. "So this is your latest girlfriend, Damian," she said curtly, looking Carla up and down with a look of utter disapproval.

Carla felt her confidence shrivel up and die. She turned to Damian for support.

"Yep! This is Carla, Ma – the love of my life."

He sounded as if he meant it, but Carla decided not to get too excited over it. She extended her hand to his mother.

"Pleased to meet you, Mrs Goldby."

The woman took Carla's hand and held it for a second before letting it drop. There was no grip, no warmth, just an icy chill that ran up Carla's arm and touched her heart.

"What happened to that other girl – the pretty one?" demanded his mother.

Carla's eyes fluttered shut with humiliation.

"She dumped me for someone else, Ma," Damian replied acidly, but his hand tightened around Carla's and his finger tickled her palm. "Anyway, Carla's by far the prettier, don't you think?" And to Carla's mortification he tilted her chin so that his mother could look directly into her face.

Her expression was glacial. "Don't be ridiculous, Damian!" Carla twisted her head away as Mrs Goldby stalked off. "If you two want to do something useful," she tossed back over her shoulder, "go and fetch Hannah down for dinner. We can't wait any longer for Jason."

"OK Ma," said Damian tugging at Carla's hand. "Do you want to come up and meet my dotty old step-gran, or would you rather help Ma in the kitchen?"

Carla pulled a face. "I'll come with you, thanks very much!"

He smiled ironically. "I did warn you!"

She followed him up the wide sweeping stairs to the balcony at the top. "Why do they live in a place as massive as this?"

"Because they can afford to! Personally I'd sell up and buy a little bungalow. Then the money from this place could come to us just a little bit sooner."

"Money-grabber!" she laughed, not taking him seriously. "Anyway, how can an old couple manage a place this size?"

"Ma's always popping in, and me and Jason and Liz call regularly – just to check on our inheritance. One day, when Hannah pops her clogs too, all this will be ours." He wiggled his eyebrows. "One down, one to go!"

Carla stared at him. He *really* did have the strangest sense of humour.

They halted outside a bedroom door and Carla heard someone arguing – a gruff, gravelly voice. "Is that your gran?" she whispered.

Damian nodded. "She's talking to herself. She hears voices. She's either possessed or demented. Oh, by the way, you'll be sleeping in the next room."

"Thanks," she grimaced.

Damian winked and tapped the door before going in.

Hannah was sitting in a crumpled armchair, facing the television, with its sound turned down. A cup of cold tea on the floor, sweets and sweet wrappers around her slippered feet. She looked startled as they entered.

"It's all right, Hannah," Damian said softly. "It's me, Damian, and I've brought my friend Carla to meet you."

Carla knelt down by the old lady. "I'm pleased to meet you. I'm sorry about..."

Damian put a finger to his lips and shook his head. Whispering, he said, "Leave it, it'll only confuse her."

Carla held Hannah's hand. "Your dinner's ready, shall we help you downstairs?"

Tired, confused eyes peered out from deep sockets. "Dinner? But I've only just had my breakfast."

Carla had expected the old lady's voice to be deep and gruff, yet it was quite normal, quite sweet really. "Do you have a hairbrush? Your hair's a little ruffled from where you've been sitting."

She was aware of Damian smiling as she brushed the old lady's hair and made her look presentable.

Surprisingly, Hannah was quite steady on her feet, and only needed a reassuring hand as they went downstairs for dinner.

The dining room had the same heavy, stuffy air as the rest of the house. It was dull and gloomy and Carla longed to throw all the doors and windows open and let some fresh air in. It was hardly her place to do so, however, and no one else seemed to bother.

The old lady eagerly made her way to her place at table. Seated already was a girl of about Carla's own age. With sleek fair hair and a face that lit up at the sight of Damian.

"Damian! Great to see you."

"Liz, hi!" greeted Damian, kissing her, and Carla felt a twinge of jealousy. "Carla, meet Liz, my twice-removed distant cousin or some such thing."

"We've never been able to figure it out," laughed Liz. She had strange eyes that narrowed to slits when she smiled – cat's eyes. "Of course, the simple solution would be for me to marry one of the gorgeous Goldby boys."

"Oh, which one?" Carla retorted, before she could stop herself.

Liz looked like she was purring to herself. "I haven't made up my mind yet."

Mrs Goldby strutted in with the gravy boat and instructed everyone to start. "We can't wait for Jason any longer. I'll warm his dinner up when he gets here."

She had prepared a banquet – turkey, cranberry sauce, everything, as if it were some kind of celebration. But she glanced at her watch constantly as they ate, waiting no doubt for Jason.

They talked non-stop – Damian, his mother and Liz. Chatting about things which Carla had no connection with. Each time Damian included Carla in the conversation, either Liz or his mother would effectively block her out.

Carla tried not to let it irritate her. She turned to Hannah, hoping to find an ally there. The old lady wasn't eating. And not only wasn't she eating, she was holding her knife the wrong way around – gripping the handle with the point downwards, like a dagger.

"Are you all right, Hannah?" Carla asked kindly.

The woman didn't answer. She looked strange, and she began jabbing the knife into the table.

"Oh, don't, you'll scratch it," Carla said gently, but the jabbing became fiercer, and her small eyes looked wild.

"Damian..." Carla breathed, alarmed. "Damian..."

They were all laughing about something, lost in delightful reminiscences that excluded her.

"Damian ... your gran ... she's gone a bit odd."

All hell broke loose.

Mrs Goldby dived across the table at the old lady and snatched the knife off her. "Who the devil gave her a knife and fork?"

"I did," Carla admitted. "She only had a spoon."

"Of course she only had a spoon," raged Mrs Goldby. "She can't be trusted with anything sharper."

"I'm sorry," Carla murmured, looking helplessly to Damian. "I didn't know."

Liz was smirking, finding the whole thing hilarious. "No point in blaming Carla, I'm sure she didn't *tell* Hannah to gouge holes in the table. Did you, Carla?"

"Of course I didn't!"

"Only the old dear responds well to orders and instructions, watch this – Hannah, you're holding your spoon the wrong way round."

"No, she isn't," said Carla, puzzled.

Liz silenced her with a dismissive wave of the hand. "Turn your spoon over, Hannah."

The old lady did as she was told.

"Now pick up your peas on it."

Hannah tried to scoop up her peas on the rounded back of the spoon. As they rolled off Liz laughed hysterically. Even Mrs Goldby chuckled.

Carla was horrified. "How could you?" She spoke softly to the old lady. "Turn your spoon over, Hannah, that's right."

As the old lady began to eat normally again, Carla glared at Liz. "That's sick!"

Liz flashed her cat-like eyes. "Her mind's gone. All she does now is argue with those voices in her head and follow orders." Her eyes glinted wickedly. "Why I bet, if someone had told her to push Grandad down the stairs, she would have."

Carla was beginning to feel nauseous. In a hushed voice she asked, "How did he die?"

Damian spoke up, his voice was hard. "The clumsy old geezer tripped over his own feet and fell down the stairs. And ignore Liz, she's warped."

Her eyes narrowed to slits. "Don't be so naïve, Damian. Surely you haven't forgotten what she did to her cat last year."

"Oh shut up, Liz."

Carla's mouth dried, the words scarcely came out. "What did she do to it?"

"She stabbed it with her knitting needles," Liz said, with an air of sadistic glee. "She said the voices told her to."

Carla felt sick. "Oh God!"

Damian glared. "She was confused. She's been on

medication since then. And she's done nothing else like that since."

Mrs Goldby's pencilled eyebrows arched. "Hasn't she?"

Silence. No one spoke, but Carla was convinced they were all thinking about their grandad. Had the voices made her do that too?

Liz was first to break the silence. "God, you should have seen the blood! You wouldn't think a little cat would have had so much."

Carla put her hand over her mouth, fighting down the feeling of nausea.

Beneath the table, Damian squeezed Carla's knee. Quietly, he said, "The cat recovered ... but we had to give it away."

"Couldn't risk keeping it," Liz remarked, slyly adding, "Damian, you really should have warned your girlfriend about the streak of insanity that runs through this family."

Carla glanced at Hannah sitting there in her own little world. "Hardly insanity, Liz, Hannah's just getting old..."

"Who's talking about Hannah?" Liz said – and laughed.

Somehow they got through the meal. As soon as Mrs Goldby had finished, she started clearing away, regardless that others were still eating. Once she had gone through to the kitchen, Carla turned to Damian.

"You've never told me about your father, Damian, are your parents separated?"

"Divorced, years ago," he replied brusquely.

"Give the girl a few of the gory details, Damian."

"There are no gory details, Liz," said Damian curtly.

"Oh, come on! I'm family, we've all heard how your

mother stole your father from his first wife, just because he was gorgeous and was the father of four boys." She turned to Carla. "Everyone else in her family had given birth to girls – Mrs Goldby only wanted boys, so this man looked a likely candidate to father the sons she craved for."

Damian looked embarrassed. "We don't know for sure what went on."

But Liz wasn't to be silenced, she munched contentedly on a chunk of turkey as she continued, mischief dancing in her feline eyes. "Let me give you an example of what his mother is like, Carla. Have you ever heard of the black widow spider?"

"Yes."

"Well, once Mrs Goldby had the two adorable little baby boys that she'd set her heart on, she had no further use for their daddy."

"So?"

"So … she simply ate him up…" Slowly Liz pulled a turkey bone from between her teeth, Carla watched mesmerized. "And then, Carla dear … she just spat out his bones!"

Jason eventually arrived just before bedtime. His arrival felt like a breath of fresh air. Liz had monopolized Damian all evening – sitting much too close to him, laughing at everything he said, hanging on to his every word.

Carla was on the point of saying something when Jason strode through the door and Liz instantly dropped Damian in favour of his elder brother.

Jason had Damian's golden blond hair, worn slightly longer, and the deep, deep blue eyes of the Goldby family. He was inches taller than Damian, with a broader physique, and a face that wouldn't have looked out of place on the movie screen.

Mrs Goldby and Liz fluttered around him like moths around a flame.

Jason Goldby had been the centre of attention for some minutes before anyone noticed that he hadn't arrived alone.

Ruth was very small, very pale, with mousy hair and a mousy little face. So that when Jason introduced her as his wife of two days, a stunned silence fell like a lead balloon.

Even Carla was astonished that someone so plain had landed a hunk like Jason. It took her only seconds, however, to realize how awful Ruth must be feeling, to be faced with a stunned reaction like this from her new husband's family.

"That's fantastic!" Carla exclaimed. And she rushed forward and hugged the little mouse and tried to shield her from the venomous glares darting her way from Mrs Goldby and Liz.

"Congratulations," Damian said woodenly to his brother. "Does this mean you won't be stealing my girlfriends again?"

"Absolutely!" Jason said with a smile and a wink at Carla that made her blush.

Damian looked at her, saw the rising colour in her cheeks and for one awful moment, a look of despair flittered across his face.

Carla threaded her arm through his. She was trying to show him that if his brother had stolen any previous girlfriends, he wasn't having this one!

She glanced up at Damian. He wasn't looking at her any more. He was glaring at his brother, a look of utter hatred in his eyes.

Carla shivered.

Liz moved between Jason and his new wife. She was much taller and slimmer than Ruth. And even Carla silently admitted that Liz and Jason looked more natural together than Jason and Ruth.

Ruth cast a nervous, twitchy smile around the hostile faces. "Hello everyone, it's nice to meet you."

Liz flashed an angry look at Jason before speaking to his little wife. "I can hardly believe you're married. How long have you known each other?"

Ruth giggled. "Ages actually, we're at the same college. But we only got together after I'd invited Jason and absolutely everybody to a do at my parents' place on the coast. We just sort of hit it off after that."

Jason eased Liz aside so that he could stand with his new wife. Liz looked as if she could spit fire.

Carla looked at the scene with dark amusement.

There was Damian, glaring at his big brother with nothing less than hatred. And his mother, tight-lipped and disapproving. And Liz, green with jealousy.

And innocent little Ruth, cuddling up to her hunky husband, like a soft little kitten with a big bad wolf.

She couldn't help but wonder who would bite first.

Voices awoke Carla from her sleep that night. At first she thought it was Hannah next door, arguing with the voices in her head. But it came from the landing – Mrs Goldby and Jason. Speaking softly, but quite audibly in the silence of the night.

"Are you out of your head?" Mrs Goldby hissed. "You're too young to get married."

"Funny," replied Jason, calmly. "But the registrar didn't ask if I'd got a note from my mummy."

"Don't be facetious!" she snapped. She couldn't

conceal her anger. "For heaven's sake Jason, it's only three days since I saw you – when your grandad died. Why couldn't you have told me about your plans then? You must have married the very next day! Oh, I can't believe you'd be so thoughtless."

"I knew you'd disapprove, Mother. I only called by the other day to tell Grandad and Hannah – I thought they at least might be pleased for me." His voice trembled. "Only I never got chance to tell them. Poor Grandad was lying dead. You know, if it had been left to Hannah, he'd still be lying there. Hannah's totally insane – you know she's hearing voices, don't you? She hears voices telling her to push people down the stairs ... down the stairs, Mother," he repeated pointedly.

"I know, I know."

"And you still don't think we should have told the police? Grandad's death probably wasn't the accident we're all taking it to be."

Mrs Goldby's tone was harsh. "Do we really want to bring a scandal on this family by involving the police, Jason? Besides, there's nothing we can do about it now. Your grandad's dead and some might say that if Hannah did push him, she's done us all a favour!"

"But she can't be allowed to get away with it, Mother ... if those voices in her head are telling her to push people downstairs she's just as likely to push one of us next – have you forgotten what she did to the cat?"

"Jason, aren't we getting away from the issue? We were talking about your ridiculous marriage." Her voice softened, became pleading almost. "Oh Jason, I had such plans for you. If you wanted to marry, why didn't you choose a really nice girl, like Liz for instance."

"Because I happen to love Ruth."

"Love!" snapped Mrs Goldby. "How can you be

in love with her? She's a little nobody with looks to match."

"I think she's beautiful, and as for being a nobody, she's got more money – correction, *we've* got more money than this family will ever have. I've married a very wealthy girl, Mother."

Mrs Goldby uttered a harsh little laugh. "Hah! So you married her for her money, I might have guessed!"

Jason sounded hurt. "I didn't marry Ruth because she's rich. I'm just telling you that to try and make her more acceptable to you."

"Well, she's *not* acceptable in this family, Jason," Mrs Goldby stated icily. "Do you hear me? And I won't have her in this family. She's not welcome here!"

"Well, that's tough, Mother," Jason snapped. "Because you're just going to have to get used to her."

But in fact no one had a chance to get used to Ruth Goldby – mousy little Ruth Goldby, who wouldn't have hurt a fly.

Because Ruth was found dead. Lying in a crumpled, pathetic heap at the bottom of the stairs the following morning.

Her neck broken.

Jason was distraught, inconsolable. Tears streamed down his cheeks as he cradled his wife's limp body in his arms.

"What happened? Did anyone see?" Mrs Goldby demanded, standing stiffly over the scene.

"We don't need to see!" Jason cried. "I warned you, didn't I ... I warned you what would happen if they didn't lock her up."

Carla clung to Damian, horrified and shaking. "Who's he talking about?"

Like his mother, Damian stood statue-like, emotionless. "Hannah, I guess."

Jason's tears streamed over his dead wife's face. "She's insane! She ought to be locked up. Bad enough she pushes the old man down the stairs, but why Ruth – oh, why my little Ruth?"

Carla stared in horror at her boyfriend. "I thought you were all joking about Hannah killing your grandad..."

"No one saw it happen but it's common knowledge that the old girl hears voices."

Liz ran to comfort Jason. "Jason's right. Hannah is completely insane. She's a danger to us all. We all pushed it to the backs of our minds, didn't we, what we really thought – that she'd finally flipped and killed the old man – well, look where our loyalty has got us. She's killed a perfectly innocent girl now!"

Carla stood white-faced, trembling from head to foot. "Why are you blaming Hannah? You've no proof..."

Jason lifted his tear-stained face. "Proof? She hears voices – voices that tell her to do things – like pushing people down the stairs. Isn't that proof enough? Go on and ask her if you don't believe me. She makes no secret of it."

"It's true," Mrs Goldby uttered stiffly. "Her doctor's aware of her situation, but the medication doesn't seem to make any difference."

Carla turned to Damian. "Damian?"

He looked pale, but there was little sympathy in his expression as his older brother continued to weep bitterly. "Who knows?" he murmured quietly.

Liz stroked Jason's golden hair, pressing kisses into it as if they would ease his pain. It struck Carla that from Liz's point of view, things were looking up.

Jason continued to sob. "She ought to be locked up ...

someone get the police … she's insane!"

As if on cue, Hannah appeared at the top of the stairs. Jason let out a strangled cry of rage and stumbled up the stairs on all fours like a demented animal to get at her.

"Stop him!" shrieked Mrs Goldby, and Damian, Liz and Carla all pounced on Jason and held him captive until he had calmed down.

Hannah looked down on the scene in blissful innocence. "Is dinner ready yet?" she asked, brightly.

The police explained that an autopsy would have to be carried out although they seemed confident that Ruth's death was nothing more than a tragic accident. Oddly, neither Jason nor anyone else said a word about Hannah when it came to the crunch.

Family loyalty was a strange thing, Carla realized.

The first mourners arrived to pay their respects to Grandfather Goldby just after the ambulance had taken Ruth's body to the mortuary.

Carla wondered if the day could get any worse.

It could, and did.

While relatives trailed in and out of the front room, prior to the funeral, Carla went in search of Damian. She found him in the kitchen with Jason. Carla assumed he would be trying to comfort his elder brother, and turned to go before she interrupted them, but what she overheard left her stunned.

"It hurts, doesn't it, big brother?" said Damian coldly. "Losing someone you loved? It's like a knife cutting through your heart. You feel sick, lost, empty … you almost want to die yourself."

"I knew I could rely on you," Jason uttered brokenly.

"Now you know how I felt," Damian went on. "Every time you stole a girl from me."

"I didn't steal – they came willingly."

"You used to go all out to take every girl I ever had from me. Even when you didn't fancy them yourself. Just so long as you took them away from me."

"It's not my fault you couldn't hang on to them once they'd met me," Jason retaliated.

Damian sounded bitter, full of hatred. "Yeah, well I'm just glad that you're feeling the pain of losing someone – really glad."

"Yes, I can see how pleased you are," said Jason. "It's almost as if you were happy that Ruth is dead. It wasn't you who killed her, was it, by any chance, Damian … just to hurt me?"

Carla couldn't bear to listen to any more. She ran and hid in her room until it was time to go.

Rain streamed down the steamy limousine windows as they followed the hearse to the cemetery. Mrs Goldby sat brushing invisible flecks from her immaculate black suit. Liz sat clutching Jason's hand as he stared blankly at the misted window. Damian stared broodily straight ahead. Sitting next to Carla was Hannah, smiling and looking as excited as a child on an outing.

Carla studied the gloomy faces. Mrs Goldby had her wish granted. The young wife she so heartily disapproved of had been wiped out of her precious son's life. And Liz – she'd be indispensable now. Jason would need a shoulder to cry on, and Liz's shoulder looked very willing.

No one wept as the coffin was lowered into its grave. Hannah held a flower in her hand and counted the petals. Everyone else stood eyes downcast, lost in their own private thoughts.

Carla stood between Damian and Jason. Poor, poor

Jason. Soon he would have to attend another funeral – his wife's. It was so tragic. She was dead before they'd even had a life together.

The sadness of the situation brought tears to her eyes, and she rubbed them away before they fell. Both Damian and Jason glanced at her, and then she sensed them looking daggers at each other over the top of her head.

Jason whispered in her ear. "He's gone to a far better place, you know."

"I wasn't crying over him," she admitted, quietly turning her head so that no one else could hear. "I was crying over Ruth."

"Thank you," he said, gently patting her arm, and ridiculously she felt better.

Mourners crowded into the house, feasting and drinking, the sadness of the occasion apparently forgotten.

"Liz is making the most of it," Damian remarked, eyeing Liz, who hadn't budged from Jason's side.

"Perhaps he needs a bit of comfort after what's just happened," Carla said, thinking how unkind Damian had been to his brother.

"Maybe … maybe not." He sighed. "Makes you wonder though, doesn't it?"

She stared at him. "About what?"

"Well, I'm not a great believer in coincidence. I wonder what the odds are of two people accidentally falling down the same flight of stairs and killing themselves in the same week?"

"Pretty remote, I guess."

"Makes you wonder if they were accidents at all – doesn't it?"

"Hannah, you mean?"

He had a mysterious expression on his face. "Actually,

I wasn't thinking abut Hannah."

"What are you getting at, Damian?"

He shrugged. "Just my suspicious mind ticking away. I mean, Liz has always fancied herself as the future wife of Jason or me – preferably Jason, I guess. Finding he'd nipped off and got himself a wife must have come as a bit of a shock. Perhaps it was Liz who gave poor little Ruth a push – or put the idea into Hannah's head. Very susceptible to suggestions is our Hannah."

Carla stared incredulously at Damian. "And what's your theory about your grandad? An accident ... or Hannah ... or Liz? Did she have a reason for getting rid of him, too?"

Damian grinned. "I'm not suggesting Liz is a homicidal maniac – mind you, the sooner Grandad and Hannah depart from this world, the sooner we get our inheritance – Liz included."

She couldn't take any more. With a shake of her head, Carla stalked off into the kitchen for a glass of iced water. All these accusations were making her head ache.

She took her drink, chinking with ice cubes and went into the garden. She should never have come. It wasn't just Damian's family who were weird. It was him as well – perhaps he was the worst of all...

Cold raindrops showered down on her face, refreshing her, washing away the dark oppressive atmosphere of the funeral. But she jumped as she sensed someone standing behind her.

"Are you all right, Carla?"

She swung around to find Jason looking down at her. "Yes ... yes, I'm fine, thank you Jason."

He looked awkward, and shuffled his feet nervously for a moment. "You know, if you want someone to drive you home ... if all this is getting too much, I've got a car. I mean, if Damian is worrying you..."

"Why should I be worried about Damian?" she gasped.

"He's a strange guy ... I feel disloyal saying this but he's done some crazy things, someone ought to have warned you..."

"Warned me about what?"

"He gets jealous – and I mean *really* jealous. Insanely jealous..."

Liz's remark echoed through Carla's head suddenly – without warning ... *you really should have warned your girlfriend about the streak of insanity that runs through this family...*

Defiantly, Carla looked Jason in the eye. "As far as I can see, Damian has had good reason to be jealous. After all, you have stolen his previous girlfriends away from him."

"That's not true," he insisted gently. "It's how Damian sees it, but he's sick, paranoid. It worries me sometimes thinking of what he might do ... what he may already have done..."

"I don't know what you're talking about!" Carla said defensively, but the conversation she had overheard leapt into her head, forcing her to listen...

It wasn't you who killed her, was it, by any chance Damian ... just to hurt me?

The pounding in her head grew worse, like sledge-hammers beating a tune on her brain.

One down, one to go.

"Carla, are you all right?"

"Excuse me." She ran indoors, pushing past the guests to reach the sanctuary of her own room. But Damian was at the bottom of the stairs, with Liz.

"Carla ... what's up?" Damian asked, taking hold of her hands. His were cold, like ice – like death.

"Damian, why are your hands always so cold?" she cried accusingly.

He smiled. "You know what they say, cold hands warm heart."

She looked into his face. The face of a killer? Surely not. If anyone had committed murder it was poor confused Hannah. Not Damian ... not her Damian.

"Have you seen Jason?" Liz asked.

"Yes, in the garden," Carla replied, trying to sound normal.

"Good, see you later."

Liz could have killed Ruth, Carla realized as she watched the girl go eagerly in search of Jason. Jealousy could have driven her to push Ruth down the stairs.

"You're trembling," said Damian, putting his arms around her. "She doesn't scare you, does she?"

"Who?"

He grinned. "Liz ... the mass murderer!"

"Don't be ridiculous, Damian," she said, avoiding his eyes, trying not to remember what Jason had said about Damian. *Someone ought to have warned you about Damian.* Was that the real reason Damian had kept her away from his family, so that no one could warn her about his insane jealousy ... about the crazy things he had done?

Oh, but which crazy things? Pushing an old man down the stairs as a step nearer getting his inheritance? Killing Ruth to make his brother suffer? So who would be next – Hannah?

The sledgehammers in her brain thudded louder and louder, jumbling her thoughts, making her head swim, she felt lightheaded, faint...

"Just think," continued Damian. "If Liz had got the hots for me and not my brother, that could have been you lying there with your neck broken."

"What?" she breathed, as a hot sickly feeling made her reel. What was he saying ... Liz could have killed *her*?

He *was* sick. She stumbled up the stairs.

"Carla – hey Carla! I was only joking ... Carla!"

He caught her as the hot sweating sensation changed to blackness. And a swampy, icy mist enveloped her. The strength left her legs and she fainted.

"Is she coming round?"

"What happened?"

"She fainted."

"Give her some air."

Slowly Carla came to, and found a sea of faces staring down at her. A damp cloth was pressed to her forehead.

"What's happened?" Jason demanded, pushing his way through the crowd of onlookers. There was fear in his eyes as he looked from Carla to Damian, then back to Carla. "Are you OK?"

"Yes," she murmured, struggling to get up. "I just fainted."

"She needs to lie down," he said, scooping her up and carrying her upstairs with Damian and Liz at their heels. He laid her carefully down on the bed. "Do you want me to ring for the doctor?"

"She only fainted, for heaven's sake," muttered Liz. "Come on Jason, I'm sure Damian can take care of her."

"A glass of water then?"

Carla nodded, "And two aspirin, please."

Jason seemed reluctant to leave her alone with his younger brother, and left only because Liz practically dragged him away.

"I could have carried you," said Damian sulkily.

"Does it matter who carried me?"

"Yes."

Her head was beginning to thump again. "Damian, I'm so tired – would you mind going?"

"If that's what you want," he said dejectedly.

"It is."

She watched him go with a mixture of relief and anguish. She cared so much about Damian, but if he was as unbalanced as Jason said, then she was in trouble.

Or danger!

When her bedroom door opened a few moments later, Carla assumed it was someone returning with her aspirin. The sight of Hannah standing there made her sit up in fright.

The old lady looked confused. "I'm looking for Byron, my husband, have you seen him?"

Carla hurriedly took the old lady's hand. Softly she said, "Don't you remember what happened to him, Hannah?"

The old lady's face creased as she struggled to think. And then with a look of utter relief, she exclaimed, "He fell, didn't he! Down the stairs." Her eyes sparkled. "He's dead, isn't he?"

Carla nodded.

"I didn't push him down the stairs, you know," said Hannah brightly. "I wouldn't, that's not nice."

"Of course you wouldn't."

"Even when they tell me to."

Carla stared at the old lady. "Who tells you to?"

"The voices … they tell me to do all sorts of things, but I won't."

"What sort of voices do you hear?" asked Carla, intrigued.

Hannah frowned, the lines down her face deepening as she tried to make sense of it all. "Sometimes the voices are in here," she said, tapping her head. "They talk rubbish and it makes me so angry. But sometimes..." she looked helpless. "The voice just floats around outside my head." She suddenly chuckled. "Maybe I'm going daft."

Carla smiled kindly. "What does *that* voice say?"

"It tells me to push people down the stairs, but I won't!"

Poor Hannah, Carla thought. If the police were ever to question her regarding the two deaths, she would be the obvious suspect. She admitted to hearing voices that told her to push people down the stairs, and two people had fallen to their deaths down the stairs.

They'd lock her up and throw away the key.

Mrs Goldby walked in then with Carla's aspirin. She put the glass and the tablets on her bedside table without a word to Carla. "There you are Hannah, come on downstairs, the guests are leaving, they want to say goodbye to you."

"Leaving so soon?" murmured Hannah. "But they've only just arrived."

Carla took her aspirin and sat on the edge of her bed, thinking. It looked as if Hannah was the guilty one – she followed orders unquestioningly, she was hearing imaginary voices. The chances of two people *accidentally* killing themselves on the stairs was very remote.

Hannah was probably guilty without even knowing it.

Yet, it was strange – the two people who had died were wanted out of the way by some members of this family. In fact just about everyone here had reasons to be rid of their grandfather and Ruth.

With their grandfather dead and gone it was a step nearer to all of their inheritances. And no one, it seemed, wanted poor Ruth. With her out of the way it left the way open for Liz; Mrs Goldby heartily disapproved of the marriage, too; and as for Damian…

Her stomach churned over, she didn't want to think about his reasons – pure hatred of his brother.

Carla rested her head in her hands. No! It had to be Hannah, it had to be.

But what if Hannah *was* innocent?

What if someone was making her a scapegoat for their own crimes?

She needed to talk to the old lady. Find out more about this voice she was hearing. If someone was putting suggestions into her head, so that she took the blame, then maybe Hannah could say whose voice it sounded like. Even revealing the sex of the speaker would narrow it down.

Her mind made up, Carla hurried along to Hannah's room, tapped the door and went in. Then she remembered that the old lady was downstairs saying goodbye to everyone.

She hesitated in the doorway.

If someone was whispering suggestions to Hannah, it probably took place in here, in the old lady's room, where no one else could hear, or observe.

Carla wandered around the room, keeping one eye on the door, looking for a tape recorder or a hidden speaker or something. There was nothing like that, nothing that she could see, not even under the bed.

But there was *something* under the bed – a circular ring type of thing against the skirting board. Intrigued, Carla stretched under the bed and tried to pull it out. It wouldn't budge but the feel of it told Carla it was a piece of hosepipe – sticking through the skirting board from the next room – her room!

Fascinated, Carla went back into her own bedroom,

and found that the hosepipe did indeed lead into her own room. Stapled against the skirting board beneath the edge of the carpet, out of sight.

On hands and knees she followed it. It led through to the next room again. Curiosity mounting, she followed its trail. Again finding that the hosepipe was stapled all around the skirting boards beneath the carpet, quite invisible to the eye. Behind a bed, behind the wardrobe, behind a dressing table...

Where it ended.

And fixed to the end – was a funnel.

Carla stared at it, realization dawning. If someone talked through this end, their voice would travel into Hannah's room.

No wonder the poor old dear thought she was hearing things!

To check her theory, Carla put a radio on next to the funnel, then dashed back to Hannah's bedroom.

She could hear the faint eerie sounds of music the moment she entered the room.

Her heart thudded.

So someone *was* trying to incriminate Hannah for the crimes *they* were committing!

She sank down on to Hannah's bed, listening with a growing sick feeling in her stomach to the voice of a disc jockey telling her all about the number one album in the charts.

Poor Hannah!

She was the perfect scapegoat. She'd told all her family that the voices she hears tell her to push people down the stairs. She'd even told her doctor. So even if she denied doing the actual pushing till she was blue in the face, who would believe a crazy old woman?

Someone in this family was evil. Utterly evil!

But who?

Mrs Goldby, or Liz, or Jason … or Damian?

There was a click.

The disc jockey on the radio was silenced and in its place came a voice that she knew so very well, and her heart leapt into her throat.

"Clever, clever girl…"

Carla shot up, her heart pounding, skin crawling with terror.

The disembodied whisper continued, freezing the blood in her veins, making every hair on her body stand on end.

"So now you know," said the whisper. "Only we can't have you sticking up for crazy old Hannah can we … we can't have you telling everyone about my little trick, can we?"

"Oh God!" Carla breathed, her head spinning. She stumbled towards the door. She had to get downstairs, to the others before it was too late.

"Carla…" breathed the voice. "I can't let you tell, you know that don't you? I'm so sorry…"

She was moving in slow motion, the door seemed a hundred miles away, she reached out…

Suddenly, from the other side came a sound, and then the door burst open and he lunged at her.

There was no time to scream. His hand over her mouth silenced her. He was strong … she had no idea how strong he was, until now.

And he was insane, she saw it in his eyes. Wide and blue and totally crazy.

"Now, how shall we do it?" he murmured callously into her hair as his grip tightened. "Another tragic accident? That's worked exceptionally well so far."

She couldn't scream, couldn't breathe.

"Better break your neck first, before I throw you

downstairs, that certainly did the trick with Grandad and little Ruth."

"Don't … please don't…" she spluttered, writhing and kicking, her heart pounding against her ribcage.

Then somehow his finger was between her teeth and she bit down hard. As hard as she could.

With a cry of pain and rage, he pulled his hand away. Just for a second. But long enough for Carla to scream at the top of her voice.

"Damian!"

Damian bounded up the stairs three at a time, calling out her name. Mrs Goldby and Liz chased up after him. All three converged in the doorway just as Jason's arms twisted around Carla's neck.

"Let her go!" Mrs Goldby shrieked.

For an eternity no one moved.

Carla could feel her eyes bulging, her breath constricted. Blurred faces stared at her. Horrified … terrified.

Then Damian lunged towards them.

Jason moved swiftly, pushing Carla into him, so that they both staggered backwards into Mrs Goldby and Liz gathered in the doorway, scattering them.

"Get out of my way!" Jason screamed, elbowing through them all.

Damian raced after him, tackling him at the top of the stairs. There was a terrific scuffle, then … the horrible sickening sound of someone falling down the stairs.

The sound of bones and stairs coming into violent contact. Thud … thud … thud … from top to bottom.

And then a deadly, heart-stopping silence.

For an eternity, Carla was afraid to look. Afraid to see who had lived and who had died.

The cold sensation of death wrapped itself around her,

touched her heart and sent a deathly chill through her body.

Please, please, not Damian… she breathed. Don't let Damian have fallen…

Slowly, deadly slowly, she dragged her feet on to the balcony. Liz and Mrs Goldby stared down at the scene, their shocked faces frozen with horror.

Carla looked down, over the balcony.

He lay still at the foot of the stairs, his golden blond hair streaked with red. No one had to tell her. She knew.

He was dead. Jason was dead.

She raised her eyes and looked at Damian, standing there, shaking from head to foot, tears in his eyes.

"He overbalanced as we fought, I tried to catch him, but I couldn't."

Mrs Goldby touched Damian's cheek as she slowly descended the stairs. Liz followed her, silently.

Carla ran to Damian and locked herself into his arms.

Safe.

"Was he insane?" Carla asked, as much later she and Damian walked towards her own house at the far side of town.

"Insane, clever – greedy. His prime objective was to get Ruth's money; he made her death look like the actions of a crazy old lady. Killing Grandad was just a bluff – it made Hannah look more guilty and took the impact off Ruth's death … made it look like just another example of Hannah's crazy behaviour.

"I suppose the fact that Hannah really did hear imaginary voices as well as Jason's voice added to her confusion. Her doctor would have assumed it was *all* in her head."

Damian nodded. "Jason created the perfect cover-up.

First Hannah supposedly pushes her husband down the stairs, then she pushes Ruth… If you hadn't screamed – you could have become his third victim!" His arm went protectively around her. "I would really have lost you to him then, wouldn't I?"

Carla stared down at the ground. "Would that have worried you very much?"

He swung her around to face him. His eyes were creased with pain. "Carla, I couldn't bear to lose you – not in that way … not in any way."

She met his gaze – and saw the love shining there, and her heart soared. "Oh Damian, there were times over the last two days when I didn't know what to think… I even wondered if you'd had anything to do with the deaths."

He brushed a dark curl from her eyes. "I can't blame you for that – the way I've acted. That's what having my family around does to me. I knew Ma wouldn't approve, and I guessed Liz would probably try and make you jealous … and I was positive Jason would make a play for you once he set eyes on you. Everything warned me that I was going to lose you – one way or another. That's why I didn't want you to meet them … I was scared of losing you. Though nothing prepared me for what nearly happened … God Carla, I'm sorry I put you in that danger."

His voice trailed away and Carla wrapped her arms around him. "It's over now, Damian – it's over. Your mother and Liz are just going to have to get used to me. And as for Jason – killing me was the only way he'd have taken me away from you … the only way."

X IS FOR EXECUTION

They were both dead, there was no doubt about that. Eyes and mouths open, faces smeared with blood. No emergency service could do anything for them now. It was time to move on, get the job done… But wait. What was that there? Reaching down, in the front of the passenger seat, among the litter of glass shards, lifting out a bulky buff envelope, then holding it up to the light to read the one letter inscription: "X". Hands trembling slightly as the flap ripped open and fingers slid in to find … white grooved tablets and a note. "Dear X. Your share. Enjoy!"

Enjoy…

The party had been going for the best part of an hour by the time Zak showed up. He came into the room, dressed in full biker's leathers, a scarf even, like it was the middle of winter, not a fine July evening. Blocking the doorway, with the host, James, looming behind him, Zak accepted the mixture of catcalls and laughter that greeted his appearance. Then he shrugged and raised one eyebrow comically.

"Anyone for strip poker?" he enquired.

It was a typical Zak entrance. For once, though, he wasn't the last. William and Mary still hadn't showed and nor, most untypically, had Olly.

"Hey, if I'd known, I'd have taken my time," Zak said.

"You always do, Zak," said James, who, at six feet three and in a bright yellow and black spotted Paul

Smith shirt, looked even more giraffe-like than usual. Even his hands had black and yellow marks on them – traces of some chemical or other. Science, chemistry especially, was his major interest.

"So we heard," leered Lee, with characteristic innuendo. His mouth opened in a sort of leer that drew attention to the gap at the centre of his front teeth, their whiteness contrasting with the darkness of his complexion, his black eyes and black curly hair, black T-shirt and Levis. A small silver ring gleamed in his ear.

"You'd be late for your own funeral," added Sam, walking across from Rachel and Dee to join the three boys. She was a tall, bony girl with short, bobbed hair and a ruddy complexion.

"Nah, I'm not going to die," said Zak seriously. "I'll leave that to you guys. I fancy being immortal..." He let his pronouncement hang in the air, raising one eyebrow again.

At that moment, Olly arrived.

"Ol, my man, you are *en retard*," Zak greeted him. "How can this be?"

Olly grinned sheepishly and pushed at his glasses. "I had a flat," he said.

"We thought maybe you'd got trapped in Smiths," said James. It was an old joke. Olly spent a great deal of time in Smiths. Not looking at the books, but indulging his extraordinary appetite for stationery. Olly loved stationery. He had more pens and notepads, the joke ran, than Imelda Marcos had shoes.

"Only you could change a flat tyre and still look like you've just climbed out of a trouser press," James continued. It was true. Olly, as usual, looked perfectly groomed in his pressed shirt and trousers, formal jacket, shiny black speckless shoes, his flat Action Man hair immaculate. He grinned a little more sheepishly.

"I had some overalls in the back of the car," he explained. "Just in case."

"Incredible," Zak declared. "But true."

"What else do you keep in the back of the car?" asked James.

"A few exercise books, maybe," said Zak. "And some pens..."

"We should ask Dee," Lee suggested, with a leer. Olly and Dee had struck up a relationship at a party a couple of weeks back and had since become a couple.

"I heard that, Lee," said Dee, who'd come across to greet Olly. Dark, green-eyed, slim, she was the prettiest girl in the group and knew it. She and Lee clashed frequently.

"Mind your own business," she said, glaring at Lee. His leer just got broader. He knew she didn't like him and he didn't care. They'd had a bit of a fling a year or so before; now they avoided one another as much as possible, which wasn't that difficult as Lee wasn't at school any more, unlike the rest of them. He'd left the previous winter to go into the music business, after answering an ad in the paper for "incredibly good-looking guys with great voices to form an all-male singing group". The new Take That they were going to be – but so far they hadn't had a single hit. That didn't stop Lee being as vain, arrogant and obnoxious as ever, in Dee's opinion. She turned her back on him now and walked back over to Rachel. Olly followed a step or so behind.

"You'd better watch yourself, Lee," James said.

"Huh," said Lee with a shrug. "I don't give a toss what Miss I'm-So-Beautiful thinks. It's a free country, isn't it?"

"So I've heard," said James. Then he and Lee went to get a drink, leaving Zak and Sam together.

"William and Mary're late," said Sam. "I wonder what could have happened to them." She expected Zak to make some wisecrack, but he didn't.

"Yeah," he said, with an unusually reflective air.

"Do you think something could have happened to them?" pressed Sam more urgently.

"Yeah," said Zak again. "They could have turned into butterflies and fluttered away into the sunset. Or been captured by aliens. Or decided to give the party a miss and go fishing. On reflection, though, I'd say they were probably just late."

"I suppose so," Sam agreed. There was a moment's awkward silence, then Sam said, "How's Chris?" Chris was Zak's twin brother. Identical in looks, they were just about as different as could be personality wise. Zak was a clown, always joking, happy-go-lucky about everything, the life and soul of the party; Chris was deadly serious. He never went to parties, never went out at all as far as Sam could gather. He preferred to stay in and study – he was always studying.

"He's, well, Chris," said Zak.

"How about you?" Sam asked. "Are you OK?"

"Hey, I'm fine," said Zak. "Simply raring to go. I can't wait for the fun and games to begin." He frowned. "There are going to be fun and games, aren't there?"

Sam smiled. "You bet," she said.

The party was to celebrate the end of another school year – the penultimate. This time next year they'd all have finished their exams and left for good. The house belonged to an elderly relative of James who'd recently moved in to a nursing home. It was the perfect venue for an overnight party: a big old house out in the country, all on its own, so that they could make as much noise as they liked and not disturb anyone. They could party all night and all the next day too if they wanted. They'd all been looking forward to this for weeks: a chance to let their hair down with people they knew well. A reward for those last weeks of slog at school.

"Hey guys, how about a game?" James suggested after a while. There was a murmur of approval, fuelled, at least in part, by the punch.

"Shouldn't we wait for William and Mary?" queried Rachel, in the sort of sing-song little-girl voice she sometimes adopted, pursing her lips and opening wide her cornflower blue eyes. When she spoke that way it was difficult to know whether she was being serious or ironic.

"We could wait all night," said Dee. "Let's get started. They can always join in when they get here."

"*If* they get here," said Lee darkly.

"They'll get here," said Zak breezily. "Or I'm a Dutchman." He paused for an instant, then, "Let me show you my new clog dance," he added and Sam and Rachel laughed.

"So, hide and seek then?" said James.

James had told them all about the great games of hide and seek he'd played here with his cousins as a child.

"Hide and seek!" scoffed Lee. "We're not eight years old."

"We're not?" said Zak with mock bemusement.

"Lighten up, Lee," said Dee. "I thought boys like you just wanted to have fun, fun, fun." It was a cutting reference to Lee's last single, which hadn't even reached the top fifty. Lee's face tightened with anger, the sardonic leer gone.

"Look here, you..."

"Guys, guys!" James interceded. "This is a party, remember. We're supposed to be enjoying ourselves."

"Yeah, come on," said Sam. "Let's play."

"Well, I'm going to the loo," said Dee, and Lee sniggered. It was a generally-held belief that Dee spent as much time in the loo as Olly spent in Smiths.

"OK, this is the idea," said James, when Dee had gone. "The first person found gets a forfeit and the last person can decide what it should be." The suggestion received unanimous approval.

"Hey, nice one, James," said Zak.

"Well, thanks, Zak," said James. "I'll seek then. How about I give you ten minutes?"

"I'll tell Dee on the way," said Sam.

They soon found that James hadn't been exaggerating when he said the house was a hide-and-seek paradise. At eight years old, the options must have seemed endless; even with their much larger seventeen-year-old frames, the friends found no shortage of hiding places.

Rachel went up higher than the others, mounting two flights of stairs until she came to a gloomy landing. To one side of her was a small door. She reached out and opened it, expecting a cupboard but surprised to discover instead another staircase – a narrow one this time. Climbing it, she found herself in a small, empty attic room. Being short, she could just about stand up straight without touching the ceiling. She reached up and released the catch to open the single sloping window. It swung up and a small gust of breeze invaded the stuffy room. She climbed on to the deep window shelf and put her head out into the fresh evening air, closing her eyes and drawing a deep breath… Then she started thinking.

She was on her own often these days. Even when she was with the others, she felt kind of lonely, isolated. Ever since the split with William: that pig William, dating Mary behind her back, then chucking her altogether when she found out and had the temerity to complain. It had happened nearly a year ago, but it still hurt. Having to see them all the time didn't help any, of course. The worst thing of all had been the way the others just shrugged and accepted the situation, welcomed Mary into the group, said nothing to William at all. He'd got off scot-free and it wasn't right. She, Rachel, had had to bite her tongue and swallow her pride to stay part of the group. Well, she was damned if she was going to let Mary take her friends as well as William. Mind you, she'd done a pretty good job. The others all thought she was wonderful: beautiful, funny, fascinating Mary... Rachel hated her. She hated William too, with his unshakeable self-confidence, his easy charm. It was great that they weren't here – they didn't deserve to be here, laughing, having fun...

She was so caught up in her thoughts that she didn't hear the attic door opening quietly behind her. It was the creaking of the stairs that alerted her to another's presence in the room, but by the time she had ducked and turned, he was already on her. Losing her balance, she fell into the room, crying out in fear and panic...

Firm arms caught and held her.

"Rachel, Rachel." The voice was surprised, amused. She looked up.

"Zak!" she cried. "You scared me to death."

"Hey, I'm sorry," he said. "I didn't know there was anyone in here. I was just going to tell you not to do it."

"Do what?"

"Jump." He raised an eyebrow and grinned.

"I wasn't going to jump, you idiot," Rachel said. "I was just getting some air." Zak released his grip and

Rachel moved away. She sat down on the window seat. Zak sat down next to her.

"Sorry to gatecrash your hiding place," he said.

"There's room for two," she said. "Just."

Zak was OK. If she'd had a choice, she'd rather it had been Lee she was alone with. Surprisingly, Lee was the one who'd been most sympathetic. He didn't like William either – and underneath all that sexist talk Lee was actually quite a warm, sensitive guy. She didn't quite know what to make of Zak, the clown. He was OK, though. He was unattached, too, and so was she – and she was sick of it. "Maybe they'll never find us," she cooed, opening her blue eyes wide.

"Oh, they'll find us," said Zak. He looked about him, then added, "This used to be James's favourite haunt."

"Really?" Rachel said.

"Yeah," said Zak. "Chris used to be best friends with James, you know, when we first started school. He came here a few times. They used to climb out of this window on to the roof as a dare."

Rachel shivered. It was a long way down. "They must've been mad," she said. Then she remembered she was talking to Chris's twin. "No offence," she added. Zak shrugged.

"How come James and Chris aren't friends any more?" Rachel asked.

"Oh, you know," Zak shrugged again. "James discovered chemistry; Chris discovered books."

"He certainly loves books," Rachel agreed.

There was a groan from below, followed by a sort of dirty snigger.

"Lee," said Rachel. "They must have found him." She sighed. "You know, he's been having a tough time recently," she said seriously. "His group's on the verge of making it, but the record company's threatened to drop him if he puts another foot wrong."

"Yeah, what's he done now?" Zak asked.

"Oh, you know Lee..."

"Yeah, I know Lee."

"Well, it's William's fault really," Rachel said, her anger returning. "He started Lee on the drugs. Lee really hates him."

"William?" Zak queried. "William's into drugs?"

"Come on, Zak," Rachel snapped. "Don't kid around all the time. You know William pushes drugs – and Mary. They..."

The door exploded inwards and suddenly the room was full of noise and people.

"Found you!" James shouted.

"Hey, what are you two up to?" Lee enquired with a leer.

"Well, Lee, we were just about to make wild passionate love," said Zak. "But now you lot have finally showed up we can do something interesting." Rachel cuffed him playfully.

"Are we the last to be found?" she asked, hopefully.

James shook his head. "We still haven't found Dee," he said.

"But we've looked everywhere," said Sam. "Where on earth could she be?"

"Search me," said James. "You did tell her what we were doing, didn't you?" he asked.

"Of course I did," said Sam, reddening with indignation.

"She couldn't still be in the loo now, surely," said Olly.

"Want a bet," said Lee.

"OK, everyone, let's go down and look," said James. "Maybe she's waiting for us in the sitting room. Maybe

William and Mary have arrived and she's chatting to them..."

Noisily they clomped down the wooden staircase until they reached the hall. James went over and opened the sitting-room door opposite the bottom of the stairs. He leant in, then a second or two later came out again.

"She's not there," he said. "No William and Mary either," he added with obvious disappointment.

"Let's try the toilet," said Sam and she strode away along the hall towards the back of the house, the others following.

The door to the downstairs toilet was locked.

"Dee!" Sam called. "Come on. We've finished." She knocked on the door. There was no response. She knocked again. "Dee!" she cried.

"Come on, Dee," said Rachel.

"What can she be doing in there?" Zak asked. It was a question that had often been voiced and usually raised a snigger. But not this time.

"Perhaps she's asleep," said Olly.

"What, with all this racket?" said James.

"Maybe she's not well," said Rachel anxiously.

"Are you OK, Dee?" Sam enquired through the closed door. They knocked once more, but still there was no response.

"What are we going to do?" Rachel asked.

"We could break down the door," Lee suggested happily.

"Oh, great, Lee," said James, looking pale.

"Maybe we could force the lock," said Olly. "I've got some tools in the back of the car."

"Well done, Ol," Zak enthused.

Dee's continued silence had put them all on edge now. Something definitely wasn't right, they knew. They knew too that they had to do something. In the end, they decided to prise open the door with a tyre iron supplied by Olly. They managed to insert it into a narrow crack between the door edge and frame and then, together, James and Olly leant on the iron, until, at last, with a loud crack, the door flew open and the two boys fell into the room. There was a second's shocked silence as everyone took in the fact that the room was empty. Then Sam raised a hand and pointed.

"Look," she said, "the window's open." She started to cross the room to investigate, but a voice from behind made her stop in her tracks.

"Hey, well, thanks for the help, guys."

Everyone turned. "Dee!" they cried in unison. Dee was standing in the hallway with her hands on her hips, her normally pale complexion ruddy, her dark hair uncharacteristically messy.

"Dee, where have you been?" said Rachel.

"I was locked in," Dee said. "I was knocking and shouting for ages. In the end I climbed out of the window. But then I couldn't get back in again. Didn't you hear me banging?"

"We were all upstairs," said James.

"I had to climb over a wall and come in round the back," Dee said. She held up one hand. "I've ruined my nails," she moaned. The remark broke the tension and there was a ripple of laughter.

"What happened to the key, then?" James enquired.

"What key?" Dee said. She put both hands out in front of her – surprisingly large, fleshy hands for someone otherwise petite. "There wasn't any key."

"Then how did you manage to lock yourself in?" said Lee sharply.

"Maybe the key fell down a crack in the floorboards,"

Olly suggested, peering down.

"Maybe it's in Dee's bag," quipped Rachel. "Like everything else." Dee always carried with her a long brown handbag that was stuffed full. She pulled a face.

"There wasn't any key, I tell you," she said. "I didn't lock the door."

"The lock must have jammed," James said, trying to restore peace.

It was then that Lee noticed the writing on the mirror. A message, scrawled in what looked like lipstick. Bright red lipstick.

"Hey, Dee, is this supposed to be a joke?" he said. Then he read: "*X is for EXIT STAGE LEFT.*"

Dee frowned. "What are you talking about, Lee?" she said. She stepped into the small room and looked up at the mirror. The ruddiness drained from her face and her cheeks, if anything, were paler than ever.

"I – I – I didn't write that," she said, quietly.

"Come on, Dee," Lee scoffed. "Who did then? Did you have someone else in here with you that we don't know about?"

"Of course not, Lee!" Dee snapped. "But I didn't write that." She smiled tentatively. "This is a joke, right?" she said. "You lot are playing a joke on me." She eyed them all keenly. "OK, which of you jokers was in here and wrote that message?"

"Don't look at me," said Zak. "I don't use lipstick. A little eyeliner now and then..."

"I don't wear lipstick, either," said Rachel.

"Nor me," said Sam.

"It must be you then, Olly," said Rachel.

"It was Dee," said Lee. "Of course it was."

"It *wasn't* me," said Dee shrilly.

"OK, OK," said James. "Let's forget about it. How

about we play another game?"

"Hey, good idea," Zak enthused. "Strip poker anyone?" He turned to move away up the hall. "I'll just go and get my gear on..."

"Yeah, Zak, we got the joke the first time," said Sam, shaking her head.

"I know," said Rachel. "I've got the perfect game." The others looked at her. She opened her eyes wide. "Murder in the dark," she announced hammily. The others laughed.

They chose what James called "the master bedroom" to be the scene of the crime. It was a huge room with a large four-poster bed and offered plenty of scope for extravagant postures. Rachel was to be the detective as the game was her idea. They drew lots to decide who was to be the murderer.

"If Lee gets murdered, I'm nabbing Dee," Rachel whispered to Sam.

"Or vice versa," Sam retorted. They both sniggered.

"Hey, stop that you two," James reprimanded. "Murder's a serious business, you know." He pulled shut the heavy velvet curtains and at once the room grew dim and shadowy. "OK, it's lights out time. Flick the switch, Rachel. Then vamoose, OK, and wait for the scream." Rachel did a mock curtsy, then flicked the light switch. There was a mixture of gasp and giggle as the room suddenly became pitch black.

"Ooo–ooh," moaned a voice spookily and there was more laughter. For some minutes they moved about without speaking, bumping in the dark, the odd titter breaking the silence.

Then there was a scream. A terrible, high-pitched scream. A scream to wake the dead.

The door opened, the light switch clicked … and the room remained dark. A groan went round the room.

"Hey, the light's not working!" Rachel announced.

"What timing," sneered Lee. James and Olly started to tug back the curtains. It was twilight outside now but enough light spilled in to bring dim visibility back to the room.

"Imagine the bulb blowing like that," said Dee, shaking her head in amazement.

"It didn't blow," said Sam quietly. "Look. Someone's taken the bulb."

"Look's like this guy's a pro, Rachel," said Lee.

"Who's dead, anyway?" said Rachel.

"It's Dee," said Sam and she nodded at the bed, where Dee was lying, motionless, carefully arranged to show off her slender, shapely legs.

"Lee did it," said Rachel.

"I wish…" Lee muttered, just loudly enough that Dee would hear.

"Hey, you're supposed to ask us questions," James said.

"What's the point?" Rachel retorted.

James opened his mouth to reply, but was halted by a muffled moan.

It seemed to come from one of the large wardrobes. Frowning, James went across and pulled open the doors.

"Zak!" he said with a hint of reprimand in his voice. Zak was hunched on the wardrobe floor with his head bowed.

"We've got a corpse already, Zak," said Sam.

"Maybe it's a serial killer," said Rachel.

Zak lifted his head. "Aaah," he moaned again.

"Come on, Zak," Sam chided. "You're ruining Dee's big moment."

"Yeah, stop fooling, Zak," James added. Zak coughed and then rubbed his neck gently with both hands. There was a look of bewilderment in his eyes.

"Someone tried to strangle me," he said hoarsely. The others groaned.

"Zak! Please!" cried James, throwing his arms out in front of him.

"I'm telling the truth," said Zak. "Really." Again the others groaned – except for Sam. She alone responded sympathetically to the unusual earnestness of Zak's tone. She crouched down and put her hand on his shoulder.

"Zak," she said. "Are you OK?" Then, less sympathetically, "If you're kidding me, I'll kill you."

"I'm not kidding," Zak grumbled.

Sam opened her mouth to speak ... then shut it again. Her eyes were gazing at a place high on the wardrobe wall. Her pink cheeks had gone pale.

"Oh," she said quietly and something in the icy seriousness of her voice drew the others' attention at once. They came and stared at what she was staring at. A message on the wall, written smudgily in red lipstick and in the same style as the one on the mirror in the bathroom. The words were different though, threatening. Reading them, Sam shivered.

"*X is for EXTINCT. You soon will be.*"

The party was split. There was a strong feeling, voiced most zealously by Dee, that Zak had stage-managed the whole thing and was playing one of his "idiotic" jokes on them all. Sam wasn't so sure. She said she believed Zak. She agreed, though, that someone was playing a joke and that it wasn't very funny. In the end, they decided to decamp downstairs – get some refreshment, lighten the mood. Maybe William and Mary would arrive; it was about time.

"You've really upset Dee," Sam said to Zak, as they trudged slowly down the long staircase.

"I was telling the truth," Zak said, all innocence.

"It would have to be someone with gorilla mitts to get round your neck," Lee remarked sharply.

"What, like Dee you mean?" said Rachel.

A couple of steps below them, Dee stopped and turned, her pale face flushed. "Don't be stupid, Rachel!" she said, without amusement.

"It was only a joke," Rachel said. "Anyway, you were dead, right?"

"Let's just drop it," said Zak. "If some crazy gorilla wants to kill me, well, it's a free country..." The others groaned.

James reached the bottom of the stairs first and led the way across the hall to the sitting room.

"The drinks are on me," he announced in a corny American accent. He walked over to the table where the bowl of punch stood. But when he reached it, he stopped suddenly and jumped back, almost knocking Sam over.

"Aah!" he exclaimed.

"Careful, James!" Sam cried.

"What on earth is it?" Rachel asked. She stepped past James to the table. Her body stiffened and her face screwed up in disgust. "Ugh!" she said. "Gross." Tentatively, the others moved forward beside her.

Lying in the punch bowl, stretched out, its small eyes staring, its sharp teeth bared, its long, thin tail curled behind it, was a dead rat. Dee started to retch and ran from the room. There was a moment of appalled silence. Then Zak spoke. "Now," he said, "that's what I call getting rat-arsed." No one laughed. They were watching apprehensively as Rachel picked up the piece of paper propped against the bowl. She opened it out and read the message written there in the familiar, red lipstick.

"*X is for ECSTASY. Hope you're happy now.*"

Without a word, James turned at once and grabbed Zak by the shirt front. "I'm going to kill you, Zak!" he hissed. "You're a prat and you're ruining everything." Zak shrank back, bemused. He held up his hands in protest.

"Hey, I'm a victim, remember," he said. Sam stepped forward and put her hand on James's arm.

"Look, let's just calm down," she said. James let go of Zak and Sam stepped back so that her eyes could take in everyone in the room. "And whoever's doing this," she went on, "the joke's over, OK?" No one said anything.

"Now, how about we go for a walk?" Sam suggested. "Get some fresh air."

"Yeah, good idea," Rachel agreed. "How about it, guys?"

"I'd better check that Dee's OK," said Olly, meekly.

"I fancy a game of pool," said Lee. He turned to James. "Didn't you say there was a table here someplace?"

"Across the hall," James said.

"You want to play?" Lee asked.

James shook his head.

"Zak?" said Lee.

Zak shrugged. "OK," he said.

James said he'd stay where he was, try and chill out a bit. When Dee returned, she decided she'd stay too and keep him company. Olly could go for a walk with the girls, she said.

"You can take my coat, if you like," she told Rachel, whose short black satin dress was hardly the most suitable of outfits for a late-night stroll.

"Thanks," said Rachel. Then she, Sam and Olly departed.

It was cool in the open air. The sky was dark and cloudy, the moonlight thin. They decided to stick to the road where at least they could be sure of what they were walking on and wouldn't get lost. The talk was restricted to the progress they were making and no mention was made of the evening's traumatic events. A bat swooped out of the gloom and made them jump. The girls shrieked, then laughed, which seemed to release the tension that had built, so that there was a new lightness to their step as they approached the end of the lane.

"Shall we go back now?" said Sam, when they'd reached the main road.

"OK," said Olly. Rachel walked on a few yards further. Suddenly she stopped and cried out.

"What is it?" said Sam. "Another bat?"

"No," said Rachel. "Look!" She pointed a shaky finger at a large tree beside the road about fifty metres away. "There's something there. A car."

"A car?" queried Sam.

"Yes," said Rachel, her voice trembling a little now. "I'm sure of it. There's a white car."

There was a chilly apprehension in her voice that immediately found its mark in the others. The same unspoken thought struck each of them: *William drove a white car. William and Mary hadn't showed up*. They moved quickly through the gloom towards the tree.

It *was* a white car. It *was* William's car and it was a total wreck – the whole front crushed and twisted by the impact with the huge tree. But worse, much worse, it was obvious at once that the two people inside the car, William and Mary, were both dead. Sam fell against Olly, tears in her eyes, while Rachel leaned in and touched the cold faces – William's almost entirely obscured behind a red mask of dried blood – feeling vainly for some sign of a pulse...

Pulling her head out of the car again, Rachel glanced towards the rear of the wrecked vehicle and gasped. There was a message lipsticked across the back window ... and this time there was no mistaking its meaning or the malice of its intent. *X is for EXECUTION*, it read.

"Oh, my God," said Sam, feeling goosepimples forming on the skin of her arms inside her thick cardigan. "This is just too awful, too awful." She looked down and, through misty eyes, saw a thin buff envelope on the ground beneath the car. In a daze, she bent forward and picked it up. She glanced at the envelope, then, frowning, slid her fingers inside, removing a piece of paper. She read it, then grimaced.

"This letter," she said, rising. "It's addressed to X." She handed the paper to Rachel.

"Dear X. Your share. Enjoy!" Rachel read aloud. Then she frowned. "What does it mean? Who's doing this?" she said.

"I don't know," said Sam. "But I think it's got something to do with drugs."

"X is for ecstasy," Olly murmured, repeating the message they'd found by the punch bowl.

"Yes," said Sam grimly. "We'd better get back and call the police."

"And warn the others," said Rachel.

They ran through the darkness, Rachel and Olly ahead, Sam at the rear, thinking, worrying. There was a murderer on the loose and, she was pretty well sure, it was one of them. The messages were too personal, too clearly linked to the note they'd just found for it to have been some outsider. No, it was one of them. But who? It just seemed absurd that one of them could be a murderer. They were all friends, weren't they? They had their differences, OK, but murder? If this were all about drugs then Lee had to be the main suspect. His life was pretty desperate at the moment and everyone knew he was into drugs… But Lee, a murderer? Her gaze fell on the two figures ahead of her. Olly had been the last to arrive at the party and he *had* been uncharacteristically late… But, well, what motive could *he* possibly have – and anyway she couldn't recall ever having heard Olly raise his voice, never mind do something violent. And Rachel? Well, Rachel certainly hated William and Mary. She made no bones about that and Sam hadn't seen her shed any tears yet… The notes, too – Sam could imagine Rachel writing those. Murder, though, that was something else…

By the time they reached the house, they were all three quite breathless. They stood for an instant outside the front door in the porchlight.

"Has anyone got a tissue?" Sam said. Her nose was streaming from her tears and the running. The others felt in their pockets.

"Sorry," said Olly.

"I've got one," said Rachel. She pulled her hand out of the pocket of Dee's coat and a wad of tissues appeared. She passed them to Sam and, as she did so, something dropped from among them and clattered on to the concrete. She bent down and picked it up. Then straightened slowly – her eyes fixed on the object in her hand: it was a lipstick. But the way she was gazing at it, it could have been a gun. She knew this lipstick – the distinctively ornate maroon casing, the florid brand letters. She knew only one person who used this particular lipstick.

"It's Mary's," she said, sombrely. Gently, she removed the top and screwed out the lipstick. The colour was bright red.

"Oh no," said Sam.

"Dee?" said Olly incredulously. "It was in Dee's pocket?"

Dee! Sam thought, her mind whirring again. All that business with the locked toilet and the lost key that had never been satisfactorily explained. All that time she'd had on her own. And, of course ... her hands! Those big hands. Zak *had* been telling the truth. But *why* would Dee try to strangle Zak? Why would she want to kill William and Mary?

"Come on!" cried Rachel. "We've got to find Dee. Quickly."

As it turned out, the task was an easy one. Dee was still in the sitting room – and Lee, of all people, was with her.

"Oh, hi guys, Dee and I were just getting a few things sorted," Lee said, casually. Then he saw the serious expressions on the faces of the three new arrivals. "Hey, what's up now?" he said.

Rachel thrust her open hand at Dee. "This," she said.

"It's a lipstick," said Dee, bemused.

"It's Mary's lipstick," Rachel said.

"Yes," said Dee. "So?"

"William and Mary are dead," Sam said, her voice shaking.

"Dead?" queried Lee.

"Yeah. William's car's out there, wrapped around a tree," Rachel said.

"With another message," said Sam.

"Someone murdered them," Rachel added. Her eyes found Dee's. "We found Mary's lipstick in your pocket, Dee. It's the one that's been used for all these sick messages."

Suddenly Dee realized that she was being accused. Her green eyes widened in horror. "I don't know anything about the lipstick," she said. "This is nothing to do with me. You can't believe I'd do anything like that." She started to sob.

"We'd better phone the police," said Rachel.

Sam glanced about her. "Does anyone know where the phone is?" she said.

"For all I know this crummy place hasn't even got one," said Lee.

"Let's ask James," said Rachel.

"Where *is* James?" Sam asked. Lee shrugged.

"H-he's gone off somewhere – with Z-Zak," Dee stuttered.

"They've probably gone to score some of James's homemade E," Lee said with dark amusement.

"James makes Ecstasy?" Sam said dumbfounded.

"Yeah," said Lee. "Of course. What do you think he does with all that chemical stuff? Make salt?"

"*X is for Ecstasy*," Sam said quietly. She looked at Rachel and read the same message in the other girl's eyes: X was James.

"We've got to find him," Rachel said urgently. She turned to Dee. "Have you got any idea where they went?" Dee shook her head.

"There's something else you should know, though," she said unhappily. "When James and I were alone? When you went out for your walk? He really laid into Zak – went on and on about how much he hates him. He said it was all Zak's fault that he and Chris aren't friends any more. He said – he said…" Her words tailed off into renewed sobbing. Olly put his arms round her.

"Come on!" said Sam. "We've got to get searching. Lee, Olly."

"I'll find the phone," said Rachel.

"Right," said Lee.

Sam was already halfway to the door now and Lee and Olly moved quickly to join her. They were just about to go out into the hallway when Rachel's voice stopped them.

"Wait!" she called. "I think I know where they are."

They climbed the staircase with almost frenzied haste, praying that Rachel's hunch was right; praying too that nothing awful had happened… Sam was still half hoping that there could be some other explanation for all this – that James wasn't to blame… Yet it was a forlorn hope, she knew, because the evidence was all stacked against him. It had been James who had led the games, told them where to go; it would have been easy for him to write those messages… He, alone, knew the geography of the house…

They reached the top of the house at last and, in a moment, were through the small door and climbing the staircase to the attic room. Lee led the way.

"Zak! James!" he shouted. He stepped into the room.

"Don't come any further, Lee," an icy voice threatened. "No one come any further." The others joined Lee now and saw what he was seeing: Zak crouching on the window shelf, leaning against the slightly open window. Trapped in the narrow gap was James's head, his hands grasping the sill, a look of terror on his face.

"Zak!" cried Sam.

"He's trying to kill me," said James.

Lee took a step forward.

"Don't!" Zak hissed. "Or I'll let him drop." Lee stayed where he was.

"Come on, Zak," he said. "This is a joke, right? Zak?"

"The police will take care of it, Zak," Sam said. "Come on, let him up. Please, Zak." Zak made no response to her plea, in fact he made no acknowledgement that he'd heard her at all. It was James who spoke. His hoarse, squeezed voice was on the verge of hysteria.

"It's not Zak," he wheezed. "It's Chris!"

The news took an instant or two to sink in. Then: "Chris," Sam said softly. "You're Chris." Suddenly, it seemed obvious.

"But why are you doing this?" Lee queried. "Why do you want to kill James?"

Chris had dropped his Zak act now. His face was stony. "Because James made the drugs that are killing my brother," he said.

"Zak's dying?" Olly said.

"He's in hospital, in a coma. He may never come round. And it's James's fault." Chris glanced down at his one-time friend with a look of deep loathing. "He and William and Mary decided they weren't making enough money dealing drugs so they decided to manufacture their own. Only they didn't bother too much about what they put in. Aspirin, rat poison, whatever..."

"Oh no," said Sam.

"Oh yes," said Chris, bitterly.

"So that's why you killed William and Mary..." Sam let the suggestion hang, playing for time, trying to keep him talking. Chris shook his head.

"No," he said. "I didn't kill them. I would have. But they were dead already. William was probably tripping and lost control of the car..." He smiled grimly.

"There's a certain poetic justice about that, I suppose. I appreciated the irony; that's why I wrote the message across the back window with Mary's lipstick… Then all I had to do was find X. But when Olly arrived after me I thought my chance was gone. I thought he'd've seen the car. But obviously he didn't."

"I came the other way," Olly said, glumly.

"Yes," said Chris. "That was a real stroke of luck." He spoke steadily, without showing any sign of strain from the exertion of holding the window down. James had ceased to struggle.

"So then you wrote those messages," said Rachel.

"Yeah. I had to flush X out," said Chris. "I thought eventually someone would betray themselves."

"It was you who locked Dee in the toilet, right?" said Sam.

"Yeah," Chris said. "I took the key when I first arrived. Then, when you were all upstairs, I locked Dee in, put the rat in the punch bowl." He smiled coldly. "Nice touch that, don't you think? Then I wrote the messages."

"So no one tried to strangle you in the wardrobe," Sam probed. James looked like he was losing consciousness. If the police didn't arrive soon then they'd have to do something…

"No," said Chris. "I just wanted to get your attention so that you'd see the message and then I'd be in the perfect position to watch everyone's reaction."

"Clever," said Lee admiringly. "Real cool."

"It had to be done," said Chris, matter-of-factly. "Just like this has to be done…" He started to straighten, releasing the window. Then he leant towards James, arms out, preparing to push…

"No!" Sam shouted. Lee leapt forward with Olly a

step behind him… They'd never have made it in time, though, if, Chris hadn't hesitated suddenly and then drawn back, allowing Lee to barge past him and grab hold of James's hands just as they were slipping from the sill… Then, together, he and Olly pulled James in. Carefully they put him down on the floor. When they turned again to Chris, there was a strange, tranquil smile on his face.

For a moment or two the only sound in the room was the noise of James, gasping for air. Then the wail of sirens intruded. Loud footsteps clacked up the stairs. Rachel appeared, pink-cheeked and panting.

"That's not Zak, that's Chris," she said breathlessly, waving an arm. When no one reacted, she frowned and turned to Chris. "There was a phone call," she said. "Zak's out of the coma. He's going to be OK."

The smile on Chris's face widened slightly. "I know," he said. "He already told me. In here." He tapped his head. "We're twins, remember." He raised one eyebrow and, in a voice so exactly like Zak's and so inappropriately full of amusement that it sent a deep chill through the room, he said,

"X is for excellent ending, wouldn't you say?"

COLONEL MUSTARD IN THE LIBRARY

The weather was terrible the night we found the old "Cluedo" set. Twelve of us, year-elevens from Clappertown Secondary School doing GCSE geography, were on a field trip to the Lake District. We were staying in this Youth Hostel, a big, old and decrepit house. Now, lots of people love the Lake District. I don't. I *hate* it: it's a lot of wet and a lot of steep – things to fall in and things to fall off. And, come to think of it, I hate geography too. What possessed me to do it for GCSE?

My name, by the way, is Laura Lomas. Everyone calls me Lottie. Well, let them. Four of us on the trip stuck together most of the time – Jason Stanley and Kirsty Walters who *always* clung to each other: Ben Robinson, who tried to cling to me though I kept him at arm's length. The trouble was, I still fancied Jason a bit: we'd gone around together for quite a while before he dumped me for Kirsty. Yet I still stayed in a foursome that he was also in. It must be my forgiving nature.

Anyway, one thing united us. We *hated* Mr Mustoe. He was head of geography and the teacher in charge of the field trip. Teacher? He couldn't have trained at a college: it must have been Prison Warders' School or the Army Corps of Screaming. And after a day out in the rain, with all the aforesaid falling in and falling off, with Mustoe shouting at us like it was an assault course – as if we had to attain some Grail only he could see – we came back in the evening to the hostel (I *have* to say this) ready to *kill*.

And once in the hostel? Well, after showers and a hot meal which should have cheered us up a bit, we had an evening to while away. Mustoe wouldn't let us go down into the town. Mrs Mellow, his side-kick, would have done, but Mustoe ruled. So what delights did the hostel have to offer? A TV in the lounge (no Sky), a few old and dog-eared books in the tatty room dignified with the name of library, a dingy games room where the pool table was broken. We all sat round the TV for a while, arguing about channels – then the four of us got bored and left the rest to it.

The games room had little to offer. No pool. Jason and Ben wanted to play darts: Kirsty and I didn't and we certainly weren't going to watch and keep the score. So I sorted through the pile of battered old boxes of board games – and found "Cluedo".

I remembered "Cluedo". When I was little and the family was all together we often – Mum, Dad, little brother Baz and me – got real fun out of it. I remembered the last time I'd played. I was eleven: it was the last night our family all lived under one roof. We'd all laughed – for the final time. "Colonel Mustard, in the library, with the candlestick." I'd never forget it. Or that Mum's and Dad's laughter was forced and they didn't ever look at each other and next day Mum went away to join this other man and never came back and we stayed with Dad and cried every night for a year because she didn't seem to want to see us again.

But that was years ago now.

"Let's play!" I shouted. The others didn't say no.

So we played. "Cluedo" isn't that hard a game and we soon remembered it. So time after time we played through it and sampled the possibilities offered by this many-roomed house, with the odd characters doing poor old Dr Black in with simple weapons.

Weird. It kept on coming out that the one who was Dr Black's slayer was Colonel Mustard. Colonel Mustard, in the study, with the gun. Colonel Mustard, in the ballroom, with the lead piping. Colonel Mustard, Colonel Mustard…

After six times in succession, Ben spoke. "This is ridiculous. Are we being told something?"

We looked at each other. Well, were we?

"Of course not," said Kirsty. "This is coincidence."

"I don't know so much," said Jason. "Mustard, Mustoe, it makes you think."

"You'd think by now this evening Dr Black would have cottoned on that this man had got it in for him. Why doesn't the victim rise up and clobber Colonel Mustard?" said Ben.

"If it was Mustoe, not Mustard, he'd deserve it. We're all Mustoe's victims," said Kirsty feelingly.

"What do you reckon, then?" said Jason. "The rope in the kitchen?"

Nobody laughed. There was sudden tension in the air.

"Mustoe goes too far," said Jason. "You know he had my brother expelled from school? Just before he took his A-levels. Our Jack wanted to get to university. He's on the dole now."

"My elder sister came on one of these field trips two years ago," said Kirsty. "She fell off a rock: broke her leg in three places. She still doesn't walk properly. It was Mustoe's fault – not taking enough care. But nothing happened to him because of it."

"Why did you come, then?" I asked – a bit rudely, perhaps.

"Because Jason did," she replied, snuggling up to him. I could have hit them both. "Besides," she went on, "I had to show it wouldn't happen twice."

"He had a big fight with my dad one parents' evening," said Ben. "He told him I was just a scruffy layabout, and my dad nearly duffed him up. The Head had to separate them. I have to ask my mum to come on her own to parents' evenings now."

"What about you, Lottie?" said Kirsty.

"Only the usual," I replied. "He's put me in detention a couple of times when I didn't do anything. Once he lost my homework, swore blind I'd never handed it in and made me do a double lot. Just what you'd expect from an obnoxious twerp like him."

"That's not much," said Jason scornfully.

"I know," I said. "Neither's Ben's. But what he did to you and Kirsty – well, they're a bit different, aren't they? Don't you think he deserves something back?"

For a second or so, Jason clenched his fists until they were white round the knuckles and his lips went very tight. Then he relaxed.

"If only..." he said.

I couldn't tell if his anger was at me or Mustoe.

"Let's play some more," I said. "It can't come out Colonel Mustard seven times in a row. It'll be Professor Plum who disposes of Dr Black next and we can forget all about it."

We played. The wind sighed round the old house and raindrops beat on the window.

It was Colonel Mustard, in the library, with the candlestick.

Mustoe might have grounded us, but he'd made sure that didn't apply to him. He'd walked out of the hostel after dinner. Mrs Mellow, we noticed, didn't go with him. She stayed with the warden, his wife and their dog and I should imagine their evening was a powerhouse of fun.

So where did Mustoe go? Obvious. Down the town and into the pubs. We could tell that easily enough when he came back.

There were twelve in the party altogether: the six girls slept in bunk beds in the front dormitory. The window looked out on to the front garden and the long sloping drive with trees either side and the lights of the town below. Beyond were the level dark waters of the lake. It was well past midnight when we heard a slurred voice outside and footsteps coming up the drive.

I slept in the top bed: Kirsty was underneath. I swung myself down, making her say sleepily, "What are you doing, Lottie?" I put the flip-flops on I prefer to slippers when I'm in places like this, flung a dressing gown over my shoulders and dashed to the window. I looked out.

"This you must see," I said.

At once, all the rest were with me, staring at the scene below.

The rain had stopped. Mustoe, in boots and cagoule, plodded upwards, swaying slightly and finding it difficult to stay in a straight line. He was singing – or trying to: some traditional Cumberland ditty he'd no doubt picked up in the pub.

Kirsty laughed delightedly.

"If he hasn't got a key, there's going to be a big row now."

He hadn't and there was.

Huge reverberations sounded through the house as Mustoe pounded on the front door. Eventually it was opened. There were angry shouts: we couldn't hear the words but the sense was plain enough. The warden was furious that Mustoe had knocked him up hours after locking-up time: Mustoe was outraged because he was teacher in charge and without him who would pay the warden's wages? So why should he be slagged off like this? Eventually things quietened down: the heavy door was closed and clumping footsteps came up the stairs. There was the sound of a flushing loo, then all was silent.

The hostel was soon full of soundly sleeping people. Some of us heard strange noises in the night. We presumed they were part of our dreams, turned over and went on sleeping.

We were woken by Mrs Mellow. "Come on, girls," she said. "It's a lovely day today and we've a lot to get through."

She was right. The sun shone, the lake gleamed: I could almost bring myself to like the place.

We were first down to breakfast. The boys shambled in some minutes later, bleary-eyed.

"Mustoe must have had a skinful last night," said Ben. "He's fast asleep still. Mrs Mellow had to get us up."

Mrs Mellow wasn't there either. She and the warden were upstairs. When they appeared in the dining room they looked puzzled.

"Perhaps he went for an early morning walk," she was saying.

"Impossible," said the warden. "The front door's still bolted the way I left it last night."

Mrs Mellow called out to us all. "Has anyone seen Mr Mustoe?"

No one had.

"Would you leave your breakfasts and help me look, please?"

Grumbling and leaving our plates of sausage, bacon and baked beans to congeal, we all shambled off looking into different rooms. It was Kathy who first went to the library.

Kathy. Now she's a tough character. As she stood at the open library door and I traipsed along the corridor, she said in her normal voice, "Lottie, come here."

I joined her, looked through the door and then called the rest.

Mr Mustoe lay sprawled, face down, on the floor. It looked as though he had been hit hard on the back of the head with a heavy object. Blood seeped from where his skull was smashed in.

Mr Mustoe, in the library, with the candlestick.

The warden dashed off to the phone and the police cars were there in ten minutes. But before they came – and after all those who wanted to scream, throw up (quite a few of them) or cry (not many of those) had dashed out and during the transfixed half minute before Mrs Mellow shoved the rest out and closed the door – I had a quick look round. Now I reckon I'm going to join the CID when I leave school because I'd be a pretty good detective. What must have happened looked clear enough to me. Mustoe was wearing a red tracksuit top and blue bottoms. Though he'd plainly been hit by something heavy, there was no weapon in sight. The sash window looking out over the drive and garden was open. The lowest pane was smashed – from outside, because there was broken glass all over the floor. There was mud on the sill and on the floor between Mustoe's body and the window, but no disorder as there would be if there had been a struggle.

And that was all I had time to suss out (I believe "suss out" is something we detectives say) before Mrs Mellow seized me by the shoulder and hustled me away, saying, "Laura, I can't possibly let you look at that sort of thing."

The blood had drained from her face: she was obviously very shaken. She turned to us all, standing dumbly in the corridor.

"Everybody in the dormitories, please. The police are coming and they'll want to talk to you all. Go there and wait."

So we went upstairs and sat on our beds, as shaken as Mrs Mellow was.

Nobody spoke for a while. Suddenly, Kirsty burst out crying.

"It was the 'Cluedo'. We shouldn't have played the 'Cluedo'."

"What's that got to do with it?" I demanded.

"It kept coming out Colonel Mustard," she wailed. "Ben asked if it was a message to us and it was."

Manjit was interested in this at once.

"Tell me," she said.

So we told about last night's amazing sequence.

"Oh, no," Manjit said confidently. "Mr Mustoe wasn't killed *because* it kept coming up Colonel Mustard. It was more a warning that he would die that night. With such an omen, nothing could stop it. It was the hand of fate showing itself, not your fault at all."

Manjit takes notice of things like this.

Kirsty cheered up at once.

"What we've got to think about," said Kathy, sitting on a top bunk in the corner, "is who had cause to kill him. The police will be looking for motives first."

There was silence. Then Kirsty said, "Oh, dear. What did Ben say last night? About Mustoe and his dad having a fight?"

I was getting really fed up with Kirsty. First of all she pinched Jason off me and then she was wimpish just now about the "Cluedo".

"What's that got to do with it?" I said. "Jason's still sore about Mustoe and his brother, and your sister's still limping."

"Jason wouldn't do a thing like that," Kirsty said.

"Nor would Ben, even if he is a creep," I answered. "That leaves you. I thought it was strange that you came on the trip after what happened to your sister."

Everyone looked at Kirsty with new interest, not unmixed – I was disgusted to see – with admiration. But that quickly disappeared when she started crying again.

"Anyway," I said, "I don't know why you're all getting worked up. Whoever killed Mustoe had to come in from outside."

That remark seemed to drop right through a hole in the floor, because Jessie suddenly shouted, "They're here."

She was looking out of the window at the ring of cars on the drive outside, blue lights flashing. Two men in civilian clothes were walking up to the front door, with five uniformed policemen and a WPC behind them.

"They'll be more interested in whether we heard any strange sounds last night than what we had against Mustoe," I said.

"Well, I heard nothing," said Kathy. "I slept like a log. I always do."

"Now you mention it," said Jessie, "I woke up in the middle of the night and thought I heard a noise like breaking glass."

"That's funny. So did I," said Manjit. "Only I thought it was part of my dream."

"There you are," I said. "The library window was smashed."

Jessie gasped and put her hand to her mouth.

"I heard the murderer," she gasped.

Just then, Nerys came in. She was still a bit green about the gills, having been the first to rush off and throw up. But she was more composed now and had some news.

"The police have set themselves up in the lounge," she said. "There's an inspector who's quite old and a sergeant who's really rather dishy. And Mrs Mellow says they're going to see us one by one, in reverse alphabetical order of surname."

That meant Kirsty would be first.

"Don't forget to tell them about your sister," I said.

"I'll do no such thing," she replied, with a nasty edge to her voice. "But I *will* ask them to find out how you knew the murderer came in from outside."

That Kirsty, she doesn't miss much. She's not as daft as she looks.

Actually Kathy and I had both been right. The police did want to know what we thought about Mr Mustoe as well as what noises we heard that night.

Nerys had been right as well. The inspector looked quite old, with a grizzled, weatherbeaten face and eyes which looked right through you. He had a lovely rich Lakeland accent. The sergeant was young, dark-haired and – well, yes, he was fairly good-looking. His voice showed he came from Liverpool.

The first questions all concerned my feelings about Mr Mustoe. Well, what could I say? I didn't like him, thought he was a rotten teacher – but did that warrant his murder?

What about noises in the night? Breaking glass? No. Running water and flushing loo? Yes. What time? 2.30. I know because it was me: I'd got up and gone to the girls' washroom. No, I hadn't seen or heard anything suspicious.

This was dead easy, I was thinking. But then came the nasty one.

"I'm puzzled, Miss Lomas," said the inspector. "One of your friends has told us something very interesting. You seem to have very firm ideas about how this murder was carried out. How can that be?"

So Kirsty had meant what she said. Right, Kirsty, we'll see what we can do to make you regret that.

For the moment, though, I just told the inspector all the things I'd thought when I first looked in the library.

"I see," he said. "Very interesting. And correct me if I'm wrong, but some of you girls don't seem entirely surprised at what's happened. Now why might that be?"

There was only one thing he could be getting at here.

"Because of the 'Cluedo'," I said.

"Ah, yes, we've heard about this famous game of 'Cluedo'. Tell us more."

So I did and they listened.

"It was playing 'Cluedo' when I was a little lad made me want to be a detective," the inspector said when I'd finished. He turned to the sergeant. "How about you?"

"*Starsky and Hutch*, sir," the sergeant replied. Then he looked at me keenly. "Someone manipulated the game so it kept coming out like that. Isn't that true?"

"It's only a board game," I said. "I don't see how you could cheat. It was just that it seemed someone was giving us a message and that's all we could think of when we found Mr Mustoe was dead."

"How did the last game end?" said the Inspector.

"Colonel Mustard, in the library, with the candlestick," I replied.

"Well, apart from the fact that Colonel Mustard's supposed to be the murderer, that's two been got right. What about the weapon? On your present form, that should be an easy one."

OK, Mr Inspector, what about this?

"Well, I suppose you're going to find a bloodstained candlestick in the garden where the murderer threw it as he was running away."

Just then, a policeman came through the door.

"Excuse me, sir," he said. "We've found something."

The inspector rose and followed the uniformed constable out of the lounge. The sergeant sat watching me, saying nothing. The silence was awful.

When, two minutes later, the inspector returned he was carrying an object in a polythene bag.

"Tell me what this is," he said.

That was easy. "A big silver candlestick," I replied.

"Oh, I doubt if it's silver. More likely base metal with a thin silver plating. The warden tells me he put it on the mantelpiece in the library because it's too hideous to have in his own rooms. Where do you think we found it?"

"In the garden?"

"Correct. Guess what was all over the base."

"Blood?"

"I really think it might be best if I handed the case over to you," the inspector said wearily.

Now the sergeant spoke. He wasn't weary, nor was he friendly. "You know too much about this and I'm going to find out why."

"I told you," I said. "It started with the game of 'Cluedo'."

"Don't give me that rubbish," he snapped. "It's impossible that the game should come out the same way seven times in a row. The odds must be as big as me winning the Lottery."

"No, they're not. Every time we play it's a fifty-fifty chance. It'll either come out that way or it won't. So it's no big deal."

"I don't want a maths lecture," said the sergeant.

"Manjit said it was the hand of fate showing itself."

"I don't want a philosophy lecture either."

The constable entered again. He held a small piece of paper which had been smoothed out after being scrunched up in a ball. The inspector took it, read the words which must have been written on it, then handed it to the sergeant. He too read it, then nodded to the constable, who left at once. Then he fixed me with an intimidating stare.

"You think you're clever, don't you," he said.

"Look, what is this?"

"What did you *really* think of Mustoe?"

"I've told you."

"No more?"

"No." I was pretty angry by now. "Why go on at me? This must have been done by someone outside."

"Why do you say that?"

"I've told you already. Broken window, glass on the floor, mud on the sill, weapon in the garden."

"We *are* the detective, aren't we? So *why* was Mr Mustoe in the library? That should be an easy one."

"He heard the intruder. His room's quite near the library so he went to investigate."

"You don't think he went to meet somebody there?"

"Who? Why should he?"

The Sergeant held the piece of paper up. Round, rather childish writing, done in pencil.

Take me back. I am waiting in the library. Cleo.
"Who's Cleo?" he said.
"How should I know?" I cried.
"Think hard."
"*I don't know any Cleo.*"
"We'll find out if you do," said the sergeant. "And we'll find out if anyone else does."
I was really angry now. I didn't care what I said.
"If you think Cleo did it and had an accomplice inside, why didn't the accomplice leave the window open for her instead of making her break it? And how did Cleo get the note to Mustoe? How do you know the note's got anything to do with this? It might have been a bit of rubbish on the floor for days that he picked up and meant to put in a litter bin. It might not mean this library at all. It might be the school library or the town library."
I finished, quite out of breath. The two looked at each other. I think deep down they really thought I *would* make quite a good detective. That must be why they always seemed to confide in me.
"My, we have got all the answers, haven't we?" said the sergeant.

They let me go soon after that. Though they said they'd want to see me again.
All that day police combed the hostel and the grounds for evidence. Samples were picked up and taken away. No doubt in the town police were going from house to house and no doubt scores of local burglars were hauled into the station for grillings about where they were last night. The questioning of us went on: when the girls were finished, the boys were started.
Meanwhile, we just had to stay in our dormitories and wait.

By now, everybody knew the details of the murder. Nerys was intrigued by the note.

"Oh, it's really romantic. It's a crime of passion," she breathed.

"Passion?" Kathy exclaimed. "For Mustoe?"

"Oh, yes. Cleo was a woman he had an affair with and he left her. And she was distraught and followed him here. She broke through the library window, slipped the note under his door and waited in the dark. At last he came, half-believing this was a hoax. She *pleaded* with him throughout the night to come back to her. But he rejected her yet again and, blind with thwarted, jealous rage, she picked up the first thing she saw. It was the candlestick. She smashed it over his head. He fell, skull crushed, blood everywhere. Distraught with horror, she scrambled back through the window, ran down the drive, realized she still had the candlestick, threw it away and then was gone for ever, far away into the night."

"And where's Cleo now?" said Kathy.

"Racked with grief and remorse, she's probably thrown herself off a mountain or drowned herself in a lake," said Nerys. "Her body won't be found for months, but when it is the mystery of the murder in the library will finally be solved."

"What a load of old cobblers," said Kathy.

"No," said Manjit. "Nerys is right. A remorseless fate has dogged Mustoe's heels for years and has finally caught up with him. The omens cannot lie."

"I wish Nerys was right," said Jessie sadly. "But it will only be some burglar breaking in. Mustoe heard the noise and went to see what it was."

"He must be a desperate burglar to come here," said Kirsty.

"Lottie, what do you think of all this?" said Kathy.

I never had time to answer. Mrs Mellow knocked at the door.

"Laura, they want to see you again."

The two of them were still there. By now they looked flushed, fatigued and fed-up. They seemed to be making heavy weather of what should surely have been a pretty simple investigation. Even so, the inspector spoke to me with extreme politeness.

"Miss Lomas, you seem to be one step ahead of everybody today. So let me ask you a few more questions."

What now? I felt a sinking of the heart.

"Earlier you seemed very sure this was an outside job."

"Of course. The broken window, the mud, the candlestick outside..."

"Yes, I know. Very plausible. Have you considered that this may be somebody trying to make us *think* it's an outside job?"

I stared.

"Yes, Miss Lomas, someone in the hostel, perhaps more than one: people *you know* did this."

"Oh, come on."

"You'd be surprised what nice people commit crimes," said the inspector. "We're not any more."

"It wasn't the warden," said the sergeant. "It wasn't his wife. It wasn't Mrs Mellow."

"And now you're going to say, 'It can't be one of my friends. We're just kids,'" said the inspector.

I nodded, unable to speak.

"Well, don't you believe it," said the sergeant.

"You'd need a pair," said the Inspector. "One to get him downstairs, one to pretend to break in. Two people who hate him so much they'd kill. Now, who do you know who fits the bill?"

"Nobody," I said. But I was getting a nasty feeling about who they had in mind.

"Let's go back to the fateful game of 'Cluedo'," said the sergeant. "We've heard quite a lot about it."

"And a few hints about people who were quite open that they had a lot of cause not to like Mr Mustoe," the inspector added.

Yes, Kirsty, Jason and Ben. Nobody would be interested in my detentions and lost homework, surely? But I wasn't going to say *anything*.

"What was it? Ben's father? Kirsty's sister. Jason's brother? They were the ones, weren't they?" said the inspector.

"You see, we know all about that," said the sergeant. "They've told us bits themselves, even if they didn't mean to. And Mrs Mellow has kindly filled in the details."

Blabbermouth Mellow.

"We're not interested in Ben's dad," said the inspector. "But Kirsty's sister and Jason's brother – that's big stuff. One scarred for life, the other with all his prospects ruined – add those two together and you've powerful motives, I'd say."

"Perhaps not each on its own," said the sergeant. "But together…"

"They *were* together, weren't they, Miss Lomas?" the inspector continued.

"How do you mean?"

The inspector looked disappointed. "Miss Lomas, we come to *you* for the answers in this investigation. *Were Kirsty and Jason especially friendly?*"

I couldn't deny it. The fact had kept me furious for the past three months.

"So try this for size. They plan this very carefully.

They see the candlestick in the library: they build the plan round it. They each creep out of their dormitories at a prearranged time. Jason carries clothes he can slip on downstairs so he leaves no incriminating track of mud. He clambers out of the window, breaks it from outside, opens it, clambers back in. Meanwhile, Kirsty has lured Mr Mustoe out of his room and into the library. How, I'll leave it to your imagination. The note from Cleo may or may not have something to do with it. But she'd probably got him up saying she's heard this noise in the library and she's frightened. Mustoe comes downstairs and into the library, sees the broken glass, stoops to look at it and, wallop! – Master Jason's candlestick's done the business, he's out of the window again, Kirsty's back upstairs, Jason throws the candlestick away, climbs back in, slips off the boots and trousers he's worn and puts them back where everybody else's are covered in mud, then into bed again and the sleep of the righteous, or so he thinks, until morning."

I *couldn't* answer. I just didn't believe a word of it. Kirsty, I wanted to get back at you, I admit. But nothing like *this*.

"Not a fingerprint in sight," said the sergeant. "Nobody did this on impulse."

"Gobsmacked, are you?" said the inspector.

I nodded.

"I'm sorry. Because I really want you to tell us our theory *can't* be right."

I couldn't, I said so.

"But I just don't *believe* it," I said.

I left the room in a daze. I couldn't speak when I got back into the dormitory and I couldn't look Kirsty directly in the face either. This was not a proper ending to the day.

After a while the WPC came upstairs and asked for Kirsty, who followed her out looking puzzled. We heard Kirsty's voice saying, "Hello, you as well?" on the landing outside and Jason's answering, "Yes, what's all this about?"

We waited. Soon there was a noise downstairs. We saw Kirsty and Jason led out, pushed into the rear seats of separate cars. The whole convoy left the front of the hostel, leaving the drive like a churned-up battlefield.

Mustoe would be in the mortuary by now. The atmosphere in the hostel was little different from what he'd left us for. Nobody was allowed out; we were to stay there until the police let us get into the minibus and go back home. There were still policemen around, searching. Dinner was a silent meal, ending with ten still-full, picked-over plates. Kirsty and Jason didn't come back that night and there wasn't a lot of sleep.

At least, not for me. I stayed awake all night, tortured about what might happen to Kirsty and Jason. Yes, I'd been a bit angry and a bit jealous of them. But not *that* much. And I wasn't now. I wanted them back.

Morning came. Breakfast was another sullen, moody meal.

Just after breakfast, Jason and Kirsty were brought back. Kirsty had been crying, Jason looked angry. He shouted to everybody as he entered the door.

"You won't believe this, but they tried to pin it on Kirsty and me."

He must have noticed that I couldn't look surprised.

"They've let us go," said Kirsty. "They had to. They told us they were wrong and they were sorry."

"That's not good enough. We're going to get our parents to make an official complaint."

Suddenly he looked at me. His eyes burned with anger.

"And don't think we don't know who put us both in the nick last night, Lottie Lomas. It was all *your* fault. I'm never going to speak to you again."

"And that goes for me too," said Kirsty.

The way everyone was staring at me showed they agreed.

By the time the minibus turned up the school drive two days early I was used to being ignored. It might, I thought, make a restful change for a while. After all, they'd forget it in the end. They'd come round. They'd soon realize that to have Jason and Kirsty charged with murder was the very *last* thing I wanted.

Even so, they didn't know the half of it...

The police had to abandon their theories about an inside job. But they never found anyone outside either. Soon they wound the investigation down. It still ranks as one of the great unsolved murders. Nobody knows what happened that wet and windy night at the Youth Hostel.

That's not quite true. *One* does...

Right at the start, Kathy had said the police would be looking for motives. And when they put Jason and Kirsty together, for a moment they must have thought they'd hit the jackpot.

But they didn't look far enough.

Colonel Mustard. What a man! Remember I told you about the last time he turned up in my presence? That game of "Cluedo" the night before Mum left home to live with another man?

I never told you who that man was, did I?

I didn't know myself for a long time. I don't think Dad did either, not at first anyway, or I'm sure he wouldn't have let me stay on at the school. I found out by accident when I was thirteen.

I'd been round to spend the evening with Amy, then my best friend. We sat eating at the table with her mum and dad. We were talking about school and Mr Mustoe's name came up. Amy's mum said, "I don't like him one bit. I can never understand why your mother went off and..." Then Amy's dad shot her a furious look and must have kicked her under the table because she put her hand to her mouth, gasped, "Whoops! Sorry. Forget I said that," and changed the subject.

When supper was over and before Dad came to collect me, I said to Amy, "What was all that about?" and Amy said, "Didn't you know? Your mum went off with Mr Mustoe."

Well, by the time Dad arrived I was in a right state and I shouted at him why didn't he tell me and why didn't he go round and get her back and punch Mr Mustoe up like other fathers would? And he shouted at me that it was none of my business and I was too young to be involved and he never wanted her name mentioned again.

I love my dad but between you and me I think he's a prat and a wimp.

Anyway, two months later we moved to where we live now, a hundred miles from where that all happened. New school, new friends, new start, forget it all.

And what happened then? Yes, you've guessed it. Mr Mustoe turned up a year later at my new school. He'd been made head of geography.

I didn't dare tell Dad.

But I watched Mustoe from afar. I found out where he lived – in a village eight miles away. I cycled there one afternoon and waited outside his house. A woman came out.

It wasn't Mum.

So now I asked Dad to tell me the truth this time. And he said, yes, Mum went off with Mr Mustoe (can you *believe* that?) but he kicked her out after two years. By now Mum and Dad were divorced. But when he heard what had happened, Dad wrote to her and asked her to come back. She wouldn't. She said she'd forfeited all right to him and to us. She was going away. We'd never hear from her again. And we didn't.

I hated Mustoe. Oh, yes, he knew who I was all right. But I never let on that I knew him. Nor he, it seemed, about me. I just sat in his lessons and stared at him – the spectre at the feast, a living reproach. "I'll never forget" – that was the message I silently sent to him every day.

I didn't really want to do geography for GCSE. Mustoe didn't want me to either. But I put down for it to keep the pressure on and Mustoe couldn't think of any reason why I shouldn't. He *needed* me, to make his group – what's the word? – *viable*, otherwise he could be out of a job. What could he say? I was good enough and if he objected the Head would wonder why.

So there I was, on the field trip. And there we were, playing "Cluedo". And my mind went right back to that long ago evening: Mum, Dad, Baz and me – *Colonel Mustard, in the library, with the candlestick*.

I didn't manipulate the cards. How could I? Colonel Mustard always coming out as the murderer was complete coincidence. It was, it was.

But next day, Manjit said it was the hand of fate. She's right there, too. It was. Because when Jason said it was a message – and when Ben said Dr Black ought to know who's after him by now: why didn't he rise up and clobber his pursuer back? – well, I couldn't help what I thought. *My whole family is the victim. Like Dr Black. So why don't we rise up and clobber our Colonel Mustard?*

The whole plan came to me at once, fully-formed and in complete detail as I lay in the top bunk. I'd been in the library and seen the candlestick on the mantelpiece. I worked out how to make it seem like someone broke in from outside – the inspector was *exactly* right there. But how to get Mustoe into the library?

Of course. I once took delight in forging Mum's big, rather childish handwriting. I was sure I still could. And her name was Antonia: she'd always, since a girl, been nicknamed Cleo.

So that was it.

I waited until everybody was asleep. Now *had* to be the time. I slipped off the top bunk, put dressing gown and flip-flops on, took a cleaning cloth I'd brought for my boots to wrap everything in and avoid fingerprints. I tiptoed down into the lounge, switched on my torch, found paper, wrote *Take me back. I am waiting in the library. Cleo* on it in Mum's handwriting, went to the library, opened the window, slipped out and found a stone to break it with, left it ready on the wall, slipped back inside, dashed to Mustoe's room, shoved the paper underneath the door, knocked on the door, dashed back into the library, out of the window, brick through the pane, into the library again, seized the candlestick, crouched behind a bookcase and waited.

He came in, very soon. He stood there, looking round.

My nerve failed me. I froze.

"Cleo?" he called softly. "Are you really here? Well, if you are, let's get one thing straight. It's over. We're finished. I don't want you."

That restored me. I was suddenly *so* angry. I rose

up, raised the candlestick and smashed it down on his head.

"*That's* for what you did to my mum and dad and Baz and me," I hissed.

I didn't need to check that he was dead. I was out of the window again and down the path. I threw the candlestick away, then back to the window, inside the library, not looking at Mustoe's still body, took off my flip-flops, rushed to the washroom and got the dirt off them under the tap, checked there were no bloodstains on me and was back in bed where I slept long and deeply.

And I *still* don't feel remorse for what I did.

And things have got better since. Dad's happier. I even think he's seeing someone on the quiet. He'll tell us in his own time. We've still never heard from Mum. One day I'll go looking.

Kirsty and Jason have forgiven me. The others talk again as well.

Mrs Mellow's head of geography now. She's all right.

Even so, I felt I'd got to tell *somebody*.

Remember, though, only *you* know.

Don't tell a soul.

Otherwise, one night I might be outside *your* window.

And this time I'll bring the candlestick with me.

DEAD LIKE ME

My name is Lauren, and I'm notorious in these parts. You may have heard of me – I'm a convicted killer, you see. Or at least that's what everyone says, from the steely-eyed judge in the Miami courtroom, to those twelve good men and true who all decided that I was guilty of murder four long years ago.

I pleaded innocent, of course, told them that there was no reason I would even dream of hurting a fly, let alone cutting short the life of another human being. You see, I told them over and over until I was hoarse, I simply didn't do it.

But then everyone says that, don't they? I imagine if they'd ever have caught Jack the Ripper red-handed back home in England, he would have said the same thing. And why should you believe me? After all, I was found guilty by the due process of law in one of the most democratic countries in the world, and I guess you can't get fairer than that, can you?

And even I'm not so sure any more. There are things I can't remember, little blanks in my life when I have no idea of what I've been doing. Long before the murder, Doug had laughed when I told him about these gaps, and he said that I was probably a schizophrenic, leading a secret double life. His woman of mystery he'd called me, and didn't understand why I started to cry when he continued to tease me. Because I'm not mad, am I? I really am innocent.

Aren't I?

But there's going to be no secrets between us. Not here, not now. So I'll be frank with you: I do have these odd blackouts from time to time. Nothing too serious, you'll be glad to know. The doctor told me that I'm probably a narcoleptic: that means I go into a deep sleep sometimes without any warning at all. There are also times when I walk in my sleep: somnambulism, I think the doctor called it. I remember once Uncle Freddie found me out on the lawn, at three o'clock in the morning, wearing nothing but my nightgown, and having no recollection of how I got there. He guessed I was stressed by the death of my parents, and I suppose he's right.

I wish I could fall asleep so easily late at night when the prison warders are locking up, and the crazy woman in the cell down the corridor starts screaming and wailing for her babies.

But then soon I'm going to have no problems sleeping at all, am I? I'm writing this at midnight, with the full moon streaming in through my cell window, and I know that in eleven hours' time I will be sleeping the longest sleep of them all...

I enrolled at Roscoe Academy six years ago when I was fifteen. I'd lost Mum and Dad in a car accident back home in England; I had no brothers and sisters and my closest relative was my Uncle Freddie who lived here in Miami.

Well, I call him my Uncle Freddie, but he wasn't really the brother of either my mum or dad at all. Dad was American – even though I've lived in England most of my life I still have an American passport – and Uncle Freddie was Dad's cousin once removed, I think. I often wonder why he agreed to look after me when my parents died. I would come into a substantial trust fund, payable to me on my twenty-fifth birthday, and in the early days I sometimes wondered whether Uncle Freddie was interested not in me but the money I'd inherit in a few years' time.

As time went on I realized just how uncharitable I was being. Uncle Freddie made sure that I wanted for nothing, and I couldn't have wished for a nicer, or more generous grown-up. And why ever should he be interested in my money? After all, he was doing very nicely for himself, thank you very much, as the owner and general manager of HappyLand, the amusement theme park out there by the Keys.

Of course, all this is academic now. I'll be dead in eleven hours' time, and all the money in my trust fund automatically goes to my next of kin. Uncle Freddie will get the money now, whether he wants it or not. Maybe he'll use it to pay off the IRS: ever since I've lived with Uncle Freddie, he's had problems with the tax people. I imagine the money from my trust fund will come in handy for him. A bit of a lucky break for him, really.

As you've probably guessed by now, Roscoe Academy is a pretty exclusive sort of private school. Most of the kids who go there are the sons and daughters of really important people – politicians, diplomats, even the occasional rock star thrown in to give the old place a vaguely Bohemian image. You don't have to be rich to attend Roscoe – the Principal gives out a few scholarships a year to the more academically gifted amongst us – but it sure helps. And that's why I think it was so great of Uncle Freddie to get me a place there; I mean, it's still a few years before I come into my inheritance, and I certainly couldn't have afforded it by myself. I suppose it just shows how unselfish people can be sometimes. But sometimes I do wonder.

There I go again, looking a gift horse in the mouth. It's just that ever since I've been in this place I've learnt not to trust anyone. There are inmates here who say that you're their very best friend, and then go talking about you as soon as your back's turned. It's hard to trust people.

So Uncle Freddie paid my fees and I'm really grateful to him for that, because I know that I wouldn't have got in purely on academic merit. I might have always received B-pluses in my physics and engineering exams, but that's nothing compared to the straight As people like Kim and Doug used to get.

Kim was just about the best zoology student ever and there were times when her teacher was tempted to give up and let her take over the class. And Doug – well, Doug was just Doug. He had one of the sharpest mathematical minds around; but, even if he hadn't, he could've charmed a string of A-pluses out of his teacher with just a wink of those dark-brown, long-lashed eyes of his.

Everyone was in love with Doug. All the boys wanted him for their best buddy, and there wasn't a single girl who didn't dream about the time when he would come up to her and ask her out to the end-of-term ball.

And I loved Doug too, and was one of the few people he did actually take to the ball. And no matter what people say – what people *have* said – I don't believe that the sort of love I had for Doug could ever turn to the kind of hate that is capable of cold-blooded murder. I mean, life isn't like that, is it? Love is love. And hate is hate. You might as well try and tell me that black can turn to white. It just isn't possible, is it?

But that's all in the past now. And so is Doug. And Kim. And soon I'll join them, and maybe then I can ask forgiveness for whatever hurt I've brought to them. Maybe I can find out the truth, unravel that mystery which started with Kim's death, on a warm June day at the beginning of summer. In the Roscoe Academy, Florida, USA, the place where the sun shines all the time and nothing untoward ever happens...

Kim died. No warning, no fuss. There was just one morning when she didn't wake up. Even now Janey, who boarded in the same house as Kim, shudders at the memory she'll never forget. It was Janey who discovered Kim's body, you see, cold to the touch, on the floor of her bedroom.

Kim's left arm was stretched out at an awkward angle, reaching for a photograph which had apparently been knocked down off her bedside cabinet. It was a framed photo of Kim and Doug, taken a few months before when they'd flown off for a secret weekend *à deux* by the Niagara Falls. February 15th, the day after Valentine's Day, to be exact.

You ask how I can be so sure of the date? How could I forget it? Doug and I were supposed to go to a concert up in Orlando that weekend, and he'd cancelled at the last moment. (He'd spun me some fairy-tale that he had a lot of studying to do for next week's computer exams.)

When they returned, Kim holding him around the waist as though she'd never let him go, he'd told me that it was all over between us, that he and Kim were now an item, and he liked me a lot, and couldn't we just be friends from now on, please? I felt betrayed, disgusted that my boyfriend was having an affair with one of my best friends, the friend who stayed overnight at my house so often that she even had her own set of keys.

I hated Doug for that, wanted to kill him. Didn't my

love, the times Doug and I had shared together, mean anything to him? I wanted to kill Kim too, to have my revenge on her for stealing away from me the most beautiful boy in the world.

Of course, I didn't mean it. You say a lot of things you don't mean when you're angry and upset, don't you? And so, when Janey, and Jean-Marc, and Scott, and Andy, had all looked worriedly at me, I'd reassured them that I'd be fine in a couple of weeks. They were great during that terrible time when I was coming to terms with Doug and Kim's relationship; they weren't so great later when they all took the witness stand against me, though, and reminded me, the judge and the jury, exactly what I'd said that day in the heat of the moment.

No, I'm being too harsh, too bitter. How could they have done anything else? After all, it was the truth: I *had* said that I wanted to kill them. It was just the prosecution that twisted their words so much to make me seem a cold and vicious killer.

Because I truly didn't mean it. But whatever I meant, and whosever story you believe, one thing still remains unchanged: Doug and Kim are dead.

But back to Janey. Janey is the sort of girl who cries at romantic movies, hides behind the sofa when *The X-Files* is showing on the TV, and reads Agatha Christie novels like they're going out of fashion. Jean-Marc says that she's got an overactive imagination, so it's hardly surprising that she was the first person to decide that Kim had been murdered. OK, I agree there was something a little odd about Kim's death; but it was just bad luck that it had had to have been the over-imaginative Janey who found her body and announced her crazy theory.

"Come off it, Janey," I pooh-poohed. It was a few days later and we were all having lunch at Suzuki's, the sushi and noodle bar that used to be Kim's favourite when she was alive. "You heard what the doctor said. Kim died of natural causes."

"Then maybe the doctor was wrong," Janey said, determined that her story of murder most foul couldn't be contradicted.

"No way," Andy said confidently and sipped at his bowl of green tea. "That Namihoko guy is the best doc money could buy. And don't you think he'd have something to say if he even suspected that his favourite niece had been murdered?"

Janey shrugged; she wasn't going to give it up without a fight. "Doctors – even doctors who also happen to be the victim's uncle – do occasionally get things wrong," she said, and then added pertinently: "You, of all people, should know that, Andy."

Andy glared at Janey. She'd struck a raw nerve, and we all knew it. Andy was Roscoe's all-round, all-purpose jock: weight-lifting, wind-surfing, white-water rafting – you name it and Andy had done it. A couple of months ago, though, he'd been tested positive for steroid abuse, and was about to be expelled from school. He'd insisted to the Principal that he'd never taken any drugs in his life, but it was only when another doctor had offered his second opinion (funnily enough, Kim's uncle, Doctor Namihoko) that he was given the all-clear.

I was glad that Andy hadn't been expelled – he's a really nice guy when he hasn't had one too many Buds – but I was still concerned that he had managed to fool Doctor Namihoko. After all, even though I had no proof, I suspected that Andy really did have a steroid problem. I remember Scott, one of his work-out buddies, once telling him that drugs were for losers and Andy had flown into a rage, really lost his top. A 'roid rage is what

I think they call it. But what could we do? If we'd talked to the teachers, Andy would have been expelled. And if we discussed it with Andy himself, there was no telling how he would react. Sometimes he reminded me of a volcano, just waiting to explode.

I often wonder if Kim had had anything to do with Doctor Namihoko's second opinion. Before she started going out with Doug, Kim had always carried something of a torch for Andy. Not that it had done her much good. Andy was the kind of guy who wasn't interested in girls, preferring to spend all of his spare time working his body in the gym. He'd told Kim that in no uncertain terms and Kim, who could usually get any man she set her eyes on, had seen red. I remember her telling Andy that one way or the other he'd come to respect her.

Certainly, after the drugs scandal, Andy had been a lot more deferential to Kim. I mean, I don't want to speak ill of the dead, but Kim had started bossing him around a bit, and it seemed that she was enjoying it immensely. It was clear that that was something the oh-so-macho Andy didn't like at all.

"Calm down, guys," Jean-Marc cut in, his smooth French accent once again defusing a potentially explosive situation. "We've just lost a friend. Let's not disgrace her memory by squabbling over how she died."

"She was supposed to be your friend," Janey said, "but you seem to be strangely uninterested in the whole affair..."

"Jean-Marc's tired," I said, rising to the French boy's defence. "He's only just flown in this morning by Concorde."

It had been me who had rung up Jean-Marc, who had been taking a vacation with his parents in Paris, to tell him of the bad news. He had immediately wanted to make arrangements to attend Kim's funeral, until I'd told him that her body had already been shipped back to Japan for a small private family burial. Still, he'd flown over to be with us all, cutting short his holiday.

But that's the way Jean-Marc is: the greatest guy you could ever wish to meet. He's so sweet, so kind, so thoughtful. Or at least that's what I thought until the judge called him to the witness stand.

"I liked Kim, *elle était très sympa, très extra*," he had told the prosecution, and then chuckled, despite himself. "She wasn't just a great biologist but she was a fantastic artist as well. I don't know if I should be telling you this, sir, but she often used to forge sick notes for us when we wanted to skip school! But there was always something strained between her and Lauren. I suppose it was because Kim stole Doug from her. I remember when Lauren found out ... well, if I hadn't have been there at the time, I'm sure that Lauren would have..."

His voice had then tailed off, as if he had suddenly realized that he had perhaps said more than he should have done.

"She would have done what, Monsieur Petit?" the judge had asked.

"If I hadn't had been there she would have killed her." Jean-Marc had turned to look at me in the witness stand, his eyes tearful and begging forgiveness. I hated him at that moment, cursing him for being tricked by the prosecution into that admission. But afterwards I realized that I couldn't really blame him: it was the truth after all...

But Jean-Marc's damning accusation would be in the future. Back then, four years ago in Suzuki's, I didn't realize that the conversation we were having would lead me to this tiny moonlit cell on Death Row.

"I'm sorry, Jean-Marc," Janey apologized. "But it's still kind of strange – a perfectly healthy Japanese girl of eighteen dying of 'natural causes'!"

Scott nodded. "Janey's right," he said. "Kim's always been in the best of health before... And now that her body's back in Japan, we'll never know if something happened to her..."

I slammed my hand down on the table. "Can we stop all this conspiracy theory stuff, please?" I said, displaying more feeling than perhaps was wise in the light of later events. "Kim died of a heart attack, pure and simple. It's rare in someone her age – but it happens."

Andy agreed; he seemed kind of anxious that this conversation should be ended too. "It's been a shock for all of us," he said.

"You never liked Kim," Janey said.

"It's still a shock," he protested, "when someone your own age dies." He shuddered. "Remember Amanda James?" he asked, and Janey nodded. "Where were your conspiracy theories then?"

Amanda had been a fellow pupil of Janey's, a diabetic, who had died suddenly four months before. Amanda had been such a fun-loving, free-wheeling sort of girl and now she was gone. She had been a good friend of Janey's and the death had upset her a lot. After all, teenagers like us aren't supposed to die, are they? And when they do it puts you in mind of your own mortality. It makes you realize that maybe you're not quite as invincible as you think.

"I'm sorry," Janey said, and maybe she meant it. "It's me and my big mouth again. Sometimes I just don't know when to shut up."

"Too right," Scott muttered, not quite under his breath.

"Let's all calm down, shall we?"

This was Jean-Marc again: sweet Jean-Marc who never wished anyone any harm. Still, maybe Janey had a point. Considering that Jean-Marc had been Kim's best friend, he was bearing up well under the pressure. I mean, I thought that French people were really expressive with their feelings, but he was showing a remarkable degree of self-control.

Maybe *too* remarkable. If I'd just learnt today that my best friend had been murdered – sorry, if she'd just died of 'natural causes' – then I'm sure I'd have been devastated. Me and Kim hadn't seen eye to eye, certainly, but I was still shocked over her death.

Jean-Marc nodded at the Japanese waiter who was mincing over to our table with the order. We would talk about the circumstances surrounding Kim's death later, he said; right now we should change the subject.

Suzuki's was a sushi bar and I'd always balked at the idea of coming here before. It had been Kim's favourite restaurant, and it seemed a little weird that Scott should insist that we come here now, so soon after Kim's death. All the same, raw, uncooked fish wasn't my idea of a gourmet meal, as my expression showed when the waiter placed down in front of us several dishes of decidedly unappetizing seafood.

"It's supposed to be trendy!" Scott said, when he saw my reluctance to pick up a piece of abalone with my chopsticks. He raised a piece to his lips, holding the chopsticks in his left hand. (Scott was right-handed, but had strained his right wrist lifting some weights in the gym, he had told us.)

"Trendy or not, it's still raw fish," I said gloomily. "It's a miracle that we don't all drop down dead with food poisoning!"

"It's all fresh," Jean-Marc said, and popped a piece of tempura into his mouth. "Killed only minutes ago in those salt-water tanks at the back. And it's healthy!"

"Healthy?" asked Andy, whose culinary experience began and ended with the McDonald's down the road. "How do you make that out?"

"Fish is the staple diet in Japan," Jean-Marc explained. "And the Japanese have one of the lowest incidences of heart disease in the world."

"That didn't help Kim though, did it?" Janey said. Blast her! Bringing the subject back to death!

"Well, I've heard all sorts of horror stories about people getting ill from raw fish," I maintained, as the waiter returned to our table with a huge bowl of steaming noodles. He chuckled at me.

"You're perfectly safe, young lady," he reassured me, and then frowned. "You're not the first person to ask me how safe seafood is though... Your friend – the Japanese-American girl – was here only a few days ago," he said. "She was chatting with the chef. She seemed very worried about something, as though her mind was elsewhere... Is she not here tonight?"

"No, she's not..." Scott said, and a silence descended on our table. The waiter obviously hadn't heard of Kim's death. But then why should he have done? Kim had died of natural causes, and, no matter what Janey said, she hadn't been murdered.

Had she?

"See!" Janey crowed, when the waiter had left our table. "He said that Kim had been worried about something! She knew that someone was out to get her!"

"Shut up, Janey!" I said. Honestly, if she didn't put a stop to this soon I swear I was going to kill her!

"You're letting your imagination run away with you,"

Jean-Marc reproved. "Who'd want to murder Kim? Who would have a motive?"

Janey sat back in her chair and regarded each one of us in turn, just in the way she'd seen her favourite detective do on that TV cop show she was always watching.

"Any one of us here," she announced finally.

"Don't be stupid," Andy said, and averted his gaze from Janey's accusing eyes, and busied himself with his noodles and tempura.

"We've all seen how Kim's been treating you over the past weeks," Janey said, and Andy knew that he couldn't deny it. "You've been nothing more than her little lap-puppy. Looks like she was getting her own back for you turning her down all that while ago. Maybe you decided to stop her once and for all."

"That's stupid and you know it," Andy said, and coloured. We all knew how much he had hated being pushed around by Kim.

"And what motive might I have for killing Kim?" Jean-Marc asked and glared at Janey, determined to disprove her theory once and for all. "*Mon Dieu*, she was one of my best friends!"

"And you owe her money," Janey said, and reminded him of the several thousand bucks Kim had lent him a few months back when his parents' cheque hadn't come through on time. Jean-Marc was something of a party animal – if you ask me, he partied too much for his own good, occasionally mixing with some very dubious people – and when his money had finally arrived, he'd discovered that he'd already spent most of it on his credit-card bill. Kim had recently been bothering him for the return of her loan, and it had been putting a strain on their friendship.

"I was going to pay her back soon," Jean-Marc claimed, and shifted uncomfortably in his seat. Jean-Marc was a pretty independent guy, who hated having to rely on anyone. Even though Kim was a good friend of his, it must have been pretty difficult for him to admit that he needed her help.

"And who would kill for just a few thousand dollars anyway?" I asked sensibly.

"Who says it's just a few thousand dollars?" Janey asked, once more warming to her theme. "That could just be the tip of the iceberg." The implication was obvious: if Jean-Marc had been so short of cash, how had he afforded that holiday to Paris, and the return flight by Concorde? Jean-Marc would say later that the vacation was a gift from his parents for his eighteenth birthday. But still...

Janey looked over at Scott. "And I know that you and Kim haven't been getting on lately. Kim told me that she knows what you get up to on a Saturday night."

Scott shifted uncomfortably, remembering the night when Kim had surprised him in a major clinch with the daughter of his father's best friend. As the daughter was engaged to someone else, and as his dad was about to enter into a big business deal with her father, he hardly liked to think what would happen if Kim decided to make the affair public knowledge. Kim had already told Janey: who else might she tell? Maybe he thought that he could shut her up for good.

"And of course, Kim was the person who stole Doug from Lauren here," Janey concluded her summation, "and you all know what they say about hell having no fury like a woman scorned!"

"And I suppose you're the only one with no motive?" I asked her, and she smiled smugly and nodded.

"That's right," she agreed. "I bet even Doug has a motive!"

"*Mon Dieu!*" Jean-Marc said. "The guy's girlfriend has just died, Janey! How can you be so thoughtless?" He nodded to the door: a tall, good-looking boy was entering, drawing the admiring attentions of some of the female diners. Janey knew that she had gone too far, and she shut up, as I invited Doug over to our table.

Jean-Marc stood up and offered his chair to Doug, who accepted it. His normally handsome face was pale and drawn, and his red-rimmed eyes showed he hadn't had any sleep for several nights. That was hardly surprising, I suppose.

"How are you, *mon ami*?" Jean-Marc asked, his voice full of concern.

"I can't believe she's gone," he sighed. "Only a week ago, she was so full of life, and now she's back home in Japan, buried in her family vault. There wasn't even time to say goodbye..."

"It's a shame none of us could go to the funeral," Scott agreed. "But I guess if her family wanted it to be a strictly private affair then that's their own business."

"There are so many things left unsaid," Doug breathed. "So many important things I wanted to tell her..."

"Things left unsaid?" I asked, and Doug sighed again.

"Private things," he said, after some hesitation. "About our relationship..."

I frowned, wondering what he meant, but said, "Don't worry yourself over it," and laid a comforting hand on Doug's. He placed his other hand over mine and looked up at me; his eyes misty with tears that were not falling.

I shivered, experiencing once again the same sort of

feelings I had had for Doug when we had been going out together, before he ditched me for that … for poor Kim.

I took my hand away, and cursed myself. I was always letting my emotions get the better of me, and that was why over the past months I'd kept my distance from Doug. Janey had remarked on my apparent coldness towards him, but it was only because I knew that if I hadn't acted like that then I couldn't be held responsible for my actions.

"I'll miss her," Janey said, although we knew that she didn't mean it. Janey had always been jealous of Kim's good looks, and her sophisticated lifestyle. In fact the two girls were complete opposites, and, even though they boarded in the same house, they hardly ever spoke to each other.

It was strange then that it should have been Janey who had found Kim's body in her room. Janey had told us that Kim had asked for some help on a joint science project. And that was odd too because the straight-A Kim had never needed any help on her natural history course before.

"Kim will always be with us in our memories," Scott declared, and the look on his face suggested to me that he wanted a final end to the conversation. He reached out his left hand for his cup of green tea. "But now we must look to the future." He stared at Janey. "And no more talk of murder, OK?"

"To the future," I agreed, and we all raised and clinked together our cups of green tea. "To a better tomorrow for all of us."

How naïve I was back then! For two of us sitting down there in Suzuki's that better tomorrow would never arrive…

* * *

I got the phone call from Jean-Marc about half past ten the next morning, when I was ... well, I'm not quite sure what I'd been doing. Remember I told you I get these blackouts from time to time? I remember waking up that morning and showering. Hot showers always make me sleepy, even so early, and I'd hardly got any sleep that night, thinking about Kim, so I'd gone for a quick lie-down on the sofa. The next thing I knew the phone was ringing. I'd dressed in the meantime – jeans and a white sweat-top.

Anyway, I answered the phone, and listened with a sinking heart as Jean-Marc told me his news. As he'd flown straight in from Paris the previous evening, when he'd returned to his apartment (unlike most of the others at Roscoe, who lived in shared dormitories or with their parents, he had his own place on the outskirts of town, near Uncle Freddie's HappyLand, in fact) he'd gone straight to bed, without checking the messages on the answerphone. When he'd rewound the tape this morning, there, among all the other messages had been one from Kim.

She had rung the day before her death, in a state of panic. Someone was out to get her, she said, and she was scared for her life. They wanted revenge, she said, and they'd stop at nothing, not even murder, to get it.

Jean-Marc was pretty shaken by the message. Ever the practical Englishwoman, I told him to make himself a strong cup of tea, and that I'd be right over.

"Revenge? What did she mean?" I asked, when I reached Jean-Marc's place.

"She said someone was jealous of her happiness," Jean-Marc said.

"Play me the tape," I said, and Jean-Marc jabbed at a button on the answer-machine. But all that came from the machine was a long silence. We exchanged a confused look, and then Jean-Marc cursed in French, as he indicated a small flashing red light on the machine. He'd accidentally pressed the erase button by mistake, wiping Kim's message.

If, of course, it had ever been there. Looking back now, I wonder why Kim had rung Jean-Marc on that day and left a message when she knew that he would be in Paris. Had she really left a message on the machine? And if she hadn't, why would Jean-Marc say that she had? Unless…

Damn it! I'm getting as bad as Janey! I told myself angrily. Seeing something sinister in everything. I raised a hand to my forehead: I was getting a headache.

"Should we tell the police?" Jean-Marc asked, and I shook my head. With the tape wiped we had no evidence and they'd probably just write us off as a bunch of stupid kids anyway.

It's sad how you can forget people so quickly. A few weeks passed as the summer term drew to a close, and people stopped talking about Kim. Even Doug hardly mentioned her at all; in fact, he and I were spending a lot of time together. There were moments when … well, maybe it was wishful thinking on my part, but I sometimes thought that he wanted to go out with me again.

But whenever it seemed that he was about to broach the subject, I would freeze him out. After all, it had been him who had dumped me, and I don't forget or forgive quite that easily; and it was hardly respectable to start going out with your ex only weeks after your girlfriend had died.

The last day of term finally arrived, and I suggested

that to celebrate we should all take the day off and spend it at Uncle Freddie's HappyLand. Initially Doug refused to go, but I insisted, and he finally bowed to pressure. I was always good at changing Doug's mind when we were going out together, and it seemed that I still hadn't lost the knack. As I rifled through my wardrobe for some clothes to wear, I noticed my favourite white sweatshirt hanging there, a rip in the left-hand sleeve. I frowned: I didn't remember tearing it. But then my memory was never that good at the best of times. Was it?

The Techno Terror was one of the newest and most hair-raising rides at HappyLand, a sort of gigantic big dipper with more twists and turns than a conger eel. Uncle Freddie had initially had some doubts about buying it for the park – it would take up a sizeable chunk of his budget for the year – but I'd finally persuaded him. I'd studied the plans and specifications with him one night, and had declared that it promised to be the most thrilling attraction he could ever have, guaranteed of bringing huge crowds into HappyLand.

I'd been talking up the ride to the others for ages, even before Kim died, and today was the first day it would be in operation. Uncle Freddie had agreed that we could be the first ones to try it out; I remember that Kim had been really excited about that.

"Come on, Doug, it'll be fun!" I said, as we walked up to the waiting buggies. Janey and Scott, and Andy and Jean-Marc were already climbing into their two-seater cars.

"I'm not so sure..." Doug said doubtfully. "You know I've got this thing about heights..."

"I remember," I said, recalling that time when we'd gone to the top of the Two Towers in New York. Back when we were still a couple.

Before he dumped me.

I took hold of his hand. "Don't be such a baby!"

Doug smiled and relented, and walked over to the buggy behind Janey and Scott. I pulled him away and led him to another one. The last time Janey had gone on one of these rides, she had thrown up, I joked; the further away from her the better!

The Techno Terror started to rumble into action, ready to make its maiden journey. Janey grinned back at us, as the cars started to move slowly up the track.

"My bag!" I said. When I'd been leading Doug to the ride, I'd dropped my shoulder bag on to the ground, and had forgotten to pick it up. I knew it was against all the safety regulations but I jumped out of the buggy and raced across to retrieve it. Doug cried after me, but didn't dare get out of the buggy himself, as it started to gather speed.

"Looks like you and the Techno Terror will have to get off to a flying start without me!" I said, and waved him goodbye, as the cars began their ascent.

The ride looked exciting as the cars reached their full speed of some thirty miles an hour, and twisted and turned and looped and rolled around. People were screaming with delight, as the Techno Terror turned them upside down and sideways, seemingly defying all the proven laws of gravity. I'd definitely made a great choice when I'd persuaded Uncle Freddie to buy in the ride.

And then the cries of delight turned to screams of terror, as there was a massive shower of sparks, and a harsh ripping and scrunching noise which could be heard even above the roar of the crowds.

One of the buggies detached itself from the track, and was sent shooting off into the air, a streak of red against the blue of the summer sky. Strangely I felt no feeling, just a strange numbness, as I watched it arc over the amusement park, and crash to the hard concrete ground about twenty yards away.

I was the first on the scene, and when the others reached me, after the ride had finished, I shook my head, before the numbness lifted and I burst into a fit of shaking and uncontrollable tears. There was nothing any of us could do. In the mangled remains of the red buggy, Doug's broken and bloodied body had been crushed almost to a pulp.

It was a tragic accident, everyone had said; or at least they did until the police and the insurance men came around to check the damage, after HappyLand had been closed for investigation. As Uncle Freddie's niece I was allowed access to the park at all times, and I was there when they discovered that the ride had been tampered with. Someone had deliberately cut and weakened the cables of one particular buggy, they said. But that was impossible, Uncle Freddie had told them; he had done a thorough safety check on it just the other day. Then the ride must have been tampered with last night or that morning, they concluded. I remembered the tear on my sweatshirt, and how I couldn't recall where it had come from.

"Someone wanted to kill Doug," Janey decided, after we had all returned to my place when the police had gone.

"Not again, Janey," Jean-Marc said. "First you think that someone murdered Kim, and now Doug. It was an accident: it could have been any of us in that buggy."

"No, it couldn't," Janey said, and then looked accusingly over at me. "Why did you and Doug choose to sit in that particular car?" I told her – it was a coincidence, nothing else – but she didn't believe me. "And just as the ride began you leapt out of the car."

"I had to get my bag," I said, and looked imploringly at Jean-Marc for help.

"Just what are you trying to say, Janey?" he asked, although he had a pretty fair idea.

"To sabotage the ride, someone would have to have access to the park," she said. "And they'd have to have a fair degree of technical knowledge as well." She glanced meaningfully over at my engineering textbooks on the shelf.

"Why would I want to kill Doug?" I asked. This was the craziest thing I'd ever heard of in my life. "We used to go out with each other, for heaven's sake!"

"Exactly!" Janey said. "Until he ditched you for Kim! You wanted to get your revenge on both of them! Pay Doug back for dumping you, and Kim for taking him away from you!"

"Kim died of a heart attack!" I said, and looked over at Jean-Marc. He was rubbing his chin thoughtfully, remembering the message on his answerphone.

Revenge...

"We all of us had a motive for killing Kim," Janey said. "Let's face it, if not for the help she gave us sometimes with our homework and exams we'd never have been so friendly with her –"

"*Ce n'est pas vrai,*" Jean-Marc protested, but Janey ignored him and continued: "We all had a motive for killing Kim," she repeated, and stared at me. "But you're the only one who had a reason to murder Doug as well."

"This is nuts," Andy said, and went into the kitchen to fetch himself a Diet Coke, while Janey continued her crazy accusations.

"Where were you this morning, Lauren?" Scott asked.

"At Jean-Marc's, you know that," I answered, and reached for the tear in my sweatshirt. How had I ripped it? I must have caught it on something when I was sleep-walking. If only I could remember, then I could prove that I hadn't planned Doug's death.

"And before that?" Jean-Marc asked. Was even he now taking up against me?

I buried my face in my hands. "I don't know!" I sobbed. "You know I sometimes have these memory lapses. I can't remember!"

"How very convenient," Janey said, her words loaded with meaning. At that point I really did want to kill her.

Suddenly all eyes turned to the door leading to the kitchen. Andy was standing there, holding some objects in his hands. "I found these next door," he said, and laid them out on the table. They were a selection of tools – heavy-duty cutting equipment, spanners and the plans for the Techno Terror.

"I'm an engineering student," I protested. "Of course I'm bound to have some tools around the house..."

The truth was that I didn't really know what the truth was any more. I couldn't have murdered Doug or Kim, I kept on telling myself. I couldn't kill anyone. But then hadn't I just wished Janey dead? And what had I done that morning, in that blank spot in my memory? I remembered Doug teasing me about my "secret life". Was that life the life of a murderess?

Someone had to have murdered them. So why couldn't it have been me?

Jean-Marc rested a hand on my shoulder. There was no proof that I had murdered Doug, he told me. Even the tools in the kitchen were only circumstantial evidence: they would never stand up in a court of law. Short of someone actually having seen me sabotage the Techno Terror, or a full-blown confession, there was nothing anyone could successfully accuse me of.

"Try and think, Lauren," he said softly. "Where were you this morning?"

Suddenly I smiled. "My diary," I said, and rustled through my shoulder-bag. "I always write it up first thing in the morning. Maybe something there will give me a clue!" I took it out of the bag and handed it over to Jean-Marc. "Read it out to me..." I said, sure that if I read the entry the suspicious Janey wouldn't believe me.

Jean-Marc flicked through the pages until he found the entry I'd made this morning, before he had phoned me. His face fell, and the words tumbled leadenly from his mouth as he read aloud what I had written in my diary.

"How I hate them both. That vicious Japanese witch who stole my Doug from me. And Doug himself, dumping me when he no longer had any use for me. Discarded like yesterday's newspaper! But I'll get my revenge. Oh yes, he'll pay. He won't be such a good-looker when they pick him out of that mangled mess of metal..."

I grabbed the diary from Jean-Marc's hand. "I didn't write that!" I insisted, but when I looked at the diary entry I recognized my own handwriting.

I had condemned myself with my own words. I had murdered Doug, and probably Kim as well.

As you all know, if you read the papers, they found me guilty of Doug's murder. Uncle Freddie got me one of the best lawyers in the country, but even he couldn't get me a lighter sentence on the grounds of diminished responsibility. A handwriting expert was called in to look at my diary, and she had declared that I was particularly lucid, and certainly not insane, when I had plotted my revenge on Doug.

They tried to accuse me of murdering Kim as well, but it was decided that there wasn't enough evidence. Her uncle had made it clear that he didn't want his niece's death investigated, and had then relocated back to Japan, where no one knew how to contact him.

Those are the facts but I still can't believe that I murdered Doug. I mean, I loved him. But what is it they say about love and hate? That they're just two sides of the same coin? I guess being betrayed by him hurt me more than I thought.

And if I didn't kill Doug then who did? I can't believe Andy or Scott did. After all, what was their motive? And the only murders Janey gets involved with are in her trashy detective novels. Sometimes I wonder about my Uncle Freddie. After all, he was the only one apart from me with access to HappyLand. He could have sabotaged the ride, I suppose. But what would be his motive for killing Doug and framing me? The money from my trust fund that will come to him on my death? Somehow I can't believe that. People can't be that cold and calculating, can they?

I hardly ever see them now, although Jean-Marc visits me once in a while. I appreciate that. He's a nice guy, although I can tell by the way he looks at me that he can't quite stomach the fact that one of his oldest friends is a cold-blooded murderer.

And I guess that's what I am. I killed Doug, and probably Kim as well, during one of my blackouts. And I'm going to have to get used to the fact. There's only a few hours left anyway. It's daylight now, and I've seen my last ever sunrise. Soon it will all be over.

There's a rustling of keys outside my cell, and I look up urgently, my heart beating expectantly, as the cell door creaks open. Could this be a last-minute reprieve?

Of course not. Things like that happen in story books and movies, but not in real life. It's just Baker, the prison guard, checking up on me. She's not an ogre like some of the others here; she gets on with me and has even been known to bend the rules for me on occasion. She smiles, like she must have smiled at other condemned women down the years.

"You've a visitor, Lauren," she says. "I thought you might like to see them in here..."

"A visitor?" I ask. "Who is it? Uncle Freddie? Jean-Marc?"

"It's your half-sister," she says, and turns to invite someone into my cell, before leaving me alone with the newcomer.

My half-sister? But I don't have a half-sister. Or is that something else I've forgotten?

She's about my height and size, and is dressed stylishly in a black, expensive-looking dress. She's wearing a large, floppy hat, so that I can't see her face until she takes it off, throwing her long, dark hair back as she always used to do.

It's been over four years since I last saw her, and she looks older, with tiny lines around her eyes, but I recognize her instantly.

"Kim," I hear myself saying, and I reach for the desk for support. It's like seeing a ghost, but I reach out and touch her: this "ghost" is very definitely alive.

"Hello, Lauren," Kim says, and smiles.

"But ... but you're dead..." The words seem trite. How can she be dead? She's standing right there in front of me.

"That's correct," Kim says, and adds with vicious irony: "And soon so will you be. I passed the electric chair on my way here. Everything's ready for the fireworks later."

"I don't understand," I say, and raise a hand to my forehead. It's bathed in a thick layer of cold sweat.

"We Japanese are a patient people," she says. "It's taken me four years but I've finally got my vengeance on both you and Doug."

"Vengeance? *You* killed Doug," I suddenly realize. "But how? Why?"

"I found out that he was going to leave me," she reveals. "He was going to go to you, ask you if you would take him back... I couldn't let that happen. I loved him and if I couldn't have him, then no one else could either. So I sabotaged the Techno Terror..."

"But how did you get into HappyLand?" I ask. "The gates are locked every night..."

"We were friends once," Kim reminds me. "Remember that time when I stayed at your place after a night out at Suzuki's to help you with your homework? You gave me a set of your keys and I never returned them. It was easy enough to sneak into your house when you were out and get the keys to HappyLand. I'm a science student too, and it was simple fixing the buggies on the ride – I knew that you wanted to be the first to take the Terror. You went on about it enough when I was 'alive'."

"But you could have killed any of us," I say. "You couldn't be sure that it would be Doug..."

Kim nods. "If Doug hadn't have been killed then, I would have found another way to punish him," she says. "The important thing was that someone got killed – and that you were blamed for the murder. I wanted to know that you were suffering, that the person who Doug loved above all else was going through hell."

"But the diary..."

"Remember how I used to forge sick notes for you all?" Kim asks. "It was simplicity itself to write in your handwriting, admitting to plotting a murder. The fact that you suffered from blackouts only made my hoax more convincing. If you started doubting your own innocence, then that would make others suspect you even more. It was all planned, you see, dear Lauren, from the message I left on Jean-Marc's answerphone, to the cutting tools I planted in your house when you were all at HappyLand."

I look to the door. I have to call Baker, tell her that I really am innocent, that I didn't kill Doug four years ago. I glance at Kim's watch – an expensive Rolex. In two hours' time they'll lead me down to the electric chair. And then a horrible thought strikes me. With my memory blackouts they think I'm mad already; why should they believe me now? I look at Kim's smiling face again.

"You're dead," I repeat, despite all evidence to the contrary. "Janey found you in your room, dead of a heart attack."

"I planned for Janey to find me that way," Kim explains and chuckles. "She always had a fevered imagination. I calculated that she'd suspect foul play and set the whole sequence of events into motion which would lead to your execution. Janey was always looking for something fishy." For some reason this last sentence amuses her and she lets out a loud and delighted laugh.

"You're dead." I can't get the thought out of my mind. Kim shakes her head.

"Something fishy again," she explains. "I'm a zoology

student, Lauren. And my speciality is fish. The puffer fish especially..."

"The puffer fish?"

"It's a great delicacy back home in Japan," she tells me, and I suddenly remember that once it appeared on the menu at Suzuki's. I also recall the waiter telling me that a few days before her "death" Kim had been very interested in the fish at the sushi bar.

"You have to be very careful how you prepare it though," Kim tells me. "Because it contains tetrodotoxin, one of the most powerful poisons known to man."

"I don't understand..."

"It can kill, but if prepared in the right quantities, by an experienced zoologist, for instance," she tells me, "it can also create the appearance of death. All the bodily functions are reduced to a minimum, but the person doesn't die."

"You staged your own death!" I realize.

"I murdered myself, that's right," Kim confirms. "And an empty coffin was sent back to Japan. I'm an orphan like you, Lauren, so there was no tiresome business with parents. And then I stayed on till I could kill Doug, the man who ditched me for you, and see you framed for murder, before I made my own way back home, knowing that I'd had my revenge."

"You couldn't have done it all by yourself," I say.

"Unfortunately no," Kim confirms. "My uncle took care of all the funeral arrangements. He was only too glad to help me out when I threatened to tell his superiors that he had lied when he said that Andy's steroid tests were negative."

"But why?" I ask.

"Remember Amanda James?" Kim asks, and I nod, recalling the young girl who had died a few months before Kim and Doug.

"My uncle was treating her," Kim tells me. "But he made a genuine mistake in the medicines he prescribed her. That was why she died. I knew – I was helping him out in his surgery at the time. But I agreed to keep quiet – for a price."

"You used your own uncle," I realize. "Just as you've used all of us. But when Doug died..."

"I don't know what Uncle thought when Doug was murdered, but by then he was in too deep... He's back in Japan now, nursing a guilty conscience and his suspicions... But for we Japanese there's nothing more important than family loyalty. Even if he does suspect me of murdering Doug, he'll say nothing. His career's on the line, after all..."

"I'll call Baker," I say. "I'll tell her that I'm innocent. They can't take me to the electric chair. I can't die for a crime I didn't commit!"

Kim laughs. "And you think that she'll believe you? Oh no, Lauren, I've won. I've got my revenge on you for stealing Doug from me. And even if she does believe you, what can they do? They couldn't convict me. After all, I've been declared officially dead. You can't bring a corpse to trial."

And then she smiles at me, an evil, superior, mocking smile that will haunt me for the rest of my life – and who knows now how long that will be?

"I'm dead, dear Lauren," Kim says. "And soon that's exactly what you will be ... dead, just like me."

POINT CRiME

Look out for the next exciting instalment from

in

Asking For It

Some people invite you to burgle them. Some still leave doors and windows open. Others have locks which can be opened with a credit card in less time than it takes to pick a pocket. Failing that, some have doors which collapse with the first kick. They have ground floor windows which cannot be seen from the street. Their neighbours make so much noise, they wouldn't hear a bomb going off, unless it happened in their living room. Yes, some people are asking to be burgled.

The thief doesn't accept every invitation. Being lazy, he only goes for places where the pickings are easy, the risks minimal. Once, he went after the usual: videos, TVs, hi-fi. But these items are bulky and conspicuous, therefore dangerous. Nowadays, he prefers to take things which fit snugly into his shoulder bag: CDs, watches, cameras, calculators. Best of all: chequebooks, chequecards, credit cards. Ideally: cash.

Where to steal from? The richest pickings used to be from the prosperous middle classes. But now they've got burglar alarms and neighbourhood watch schemes. They're best left to the professionals, who can be in and out in a minute, taking a baseball bat to anyone who gets in their way.

The children of the middle classes, however, are a different story. They have all the consumer goods, but none of the security. They're so casual about their possessions, you'd think they want to be burgled. It gives them something to talk about with their friends, one more reason to complain about the world.

The thief wanders around a university hall of residence on a Friday afternoon in early May. This hall has been good to him before, so he's hopeful. His usual technique is to show up in the morning, slipping into rooms just after their occupants have gone off to lectures. It's easy to tell which rooms are empty because the pigeonholes in the foyer will be empty, too. Friday afternoons aren't so good. The place is nice and quiet. Plenty of people are out. Some of them have gone away for the weekend. Sadly, they've taken their wallets and purses with them. All the thief's picked up so far are a bunch of indie CDs, an Olympus AF10 and a CD Walkman with portable speakers.

The stuff in his bag will bring in forty, maybe fifty pounds. But the thief wants more. He wants enough money to have a really good weekend. So he climbs another set of stairs, walks stealthily down another corridor, looking for one more room with "burgle me" scrawled on its welcome mat. With each set of stairs, there's more risk – he has further to run if challenged. The first rule of burglary is this: have a safe escape route planned – and he has. Each floor has a fire door – not alarmed – which can be opened from the inside, but not out.

The room he's going to try next had nothing in its pigeon hole. The thief knocks on the door. No reply. There's a decent sized gap between the door and its side post. The thief pulls a Visa card from his jeans pocket, pushes it into the gap so that the spring bolt is pushed back. He presses the door, wiggles the credit card and – *hey presto!* – he's in.

The room is practically empty. There's a bunch of text books on the shelf, some notes on the desk. There's a poster saying *Jesus Saves* above it. The thief looks under the bed. He goes through the desk. He looks behind the books. Finally, he pulls out the Bible, holding it open with his gloved hands so that any enclosures flutter to the ground. Out falls a shiny, plastic credit card. A broad smile fills the thief's face.

The name on the card is male, which is useful.

The thief can learn to copy the signature, then use it himself, rather than selling it on for a pittance. The way it's hidden suggests that the credit card's owner has been keeping it for emergencies. He'll have been cautious about using it, even though the credit limit will only be five or six hundred pounds. The thief will be cautious, too. He intends to get full value out of this card.

The thief tidies up quickly. If he leaves the room as he finds it, then, hopefully, it will be a few days before the victim notices that the card's gone. Maybe he won't find out until he suddenly gets a huge bill.

Satisfied that the room is straight, the thief checks that the corridor is clear, then slips out. He intends to leave the building, dump his takings in a safe place, then shoot into town for a spending spree on the credit card.

The thief reckons without the guy who charges out of his room on the floor below, barging into the thief as he passes, knocking the bag from his shoulder to the floor. The guy trots down the stairs without an apology. The thief watches the guy go, clocking his ugly, arrogant face. The guy doesn't look back at the thief, which is good. Then the thief looks back at the door through which the guy has just come. It's ajar.

If ever a guy was asking for it, it's this one. The thief picks up his bag and nudges the door open. He can still feel the throb in his shoulder from where the guy knocked against him. He will enjoy…

Something's wrong. A single glance tells the thief that this isn't a guy's room, it's a girl's room. In fact, the thief remembers, all the rooms on this floor are for women. And this one's a mess. There are clothes, cassettes, books and stuff scattered across the floor. The bed is made, yet there's the unmistakeable smell of sex. The thief realizes that he's made a mistake, that he ought to leave the room quickly, before…

Then he hears a whimpering sound, coming from the side of the bed. Common sense tells him to get out of the room this moment. A smaller, but more insistent voice tells him to stay.

"Are you all right?" he calls, softly, before taking a step forward, looking.

On the floor, a naked girl with short hair pulls a towel around her bruised body.

"Help me," she says.

Point Horror

Are you hooked on horror? Thrilled by fear? Then these are the books for you. A powerful series of horror fiction designed to keep you quaking in your shoes.

The Cemetery
D.E. Athkins

The Dead Game
Mother's Helper
A. Bates

The Surfer
Linda Cargill

Caroline B. Cooney Collection
The Cheerleader
The Return of the Vampire
The Vampire's Promise
Freeze Tag
The Perfume
The Stranger
Twins
Caroline B. Cooney

April Fools
Help Wanted
The Lifeguard
The Mall
Teacher's Pet
Trick or Treat
Richie Tankersley Cusick

Camp Fear
My Secret Admirer
Silent Witness
The Body
The Window
Carol Ellis

Funhouse
The Accident
The Invitation
The Fever
Funhouse
The Train
Diane Hoh

Driver's Dead
The Yearbook
Peter Lerangis

The Watcher
Lael Littke

The Forbidden Game:
The Hunter
The Chase
The Kill
L.J. Smith

Dream Date
The Boy Next Door
The Diary
The Waitress
Sinclair Smith

The Mummy
The Phantom
Barbara Steiner

Beach House
Beach Party
The Baby-sitter
The Baby-sitter II
The Baby-sitter III
The Boyfriend
Call Waiting
The Dead Girlfriend
The Girlfriend
Halloween Night
The Hitchhiker
Hit and Run
R.L. Stine Collection
The Snowman
The Witness
R.L. Stine

Thirteen Tales of Horror
Thirteen More Tales of Horror
Thirteen Again
Various

Dare you read

NIGHTMARE HALL

Where college is a

scream!

High on a hill overlooking Salem University, hidden in shadows and shrouded in mystery, sits Nightingale Hall.

Nightmare Hall, the students call it. Because that's where the terror began ... Don't miss the spine-tingling thrillers:

Deadly Attraction
Guilty
Pretty Please
The Experiment
The Nightwalker
The Roommate
The Scream Team
The Silent Scream
The Wish